'Venice comes alive . . . warm, engaging and truly delicious'
Rosanna Ley, author of *The Little Theatre by the Sea*

'A delicious and sensual adventure. I was whisked away to the sights and tastes of the most romantic – and mysterious – of cities. A story as evocative and captivating as Venice itself'
Fiona Gibson, author of *The Woman Who Met Her Match*

'With a wonderfully evocative setting and mouth-watering descriptions of Venetian food, *A Year at Hotel Gondola* is a refreshingly different take on the challenges of making a relationship when you're older'
Pamela Hartshorne, author of *The Cursed Wife*

We love this book . . . absolutely delicious, like a warm hug on a sunny afternoon'   *HotBrandsCoolPlaces.com*

'Full-bodied as a rich Italian red, it's a page-turner combining the missed chances of *Captain Corelli's Mandolin* with the foodie pleasures of *Chocolat*'   *Eve*

'An evocative foodfest of a novel'   *Prima*

'A slice of pure sunshine'   *Good Housekeeping*

'A lovely read . . . with a genuine heart and true observation'
Elizabeth Buchan

'A touching story about one woman's search for love'
Sunday Express

'Set against a backdrop of love, friendship and food . . . The descriptions of Italian f...

'Sink back on the sofa w...

Now Magazine

Nicky Pellegrino was born in Liverpool but spent childhood holidays staying with her family in Italy. It is her memories of those summers that flavour her stories: the passions, the feuds but most of all the food. Nicky now lives in Auckland, New Zealand with her husband, two dogs and two horses.

Find out more at www.nickypellegrino.com

Also by Nicky Pellegrino

Delicious
Summer at the Villa Rosa
(*originally published as* The Gypsy Tearoom)
The Italian Wedding
Recipe for Life
The Villa Girls
When in Rome
The Food of Love Cookery School
One Summer in Venice
Under Italian Skies

A Year at Hotel Gondola

Nicky Pellegrino

ORION

An Orion paperback

First published in Great Britain in 2018
by Orion Books
This paperback edition published in 2018
by Orion Books
an imprint of The Orion Publishing Group Ltd,
Carmelite House, 50 Victoria Embankment
London EC4Y 0DZ

An Hachette UK company

1 3 5 7 9 10 8 6 4 2

A CIP catalogue record for this book
is available from the British Library.

ISBN 978 1 4091 6768 6

Typeset by Deltatype Ltd, Birkenhead, Merseyside

Printed in Great Britain by CPI Group (UK) Ltd,
Croydon CR0 4YY

www.orionbooks.co.uk

'The wasting of time is the thing I worry about the most, because when you get to my age, you realise time is all there is.'

Gloria Steinem

A Year at Hotel Gondola by Kat Black

CHAPTER 1

There is no sadder feeling than being jealous of your own life. Do you know what I mean? Have you ever been envious of the girl you once were? Looked back on your past and realised it was more exciting than your future is set to be? Have you ever felt that way? Because right now I'm doing my best to make sure I won't.

My life has been pretty interesting since I took sole charge of it. Oh, I had the same dull start as everyone else. School and homework, late-afternoon cartoons, setting the table for a meal of soggy vegetables and chewy meat, then early to bed and lying awake for hours, staring at a crack of light creeping beneath the door, thinking and thinking. Somehow I knew better things were waiting. I just had to find them, or help them find me.

Childhood is such a waste of time, isn't it? Mine seemed to drag on for ever. As soon as I was free of it – with my back turned on my northern hometown, with the train hurtling towards London Euston and a new life – I swore I wasn't going to waste another moment.

Obviously we all have to do the laundry and vacuum the floor so I haven't been living it large every single second. But I've tried to make the most of my time.

I've ridden on horseback over the Mongolian steppe and shared yak meat with nomads. Been fed seal blubber by Inuits in Greenland. Choked down fermented shark in Reykjavik. Breakfasted on crisp pancakes cooked by street hawkers in Shanghai and spicy dosa from a roadside stall in Mumbai. I've followed my appetite around the world. You may have seen the television shows I've made, read some of the articles or books I've written? Mine has been an adventurous life; at least so far.

Then I turned fifty and something shifted. I blame my mother. 'Twenty good years,' she said. 'That's what you've got left at your age. After that you won't want to have adventures any more.'

I told her she was talking rubbish but after I'd put down the phone, I kept thinking about her words. Twenty good years didn't sound like enough. What if my mother was right? Perhaps at seventy I might feel entirely different than I did right now. Maybe there was some threshold you crossed then started craving safety and comfort. How could I know for sure?

That night I woke up at three a.m. and couldn't get back to sleep. Fears always seem so much bigger at that hour and I hoped by morning this one would be gone. But the worry had found a space in my mind and moved in. I couldn't get rid of it.

I rang my mother back. 'You've never been adventurous,' I complained. 'So how would you know?'

'Because everyone around me is old and all of us are the same,' she replied. 'We're letting our passports lapse and surrendering our driving licences.'

'God, how depressing.'

'You can find pleasure in smaller things, you know, Kat. It's rather lovely being a homebody. You'll see.'

No, I won't see. For me, life is what happens beyond my front door. It's a packed suitcase and a purse full of foreign currency. I'm not saying that I don't feel older. My left hip hurts a bit, I need reading glasses and if I didn't make a monthly visit to the hairdresser there would be much more grey in my hair than brown. I can see the signs all right. But I've made myself a promise – even if I live till I'm a hundred I'll never be a homebody.

I'm planning for things to get more interesting as I get older, not less. I won't be wasting time. And I'm not going to be jealous of my own life. Not ever.

I

Kat Black hadn't been sure if she should admit to being fifty. People pigeonholed you, didn't they? Perhaps she could gloss over her exact age and let everyone assume she was still in her forties. But then the 'twenty good years' line wouldn't work; and her mum actually had said that; and Kat had been rattled, just as she had written. Besides, it was a great first chapter and she didn't want to change it.

What was the point anyway, her age was already beginning to make a difference. Wasn't it the reason the network hadn't been interested in another series of her travel and food show *Black of Beyond*? Perhaps it was even why her publishers had halved the advance for her new book? Her agent claimed the same thing was happening to everyone, but Kat hadn't been convinced. It seemed more likely that her career was contracting. She had worked so hard and achieved so much but she could smell change in the air.

She stared through the window. From here she couldn't see much unless she opened it up and leaned out. The guest suites in the Hotel Gondola boasted all the best views. The room Kat lived in was up a steep staircase, beneath the eaves, and looked out towards the window of the hotel opposite. Still she loved it here, right in the centre of Venice, all its life humming around her. This was such a different city to live in than to visit. Everything was different now; that was the whole point of coming.

Kat stared at her computer screen, checked the word count and sighed. The beginning of a book was always the hardest part, and this one was going to be even trickier, because she was living the adventure as she was writing it.

A Year at Hotel Gondola; she had been surprised how much her publishers liked the idea. She'd had to promise recipes, of course, which were always hard work, with all the testing required and making sure she measured things down to the last teaspoon. It wasn't the way Kat preferred to cook but she could tell it was going to be a deal-breaker.

'This is going to be my biggest adventure yet,' she had promised when she was pitching the concept. 'Kat Black experiences the one journey she has never taken before – a relationship.'

It wasn't strictly true. She'd had plenty of boyfriends, but the longest Kat had managed to stick with one was eight months, and he was a photographer who travelled almost as much as she did, so it hardly counted as a proper relationship. She and Massimo Morosini, though; that was different; at least it had better be because there was so much more at stake this time.

Kat closed her laptop, stretched her arms and yawned. Perhaps if she took a walk it would clear her head. She needed to explain how she had ended up at Hotel Gondola and wasn't sure how best to tell the story. Massimo's mother would read this book and so would her own. Some of those ex-boyfriends might pick it up, and hopefully thousands of strangers would buy it. All those eyes turned towards her personal life. Sometimes Kat wondered why she'd ever thought it was such a great idea.

Cramming her laptop into her bag, Kat found sunglasses and a hat. She was cautious as she opened the door to her room, stopping and listening before setting a foot outside. The hotel was full of guests and on no account did she want to meet any of them. There were always questions to answer, problems to solve. They needed directions to the Lido or an extra pillow or ideas for where to eat that night. So Kat had taken to creeping out of her room, then taking the stairs as quickly as possible, head down, sunglasses on, hat brim pulled low. If she could get through the reception foyer without being stopped then she was almost in the clear, but she never fully relaxed until, turning off the quiet *fondamenta*, she knew the Hotel Gondola was out of sight.

Kat had only been in Venice for a short while but already she had found places she was starting to think of as her own. In search of tall, leafy trees she often walked to the Papadopoli Gardens. Even now she still got lost on her way; it only took one wrong turn, one moment of distraction. But those were the times she would stumble across some hidden spot she had heard about but never managed to find before. The little *osteria* with the handwritten menu, the bar where they served paper cones of hot fried polenta, the family-run restaurant that was always full of locals. Massimo kept telling her half the joy of Venice was discovering its secrets for herself. But this was his city; he'd been walking through it most of his life, and often had reasons not to join Kat on her daily strolls – too much work, too many commitments. So she explored alone, the way she always had.

Today Massimo was in his cubby of an office, frowning at spreadsheets filled with numbers. He owned and managed the Hotel Gondola and took his work seriously. Kat was meant to be working too; the weight of the laptop in her bag was a reminder of that. But she had never been good at thinking while she was sitting at her desk. Besides, she had a whole year ahead of her to finish this book and surely it was better to be out experiencing things, finding colour and adventure to fill it with, so she could bring Venice alive for people, make them feel as if they were actually here as they read her words.

A year in this watery, shadowy city; learning to be Venetian, to eat and love like them. When Kat had dreamed up the idea it seemed the answer to her problems. Now she wondered if all she had done was create a whole lot more. A book to conjure out of nothing was one thing; a relationship to negotiate quite another – particularly as she and Massimo were so new to one another.

'Excuse me, excuse me.'

Kat turned at the sound of the English voice and recognised the woman speaking as a guest from the Hotel Gondola. She had noticed her earlier in the reception area, sitting beneath the chandelier, puzzling over her guidebook.

'Are you OK?' the woman wondered.

'Yes, why?' asked Kat, a little too abruptly.

'I'm sorry. There was something about your expression.' The woman removed her sunglasses and gazed at Kat with bluish-grey eyes. 'I thought it was best to check there was nothing wrong. It's easier not to but then I always regret it. And I recognised you from the hotel. My name is Ruth Wilson. I've been with you a week and I'm staying for three more.'

'Yes, of course.' Kat tried to sound warmer because Massimo had told her the long-stay guests, the ones that tended to come back year after year, were like gold dust.

'I'm a fan of yours, actually,' the woman continued. 'I've watched your show on TV for years. It was one of the things that made me excited about travelling again after my husband died.'

'Oh, thank you, I hope you're having a great holiday.'

Kat began to edge sideways but the women seemed not to understand this was a signal for the conversation to end.

'I'm here to paint,' she explained, 'but I haven't even unpacked my canvases yet. I'm getting a feel for the place. I want to portray it in a way that goes beyond the clichés.'

'Difficult with Venice, so many other artists have been here before you,' Kat pointed out.

'Yes, but I'm not here to paint the canals and gondolas. It's the people I'm interested in.'

'Ah, well, there's no shortage of them. But I suppose you want to paint Venetians rather than tourists?'

'I'm not sure yet. I was wandering around trying to decide when I spotted you.' The woman's eyes searched her face again, as if there might be an answer there. 'I've been hoping to talk to you but you always seem in such a rush when I see you in the hotel.'

This woman was lonely, that much was clear. As tempting as it was to walk away from her, Kat couldn't do it. Venice seemed such a terrible place to be alone, so colonised by honeymooners and noisy groups, so prone to sudden mists and gloomy afternoons, so filled with faded grandeur.

'Would you like to join me?' she made herself ask. 'I'm heading over to the Papadopoli Gardens.'

'Oh I love gardens. Are they pretty?' Ruth sounded eager.

'It's a nice park, nothing amazingly special, but I find it's a good place to go when I need to think about the book I'm trying to write.'

'I suppose you won't be able to think properly if I'm there chattering away, will you?'

Kat murmured something noncommittal but it was enough to encourage Ruth.

'Still, if you're sure, then yes, I'd love to come.'

They walked together, Ruth matching Kat's long stride, darting round groups of tourists clotting the way, crossing bridges arching over the silty canals, keeping pace with the slow chug of motorboats.

She was a chatterer, just as she had warned. Mostly what she talked about was Kat's work; the TV shows she had especially liked, the travel books that had inspired her. She mentioned several times what a huge fan she was. Admiration always felt so awkward. It wasn't the reason Kat sent those things out into the world, to be feted and famous. They were a means to an end, a way of funding the life she wanted. At least they had been up until now.

'So what's your new book about?' asked Ruth. 'Venice, I'm guessing.'

'That's right.'

'What aspect of it are you focusing on? The history, the cooking ... Oh, I'm sorry, perhaps you're one of those writers who hates to talk about your work in progress?'

'There isn't much to talk about yet,' Kat admitted. 'The idea is that I'm going to spend a year here, and I'll write about the people I meet, the places I visit, the food I eat, that kind of thing.'

'It sounds like an adventure.'

'I hope it's going to be.'

Ruth's eyes searched Kat's face again. 'You know earlier when I asked if everything was all right?'

'I had a frown on my face? Thinking about the book, I expect.'

'Actually it was something else. I always find this tricky to explain but when I see people, I see colours.'

Kat was taken aback. This slight, slender woman seemed so ordinary. Her grey hair was neatly cut in a bob, her clothes were practical and her face bore only the lightest trace of make-up. There was nothing in her appearance to suggest she was the type to start talking about seeing colours.

'I don't mean an aura,' Ruth explained hurriedly. 'It's more an impression of colour than a halo of light. And it gives me a sense of that person, who they are and how they're feeling.'

'So all these people' – Kat gestured at a tour group heading their way – 'you're seeing colours when you look at them?'

'That's right. As a child it was a shock when I realised everyone didn't experience the world the same way.'

'What colour am I?' Kat asked.

'That's the thing,' Ruth said hesitantly. 'Your colour keeps changing. Right now you're silver. Earlier there was blue swirling around you. And yesterday you rushed past me in reception and left a trail of orange.'

'Does that not normally happen?'

'Not really, that's why I wondered if something was wrong.'

'Was I a different colour when you watched my TV shows?'

Ruth smiled. 'It doesn't work like that for me. It only happens when someone is physically present. I'm sure you're sceptical, most people are. But I'm not a madwoman, I promise you.'

Kat decided to humour her. 'So what do you think it means, my changing rainbow?'

'I don't know, only how it makes me feel. "Unsettled" seems the best way to describe it.'

'And I'm still silver, right?'

'For now.'

Kat laughed. 'I'm sorry but that's so weird.'

'My husband was the most beautiful shade of green,' Ruth said wistfully. 'It made me feel calm. And then he got sick and it dirtied to a dull khaki. Nothing the doctors did ever changed it back.'

'I'm sorry ... You said he died?'

'Yes, two years ago although he was ill for a long time before. He always used to tell me I should paint the colours I saw. It was after I lost him that I started.'

They were nearing the gardens now. Kat had managed not to take a wrong turn even though she hadn't been concentrating. 'Were the two of you together for a long time?'

'Forty years. We never had children; it was just him and me, a tight little unit. That's why I've been doing so much travelling. It's easier than being at home.'

Poor Ruth, lonely everywhere she went. Kat was glad she had invited her along even if she did seem quirky.

'So what made you come to Venice?' she asked.

'I visited once many years ago and wondered if it had changed.'

'And has it?'

'Not really; not in the ways that matter.'

The Papadopoli Gardens weren't large; you could stroll

the gravel paths in no time at all. Usually Kat found a bench, not too near the children's play area, and sat for a while listening to the sound of the breeze in the trees and enjoying the relative calm of the place. Today there was Ruth filling the silence with words and no easy way to escape her. Kat wondered how it must feel, to be so lonely. She listened to her long, rambling story of visiting Venice when she was younger, and imagined the stretch of years between then and now, all spent with one man, then left with nothing at the end of it all, just an empty house, an empty life.

'This is my first trip on my own,' Ruth confided. 'I did a couple of organised tours and a river cruise to get my courage up then decided to come to Venice. I suppose you've been here many times?'

'Actually I always avoided it,' Kat told her. 'To me the south has always felt like the real Italy and I assumed Venice was a tourist Disneyland and a bit pointless.'

'What made you change your mind?'

'Chance brought me here,' Kat told her. 'It brought me here then it kind of took over my life. That's what my book is about. The one I'm supposed to be working on right now.'

CHAPTER 2

Love and money – that's what most people want, at least in
my experience. Other things as well, but it all comes back to
those two eventually. I've always felt different. To my mind
love tethers you, it brings children and possessions and they
hold you fast. I've cherished my freedom too much for that.
As for money I have a tendency to send it back into the world
as quickly as I earn it. I'm a spender. Not on handbags and
shoes, hell no, not on sensible things like property either.
You'd laugh if you could see my apartment. It's a shoebox
in Maida Vale, a single room with a bathroom attached. I
sleep on a sofa bed and there is always a suitcase on the
floor that's in the process of being packed or emptied. My
apartment is cramped and not especially nice but that doesn't
matter because it's only ever a place to perch. I like travel and
adventures; I like a changing view; and I didn't expect any of
that to alter.

After I turned fifty I started doing too much thinking and
one of the things that struck me was I might go through my
whole life and never be truly loved by a man. Perhaps I'd
been looking at too many happy couple shots on Instagram
and Facebook but I began to wonder if a person who lives for
experiences really should miss out on such an essential one.
What if I'd left it too late? What if it was something I regretted
later on? I was surprised how much the idea bothered me; my
mind kept coming back to it. I needed to know how it felt to
be loved. I didn't want to miss out.

Of course, the thing with love is it doesn't just turn up on schedule like a train or a plane. And the truth is I had no idea where to look for it.

How do people meet each other? In the past I'd had boyfriends who crossed my path through work or were attached to a circle of friends. There hadn't been one for a while, not even a casual fling. I didn't realise quite how long a while until I counted back. Three years, unless I'd forgotten someone and I was pretty sure I hadn't – a long drought. It was time to do something about that, surely?

That is the frame of mind I was in when I was offered the Venice trip. It was an assignment for a travel magazine, flights and accommodation all covered, and the editor gave me the same brief they almost always do.

'Get off the beaten path. Find me places that aren't in the tourist guides, the things only the locals know about.'

Editors never like to hear your problems. They want you to write your piece, meet your deadline and not make any glaring mistakes their readers might pick up on. Usually I deliver but this time I couldn't help objecting.

'Is there really any such thing as off the beaten track in Venice?'

'Oh, come on, Kat, you must have loads of insider knowledge. Just hook up with your contacts and find me some juicy stuff then I can get a front cover out of it – Secret Venice.'

I didn't tell her I'd never been to Venice, that I'm a traveller rather than a tourist, and I prefer the far-flung places to the thoroughly discovered ones. I didn't mention any of that.

'OK, I like a challenge; I'll do it,' I told her, because I didn't have anything else on at the time. 'How many words do you want?'

After I put down the phone I read a few blogs and started to feel more enthusiastic. Secret Venice might be a stretch but there were definitely locals and they had to hang out somewhere. I had a whole week; surely I could come up with a decent story.

So it was chance that sent me to stay at the Hotel Gondola. Its name was there on the itinerary supplied by the magazine, and my contact was its owner/manager Massimo Morosini.

Let me tell you about the Hotel Gondola. It's a jewel-box of a place, filled with chandeliers, Murano glass mosaics and antique mirrors. Every room is different, but all have swagged satin curtains and gold-leaf wallpaper. A few of the better suites boast balconies overlooking the canal and you really can arrive at the hotel by gondola if you choose because it has its own landing. There is a breakfast room, and a small bar that opens out onto a terrace where on warmer evenings you can enjoy a cocktail before you head out to dinner.

On that first afternoon I was out of sorts when I arrived. Venice had outfoxed me. I'd been lost in a maze of narrow streets, pulling my suitcase behind me, listening to the ugly sound of plastic wheels rumbling over old stone, passing other visitors doing the same. I should have taken a water taxi but it had seemed fairly straightforward when I checked the map that was now crumpled in my hand.

When I reached the hotel at long last it was to find there was some confusion over my booking. A lot of tip-tapping on the computer and head-shaking ensued. In some parts of the world I've found the thing to do in these situations is to get a bit cross and wave your arms around. It doesn't seem to matter what you say or even which language you're speaking; it smooths the way. I tried it here but the young female clerk's expression didn't change. Genuinely pissy now, I glanced at my itinerary and raised my voice, this time throwing in the manager's name. A moment later a man appeared from a screened-off area behind the reception desk. I have no idea how he'd folded himself in there. He was tall, with wide-set shoulders, olive skin, dark eyes and one of those solid chests you feel like leaning into.

'Signora, is there a problem?' he asked, in a low, slow voice.

'Yes, there seems to be. I'm from *Travel Dreams* magazine

and I'm meant to have a room here but apparently I'm not showing up on the computer.'

More tip-tapping, more head-shaking then the pair started arguing. It ended with the young woman storming off through the reception area. The tall man muttered something to himself then looked up at me.

'I'm sorry, signora, there has been some sort of screw-up with the booking system and your room has been assigned to another person who has already checked in.'

'Great,' I said. 'Can you recommend somewhere else that might have space for me?'

He held up a hand. 'No, wait, it seems we have had a last-minute cancellation so there is another room. In fact, it is an upgrade – the honeymoon suite.'

'Really? Who cancels the honeymoon suite at the last minute?'

'Someone who has had a far worse day than you, signora.'

He introduced himself as Massimo Morosini, the hotel's owner, and then he apologised for his clerk, checked me in himself and insisted on accompanying me to my room. The lift was so tiny that to not touch at all, we had to stand pressed against its walls. That made conversation awkward but still I thought I should ask for some tips on places to check out.

'I'm looking for the secret spots, the ones the tourists never find,' I told him. 'Little bars, restaurants, music venues maybe.'

'To visit or as research for your magazine article?' he asked as the lift doors opened.

'To write about, obviously,' I said.

'I can't think of anywhere, I'm sorry.'

'Where do you go when you're not working?'

He had been about to unlock the door of my room but now he straightened up and looked me in the eye. 'We Venetians need a few places that are just for us. They aren't grand; in fact most are the opposite. Your readers wouldn't like them as much as they do Harry's Bar and Caffè Florian.'

'My readers are looking for an authentic experience,' I argued.

'But if these places fill up with outsiders they won't be authentic any longer. I'm sorry, signora, but there are some secrets I won't share.'

He opened the door, gesturing for me to go in. It was a big room and the first thing I noticed was the generous balcony that looked down onto the canal. Then I registered the red rose petals strewn across the bed and the bottle of Moët in an ice bucket beside two champagne glasses.

'Oh dear … they really were honeymooners.'

Massimo put down my suitcase, glanced at the petal-covered bed, then over at me, and smiled. His smile was the best thing about him. It warmed his face and made his dark eyes spark.

'You may as well enjoy their champagne. But I can send someone to clear the rose petals.'

'No, that's fine, leave them.'

'Well in that case enjoy your evening, signora.'

'Could you just tell me about one place?' I wheedled. 'One little favourite spot that I won't find in any of the guidebooks.'

'I'm sorry, no.' He shook his head. 'But if you look hard enough you may find them for yourself.'

Secret Venice. As the afternoon settled in, Kat Black sat on a bench in the Papadopoli Gardens, wondering if she would ever uncover it. A week hadn't been enough; a year might, but still she wasn't sure.

'The trouble is they'll only let you in so far, the Venetians,' she told Ruth. 'That's what's worrying me. A magazine article is one thing ... but a book ...'

'How long have you been here?' asked Ruth.

'You mean officially, as in living here? Just four weeks. There was some toing and froing before that but I'm not counting it as part of the year. So I do have plenty of time ahead, I suppose.'

'A year in Venice, I envy you. I expect your readers will too.'

'I'm pretty sure I've never spent an entire twelve months in one place,' Kat admitted. 'At least, not as an adult. I'm always on my way somewhere else.'

'But you'll pop back to London to see your friends and family?'

'No, I don't think so. For this to be an adventure it has to be a complete change for me. It would be cheating if I went back to my own life.'

'Really?' Ruth sounded surprised. 'Why would it be cheating?'

'What sold this book idea to my publishers was the midlife passion element,' explained Kat. 'After pretty much a lifetime of being single I've fallen for an Italian man and committed to us spending the whole year together to see if we can make it work.'

Kat gave Ruth the abbreviated version of the story. It was an explanation she had honed in the retelling. She and Massimo had met, been instantly attracted to each other and decided not to waste time on a long-distance relationship. They were both at a stage of life when it seemed wiser to get on with things.

'So we're risking everything on love,' Kat finished with a flourish, as she always did. 'Romantic, isn't it?'

There was a frown on Ruth's face. 'What if it doesn't work out? What if Massimo isn't the person you think? That seems to be the biggest risk.' She sounded genuinely concerned.

'It's only a year and anyway that's how I've always lived, taking risks,' Kat pointed out. 'This is just a different one.'

'I suppose it explains why your colours keep changing.'

'You mean because I'm scared that I've over-promised with this book?'

Ruth shook her head. 'No, not that.'

Kat had lost count of the people who'd told her not to move in with an Italian man she hardly knew. Her mother had been especially horrified, declaring that she was behaving like a teenager, which if anything had helped Kat make up her mind. When her mother disapproved of something, generally she went ahead and did it. It was a life rule that had served her perfectly well so far.

There were friends whose opinions she valued more who seemed similarly disquieted. Some met Massimo, and liked him, yet still they thought she was going too far. Don't rush in, take things slowly, give it more time, they kept saying, as if she were still eighteen with the whole of life ahead. This opportunity was here right now, she told them. She could take it and see how things turned out. Or she could wait and lose her chance.

'It will be a different book if things don't work,' she admitted to Ruth.

'What happens once the year is over? Will you stay here or go home?'

'Who knows? I can't predict what's going to happen, that's the whole point.'

'You must have thought about it surely?' Ruth sounded surprised.

'Not really,' Kat admitted. 'We have a whole year ahead of us so I expect things will work themselves out like they do in any relationship. You can't plan this stuff, can you?'

'I suppose not,' Ruth murmured.

Kat wondered how old Ruth was, in her mid-sixties perhaps? As the amber light of the late-day sun found her face it showed up lines and thread veins, it sparkled from the single strand of blue glass beads around her neck, and made her hair a halo of grey. Kat glanced away and noticed another woman, this one a mother crouching down to a child, smoothly and easily, without a hint of a twinge in her knees. She was ordinary enough but she was young and that made her attractive. Kat had the odd sense that she was caught in a crowd and being forced along in the wrong direction. In no time at all she would be old, just like Ruth. There was nothing she could do to stop it. The thought made her feel panicky.

'There's no regrets so far,' she told Ruth. 'It's all going well. Massimo works long hours, obviously. It's not easy running a place like the Hotel Gondola; he has to be everywhere. But when I can get him away we have a great time together.'

Ruth nodded, but in a manner that suggested she was unconvinced.

'So how did you meet your husband?' Kat asked her.

'Oh, it was a long time ago.' Ruth smiled. 'I was an usher at the local cinema. I used to show people to their seats with my torch once the lights went down and sell ice creams in the interval. He loved films so he was always there, with friends or on his own, and one day he asked me out. It was as simple as that.'

'How long afterwards did you get married?'

'A year, more or less.'

'And you never had any doubts, never worried what would happen if it didn't work out?'

'When you're young and in love you don't think that way.'

'So you took a risk.'

'It didn't feel like it at the time,' Ruth insisted. 'But yes, I see what you're saying. Why should it be any different when you're older?'

'Why should anything be different?'

Ruth gave a half-sigh. 'That's a big question and I'm not sure I can answer it.'

The park was getting busier, students and workers criss-crossing it on their way home. Kat wished she could follow them, see inside their apartments, meet their families, listen to them talk and taste the food they cooked for dinner.

She got up from the bench, stretched her stiff hip, and said to Ruth, 'Why don't I make you a drink and see if you can try?'

'Don't you have a book to work on?'

'I do, but right now the bar at the Hotel Gondola is calling me. I'll write another chapter later, or at least I'll attempt to.'

A Year at Hotel Gondola by Kat Black

CHAPTER 3

Nothing is ever normal in Venice; it can't be. That's what I'm coming to realise. The first night, when Massimo left me alone in the honeymoon suite, I sat out on the balcony and sipped my way through an entire bottle of champagne. Generally I'm not a big drinker but there was something about being in Venice that made me feel like celebrating.

It was early autumn and I caught the damp, slightly musty smell of the canal on the breeze. Beneath me a gondola glided past and music drifted upwards from a nearby bar. I didn't realise it then, but Venice was starting to seduce me.

I've travelled a lot but would never describe myself as world-weary. Each new destination holds something to surprise and delight. Still, these days I'd rather avoid the places that have been too tainted by tourism. It isn't easy. I've had hawkers follow me along the Great Wall of China trying to sell me fridge magnets. I've sighed at the queues pushing their way through the Sistine Chapel or the Anne Frank Museum, at the hordes taking selfies in front of the *Mona Lisa*. Oh yes, and then there is the food. I've been offered hamburgers in North Vietnam, egg and chips in Spain; it breaks my heart. So if I'm honest, I expected over-hyped, tourist-laden Venice to be a series of disappointments.

I woke at dawn on the first day so I could see the place without people. It was a crisp, calm morning and I walked through the graceful squares and cobbled streets; across bridges arching over dark water; shop windows filled with carnival masks; past an old palazzo quietly crumbling and a grandiose church. I lost myself in silent, empty Venice and it felt almost like stepping through history.

It wasn't too long before the spell was broken by the sound of a motor. A delivery barge, loaded with casks of wine and crates of beer, chugged past and moored a little way ahead of me. Men called to each other as they unloaded its cargo onto handcarts.

Suddenly the air was scented with coffee and warm sugar. I rounded a corner to find a small bar, its doorstep thronged with people drinking espresso and eating freshly baked pastries. These must be locals, I thought, squeezing past an old lady wearing a bright pashmina and a businessman in a pinstriped suit and sunglasses. Inside was a long wooden counter holding a glass case filled with more pastries, and an old Gaggia coffee machine, hissing and steaming.

I always love that first taste of coffee in the morning, the burnt bitterness of it jolting me awake. I had to wait some time for this cup, though, as I'd stumbled into a place where the regulars were served first. Standing patiently at the counter, I listened to the Italian voices at my shoulders and glanced at the man beside me deep in his copy of *La Repubblica*. It seemed this assignment might not be so tricky after all. Already I was finding the real Venice.

The rest of the day was devoted to wandering, pausing from time to time to eat or drink, to take some notes or rest my feet. What I wanted at this point were impressions rather than details. So I jotted down the names of places to return to and kept walking.

By afternoon the tourists were with me wherever I went. Piazza San Marco was a sea of them. They bobbed in gondolas on the Grand Canal, sat on the steps of the churches and swarmed along the narrow streets.

I moved to the further reaches of Venice, where there was still peace to be found if you looked carefully enough. In a park tucked away behind a palazzo or beside a canal lined by people's homes, their windows shuttered for privacy, the only sign of life the day's laundry fluttering on clothes lines.

I spent a long time wandering until I was tired and lost. Every archway or corner tempted me onwards. Finally I came across a *vaporetto* stop and took my chance to ride the crowded ferryboat back towards Hotel Gondola.

It was almost evening by the time I arrived and other guests were straggling in: families clutching maps and wearing daypacks, middle-aged women in comfortable shoes, a couple hand in hand. I glanced towards the reception desk but there was no sign of Massimo, just the unhelpful clerk from the night before.

'Is the manager around?' I asked.

'No,' she replied, doing her best not to meet my eyes.

'Do you know when he'll be back?'

'No.'

'Have you any idea where he is then?'

'He is upstairs, in the bar,' she said grudgingly in heavily accented English.

Assuming Massimo was having an after-work drink, I climbed the narrow staircase to the bar beside the terrace. Rather than relaxing at a table with a cold beer, I found him standing behind the bar, staring at the screen of his phone and frowning.

'Good evening,' I greeted him.

'*Buona sera,*' he replied distractedly.

'Are you the bartender here as well as the manager?'

'Not usually.' Massimo looked up. 'The regular barman didn't turn up this evening.'

'Is he often so unreliable?'

'He is my nephew.'

'Oh.'

'The clerk on reception is my niece.'

'Ah, right.'

'This is a family hotel and we employ relatives whenever we

can.' Massimo held up a hand. 'Please don't ask how that is working out for me.'

I laughed. 'So you're pouring the drinks this evening?'

'I've been trying but those two English women out there have ordered a cocktail I've never heard of – a Double Banger. I pretended I knew it, thinking I'd look up the ingredients. I've found a Fruity Banger, a Cactus Banger and a Harvey Wallbanger ...'

'But not a Double Banger?'

'No, it doesn't seem to exist.'

I glanced over at the pair of women at the outdoor table. They were about my age and dressed in sparkly things for their evening out. One of them was looking back at us and giggling. A Double Banger, eh? I was pretty sure they were having Massimo on.

'Let me through,' I told him. 'I'll sort this.'

'You've worked in a bar?' he asked hopefully.

'Loads,' I exaggerated. 'For years and years.'

I made a basic Harvey Wallbanger with orange juice, vodka and Galliano. Then I poured in a shot of grenadine that sank prettily to the bottom and finished with a twist of orange and a maraschino cherry.

Massimo was looking on. 'Is that a Double Banger?'

'I've got no idea but don't worry, neither will they.'

I watched him take the drinks over. He smiled and chatted to the women as he laid paper napkins and a silver dish of salted nuts on their table. The younger of the two took a sip from her glass and nodded. The other did the same. Massimo stayed beside their table, talking for a while longer, and their faces tilted upwards as if every word he said was fascinating.

As he headed back to the bar, he grinned at me. 'The perfect Double Banger apparently, well done and thank you.'

'I'm sure if you flirt with them enough, they'll drink anything,' I said drily.

He gave me a sideways look and laughed. 'I hope so.

Because I have a feeling I'm not going to be the greatest bartender.'

'You'll be OK. Surely it doesn't get too busy up here?'

'Guests come in for drinks before dinner. This time of year it's chilly on the terrace in the evening so we put out rugs, have the heaters on, there are fairy lights; it's pretty.'

'Do the locals drink here too?'

'No, they go elsewhere. This is not one of your secret spots.'

'I think I managed to find one today,' I told him. 'A little coffee shop packed with only Venetians.'

'Ah yes.'

'I'm sure you could show me better places I'd never discover on my own.'

Massimo laughed again. 'Didn't we already have this conversation? Last night, wasn't it?'

'Yes, but last night you didn't need me,' I pointed out. 'Now you're an inexperienced barman who is about to struggle with a rush of customers – imagine how that is going to play out on TripAdvisor.'

Massimo leaned back against the bar and crossed his arms across his chest. 'Clever,' he said.

I smiled. 'Yes, I know.'

'So you will help me out in the bar this evening and in return tomorrow night I show you my Venice?'

'It's a deal,' I agreed.

'But if I take you to my favourite places then you can't tell your readers where they are.'

'That's not going to work for me.'

'It's the deal I'm offering.'

'I'm not taking it.'

'Va bene.' He ran a hand through his dark hair. 'I suppose I'll have to do my best here without you.'

A couple with two teenagers appeared. They settled at a table and waited to be served. An older man came in, and did the same.

Massimo looked at me and widened his eyes.

'Oh, all right.' I relented. 'You take the orders and I'll make the drinks. But you'd better show me a really good time tomorrow night.'

'I will; I promise.'

Soon the terrace filled up and every table was taken. Fortunately most people weren't adventurous. They wanted beers, Aperol spritz, a Bellini or a margarita; nothing I couldn't manage. When the orders began to stack up, Massimo came behind the bar and helped out. He popped corks from bottles, rinsed glasses and wiped down surfaces covered with stuff I'd spilt. We worked well together. There wasn't time to talk for at least a couple of hours but then the customers began to drift out, group by group, until there was only one full table left.

Massimo poured two glasses of Prosecco and passed one to me. 'I think we deserve this.'

'How long before they all come piling back, do you think?'

'A good two to three hours but there won't be nearly as many. Are you tired?'

'No, I'm fine,' I said, although in truth, after a long day mostly on my feet, I was completely shattered.

'I couldn't have done that without you,' he said, clinking his glass against mine.

'How does your nephew manage on his own?'

'Poor Nico, I suppose I'll have to find him some help.' He breathed out a sigh. 'With a place like this there is always something I need to get onto.'

'Have you worked here very long?' I asked.

'All my life, more or less.'

Massimo told me his story between sips of Prosecco. His grandparents had started the hotel when they were young and eventually his parents had taken it over. As children he and his sister used to help with simple tasks like collecting the used linen from the rooms, or polishing the glassware and silver. His parents had them working here at weekends and after school. Then a few years ago they retired to Burano and now the hotel was his to run because his sister wasn't interested.

'All your life spent in the one place,' I marvelled.

'It's beautiful here,' he said, looking out over the terrace, with its gleaming fairy lights twisting over wrought-iron balustrades and topiary trees in terracotta pots.

'But there are so many other beautiful places in the world,' I countered.

'Yes, and I've travelled to see some of them, but I've always wanted to come home. Don't you find that too?'

'Not really.'

He shrugged. 'If your home was the Hotel Gondola maybe you'd feel differently.'

I tried to imagine living in Venice and running a place like this, waking every morning to the same tasks and routines, with guests to manage and staff to wrangle. At that point it seemed impossible. I couldn't dream up a scenario where anything remotely like it might happen.

3

Kat Black didn't especially enjoy tending the bar. But she was here, not as a guest any more, but to help run the Hotel Gondola and it was the one job she could usefully do. So every evening, before the rush for aperitifs began, she joined Massimo's nephew Nico up on the terrace and they worked together.

She was better at it now, her repertoire of cocktails had grown and she could shake, muddle and mix with the best of them. The bar had grown busier as a result and often she was recognised. Kat dreaded that moment of feeling someone's eyes lock onto her face and hearing the inevitable question: 'Don't I know you from somewhere?'

If she said yes, and mentioned her TV show *Black of Beyond*, they'd make a fuss, ask her to autograph a cocktail napkin or wonder what she was doing in Venice. Very quickly, Kat realised it was better to reply: 'No, I don't think we've ever met.' And if they managed to put a name to her face she would murmur: 'Yes, I do look like her, everyone says that.'

It seemed far easier not to get locked in conversation with any of the hotel's guests and then have to explain why she was working behind a bar now instead of in front of a TV camera. And yet today, for some reason, she had spent half an afternoon with one of them and here Ruth was still, perched on one of the barstools, staring warily at the cocktail Kat had mixed for her.

'What exactly did you say it was?'

'A breakfast martini.'

'What's in it?'

'Have a taste, it's delicious.'

Ruth took a tentative sip. 'It's rather strong.'

'Don't worry, you're only getting one of them.'

'There's a familiar flavour I can't quite put my finger on. Limoncello?'

'Marmalade,' Kat told her.

'Really? In a cocktail?'

'Yes. Gin, Cointreau, lemon juice and a spoonful of thin-cut orange marmalade. It's the cocktail of the week. Massimo is keen on it.'

Kat had discovered that making cocktails was really not so different from cooking. Half the secret was good ingredients, and having them at your fingertips. Then it was all about bringing together flavours, the sting of gin, the bite of fresh lemon, a jammy hit of sugar.

Ruth took another sip. 'Have you ever had one for breakfast?' she asked.

'No, and I wouldn't recommend it. For breakfast you'd want an espresso martini. I'll make you one of those some time.'

Kat was busy checking that the bar was stocked with everything needed for the shift ahead, while Nico was wiping down tables decorated with ugly splatters by Venice's sparrows and seabirds. Soon guests would start filtering in, ready for their first drink of the evening.

'If you're working here every night, and Massimo is busy with the hotel all day, when do you find time for each other?' wondered Ruth.

'It's not ideal,' Kat admitted. 'But sometimes there is a lull and he takes me out for dinner or joins me on one of my rambles around Venice. And, of course, when winter comes the weather will be too bad to keep the terrace open, and there will be far fewer guests. Massimo says we'll have lots of time to enjoy together then.'

'Winter is a long way off,' Ruth said, sounding dubious. 'I think you may have set yourself quite a challenge here.'

'Maybe, but just like I was saying earlier, I'm not going to give up on challenges just because I'm getting older.'

Then Kat started on all the things she tended to say when she really got into this subject. How her body might be ageing but she still felt young inside her head, how her dreams hadn't changed, how she wasn't buying into this whole business of twenty good years, how her plan was to keep on living right up until the moment she keeled over and died.

'Fair enough,' said Ruth. 'But do you have to make it so hard on yourself?'

Massimo appeared at the same time as the first group of customers. Usually he liked to look in once or twice over the course of the evening. Kat would pour him a drink and he'd move from table to table, chatting to the guests, hearing how they had spent their day and suggesting how they might enjoy the next one. He was so striking with his lean body, wide shoulders and still-dark hair. People were charmed by him and Kat could see how he enjoyed winning them over.

This evening, though, he looked distracted. He escorted a group – two American couples – to a table with a view over the rooftops, then came and stood at the small bar, as far away as possible from Ruth.

'Kat, I need to talk to you,' he said quietly.

'Right now? I'm about to get busy.' She could see Nico clutching his order book and moving towards the two couples.

'Just for a minute.'

Kat was polishing up a martini glass. 'Do you need a drink?'

'Not really but you might: my wife is coming in this evening.'

'For goodness' sake, not again.'

Massimo's wife Zita, the woman he couldn't divorce because his parents hadn't accepted they were separated. She was a tiny, copper-skinned Neapolitan with a taste for blingy belts and dangly earrings. Kat suspected she was trouble, although Massimo kept telling her not to worry.

'Is she playing some game with us?'

Massimo frowned. 'Zita isn't like that.'

Kat threw gin into the shaker, splashed in Cointreau and lime, and a dollop of marmalade. 'Why else would she be doing this?' She fought to keep her voice low, aware of Ruth sitting at the bar, quietly eavesdropping.

'Because she wants to sit on the terrace, drink a cocktail and say hello to me,' Massimo told her.

Kat shook the martini more energetically than necessary, poured it into the glass and placed it on the bar. She wondered why it was taking so long to sort out this stupid situation. Massimo and Zita had been apart for over two years. They didn't love each other, hadn't for a long time, and their daughters were both away at university in Milan. On the face of it there seemed nothing to hold him back except family disapproval.

'You're forty-seven, surely you get to run your own life now,' Kat kept saying whenever they spoke about it.

'It's different for Italians. You don't understand. This thing with you and me has moved so quickly. It's necessary to give my family more time.'

And so Massimo hadn't told his wife about Kat yet, reasoning that once he did their daughters would have to know. Neither had she met his sister, or his parents. Nevertheless, word must have got out; most likely Nico was reporting back to at least a few of the family. Zita must have heard something. At the end of Kat's first week she had appeared, hair sleek and nails freshly lacquered. She took a seat facing the bar and Kat could sense her cool, appraising gaze.

That seemed fair enough; Kat could imagine being curious enough to do the same. Except now Zita was coming back. What did she want?

'She's making sure I know this is her territory,' she told Massimo.

'This isn't about you,' he promised.

Trapped behind the bar, Kat clattered gin bottles in frustration.

'Please don't let it upset you.' Massimo leaned over and quickly brushed her lips with his. 'I don't want you to feel bad.'

Kat wondered how she was supposed to feel. Nothing in her life so far had prepared her for a situation like this.

'Zita will stay for an hour at the most,' he promised. 'I'll reserve a table for her at the far end of the terrace. If you don't want to be here then take a break and Nico will manage on his own.'

With another quick touch of his lips, Massimo turned and headed off on one of his circuits, stopping to ask this person if they wanted another drink, that one if they needed help to book a tour, no trace of tension, his usual pleasant self.

'I'm not going to run away,' Kat muttered to herself. She picked up an order Nico had left on the bar and tried to focus on mixing drinks. A negroni, a spritz, a Bellini; the cocktails everyone chose because they were in Venice. So much was inevitable when you were a visitor here, how you ate, what you saw. Perhaps it was the same everywhere. To Kat it seemed as if, in her own life, all those certainties were disappearing. She felt more lost than she ever had in all her years of criss-crossing the globe.

Ruth had finished her martini now and was playing with the empty glass. 'Do you think I might risk another one of these?' she called over tipsily.

'No, definitely not,' Kat told her.

'But it's made me feel so lovely – sort of light, buzzy and relaxed.'

'I know but a second one won't make you feel twice as good.'

'What a shame.'

'I'll make you a weak gin and tonic instead. Safer, I promise.'

'I thought you didn't do safe?'

Kat filled a tall tumbler with ice and slugged in some gin. 'You know, Ruth, you're absolutely right, I don't.'

How would she cover all this in her book? Kat wondered, watching Massimo pause at a table to chat to some guests, smiling as though he didn't have a care in the world. She wasn't even going to think about it yet. Dealing with the opening chapters was proving tricky enough and they covered the very beginning, the heady days of flirting and falling for each other, when everything still felt easy and exciting.

A Year at Hotel Gondola by Kat Black

CHAPTER 4

It was my second day in Venice and I had plans for the evening. Massimo had given me strict instructions. He'd said to meet him at six p.m. in the hotel lobby. I wasn't allowed a pad or pen, not even my phone, in case I was tempted to take down notes. I was to be as dressy as I liked but not wear high heels. And I was to expect it to be a late night.

It wasn't truly a date and yet for some reason I wanted to make an effort. Looking through the outfits I'd brought, none seemed exactly right. They were too casual and loose-fitting, too dull. I needed something fabulous.

Shopping for clothes is not my favourite thing. The problem is I'm one of those in-between women, not exactly fat but not skinny either. I've got generous hips, a bit of a tummy and although my legs aren't bad, they're not what they used to be. In the right outfit I can look OK, in an unflattering one I'm a disaster.

For my television shows, I've always been dressed by a stylist who has spent days slogging round the stores. My very best clothes are the ones I've held onto after filming was finished – tops that drape and trousers that skim. But now I needed a frock and there was no stylist in sight.

Even finding a place that sold the sort of things I like proved difficult. I wandered up to the Strada Nuova where it was all cheap leather goods and glass jewellery. Turning round, I retraced my steps, and walked on further, over the Rialto Bridge, past the bustling fish and vegetable markets and into the back streets where very quickly I lost myself.

I found the funny little shop just across a stone bridge that spanned a narrow canal. There was no signage on its awning and I might have walked straight past except a dress in the window caught my eye; a classic 1950s shape with a nipped-in waist and scooped neckline, its fabric cheerfully patterned with lemons. Pausing for a moment, I decided to go inside.

Even if the space had been twice as big you wouldn't have wanted so many clothes displayed in it. The rails were crammed, the shelves spilling over. Standing in the doorway I reeled a bit and then I heard a woman say, 'Come in, come in, you are English, yes?'

I couldn't tell where the voice was coming from, only that it was very close. 'Hello, yes, where are you?'

There was a rustling from behind a rail of tightly packed gowns then two small, fluffy dogs burst through; one yipped at me, the other sniffed my feet. The person that followed, pushing out between a black evening dress and a cream sequinned bolero jacket, was elfin and slender, with silver hair stylishly cropped, sleeves of bangles up her arms and ropes of coloured glass beads in a tangle round her neck. I noticed all of these things before realising she was rather old.

'Ouf,' she said in a gravelly voice. 'I really must clear a pathway to my storeroom. It's becoming much too hard to fight my way through with the new deliveries.'

'New deliveries?' I laughed. 'You might need to sell a few things before getting any more clothes in.'

'Ah, but the selling is the difficult part.' The woman gave a helpless shrug. 'I can't let someone walk out with a frock that is entirely wrong, you see. The thought of it hanging in the back of a wardrobe, unloved ... that's not why I'm here. I want my clothes to be worn, to give other women the same pleasure they once brought me.'

'These are all your own things?' I asked, surprised.

'Only the loveliest of them are. When I opened this shop, my friends started asking me to sell clothes for them as well.

35

And I have many friends, you see, so the shop is rather full.'

'You're a Venetian?'

'I was born here and it is where I have lived my entire life.'
She held out her hand. 'My name is Coco.'

'I'm Kat.' I shook her hand.

'So tell me, Kat, what kind of person are you?'

'I'm sorry?'

'I need to know so I can decide which dress is right for you.'

'Actually, I wanted to try on a frock in the window, the one
with the lemons.'

'No, no,' she said emphatically.

'You don't think it will fit me?'

'It might but I am not selling you that dress. You would
regret buying it before you got back to your hotel.'

'I just want to try it on,' I told her.

'No,' she repeated. 'There is a dress here that will be right
for you but it is not that one. So tell me about yourself. What
do you like?'

Clearly the old woman was odd. I considered making some
excuse and exiting the shop, but I really did want a new dress.

'I like clothes that are a little different, colourful rather than
black, and nothing too formal,' I told her.

'So you are an adventurous person?'

'Definitely,' I agreed.

'Do you always make your hair into that big ball on top of
your head?' Frowning, she traced a circle with her finger.

'My topknot? I have a lot of hair,' I said defensively. 'And
it's more practical to wear it up.'

'Practical?' She raised her eyebrows. 'Let it down, signora,
so I can take a proper look at you.'

To humour her I did as she asked. Glossy brown curls
tumbled over my shoulders and fell down my back. Coco
cocked her head then turned and started burrowing into a rail
of clothes at the furthest corner of the shop.

'We'll try the blue frock that belonged to Isabella di

Bono,' she said, her voice slightly muffled by layers of fabric. 'We'll stick with the cooler colours only. No reds, no orange, definitely no lemons.'

She pulled out four different dresses. 'This will do to begin with.'

One by one I tried them on in the curtained-off area that served as a changing room. Coco made me emerge each time and stand in front of the full-length mirror while she tweaked and tugged at the garments. To my surprise she had picked right; they did all suit me.

'I'm not sure which I like best,' I told her.

'You should take the blue one and the little white wrap-round because it shows off your shape.'

'How much are they?'

Coco named a price that seemed steep for a couple of second-hand dresses, but I did like them and, as I've said, I don't shop much.

'OK, I'll take them both,' I told her.

'No, no.'

'But you said I could.'

'And you are going to accept the first price I offer you?' Coco gave me a look that made it clear she thought I was a hopeless case. 'You are not going to haggle with me at all?'

'I wasn't planning to,' I admitted.

'Well really, where is the fun in that?'

So I haggled, half-heartedly at first and then with more enthusiasm once I realised how much she was enjoying it. In the end I got the dresses for half the price she had originally quoted.

'You have made a very good saving,' Coco said warmly, as she wrapped the clothes carefully in tissue paper. 'And you have two new dresses you will look beautiful in so long as you don't do bad things to your hair. You must be happy.'

'Yes, I am.'

'That is very good.' She seemed genuinely pleased.

It struck me that I might be able to get more than dresses from Coco. She was a local and surely would have some good tips on where to go and what to do. Secret Venice, the hunt was on and I'm not one to give up till I find what I'm looking for.

'I'd love to buy you a coffee to say thank you,' I told her. 'Could you possibly leave the shop for half an hour?'

'Of course, that is what the closed sign is for. But I am not sure what you are thanking me for.'

'For selling me two perfect dresses at a bargain price. I have a sort-of date tonight and I'll be wearing one of them.'

'A sort-of date?' As Coco laughed she looked quite beautiful in a way that seemed fragile and temporary. She moved her arms and the bangles clinked like a musical accompaniment. 'Is he good-looking?'

'Yes, very,' I admitted. 'Actually, he's a Venetian so you may know him. Massimo Morosini, he owns the Hotel Gondola.'

'Morosini ... let me think.' She frowned. 'Perhaps I do know who he is. Tall, and yes, extremely attractive with the face of an aristocrat. He had a wife from Napoli but I heard they parted a while ago.'

Coco rummaged about under the counter and pulled out a large card with the word *Closed* handwritten in different languages and colours. She hung it on the inside of the door then gave me one of her fluffy dogs to carry as we walked down the now-busy street. Its fur smelt of her fragrance, something powdery and old-fashioned that seemed to cling to me even after I put the animal down.

The place she had brought me to had tables with jauntily striped umbrellas lined up alongside the edge of the canal. 'Isn't this a bit of a tourist spot?' I asked.

She shrugged. 'Yes, maybe, but the coffee is good and it is where I always come.'

We settled at a table and the waiter appeared at her shoulder almost instantly. Coco did the ordering, without bothering to ask what I might like.

'Tell me about this evening you have planned with Massimo Morosini,' she said, turning back to me. 'Either it is a date or it isn't. How can you be unsure?'

'Most likely it isn't,' I admitted. 'I told him that I wanted to experience parts of the city other visitors never find so he's offered to show me around.'

'You are here on your own?'

'That's right.'

Coco gave this a moment's thought. 'Then it might be a date. You must wear the white wrap-round dress, that may help decide things.'

The waiter returned with our coffee and a plate of sugary-looking biscuits. He made quite a ceremony of laying it out on the table, a cappuccino for me, a double espresso and a jug of heated milk for Coco.

'These biscuits are good; you must try them,' she told me, offering me one.

I bit into thin crispness, sweetness and vanilla then had her spell out the name – *lingue di gatto* – to scribble in my notepad.

Coco fed more biscuits to her dogs than she ate herself. One was sitting on her knee, the other close beside her feet.

'I have a date this evening too,' she told me, spooning a skein of milk froth over her strong black coffee. 'One of my lovers is taking me dancing.'

'*One* of your lovers?'

'Yes,' she said airily. 'There are several.'

I smiled at her, assuming she had a rich fantasy life.

'So tell me, what is it you are hoping for from Massimo Morosini?' she asked me.

'Hoping for? A night out, a fun time …'

'And after that?'

'Um, well, I hadn't …' I was thrown by such directness.

'If I were you I would certainly make love to him,' Coco said crisply. 'You are in Venice, you are both single, it would be crazy not to. You don't agree?' She fixed me with that same look she had worn when I failed to haggle with her in the shop. 'Didn't you tell me that you are adventurous?'

'Yes,' I said, entirely taken aback.

'Then what is there to stop you? It is wonderful having lovers. It is the very best thing.'

Coco told me all about the man who was taking her out that evening. She said he was a good dancer and a smart dresser, who had a beautiful motorboat she loved to ride in.

'Of course, he has a wife so I only get to see him once or twice a week but that is perfect because we never tire of each other.'

'And I guess it means you have time for all your other lovers,' I said, still not believing her.

'Exactly.'

When we'd finished our coffee, I walked Coco back to the shop. She made me promise to return the next morning so she could hear about my almost-date.

'Remember, it is the white dress not the blue one that you are wearing,' she called to me from the shop doorway. 'And keep your hair down and put some blusher on your cheeks.'

Walking away, I couldn't help smiling. Everything about Coco seemed extraordinarily interesting: her shop, the way she dressed, and the things she said. And it struck me that she wasn't entirely wrong. I was single and Massimo seemed to be too; why shouldn't we have a good time together?

4

Kat was in one of her dangerous moods. She had downed a martini while waiting for Massimo's wife to appear in the bar, and it hadn't been the smartest idea on an empty stomach. She kept an eye on the table at the far end of the terrace but, as the rest of the place filled up, it stayed empty. Perhaps Zita wasn't coming after all. Kat was trying to decide whether she felt relieved or disappointed, when at last she made her entrance.

She was wearing a red dress made from tight stretchy fabric and carrying one of those statement handbags that cost more than some people's cars. Massimo met her with a quick kiss on both cheeks and they walked out to her table together.

'Oh dear,' said Ruth, still sitting at the bar, her gin glass now empty.

'Sorry?' In a semi-daze Kat glanced over at her. 'Were you wanting another drink?'

'No, definitely not.'

'What was the "oh dear", about then?'

'Your colours are changing, flaring red, orange and gold. It's beautiful but scary.'

Exasperated, Kat sighed. 'Sorry, Ruth, but all this woo-woo stuff, I don't believe in it.'

'That's fine. You don't have to.' She seemed unfazed. 'And actually I will have another drink; just a soda with some lime. I want to stay around and watch.'

'Watch what?' Kat asked.

Ruth gave a shrug. 'I'm waiting to see.'

It seemed to take ages for Nico to shuffle over and write down their orders. Then Zita stalled him in a long conversation – she was his aunt by marriage so must have known him since he was a child, supposed Kat – and for once he bothered to stop and clear away a few empty glasses on his way back to the bar.

Kat almost snatched the order from his fingers. The martini would be for Massimo, the spritz for his ex-wife. She made the drinks quickly and waved Nico away.

'I'll take these. You go and ask those Americans if they'd like anything else.'

She knew Massimo was watching her as she headed over, yet his expression didn't change, not even as she put down the drinks and smiled at Zita.

'Hi, I'm Kat, Massimo's girlfriend, how lovely to meet you.'

Zita jumped to her feet. 'I have been longing to meet you too,' she said, grabbing Kat's hands. 'Massimo said I mustn't rush in. I think he didn't want to scare you with his big, crazy family.'

She was all heady fragrance and soft skin. Her voice was husky, her grip surprisingly strong. Looking down, Kat saw the rings still on her finger, wedding and engagement.

'You must join us,' insisted Zita. 'Sit down, take my drink and I will ask them to make me another.'

Massimo laughed uneasily. 'Kat is the one making the drinks this evening; she can't join us.'

'But I want to get to know her,' Zita insisted.

'Perhaps another time.'

'Massimo, *caro*,' Zita said in a wheedling tone. 'Don't be so ridiculous. If Nico can't cope without her then why don't you get up and help him?'

'But I …' Massimo seemed as if he were going to argue then changed his mind. Still he sounded reluctant. 'OK, if it's what you really want.'

'*Perfetto*! Off you go and let us chat in peace.' Zita patted his arm. 'Don't worry, *caro*, you can trust us.'

This hadn't been Kat's plan at all. She had only wanted to meet his ex-wife, not spend half the evening chatting with her. But here she was being manoeuvred towards a chair, the woman's grip on her arm still strong. And Massimo was standing up and offering his surrender.

'You ladies enjoy your talk. Let me know if you need more drinks.' He gave a little mock bow. 'I'm at your service.'

Kat took a gulp of the martini he had left behind on the table. She was aware of Zita sitting beside her, leaning forward and close, the sweetness of her fragrance enveloping both of them.

'So ...' Kat began hesitantly.

'So,' Zita echoed. 'You are Kat Black. I have seen some of your TV shows. You are famous, yes? And now you are Massimo's girlfriend.'

'That's right.'

'Tell me, Kat Black, are we going to be friends or enemies?'

'Do we have to be one or the other?' Kat felt thrown off balance.

'Definitely.' Zita drummed her copper-varnished finger-nails on the table. 'It is inevitable, isn't it?'

Kat took a steadying breath. 'I don't think—' she began.

'Look at Massimo over there by the bar,' Zita interrupted. 'Can you tell what is on his mind? No, because you don't really know him. But I do and I will tell you. He is pleased that we have met because it is something he has been worrying about, but he has lost control of the situation and finds that disconcerting. You see? This is just one way I can help you if you are my friend. If you are my enemy, well ...'

'I'd better be your friend then,' Kat said, as lightly as she could. She spared a moment's thought for Ruth looking on from her perch up at the bar. If she could really see colours what sort of a show must she be witnessing now?

'Excellent; the right choice.' Zita leaned back in her chair.

Attractive as she was, Kat thought she saw a hint of hardness in her face. Best not to make an enemy of this woman.

'I'm glad you think so.'

Zita smiled at her. 'Poor Massimo, it wasn't his plan for us to meet so soon, and he is a man who can't bear it when things don't go to plan. He has always liked the world arranged his way.'

Kat thought that was probably true. Massimo was one of those people whose desk was always tidy and whose cupboards were carefully ordered. If she left a book face down on the floor, she'd return to find it neatly replaced on the shelf. If she tossed her jeans over the back of a chair, he would fold them. He made a joke about it, blamed it on his training during military service, but she could see it really did annoy him. And to be fair the room they were sharing, hidden away up in the eaves of the hotel, was cramped and easily cluttered. It hadn't been long before she'd stopped leaving her stuff in random piles, and started trying to find the right place for everything.

'I guess he has to be organised, running a hotel like this,' she said to Zita, uncomfortable to be discussing Massimo with her like this, as she was certain he would hate it.

'And so you are helping him now, working here. How is that going?'

'Fine.'

Zita gave a disbelieving lift of her eyebrows. 'Such a career you have had, all that travel, all those places, and now you are here in Venice. How are you finding it?'

'Interesting,' Kat told her, seizing the chance to change the subject. 'Quite different to any other place I've spent time in and not just because of the canals and the architecture.'

'How then?'

'To me it almost seems like two cities,' explained Kat.

'There is the Venice of the Venetians and then the place the tourists experience.'

'That is probably true,' agreed Zita. 'So many of the old families have moved to the mainland where it is cheaper and easier to live. The ones that remain know their livelihoods depend on the visitors but still they prefer to keep their distance. They are a tight little circle.'

'What I'd really like is to find my way into it. I'm supposed to be writing a book about the real Venice.'

'Good luck.'

'You've lived here for a long time, you must know the city well.'

'Yes, but not necessarily the people. You must remember that I come from Napoli. To them I am an outsider; I don't speak their dialect. Maybe in several centuries they might accept me but not yet.'

Kat felt discouraged. 'My problem is that working here in the hotel, the people I talk to all seem to be tourists. I'm not sure what I'm going to do.'

'Perhaps if you try to seek out the real Venice, it only becomes harder to find,' said Zita.

'So what do you suggest?'

'Wait for it to find you?'

'I'm not the greatest at waiting for things,' Kat admitted.

Zita smiled again. 'And so we find another thing we both have in common besides Massimo.'

The conversation flowed a little more easily after that. Zita spoke about her daughters with pride and affection. She described the Morosini family, a bewildering array of parents, aunts, cousins, nephews and nieces that Kat was certain she would never get straight in her mind. She recommended a hairdresser and the only woman in the whole of Venice who should be allowed to touch Kat's eyebrows. She finished one spritz then another, her voice growing louder, her hands tracing shapes in the air. Every now and then

Massimo glanced over and even Kat, who was only beginning to know him, could tell he was uncomfortable at the sight of them together.

'I am glad my husband has found someone like you,' Zita told her. 'I think you will be good for him. And I am certain that you and I are going to become great friends.'

The sky was darkening and the terrace emptying. With their moods softened by a cocktail or two, people were making the move towards dinner. Suddenly Kat longed to go with them. A part of her wished she could run from the whole situation – this woman, Massimo, his hotel, her book deal, all the challenges she had set herself, even Venice. Everything seemed so complicated and she couldn't remember why she had ever thought it such a good plan. The adventurous spirit that had taken Kat across the world seemed to be deserting her in this city of watery plains and shadowy canals. For the first time in her life she felt daunted. But maybe it was easier to be brave alone in the middle of some wild place than where she was right now, fitting in with someone else's life, trying to find out how it felt to fall in love.

Kat stood abruptly. 'I ought to go,' she said. 'I have things to do.'

Zita looked surprised. 'I thought we might have dinner together.'

'Some other evening,' said Kat. 'I've lost too much time today and have to get at least a couple of hundred words of my book written tonight before bed or else at this rate I'll never meet my deadline.'

'Ah yes, your book. What will it be about? Venice? Massimo? Your relationship?'

'All those things,' said Kat awkwardly.

'I look forward to reading it some day.'

'I'm still very much at the beginning,' Kat told her. 'There's a long way to go. Have a good evening, Zita. I'll see you again soon?'

'Most definitely,' Massimo's wife replied. 'Very soon, I am sure.'

Over at the bar Ruth had obviously been watching them and now was pretending to frown over her guidebook.

'I need to decide where to eat,' she told Kat. 'Should I just go to a little bar for a snack or out to a proper restaurant?'

Kat suggested a couple of places, inexpensive and close by, where an older woman might not feel too uncomfortable having dinner alone.

'I'd join you but I have to work,' Kat told her. 'And then later I really must make some progress with my book.'

'That's fine, you get on with your writing.' Ruth stared at her. 'Oh, and just in case you were wondering. You're blue now. Dark, dark blue. It feels moody and rather dramatic.'

A Year at Hotel Gondola by Kat Black

CHAPTER 5

For my night out with Massimo I wore my hair down and put on the white dress just as Coco had told me. I used a few tricks I've picked up from make-up artists along the way so my eyes looked bigger and my skin seemed dewy. As the church bells of Venice pealed for six o'clock I reached the lobby to find him waiting.

Italian men have a certain way of dressing, pale pants and close-fitting shirts in gelato colours, a look that would seem too try-hard on an English guy. Massimo was in pistachio and cream, with a sweater round his shoulders ready for when the evening cooled. His dark hair had been trimmed, his olive skin was freshly shaved. Everything about him looked immaculate.

He greeted me with a light touch cheek to cheek. 'Ready?'

'Absolutely.'

His walking pace was brisk. As we made our way through the maze of little back streets the Venetians call *calli*, he kept distracting me with questions. Where was my favourite place in the world (too difficult to choose). What was my scariest experience (anything involving dizzying heights, if I'm honest). What did I love about travelling (freedom, change, possibilities … need I go on?). I was so busy coming up with answers that very soon I'd lost any idea of where I was.

'You did that on purpose,' I said accusingly.

'Did what?'

'Made me talk about myself so I wouldn't pay attention to the route we were taking.'

Massimo laughed. 'Yes, perhaps I did.'

We were crossing a stretch of glossy water between two walls of ivy-covered stone. A golden fall of evening sunshine lit our faces and there was the soft chug of a motorboat passing beneath us.

'You want to see the real Venice? Here it is, all around us,' said Massimo. 'You just have to open your eyes.'

The first place he took me to had a single half-curtained window and a low doorway. Inside was scented with cigar smoke.

All Venetians have a favourite *bacaro*, the small bars where they like to stop at midday and in the late afternoon for a glass of wine and a few of the snacks known as *cicchetti*. This one was only slightly bigger than a hole in the wall. Its wooden counter top was worn with age and on it was a glass case filled with crostini, their toppings secured by toothpicks, as well as platters of crumbed meatballs lapped by an oily tomato sauce.

'This is one of the older *bacari*,' Massimo told me. 'They say Casanova used to come here.'

'What did Casanova drink, do you think?' I asked.

'He would have started with a glass of Prosecco and a taste of the *baccalà mantecato*. I suggest we do the same.'

New flavours are one of the things I live for, and although I'd eaten salted cod before I'd never tried it whipped into a perfectly smooth cream with olive oil and garlic and then smeared across a circle of lightly toasted baguette. I closed my eyes and chewed slowly. It was rich and savoury, with only a hint of the sea to it.

When I opened my eyes Massimo was staring at me.

'Sorry, I always do that when I'm trying something new,' I told him.

'I couldn't tell whether you liked it or not.'

'I don't know that myself yet. The first bite is always about understanding what I'm eating, trying to make sense of the flavours and texture. I'm learning about it, I suppose. The liking part comes later.'

'Is there anything you wouldn't taste?' he wondered.

'Probably not, unless it was poisonous, and even then I've tried a few risky things – pufferfish sushi in Japan and some questionable weeds and mushrooms. So far I've survived.'

'Why would you want to eat those sorts of things?' asked Massimo, screwing up his nose.

'Because food is one of the big adventures; it's a way of experiencing every part of a place, the tradition and rituals as well as the tastes and smells.'

'Maybe ... but still I couldn't eat something I didn't like. I couldn't even take a second bite. In Venice we have a saying: "Eat and drink because life is a lightning flash." Food is about enjoyment for us.'

'For me it's about curiosity,' I told him.

'OK, but either way you should try more of the *cicchetti* here because they are among the best.'

We didn't linger at that *bacaro* but stayed for long enough to eat a plate of battered white-bread sandwiches, filled with stringy mozzarella, toasty warm from the deep fryer.

Then we moved on, walking through arched passageways that led beneath ancient buildings, over one bridge then another, beside dark water glinting with reflected light.

We went from *bacaro* to *bacaro* drinking a pink wine that tasted like strawberries and devouring crispy bite-sized balls of aubergine, a salad of charred octopus tentacles, more crostini topped with smoky, cured meats and of course sardines prepared the Venetian way, sweet and sour, cloaked in cured onions and pine nuts. And we talked a lot, I don't remember about what, only that there seemed no shortage of things to say to one another.

As it grew late, Massimo took me to other places: a jazz bar behind a heavy wooden door that he had to knock on to gain entrance, the ballroom of a crumbling palazzo where people were dancing, places I was desperate to include in my article but was certain I had no hope of finding again without him.

As we were walking home, slowly by then because both of us were steeped in good food and wine, I remembered what Coco had said about having lovers; there is nothing more wonderful, she had insisted. And for a moment or two I let myself imagine taking Massimo to bed, stripping the soft linen shirt from his lean, muscled body, touching the skin beneath it. In my head I pictured us together, feeling pleasantly shivery.

A mantle of mist had settled over Venice, and the city looked dark and moody. I glanced at Massimo as he walked beside me. Might he be thinking the same thing?

I was still wondering by the time we reached the Hotel Gondola. The lights were dimmed, the reception desk empty. Massimo walked me to my room, which meant squeezing into that tiny lift again, almost touching but not quite, listening to it creaking its way upwards.

At the door to my room, we paused.

'Thank you, it's been a great night,' I told him.

'I've enjoyed getting to know you, Kat.'

He stood and looked at me. Since I'm tall, we were very nearly eye to eye. This was his chance if he wanted to take it.

'Tomorrow I have to be up early for work and there will be a long day ahead,' he said softly. 'I need to make the most of the hours left for sleep.'

'OK,' I replied, hoping to keep the disappointment from my voice. 'Goodnight then.'

He kissed me, but so quickly that it was over and he was gone by the time I realised I had been kissed. I closed my eyes to hold onto the taste of him. And then I opened the door to the honeymoon suite, stripped off my own clothes and lay down alone in that great big bed.

In the morning there was no sign of Massimo. I looked for him on the terrace and hung about in reception for a bit, hoping for the chance to thank him again for such a great evening, but he must have been hidden away in his office.

So I went for a walk, thinking I might be able to retrace some of our route from the night before. It was impossible. Even when I was convinced I must be at the right spot I couldn't find the bar where I'd enjoyed the amazing fried aubergine balls or the place Casanova had frequented.

I stopped for coffee and ate a sugar-dusty brioche as I tried to decide what to do with the day. There were plenty of walking tours and cooking classes on offer, perhaps I could book onto one of those and come up with a story angle that would satisfy my magazine editor. But that went against the grain for me. I'm all about meeting locals, going inside their lives and joining them on their own personal orbit around wherever I'm visiting. That's what my TV series *Black of Beyond* was based on and now, for this article, I wanted to write about Massimo and the places he had taken me to. In the evening, all lit up and with their awnings opened out, those *bacari* might be easier to find. Still, I needed a few pointers and wondered if the old Venetian lady from the clothes shop would be able to help.

It took a while to find her, Venice fooling me as always with narrow back streets that took me in directions I hadn't expected. It was almost lunchtime by the time I saw the shop, just across the plain stone bridge where it had been all along.

Coco was standing in the doorway, her dogs at her feet. She was wearing a cowl-necked top in a shade of burnt orange paired with flared dark-denim pants and she was talking to a gondolier. It was one of those sights so ridiculously Venice that I had to stop and take a photograph. Seeing me, she struck a pose, head thrown back and laughing, as if the gondolier had just said something marvellously amusing.

'I wonder how many holiday albums I've appeared in over the years. I ought to charge people,' she told me when I joined her on the doorstep.

'You do look great. I love the colour of that top.'

'It wouldn't suit you.' She narrowed her eyes. 'Neither does the outfit you are wearing right now.'

'What's wrong with it?' I asked, surprised.

'*Cara,* can you really not see that this is the uniform of the middle-aged woman? Dark capri pants, baggy top.' She shuddered. 'Horrible.'

'They're comfortable clothes to walk about in,' I told her.

'It is possible to be comfortable and still have some style,' she said sharply. 'You should think about the people who have to look at you.'

'I was going to suggest we went for a coffee but I guess you won't want to be seen out with me like this?' I joked.

'Absolutely not,' Coco said crisply. 'Fortunately I have a whole shop of lovely things. Why don't I lend you something?'

She hustled me inside before there was time to argue. To my eyes the place looked even more cluttered than it had the day before. There were accessories I hadn't noticed previously, felt hats, feathery shrugs and furry stoles. She steered me past all of that and towards a rail of daywear.

'Venetian women wear layers,' she said. 'In the daytime we don't like to show too much skin. The look we are striving for is smart casual but always chic.'

Coco pulled out some trousers in a soft shade of stone, a grey/blue shell top, and a longline cream jacket in the lightest of fabrics.

'This,' she said.

'Shall I try it on?' I asked.

'No, you should put it on then we can go.'

In the tiny changing area I removed the offending capri pants and the top that I'd imagined was doing a fine job of disguising my bumpy bits, and dressed in the outfit she had given me.

'A little dull but I suppose it will do for now,' Coco said when I appeared. 'Boring is better than ugly.'

She gave me a moment to check out my reflection in the mirror then steered me out of the shop.

'The time for coffee is past,' she said, hanging the closed sign and locking the door behind her. 'In Venice there is a right moment for everything and now is when we eat. So let us have lunch. Where would you like to go?'

'Somewhere full of locals,' I said quickly. 'Where do the gondoliers eat?'

'Everyone asks that.' Coco looked amused. 'The truth is there are hundreds of gondoliers and they eat everywhere. But don't worry, I know a very good *osteria*. You will like it.'

She took me on a long walk, her little dogs trotting behind, all three of them at a surprisingly fast clip.

'I can't promise you gondoliers,' she said, as we reached a place with a few shabby outdoor tables. 'Only fresh seafood and good company.'

Inside were dark, wood-panelled walls and furniture to match so the net effect was gloomy. There was no menu but Coco had a rapid exchange with the proprietor that involved a lot of head-shaking. Finally he turned and stalked through to the kitchen, reappearing with a bowl of uncooked razor clams in iced water.

He presented them to Coco who took a careful look then nodded. Then there was another long discussion, until it appeared that at last we had ordered.

'You have to be careful to get the freshest seafood,' she told me. 'They know me here but even so I like to make certain they don't serve me the fish they want to sell before it goes off.'

'Surely they wouldn't dare.' I was half joking but again she took me very seriously.

'Oh, they would. And there are other things we must watch out for. In Venice most places have two prices – one for the locals and a higher one for tourists. I made sure he knew which charge we will be paying. Also there is always a dish they only tell the regular customers about. Today it is steamed bass with stewed apples and aged balsamic vinegar.'

'Are we having that?'

'Only after we have enjoyed a simple soup of the razor clams because this is the season when they are very good. And a small *frittura mista* just to taste as the batter here is so crisp and light, and the shrimp the sweetest.'

'That sounds perfect. Do you mind if I make a few notes while we eat?'

Coco gave me what I've come to think of as one of her looks. 'Why would you do that? Are you worried the meal won't be memorable enough?'

I explained I was a writer and told her about the article I was working on. Thankfully she didn't appear to have Massimo's squeamishness about sharing insider details. Instead she seemed rather excited to help. She listened to my description of the places I had visited the night before and managed to identify three of the *bacari* and the ballroom, helpfully marking them on my map.

'I have never visited that little jazz bar, though. Find out exactly where it is and perhaps we can go together, you and I,' she suggested. 'My life is much too quiet nowadays. There aren't the parties there used to be, not among my friends. They are all getting too old to enjoy themselves properly.'

'Not you, though?'

She shrugged. 'Not so far.'

Our razor clams arrived, bathed in white wine, parsley and garlic, and splashed with grassy olive oil. I closed my eyes, filling my mouth with the first spoonful. It was simple, and very fresh, just as Coco had promised.

She ate with enjoyment, steeping slices of grilled bread in her soup, and sucking the tender flesh from the razor clam shells. Once finished she pushed the empty bowl to one side, as if she wanted nothing more to do with it.

'So, Kat,' she said. 'You haven't told me the most interesting thing about your evening.'

'What's that?' I asked.

'How did it end?'

I must have looked startled because she laughed.

'You are shocked, maybe? You think I am prying into your business.' She gave a carefree shrug. 'It is true, I am.'

'Nothing happened,' I told her. 'Just a tiny goodnight kiss then we both went to our separate beds.'

'Ah, what a pity,' said Coco. 'Still, maybe next time.'

'I'm not sure if there will be a next time,' I admitted. 'Massimo might not be interested in me. It's difficult to tell.'

'But you are reading the signs surely? What are they saying?'

'There aren't any signs.'

'Of course there are,' Coco insisted. 'With men there are always signs. It is a matter of looking properly and knowing how to read them.'

'Unfortunately these seem to be skills I lack,' I admitted.

'Kat, how old are you?' Coco asked.

'I've just turned fifty, why?'

'How can you have reached such an age and not know this?'

'It's an aspect of life I've neglected,' I admitted. 'I've been busy with other things.'

She gave me a pitying look. 'I see.'

'I've been having adventures not boyfriends,' I said defensively.

'Personally, I have always found the two go hand in hand,' said Coco in a tone of voice that suggested she didn't believe a single word I was saying.

'Well, there have been men, obviously, but they always chanced along, guys I've worked with or met on my travels. We'd just sort of get together and then there was always a point when it made sense to go our separate ways. There never seemed much effort made on either side.'

Beginning to understand, Coco nodded. 'So you are like me. You have many lovers, but no one man who is special. There is nothing wrong with that.'

'Isn't there? I'm starting to wonder. Love seems a pretty big thing in life to miss out on.'

Coco nodded, looking like a wise old owl in her round-framed spectacles.

'With Massimo do things feel different than they did with those other men?'

'Maybe they do,' I realised, searching my mind in an effort to work out why. 'With him there was this instant attraction. You know when you look at a guy and you get a bit ... um, tingly? I keep finding myself thinking about him, which isn't like me at all.'

'That's a good sign.'

'But even if he is interested in me I get the feeling he's not going to be the one to make a move.'

'Then you must seduce him,' Coco decided.

'I can't do that.'

'Of course you can.'

'No really,' I insisted, 'I wouldn't know where to begin. I've never seduced anyone in my life.'

'Then how did those other men become your lovers?'

'Oh you know ... you have a few drinks ... one thing leads to another.'

Coco frowned and sighed. 'Then I suppose you need my advice?'

The waiter appeared with our *frittura mista*, a tangle of seafood and strips of vegetables in delicate nests of batter. Still frowning, Coco picked up a slice of zucchini with her fingers.

'The mistake lots of women make is assuming men are simple creatures,' she told me, between bites. 'Give them football, wine, good food, enough money, a pretty woman and they are satisfied. But men are as complicated as we are, just in different ways. Once you understand this it makes everything easier.'

'OK,' I said, beginning to think that she might actually have some idea what she was talking about.

'I don't know Massimo Morosini well so I must guess what is going through his mind.' Coco nibbled at a piece of shrimp, her expression thoughtful. 'I think it is about decorum. Good manners are important to Venetian men. You are a guest in his hotel, writing an article for a magazine. It is a professional situation. He will be very aware of what is appropriate.'

'That could be right,' I told her. 'He seems to take his work very seriously.'

'The question is how to tempt him to abandon decorum. It is not a matter of flirting or wearing something low cut. Absolutely not.'

'What then?'

Her fingers drifted towards the squid. 'I am thinking.'

In the moments of silent eating that followed it occurred to me that it was less than normal to be taking advice on seduction from an octogenarian – I'm assuming that's her age; she's never actually told me. But what you have to realise is that Coco has this air of absolute self-confidence. Sometimes I do doubt her words later on when I'm thinking them through, but in her presence I'm almost always convinced.

She finished the final morsel of shrimp, summoned the waiter to whisk away her empty plate, and declared, 'I know exactly what you should do.'

'Go on,' I prompted her.

'You will offer Massimo dinner at Harry's Bar as a thank you for such a wonderful evening. I know what you are going to say, that it is a tourist spot, but believe me, most Venetians love to go when they can afford it. And the light in there is always flattering no matter what the time of day. You will drink a Bellini then eat the carpaccio and a risotto, the traditional menu.'

'Then what?'

She held up a hand, as if to ward off the interruption. 'Over dinner you will tell him you have finished your article and sent it to the editor. This may not be true but that is not important. What you need is for him to think you are free to simply enjoy yourself.'

'OK, that sounds doable.'

'Yes, but now comes the hardest part. You must kiss him *before* you get back to his hotel. On the way ask him to show you something – his favourite view or a place he loves. And find a reason to get closer to him. Then kiss him.'

I was dubious. 'What if he's not so keen on being kissed by me?'

'He is a gentleman so will extricate himself in way that is not too awkward. And in a few days you will leave Venice and never see him again. But I think the plan will work. What we need is to find the right outfit, decorous but still sexy. I must have something in the shop but nothing is coming to mind.'

As we ate the sea bass she held forth about fashion. Coco has very strong opinions about what is stylish and what not. Capri pants were not my only crime. Apparently jeans should not be baggy and there were particular ways that scarves ought to be arranged around a neck, it went on and on. I let her talk and savoured the sea bass and its sweet/sour meeting with balsamic vinegar and stewed apples.

'I'm not sure about this plan yet, you know. I'm still thinking about it,' I said, once I had finished eating.

Coco gave an exasperated hiss. 'You are in one of the world's romantic cities, you are fifty and badly in need of some passion. What is there to think about?'

Writing about the very beginning and those first sparks of excitement had made Kat wonder if things were progressing the way they were supposed to. She had never worked and lived so closely with someone before, she had no compass. Was it reasonable to delay meeting most of Massimo's family and friends? Should she be concerned that while she was busy writing he had decided to take his wife out for a late supper? Was he tiring of her, wishing he hadn't rushed into this, wondering how to get out of it? Kat wanted to ask him, but also didn't, in case the answer he gave wasn't what she needed to hear.

A Year at Hotel Gondola wouldn't be much of a book if it all foundered within a few weeks. Kat wanted this project to work as there was nothing else on the horizon and she'd spent a lot of the advance already. Money seemed to slip away from her. She liked to be generous, treating friends to lavish lunches and ordering champagne. And then there were the upgrades; she was the queen of those. Business-class flights, five-star hotel rooms, and when the show's budget didn't cover it, she pulled out her credit card. 'Don't worry about money' had always been her attitude. 'There'll be more tomorrow.'

It had been a shock when the network decided they didn't want another series of *Black of Beyond*. The show had run its course, was what they said. But Kat wasn't finished with television yet. She had loved it all her life and wasn't ready to be set aside. If this book were successful then surely that would help leverage something else. *Kat Black's Venice,* perhaps? Other people had done similar things but hers would be better because by then she would be a real insider. She just had to make things work with Massimo.

Physically they were well matched and, if anything, that side of it was only getting better. Kat looked back at other men and realised she'd had no idea what she was missing. It was when they were out of bed that she felt uncertain. Everything had happened so fast, just as Massimo kept saying; perhaps all they needed was more time together.

Kat gave up on writing, put away her laptop and opened the window to let in some air. Leaning out a little, she thought she would never tire of this view, Venice at night, all dark water and coloured lights. A mist had blown in from the sea and everything was softly hazed. It had been like this that first time they went to Harry's Bar. Even the light inside the restaurant had seemed to throw them into soft focus.

Climbing into bed, she pulled the covers over her shoulders. Everything was so plain in this little room. It was free of the tassels and ruffles, the gold leaf and Murano glass that so lavishly adorned the rest of Hotel Gondola. No need to bother with any of that in what was essentially the staff quarters.

She was drifting off to sleep when Massimo came in. She heard him kicking off his shoes and for once letting his clothes drop to the floor.

'Did you have fun?' she murmured.

'Sorry, I was trying not to wake you.'

'I wasn't properly asleep, only drowsing.'

'Ah well, in that case.' He turned on the bedside lamp and picked up his clothes from the floor. 'You know what I'm like.'

'You'll sleep better if it's tidy.'

'Exactly.'

Once he had hung up his clothes, Massimo slid into bed beside her, reaching out, rasping his chin against her bare shoulder and nuzzling his face into her neck. And then he sighed. 'My God but Zita exhausts me. I only have to spend a few hours with her to see why it was impossible for us to stay together.'

'What did the two of you talk about this evening?'

'Lots of things: summer and whether she would do something with the girls. Zita's family has a house near the beach in Calabria that they've always stayed at together for a week or so in August. But the girls are older now. They might want to make other plans.'

'Did you talk about me at all?' Kat asked, feeling the warmth of his mouth as it forged a path up her neck.

'Mmm.'

'What do you mean, "mmm"?'

He rolled away from her. 'Yes, of course we did. Zita likes you. She is keen to see more of you. I'm not sure why you would want that but if you do then it's OK by me.'

'I thought she was a bit scary actually,' Kat admitted. 'Sort of confrontational in the beginning but then she settled down.'

'Maybe she felt threatened by you. You are successful, you've had this amazing career.'

Kat shuffled closer to him. 'Massimo, do you think I should have Botox?'

'Where did that come from?' He sounded surprised.

'Zita must be around my age but she looks younger. I was thinking maybe I should do something about that.'

'Don't mess with yourself.' His tone was stern. 'You are beautiful, Kat.'

'I'll be fifty-one next birthday and I can see my face changing.'

'It's becoming even more beautiful.' He pulled her on top of him. 'And Botox? If your face is frozen I won't be able to tell if you're excited, if you want more of something, or if you want less. Had you thought of that?'

'No,' she admitted, pushing her hips into his, a little breathless already at the thought of what was to come.

'Well then.' His hands took hold of her just roughly enough. 'Don't mention it again.'

Afterwards he fell asleep quickly, and Kat lay listening to his breathing and letting her thoughts settle. It had been an odd sort of day: first Ruth and all that talk of colours, then Zita, and whatever was going on with her. Did either of them realise they might end up in her book? Anyone she met in Venice was fair game as far as Kat was concerned, although she wasn't sure if even Massimo fully appreciated that.

Whenever they discussed what she was writing his main interest seemed to be how it might help his business in these uncertain times. All his talk was of the way Airbnb was ruining the small family hotels, how visitor numbers were dropping and room rates bound to fall. Massimo would be happy if her book sold well enough to put Hotel Gondola on the map, if it drew in more guests and meant there was money to keep the roof watertight and the walls free of damp. He expected to read the manuscript, of course, and approve what had been said about him, but whether that would happen, Kat still hadn't decided. It depended on how things stood when the year ended. If they were still together then perhaps she would have to let him.

Kat suspected her friends were taking bets on how long their relationship would last. Several had insisted she wasn't the type to settle down, that she would find life too predictable and dull. It was amazing how wrong everyone had been about that. You couldn't feel this off balance and be bored, thought Kat, who woke every morning and wondered what the day held, just as she had when her life was all about travelling. Here there was Venice and Massimo, and she hadn't reached the heart of either.

It had only been a few weeks, she reminded herself. In

early spring she had arrived when heavy rains were still sluicing the streets and the water was bubbling up through the manhole covers in Piazza San Marco. Time had passed quickly and already Venice was less chilly and far busier. The start of summer was tantalisingly close and Kat felt like a different person than the one who had flown over with two suitcases and a laptop bag, her mind buzzing with ideas for the book she was going to write.

Sharing a life with Massimo, being with him day after day, wasn't how she had expected. She must have spent hours watching his face, trying to read his expression. Was he happy, was he sad, was he satisfied? Slowly, she was learning. At first if he frowned Kat assumed it was because of something she had said or done, when more often than not it was a work issue bothering him. When he came to bed and didn't touch her, only wanting to fall asleep, she took it as rejection, not a sign he was exhausted. If he said no – to a walk, or a dinner, or a drink – she felt snubbed, however obvious it might have been to anyone else that he was simply too busy.

Kat had arrived in Massimo's life and become a part of his everyday. It was a dance she didn't know the steps to. So no, she wasn't bored yet, even if Venice was a city that moved to its own beat, slow and centuries old; even if she was held here by a man and a book, and struggling at times with both.

Beside her Massimo snored softly. Kat envied him his talent for sleep. He seemed to be able to pass out within moments of laying his head on the pillow and then, in the morning, woke early and refreshed. After a shave and shower, he would put on something neatly pressed, drink a single espresso and leap into the day. Meanwhile, she was still tangled in bed covers and vowing to get up in ten more minutes. Lying awake now, Kat worried this might be a sign. If they couldn't even take the very first steps of a day together, how could they hope to find any sort of a rhythm in the longer term?

Glancing at the clock on her nightstand she realised it was past midnight. Kat didn't feel any closer to sleep. It didn't help that she was hungry. Dinner had been a plate of bar snacks, some olives, a few nuts, things she had nibbled on while busy writing.

The trouble was, Hotel Gondola had no proper kitchen. There had been one apparently, but when Massimo took over he ripped it out because it took up space he could use to add more rooms. So now there was only an area that was large enough to prepare the brioche and coffee they offered for breakfast and the appetisers for cocktail hour, but not suited to cooking an entire meal. She and Massimo either snacked or ate out, which meant that often at this time of night Kat heard her empty stomach growling.

There was a place she had found, not far from Piazza San Marco, that seemed to be open no matter how late. It sold pizza by the slice that was surprisingly good, thin bases covered in a sauce made from fresh tomatoes, lots of peppery salami and bubbling cheese. It was exactly what Kat felt like eating, comforting food, warm and easy.

Quietly she slipped out of bed, dressed and eased herself out the door without waking Massimo. The hotel was entirely quiet and the night manager, most likely snoozing in the office, didn't see her leave.

Venice had a different atmosphere at night, when darkness fell and tiredness swept the tourists from the streets. Kat listened to the sound of her own footsteps as she walked through pools of light shed by street lamps, beside canals as black as the night, across shadowed squares – or *campi* as she was getting used to calling them – past a few last revellers outside a bar where music was still playing. The pizza place was open, as she had hoped, and there were a couple of customers sitting on a bench outside. Kat chose two slices and ate them quickly, standing out on the *calle*, staring back through the window of the small pizzeria, watching the man who had served her. He was often here, so Kat assumed he must own the place. If she was shooting her TV series, *Black of Beyond*, she might spend a few hours with him, learn the secrets behind the zing of his tomato sauce and the perfect crisp of his pizza base. Or she would do the same thing at a *bacaro* that served really good *cicchetti*. Wherever the show took her, food was the backbone of the story that she told her audience and at some point she always ended up with a local, in their kitchen, cooking side by side.

Kat missed cooking. It was a way to make sense of a place, shopping for ingredients at a street market and discovering how to create the foods the people she was meeting liked to eat every day. More importantly, it calmed her. She felt at ease in kitchens, she understood them, wherever she was in the world. Even at home in her tiny flat in Maida Vale there was pleasure in preparing a meal – a single grilled fillet of trout with romesco sauce, one leg of chicken cooked with Marsala and sage; the whole place scented with whatever was simmering, the table set just for her. And now for all these weeks in Venice she hadn't so much as chopped an onion; another missed beat in the strange new tempo of her life.

It came to Kat as she was ordering her third slice of pizza. Food was meant to be a central part of her book but all the focus of her writing so far had been on her relationship. She had been too distracted by Massimo to look beyond that although she'd always known her publishers and readers would be expecting more. They wanted what she always gave them, lavish descriptions of cooking and eating, culinary insights and adventures, even recipes this time, and without a decent kitchen how was she going to manage any of that?

She ate her last slice of pizza as she walked back towards Hotel Gondola. This time she didn't worry about waking

Massimo. She pulled the door shut, turned on a lamp and sat down heavily on the bed.

He was blinking, half-awake. 'Kat?'

'Massimo, I need a kitchen.'

'What, right now?' He squinted his eyes open. 'Why?'

'I can't manage without one.'

He groaned, sleepily. 'OK, we'll sort something out but can we talk about it in the morning?'

'Do you think it's possible? I mean, who in Venice would have a spare kitchen? Might you know anyone?'

'Mm,' he replied, his eyes closing, already drifting back into sleep.

If she woke him again he would be cross, and rightly so, she supposed. Massimo didn't share her drive to have things done and decided right now. He was the least impatient person she knew. Things happened, but at a moderate pace and he was impossible to hurry.

Kat lay fully clothed on top of the covers and considered her options. Venice was a city where space was rarely wasted. Maybe she could share a kitchen, find a café that was closed at night or someone who didn't live in their apartment full time. She imagined herself at the Rialto market, browsing round the produce, with a basket over her arm. In her fantasy there was a Venetian at her shoulder pointing out the specialities found only here and describing how to prepare them. Kat was imagining how she would learn the perfect sweet/sour balance of *sarde en saor* when sleep finally found her. Even in her dreams she was cooking, stirring a risotto, spooning in butter and grated Parmesan, ladling it into wide, white bowls.

Massimo woke her early, with a shake of the shoulder rather than a kiss. 'Last night, did you come in late and started talking about kitchens? Or did I dream it?'

It was Kat's turn to blink drowsily. 'Sorry,' she muttered. 'I had a revelation and couldn't wait to share it with you.'

He offered her a strong, short coffee made on the Nespresso machine they had in their room. 'You had better tell me again then; I was half asleep.'

She sat up, took the coffee, and downed it in a couple of gulps. 'I have to find a kitchen. I promised my publishers there would be recipes in the book and so I need somewhere to test them, ideally a place near the Rialto market.'

'OK,' he said dubiously. 'I'll have a think and ask around. Nothing is coming to mind right now.'

'If I had a kitchen I'd be able to prepare some of my favourite dishes for you,' said Kat, hoping the promise might speed his thinking process. 'That would be good, wouldn't it?'

'Yes, it would,' he agreed. 'I can't imagine it, though, Kat. You're always saying how impatient you are. How does that fit with being a chef?'

'I'm not a chef, I'm a cook,' she pointed out. 'And in a kitchen you're always moving, playing with ingredients, transforming and creating. The reward is good food so of course I love it.'

'Then we'd better find you a kitchen,' said Massimo. 'I'll see what I can do, I promise.'

As Kat watched him getting dressed, a feeling of well-being rushed at her. Here she was, living right in the middle of Venice, with this very attractive man who made love to her almost every night and often told her she was beautiful. He was putting on a striped shirt and a linen jacket now, running a comb through his neat dark hair, taking a moment to check his reflection in the mirror. He was kissing her, his hand flat on her belly, its gentle pressure bringing on the usual stirrings.

'What's your plan today?' he asked. 'More work on the book?'

'I guess so. I'm up to the part where we have dinner at Harry's Bar.'

'Ah, that night.' He smiled at the memory. 'Don't give away all our secrets, though, Kat. Keep some of this just for us.'

Before she had a chance to ask exactly what he meant, he was kissing her again and out the door to work. The comment bothered Kat. She knew it wasn't normal, the way she lived so publicly much of the time, but she had grown used to people knowing random stuff about her. What would Massimo believe was acceptable? Where would he draw the line? Not in the same place she did, that was for sure. Kat tried to put the worry out of her mind. If she thought about it too hard, she'd never be able to write a word.

After stealing a few more minutes beneath the covers, she got out of bed, showered then went and stared into her wardrobe. She wanted to pay a visit to Coco and by now had learned that what she was wearing mattered. There would be no capri pants and forgiving tunic tops, no middle-aged uniform. Her hair was to be loose over her shoulders instead of up in a topknot. Lipstick and mascara must be applied, possibly even a smudge of brown shadow on her eyelids. Kat wasn't giving her friend any excuse to start complaining.

She was amused by the older woman's obsession with appearance. Coco wouldn't poke her nose out of the door unless she had powdered it first and expected everyone to have the same standards. So whenever they had plans to meet, Kat dressed to please her.

This morning she wore the blue dress she had bought on her very first visit to the shop. It had belonged to one of Coco's old friends and she always seemed nostalgic when she saw it. So much of life must be tied up with memories when you reached that age, although to be fair Coco didn't talk about the past very often. Mostly she seemed focused on the day and whatever pleasure she could find in it. She was pure gold as far as the book was concerned; Kat loved writing about her. And now she hoped the eccentric Venetian might be able to help her out in another way.

The corridors of Hotel Gondola were coffee-scented, as they always were first thing. A lot of the guests would be in the bar by now enjoying the brioche and *caffè con latte* that was included in their room tariff. Kat never ate breakfast with them. She had found a *pasticceria*, just the right distance away, where she could enjoy her morning brioche without anyone expecting her to force a bright conversation.

Today, though, Ruth was waiting in reception to ambush her, clutching her guidebook and feigning interest in its pages.

'Good morning,' Kat said, oddly pleased to see her face. 'What are you up to today?'

'Oh, I don't know.' Ruth sounded dithery. 'I thought I might go to the Peggy Guggenheim Collection later. It's a must-do, isn't it?'

Kat had never been but she didn't tell Ruth that. 'Yes, absolutely, if you're into art,' she said. 'I'm heading out for breakfast and then on to see my friend Coco.'

'How lovely to have friends in Venice,' Ruth said.

'Why don't you come?' said Kat impulsively. 'You might find Coco rather interesting. I'd love to know what colour you think she is.'

'So you're open to my woo-woo stuff this morning?' Ruth sounded pleased.

'It's not my thing at all. I think it's kind of nutty, to be honest.'

'But you're intrigued?'

'A little,' Kat admitted.

Ruth seemed happy to delay her trip to the gallery and accept her invitation. They headed out of the hotel together and walked along the narrow pathway beside the canal.

'You actually do think you see these colours, don't you? You're not making this up?' said Kat.

'I really do see them,' Ruth promised. 'Sometimes I wonder if it might be better not to. It can complicate things, you see. A person may be pretending to be one thing but their colour will show me they're quite another.'

'That sounds like an advantage.'

'Perhaps it is ... but we all like to portray ourselves a certain way. Being the person who can look past that changes so many little things, how you approach someone, how you talk to them, the relationship you form. Take yourself, for instance. I'm stalking you, as I'm sure you've noticed. But I can't help it; I'm fascinated.'

'What colour am I now?' Kat wondered.

'Pink, a really pretty shade, it seems happy.'

Venice was bathed in sunshine; the blue of the sky mirrored in its still waters. If she were in a hurry Kat could forget to notice the beauty of the crumbling walls, crooked windows and cobbled streets smoothed by centuries of footsteps. Today, though, her eyes were open and she felt enchanted by everything.

'It would be terrible to be in Venice on a morning like this and not be happy about it,' she told Ruth.

'Terrible,' her new friend agreed.

After two cups of milky coffee and a sweet brioche filled with vanilla custard, Kat's sense of well-being was only heightened. She was beginning to feel at home here. Hadn't the man behind the counter in the *pasticceria* given her a friendly nod? Wasn't she meeting new people? Surely that meant Venice was opening up and allowing her in. And now Kat had a good idea, which always made her feel better about everything.

'It's time to go and see my friend Coco,' she told Ruth, once she had finished eating.

As they walked towards the shop Ruth asked questions: who was this friend, how had they met, what did she do? Kat didn't say much, wanting her to form her own impressions.

'You have to meet her to believe her,' she explained. 'You'll see what I mean.'

71

They reached the shop to find Coco costumed in a blaze of bright shades – blue skirt, orange top, red shoes, green scarf.

'Colour blocking,' she told Kat, once she had greeted her with a kiss on both cheeks. 'I read about it in an old copy of *Vogue* I picked up somewhere. What do you think?'

'Stunning,' said Kat, glancing at Ruth and surprised to see she looked dismayed rather than charmed.

Coco struck a fashion model pose. 'When you have an entire shop to choose from you can try any look you want. I'm enjoying this one, for today at least.'

Kat introduced her to Ruth who still seemed oddly solemn although she made an effort to admire the shop and all the lovely things.

'There will be an outfit here that is perfect for you,' Coco promised her. 'Tell me about yourself. Who are you, what makes you special?'

'I'm very ordinary,' said Ruth.

'Never say that. No one is ordinary.'

'But I am,' Ruth insisted. 'And I've never been very good at clothes, to be honest.'

'Which is why you need me.' Coco stood back and considered her for a moment. 'You are an English rose, modest, not one to draw attention to yourself. No colour blocking for you, no clothes that shout, your style is understated.'

'That's true,' Ruth agreed.

'And you are very pretty but you are not making the most of it. Has anyone ever told you this?'

'Not that I remember,' Ruth said steadily.

'So what would I like to see you wearing?' Coco cocked her head. 'Hmm, I think ... yes, yes ... one moment, signora.'

As Coco busied herself burrowing in between the racks of clothes, Kat turned to Ruth and asked quietly, 'So what colour is she?'

Frowning, Ruth shook her head. 'Not now.'

Kat gave her a quizzical look but she refused to be drawn

and then Coco re-emerged with a couple of summery frocks. 'What do you think?'

'Very nice,' said Ruth. 'But I—'

'On the hanger they are nothing. You must put them on and then we will know if they are your dresses.'

Kat had to hand it to Coco; she knew what she was doing. Both the frocks looked lovely on Ruth and the one she decided to buy, a blue Liberty print, brought out the shade of her eyes and made her seem years younger.

'You have to haggle with her now,' Kat whispered to her. 'She insists on it.'

'I'm hopeless at haggling. I hate it.'

Coco was folding the dresses, smiling to herself, pretending she hadn't heard.

'It's just the blue one I want,' Ruth reminded her.

'Today I will make you a special deal. Two for the price of one,' Coco replied.

'Really? Do you have a sale on?' Ruth looked around as if expecting to see signs.

'No, this deal is just for you because you are with my friend Kat ... and also because I know that once you get the cream dress home you will prefer it to the other one.'

Ruth flushed. 'That's very generous of you.'

Coco nodded graciously. 'This dress belonged to a very lovely friend of mine. I will like to think of it having a new life in another country.'

As the two women completed their transaction, Kat flicked idly through the rails. She was holding a floaty summer top against her body and glancing in the mirror when Coco called over to her. 'No, Kat, you do not need anything right now. You have enough.'

'I'm surprised to hear you say that. Is it possible to ever have enough?' asked Kat.

'For me no, but I have a talent for remembering what is there and bringing pieces together. You do not.'

'That's true,' Kat conceded. 'I'm more like Ruth, I've never been all that good with fashion either.'

'I know that, my darling; there is no need to remind me,' said Coco who was rummaging in the drawer where she kept her home-made *Closed* sign. 'Now it is time for us to go and drink a coffee together, yes?'

She led them to the usual place, her little dogs skittering at their feet, and they sat at one of the canal-side tables beneath a striped sunshade. Whenever Kat had been out with Coco, she had taken over the ordering of food and drinks entirely. But with Ruth she was solicitous. How did she prefer her coffee? Would a sweet treat be nice?

Once the business of eating and drinking had been negotiated, Coco switched her attention to Kat. 'So tell me what is on your mind?' she asked.

'How do you know there's something on my mind?'

'I am an old witch.' Coco smiled, delighted with herself. 'I cannot guess what it is, though. You will have to tell me that.'

'I'm wondering if you can help me,' Kat explained. 'I'm looking for a kitchen where I can test recipes for my book. It doesn't have to be huge or have fancy equipment but I'd like it to be reasonably close to the Rialto market. I was hoping you might know of something.'

'A kitchen.' Coco thought about it. 'Has Massimo not got any ideas?'

'He's asking around but that could take a while so I thought I'd better do some asking of my own. I did wonder about your apartment.' Kat broached the idea warily. 'If I cooked there while you were working in your shop I wouldn't be a disturbance. I could leave a delicious dinner in the oven for you plus I'd pay you too, of course.'

'My kitchen?' Coco sounded confused. 'But you have never been there.'

'No, but you mentioned it wasn't too far from the market.'

'That is true but it won't do.' Coco began to laugh. 'It won't do at all.'

'Why not?'

'I will show you. We will go there when we have drunk our coffee.' She laughed again. 'Cook in my kitchen, oh no.'

Once they had paid their bill, and Coco had persuaded the waiter to wrap the remaining biscuits in a napkin for her, the three of them walked to Coco's place together, Ruth and Kat assigned to carrying the little dogs, as the streets were becoming crowded and Coco feared they might be trampled on by a passing tourist.

Her ground-floor apartment was in a pretty part of Venice, beside a narrow canal where many of the houses had window boxes filled with spring flowers. Unlocking the door, she ushered them into a small hallway.

Instantly, Kat realised what the problem was. The entrance was hung with clothes, the living area filled with more rails of them and the kitchen, when they fought their way through to it, turned out to be stacked with shoeboxes.

'The place wasn't always like this,' Coco said, looking round helplessly as if only just realising the extent of the problem. 'People kept giving me things and if they were beautiful I couldn't say no. Before long it was overflowing, because as you see it isn't large. That is when I started the shop. But more clothes just keep coming so it hasn't really helped.'

The stove top was as cluttered as anywhere else. Opening the oven, Kat realised even that had been taken over for storage. 'How do you cook a meal here?'

'I don't,' Coco confessed. 'I have lost any interest I had in cooking. It is such a fuss and besides it has never been my talent.'

'But you love to eat,' said Kat.

'Venice is full of places where I can do that.' She glanced around her kitchen again. 'So you see, no good for you at all.'

'Absolutely not,' agreed Kat.

'I had to show you or you might not have believed me,' Coco explained. 'But there is another reason I wanted you to come. Upstairs is an empty apartment. The landlord keeps it for visiting friends so won't want to rent it out. But possibly you might be able to use the kitchen. I have a key. Would you like to see it?'

'Yes, of course.'

'The stairs are steep and narrow so go carefully. Hold tight to the banister,' Coco advised, leading them upwards.

The place was perfect; Kat could see that right away. The main room was sparsely furnished with a moth-eaten velvet chaise and a small dining table. She liked the high ceilings, the blush-pink walls and the doors that led out onto a balcony but it was the kitchen that drew her, small and simple, set against one wall. Kat opened drawers and cupboards, finding mismatched saucepans and utensils, a couple of really good kitchen knives and an ancient orange Le Creuset casserole.

'I could cook here very happily,' she told Coco. 'Would you give me the number for the landlord?'

'Best leave it to me.'

'When might you be able to make contact? Will it be soon?'

'I expect so.' Coco sounded vague.

'Only I'd hate for it to be rented by someone else in the meantime. A place like this on Airbnb could make quite a bit of money.'

'As I told you earlier, the landlord isn't interested in renting ... or in Airbnb, whatever that may be.'

'So you think I have a chance?'

'I am hopeful.'

Ruth had opened up the glass doors and was standing out on the balcony, gazing through the windows of the building opposite. She sat down in one of the rickety-looking chairs, beside a waning potted geranium, and kept staring. Kat went out to join her.

'What is it you're looking at?' she asked.

'I'm afraid I'm snooping,' Ruth admitted. 'This canal is so narrow you can see right into those rooms.'

Kat followed her line of vision and realised it was true. She had a clear view right inside the apartment opposite. There was a sofa covered in a blue throw, a small dining table, and behind it copper pots hung above what must be the kitchen. No one was inside but had there been, she could have spied very easily.

'I expect that means they can look straight back into this apartment,' Ruth pointed out.

'True, but I'll only be cooking so I don't mind. And it's peaceful out here. It would be a good spot for me to get some writing done.'

Coco was still inside. She had found a broom and was sweeping the floors clean of dust and dead insects.

'You wouldn't tell me about her colour while we were in the shop,' Kat remembered. 'I imagine it must be pretty spectacular.'

Ruth shook her head. 'Not now,' she said again.

Kat wondered why she was being so mysterious. Up till now she hadn't seemed to want to hold back.

It wasn't until later, when they had said goodbye to Coco and were walking back to Hotel Gondola, that Ruth opened up.

'Grey,' she said suddenly. 'Completely grey, almost like no colour at all.'

'What?'

'Your friend Coco, she puts on a fabulous show, but that's all it is.'

'Is that unusual?'

'I've seen it before.'

'What does it mean?' asked Kat.

'I'm not sure.'

'Is she unhappy? Depressed?'

'I hope not,' said Ruth. 'But I don't know. All I saw was grey and all I felt was sadness.'

Kat reminded herself that she didn't believe in Ruth's psychic powers, but still the words formed a worry. A woman as vivacious as Coco should be a rainbow of bright colours, not grey. Could there be something wrong with her? Was she sick or only sad?

All afternoon, sitting at her desk and staring at her laptop, her thoughts distracted Kat from writing the Harry's Bar chapter of her book. This was a key scene; the big seduction. It was vital to get it right. Still her mind kept drifting back to Coco and she had a struggle to concentrate hard enough for the words to start flowing.

A Year at Hotel Gondola by Kat Black

CHAPTER 6

I'm an intrepid person, always willing to take a risk. But
Coco's plan for my seduction of Massimo had me wavering.
I couldn't even find the right time to ask him out for dinner.
Whenever I saw him there were other people around – hotel
guests, the moody desk clerk – or he was having an intense
conversation on the phone.

I was concerned he was going to notice how often I was
putting myself in his path as I went in and out of reception
needlessly several times that afternoon. At cocktail hour I was
in the bar hovering over an Aperol spritz, wearing a little black
dress I had bought from Coco and running over what I was
going to say, polishing it in my mind, like an anxious teenager.

There were other tables occupied by the time he appeared,
but it was to me that Massimo spoke first.

'*Buona sera*, Kat, how was your day unlocking the secrets of
Venice?'

'Pretty good, I finished my article actually,' I lied, just as
Coco had instructed.

'Already?' He was surprised.

'I'm very efficient ... and you were such a good guide last
night ...'

He made a tutting sound. 'So you have broken your word and
written about the places I took you to? I am very disappointed.'

I hoped he was joking. 'You knew it would happen surely?
The good thing is now I'm off the clock I can do something
shamelessly touristy. What I'd really like is to eat at Harry's
Bar.'

'Tonight? It will be busy but I can see if it's possible to make a reservation.' Massimo was back in hotel manager mode.

'Why don't you join me?' I asked, trying to sound casual. 'My treat to say thank you for showing me round, and sorry for breaking my sacred word.'

'Dinner at Harry's Bar is an excellent way to apologise but unfortunately I have some accounts to work on tonight.'

'Won't the accounts still be there in the morning?'

'They will,' he agreed.

'And wouldn't you feel terrible leaving me to eat dinner alone?'

'I would feel ... regretful.'

I searched my mind for something persuasive. 'And isn't it one of the world's most celebrated restaurants?'

'That is true.'

'So you'll come?'

He smiled. 'I will make a call and see if there is a table free.'

Massimo disappeared for five or ten minutes, and on his return smiled again. 'You are in luck. I have made a reservation.'

'A table for two?'

'For two, in the downstairs bar, which is the only place to be seen even though the upstairs dining room has the view.'

'Apparently Humphrey Bogart used to take Lauren Bacall there,' I said.

'They all went, Ernest Hemingway, Truman Capote, Aristotle Onassis, Peggy Guggenheim, various royals.'

'And now Kat Black,' I said. 'With Massimo Morosini.'

'Yes, but not until later, so I can give some time to my accounts first.'

I was so flushed with triumph I had another drink while I waited. The bar was humming and I eavesdropped on the conversations at the nearby tables. Hotel Gondola doesn't tend to attract a young crowd. They would rather stay at a cheaper *pensione*, or over on the mainland in budget accommodation.

The people who come here want a taste of Venice's grandeur. They have some money but not enough to stretch to a room at one of the luxe places like the Danieli or the Gritti Palace. There are lots of middle-aged people, some honeymooners, a few families and the odd solo traveller like me.

I heard Australian accents at the table beside me; Russian voices a little further away; English and German. Many would be having the same conversations: remarking on how crowded it was in the streets around San Marco, trying to decide whether to take a Doge's Palace tour or a boat to one of the islands, complaining about the prices or how the very thing they came to see was closed for renovation. I sipped my spritz and listened to the babble.

It was dark by the time Massimo came to collect me. My jittery mood softened by cocktails, I was looking forward to sitting down in Harry's Bar, to a waiter at my elbow and a menu in my hands.

I love everything about eating out, whether it's at a neighbourhood bistro with a candle in an old Chianti bottle or some place with starched linen and shining crystal. I enjoy the little rituals, the setting of a napkin on my knee, the moment when the specials are recited, the choosing of the wine. There is the tension of trying to decide exactly what dishes to order – do you choose an old favourite or take a chance on something new? And then the waiting, with your appetite sharpening, and the meal arriving, and that moment just before you take the first bite when it's all still possibility.

'I hope you won't be disappointed,' said Massimo. 'It's very low key.'

That turned out to be true. In fact, from the outside the place is so discreet it is only noticeable because of the legendary name etched on to the frosted windows – Harry's Bar.

Through the doors we went and into a room that was small and unexpectedly cramped, like a ship's cabin. The maître d' guided us to a corner table and sat me down on a banquette.

The place was jammed but even so the menus came quickly, followed by warm bread rolls and a carafe of red wine that Massimo had ordered.

'The food here is understated, but they do the classics well,' he told me.

We began with the carpaccio, paper-thin slices of beef drizzled with a lemony mayonnaise. Then a risotto of tender squid, richly sauced by its own black ink, with every forkful colouring our mouths, so we had to keep pausing to dab our faces clean.

'Never order this if you are on a romantic date,' Massimo advised, looking amused as he leant over to wipe a missed spot from the corner of my mouth with his own napkin. 'It is delicious but impossible to eat with dignity.'

'I'll keep that in mind,' I said wryly.

Next we shared a salad of plump scallops, peppery rocket and sweet balsamic vinegar. And even though our appetites were flagging we finished with a dish of cinnamon-poached pears and two glasses of the Moscato d'Asti.

'The perfect Harry's Bar meal,' said Massimo, clinking his glass against mine.

And right there in that intimate room that can't have changed for decades, where there was always a white-jacketed waiter when he was needed, and the lighting was a soft butterscotch haze, and the clientele a mix of tourists twitching at the prices and old people who might have been there for ever; in Harry's Bar, tightly tucked behind a table, I fell in love.

OK, perhaps not completely in love, but really quite smitten, and with Venice as much as with this completely gorgeous man. I wanted them both.

After we had lingered over coffee he insisted on paying the bill, refusing to listen to any talk that it was my treat. It was late by then but I was determined to follow the rest of Coco's plan. Somehow I had to convince Massimo into taking me to a romantic spot where I could steal a kiss.

'What's your favourite view of Venice?' I asked in what I hoped was a casual manner as we left Harry's Bar.

He considered the question. 'I think it has to be looking back at the city from an island out in the lagoon.'

'Your favourite place then?' I asked, since that was hardly helpful.

'It depends on what time of the day or night we're talking about.'

'Right now.'

He glanced at his watch. 'Piazza San Marco,' he said. 'Fewer people will be crowding it but the café orchestras are still playing. I love the atmosphere and the lit arcades, especially when the whole piazza floods and you get these wonderful, watery reflections.'

It seemed too public a spot for a seduction but I didn't have any better ideas. 'Let's walk that way now,' I suggested.

'OK, it's just around the corner.'

The only times to be in Piazza San Marco are early morning and late at night. In between it heaves with visitors who are mostly dressed in clothes that Coco wouldn't approve of, and who mill about taking photos and getting in the way of the view. Or even worse they sit on the steps to snack on a sandwich, infuriating the locals, as that kind of behaviour is strictly forbidden.

On the autumn night I first went there with Massimo the air was crisp enough for him to have donned a fine wool coat and there was only a single orchestra entertaining a sprinkling of people. We stood a little way back from the tables of Caffè Florian and listened to a Strauss waltz.

As the orchestra began to play a spirited version of Ravel's 'Bolero', I leant against Massimo, hooking my arm through his, and our bodies swayed together slightly. In the end I let the music carry me into the kiss. My lips touched his and there was a brief moment when I think he was startled and then he pulled me closer. We kissed as the drum beat out its rhythm and the clarinet repeated its tune; we kissed long and slow, as if we couldn't stop until the song did.

I have no idea how long it had been since a man kissed me like that. It's never the main course, kissing, is it, just an appetiser that's meant to lead on to something more satisfying. But in that wide, graceful piazza Massimo kissed me as if it was everything. And when the orchestra stopped playing and we parted, I felt dizzy.

'Kat, I like you a lot ... I find you very attractive,' Massimo said. 'But I have to tell you something.'

'What?' I asked, still reeling from the kiss.

'I am not going to be any woman's holiday romance, not even yours.' He said it softly but firmly.

I might have made a gasping sound; I was certainly astonished.

'Venice isn't short of women who want a good time for one night before they leave,' he continued. 'If that sounds like you then we should say goodnight now.'

Mutely, I shook my head.

'You have to understand how it is to live in this city where almost everyone is only passing through. I've had my share of flings. They never made me happy.'

'I'm not looking for a quick hook-up,' I said, a little defensively.

'What then?'

I stared over at Caffè Florian's orchestra who were now playing a cheery version of 'New York, New York'.

'Be honest with me,' Massimo said.

'You want honesty? OK then.' I took a deep breath. 'I want the one thing I seem to have missed out on so far in my life. A love affair, a mad, crazy, romantic one like in books or movies. Maybe that kind of thing doesn't exist in real life, I'm not sure, but I need to find out.'

'You've never experienced it?'

'No, and I'm worried about running out of time.'

He touched my cheek with his fingertips. His face was shadowed so I couldn't read his expression and his voice was a whisper. 'So let me get this straight. You want real passion?'

'Oh God, yes.'

He kissed me again; and this time it felt like an agreement.

There have to be some things that stay private so I'm going to take you to the doorway of Massimo's room up in the eaves of Hotel Gondola and leave you there as he and I go inside. All you need to know is what I told Coco later the next day; her plan had been a good one. A brilliant one.

In the few days I had left in Venice we did a lot of talking. Massimo stole time away from work and we spent much of it beside the bar of his favourite *bacaro*, sharing plates of seafood and sipping wine. We took *vaporetto* rides together and long, aimless walks. Or simply sat in the autumn sunshine and watched the light playing on the water of the lagoon, holding hands like teenagers.

I thought this must be it; falling in love. The more we were together the stronger my sense it was right, this thing between us; it was the affair I'd been longing for. It seemed Massimo felt the same way. By my last morning he had booked flights to come over to London for a long weekend and after that he wanted me to return to Hotel Gondola for Christmas.

There was a great deal of toing and froing over the course of that winter, a lot of nights when we couldn't get enough of each other, and every time we parted it felt a little harder. All my life I've been a person who's hated to miss out. Places, adventures, even flavours – I wanted to experience them all. Now I had my chance at the greatest adventure of all. How could I miss out on that? Before long I had made my big decision. I would carve out a year from my life to give to Massimo and Venice and see what they both did with it. I was going to spend a year at Hotel Gondola.

6

Kat felt she had handled things well, leaving the readers outside the room like that, even if it did mean they missed out
on the best part of the night. Dinner at Harry's Bar, swaying
to the music in Piazza San Marco, even the greatest kisses of
her life, paled in comparison to being in bed with Massimo.
He was tender, he was rough, he was unexpected. Even
now, after so many more nights together, Kat felt shivery
thinking about it. But she wouldn't be going anywhere near
that stuff in the book. People had imaginations, didn't they?
And anyway, she didn't want to rework the chapter. It had
taken long enough to finish it in the first place.

All the time she was trying to write, Coco kept creeping
back into her thoughts. 'Grey, almost like no colour at all'
is what Ruth had said. Kat wanted to dismiss it as nonsense
except there was something oddly perceptive about her; she
seemed to read people's moods accurately. And not to be
dazzled by Coco, with all her flamboyance and bold colour,
well that was a little strange. So Kat couldn't help feeling
anxious.

The next morning, straight after her coffee and brioche,
she headed back to the shop, half-expecting Coco not to be
there, for some disaster to have happened. But the place was
open and there was a mannequin outside the door with a
gold silk brocade jacket pinned onto it.

She found Coco deep in conversation with a customer. 'I
know you like the lace dress but when you get home it will
seem wrong,' she was saying. 'You will never wear it. The
other one, though ... people will admire you in it.'

'Yellow isn't my colour,' replied the woman, her accent American.

'Good things will happen when you wear this dress.'

'I'll just take the black lace,' the woman insisted. 'That's the one I like.'

'I won't sell it to you.'

'I'm sorry?'

'It is not for sale ... not to you ... it would be a mistake. But I will give you the yellow one at a very good price.'

'You can't refuse to let me buy the dress I want.' The woman sounded astonished.

'Yes, I can.'

'Is this how you usually operate?'

'Of course,' said Coco.

With a huffing sound, the woman turned to storm out of the shop. 'Ridiculous, absolutely crazy,' she said in Kat's direction. 'I'm not giving her my custom.'

'Wait a moment, signora,' Coco was serene. 'I have a proposition for you. I will give you this dress. When you wear it and realise I am right then you can send me a cheque for what you think it is worth.'

The woman paused in the doorway, intrigued. 'What if I hate it and never wear it?'

Coco was already wrapping the frock in tissue paper and slipping in a square of card with her name and address handwritten on it in purple ink. 'In that case no need to send me any money.'

'Are you serious?'

'Absolutely.'

'And you trust me to pay you if I wear it?'

'Signora, I trust myself. This dress and you are a perfect match.'

'In that case, I'll have to take it, I guess. Although it all seems very strange. This is certainly not how we do things at home.'

The woman still seemed flustered, even as she left the shop clutching the package Coco had tied up with a length of fraying polka-dot ribbon. She glanced towards Kat with a half-shake of her head as if encouraging her to flee while there was still time.

'Well,' said Coco, watching her go. 'That makes three good things that have happened today.'

'It does?' said Kat.

'I never thought I would find the right woman for that dress. Yellow is not an easy shade, you know. And it fitted her like a glove.'

'What were the other two?'

'I was given that wonderful old mannequin so now I can display a different item every day. And one of my lovers called and invited me to a concert this evening.' She smiled brightly. 'So three good things and it is still so early.'

Nothing was grey about Coco today; she was as cheerful as could be, and Kat was reassured that Ruth had to be talking nonsense.

'Actually, four good things in total,' Coco said. 'The last one is for you. I have some news. The kitchen is yours and the rent is very reasonable.'

'Really? You've sorted it already?' Kat was amazed.

'I told you I would. There is one condition, though. If the landlord has friends who want to stay then you must vacate the apartment for a time.'

'That won't be a problem. Thank you so much, you're amazing. You'll be the first person I cook for.'

'I am very fussy,' Coco warned her.

'Only the freshest fish, I promise.'

'In that case I had better come when you shop at the Rialto. Don't go alone.'

'When do you think I could get access to the apartment?' Kat asked.

'The place is empty so I will give you the keys now. You

can take another look and see if there are any things you need. But *do not* go to the market without me,' Coco stressed.

Kat agreed that she absolutely wouldn't go anywhere near the Rialto market and Coco produced the keys, a large old-fashioned one for the front door and a smaller one that would let her into the apartment.

Naturally it was impossible to resist walking via the market. And when she saw the stalls loaded with spring vegetables, Kat couldn't help stopping. White asparagus stood spear to spear, plump pods of peas spilt over in mounds, there were buds of baby artichokes with purple-green leaves and fronds of spring herbs tied in bundles with names on their labels that Kat didn't recognise – *bruscandoli, barba di frate*.

She waited for the vendor to finish serving another customer then asked if he spoke English. He shook his head. 'My son,' he said, holding up a finger to indicate that she should wait a moment.

Kat wondered what you might cook with these tangles of fresh spring greens. A pasta dish perhaps, or she could simply braise them with some diced pancetta and lots of peppery olive oil. She was dreaming up ideas when the vendor's son returned.

'Signora, can I help you?' he asked.

'I was wondering if you could explain what these are.' She pointed to the greens. 'Are they local specialities?'

'*Si*, signora,' he replied, picking up a bunch of what looked like long chives with sandy roots still attached. '*Barba di frate* are a kind of grass that likes to grow on the marshes. And *bruscandoli* are the shoots from the wild hop plants. Both are from places in the lagoon where the soil is salty so the flavour is very good. You will only find them here for a short time in spring; not for much longer.'

'In that case I'd better buy a bunch of each,' said Kat.

Next she moved on to the fish market, browsing among the stalls before choosing some squid. Olive oil and sea salt she found in a small grocery store nearby; and that was all Kat needed to cook her first Venetian meal.

The apartment smelt a little musty, which she hadn't noticed on her first visit, so she opened the doors to the balcony to let in some air before turning her attention to the kitchen. She found a large cast-iron frying pan, a chef's knife and a wooden board. The squid she thinly sliced then poured a deep puddle of olive oil into the pan before sautéing her spring greens until they were soft, adding the seafood at the last moment to cook through. A sprinkle of salt and a little of the white pepper she found in a cupboard, a moment of regret that she hadn't bought a lemon, and Kat was ready to eat.

She sat out on the balcony, the bowl of food on her knee, and closing her eyes, took her first taste. The greens had a mineral tang to them, perhaps because they had grown on land flooded by high tides. The squid was tender and again she was sorry not to have christened it with citrus.

As she ate Kat looked through the window of the apartment opposite, realising someone was at home. A man was stretched out on the sofa, dressed in jeans, his torso bare. At first she assumed he was asleep but then he sat up and got to his feet.

Kat kept watching, she couldn't help herself, even as he came towards the window, threw it open and leaned a little way out, breathing the fresh air deeply. His body was lean and lightly muscled, his skin fair and his hair a tangle of dark blond. When his eyes met hers, he gave a polite nod.

'*Buon appetito*, signora,' he said.

'*Grazie*,' Kat replied, embarrassed to be caught staring.

He yawned again, rumpling his hair with his hands, before turning back inside. As she finished her lunch, Kat could see him moving about his kitchen and soon the scent of coffee drifted from his open window.

Who was this man? Was he a tourist or did he live here?

And if so what did he do for a job? Kat wondered if she might get to know him or if the narrow band of canal that separated them meant they would remain only on nodding terms?

Once she had finished eating, Kat cleaned up the kitchen carefully, putting everything back exactly where she had found it, so there was no sign a meal had been made. She wouldn't mention today's simple lunch to Coco. It wouldn't be fair to rob her of the pleasure of sharing the Rialto market, revealing who had the best produce, introducing her to stallholders and haggling for a good price. And there was no harm in letting her think it was the first time she'd shopped there.

Kat walked back to Hotel Gondola in a happy haze, thinking about food. Soon she was going to buy some baby artichokes and fresh peas. When spring vegetable season ended there would be high summer to look forward to with its plump tomatoes and eggplants, autumn with squash roasted to sweetness and then winter's bitter radicchio.

Feeling hunger pangs stirring, Kat decided to tempt Massimo away from his work with promises of pistachio cake at his favourite *pasticceria*. It would be good to spend some time with him away from the hotel. She was so distracted by her thoughts she didn't notice at first that she had been caught up in some sort of protest. Ahead of her were hundreds of people with prams and shopping trolleys, marching slowly and clogging the *calle*. They were shouting slogans in Italian and Kat managed to understand a couple: 'Venice for the Venetians, tourists go home.' Some had placards demanding fair rents or a ban on cruise ships, and most were youthful and angry.

'This is not Disneyland, this is our home,' one young man yelled loudly in English. With a shock, Kat realised who he was – Nico, her fellow bartender from Hotel Gondola. And beside him was his sister Adriana who ought to have been at work on the reception desk. Both were waving placards that read, *No more tourists.*

What were they thinking? Didn't they realise their liveli-hoods depended on the visitors? For a moment Kat wondered if she should say something and then thought better of it. The pair were caught up in an unfriendly crowd, all of them chanting together now, and Nico seemed to be among the leaders. She would have to tell Massimo about this, though. And he wasn't going to be pleased.

There was no way for her to get past the demonstration so Kat detoured through a labyrinth of back streets, managing to head in the wrong direction altogether for a while, before circling back to the hotel.

She found Massimo manning reception, with a welcoming smile on his face as he checked in some guests. As soon as he had finished with them, the smile dropped away.

'Today is a nightmare,' he complained. 'Adriana didn't turn up for work and isn't answering her phone. I don't know what is going on.'

'I do, because I just saw her.' Kat was indignant. 'She's in-volved in some sort of protest and Nico is there too. There's a huge group of them. They want to get rid of the tourists, apparently, which seems pretty stupid.'

Massimo's response was unexpected. 'They don't really want to get rid of the tourists,' he told her, 'just the day-trippers who come and take a few photos then get back on their cruise ships. The young people are worried about the future. They want Venice to stay a real city where they can live and work, where there are affordable apartments to rent, and businesses other than souvenir shops.'

'So you're not going to try to stop them?' Kat asked, surprised.

'What right do I have to tell them they can't protest about something they believe in?'

'To me it seems a bad look for two of Hotel Gondola's

staff to be involved in something like that, even if you are sympathetic to their cause.'

As Kat described the placards and the slogans being shouted, Massimo frowned. 'I suppose you are right. If any of the guests recognised them it might be awkward.'

'And bad for business,' added Kat, knowing that would hit a nerve.

Massimo pulled out his phone and made several attempts at calling them. Kat could sense him growing impatient when he failed to get a response from either.

'I suppose I'd better go and find them,' he said, still sounding reluctant. 'Tell me exactly where you saw the demonstration. And will you stay and look after things here while I'm away? I'll try not to be too long.'

Kat had been planning to devote the afternoon to writing but instead she agreed to man reception and wait for Massimo's return. She didn't enjoy it much. There were long stretches of boredom when all she had to do was smile at guests as they passed through, greet them with a friendly '*buongiorno*' and ask how they were. Those were punctuated by busier periods when people wanted to be checked in or out, to complain about something in their rooms that needed attention, or to have her call a water taxi or reserve a restaurant table. By the time Ruth found her there, Kat was desperate to escape.

'Purple, but not a pleasant shade,' Ruth announced. 'A new colour for you, I think.'

'I'm not really in the mood,' Kat replied flatly.

'Evidently not.' Ruth seemed unruffled. 'Is this your new job? Where is the usual girl?'

'She couldn't make it in today.'

'And you're filling the breach?'

'Only until Massimo gets back, which hopefully won't be too much longer.'

93

'Hopefully' – Ruth's eyes swept over her – 'because I don't like the look of the purple.'

She changed the subject then, and started talking about her visit to the Peggy Guggenheim Collection. Kat listened as she raved on about the Pollocks, the Picassos and the Mondrians, about how peaceful the garden was and how pleasant the café.

'I feel so inspired now to begin a whole new Venice series, the colours of the landscapes, the water and the people,' she enthused. 'I won't ever be an artist like Pablo Picasso but I can still express myself with paint on canvas the way he did. Why not?'

Personally, Kat didn't see the point of bothering to do something unless you had real talent. But now Ruth was talking about how much her art fulfilled her so she stayed quiet and kept listening.

'It's as if there is this great creative force sweeping across the world and I'm a tiny part of it. It's magical but also scary because I have to give myself to it completely and at this stage in my life—' Ruth stopped suddenly. 'Is this too woo-woo for you?'

'A little bit,' Kat admitted.

'What I'm trying to say is that you don't have to worry about me stalking you from now on because I'm going to be busy.'

Kat couldn't help smiling. 'You're the nicest stalker I could imagine. I hope you'll still have time for the occasional coffee.'

'I'm sure I will. Actually, I was planning to head up to the bar in a little while and have you make me one of those espresso martinis you were talking about.'

'Oh shit, the bar, what time is it?' Kat checked the clock behind the reception desk and repeated, 'Oh shit.'

'Can't that nice-looking boy Nico look after things if you're stuck down here?'

'He didn't make it in today either,' murmured Kat. 'I'm going to have to see what I can sort out. Do come up later, though. Hopefully there will be someone to mix a drink for you.'

Normally the Hotel Gondola ran so smoothly that Kat couldn't quite believe how easily the wheels had fallen off. She managed to trace the staff contact list and found a number for the clerk who did the evening shift – one of Massimo's cousins. It took some persuasion and the promise of a modest bonus but he agreed to come in straight away. All she could hope for was a quiet night in the bar, particularly if Massimo was going to be held up any longer.

There was still no sign of him by the time his cousin arrived to take over on reception. Kat tried calling his mobile then sent a text when he didn't answer. She was upstairs setting up for her shift in the bar when she got a reply from Massimo at last: *Sorry, I have problems here, hope you're coping.*

Kat was simultaneously irritated that he was being so cryptic, concerned something was seriously wrong and worried how she would manage if the bar did fill up, particularly since the cocktail of the week, the *sgroppino*, was a fiddly mix of lemon sorbet whisked up with vodka and Prosecco.

The first two or three groups filtered in gradually and it wasn't too difficult to juggle taking their orders with mixing drinks. Then there was a rush, with several guests braving the terrace despite a spring breeze cooling the evening, and Kat busied herself switching on the outdoor heaters and handing out rugs.

She was darting back for her order book when Zita appeared. Massimo's ex-wife was the last person Kat wanted to see right at that moment. She looked perfect, of course, her eyes expertly smoked with shadow, lips glossy, hair freshly tonged. Kat felt ragged in comparison, wishing there had been time to do more than throw a cashmere cardigan over her dress and pull her messy curls into a topknot.

'*Buona sera.*' Zita was all smiles.

'Hi,' replied Kat, a little breathlessly. 'Sorry, I can't stop to chat. We're so short-staffed this evening.'

'Where is Nico?' Zita checked the terrace. 'And Massimo?'

Kat gave her a brief version of events as she grabbed the order book from the bar. 'There might be a bit of a wait for drinks,' she warned, 'but I'll get to you, I promise.'

'*Mannaggia.*' Zita threw her hands in the air. 'You can't be expected to work here alone. Give that book to me, and I will take the orders while you make the drinks.'

'Really?' Kat was dubious.

'Yes, yes, *cara*, I have done it before. There isn't a job in this hotel I haven't helped out with.'

Kat didn't especially like the idea but knew she was going to need the help. 'Well if you're sure ... just until he or Nico makes it back. That would be great, thanks.'

Zita took the order book and Kat watched her stalk across the terrace in high heels. She was far more efficient than Nico, moving quickly from table to table, offering mineral water, recommending cocktails, making sure everyone had a bowl of salty snacks to nibble on, clearing away empty glasses, all with the minimum of fuss.

It made Kat think about how lazy and resentful Nico could seem as he went about his work. His sister Adriana was the same. She assumed they were sulky around her because they disapproved of this English woman who had swept in and taken over. Now Kat pictured them out in the street waving placards, shouting slogans, their faces lit with anger and realised something else had been going on all along.

'A Bellini and a negroni for table four,' Zita sang out, ripping a page from the order pad and tossing it onto the bar. 'Table eight were asking for Massimo. Apparently he recommended a seafood restaurant to them and they can't remember its name.'

Kat frowned. 'Sorry, I don't know—'

'That's OK,' Zita interrupted. 'I told them Antiche Carampane because that's what he always says. But I'll need to mark it on a map for them, as it's impossible to find. Do you still keep some behind the bar?'

'Yes, of course.' Kat handed her a tourist map, then got on with making the cocktails while Zita unfolded the map and guided table eight through the back streets of San Polo.

Kat tried not to resent Massimo's ex-wife for slotting so easily back into Hotel Gondola – she was grateful for the help, after all. But it was difficult not to feel that Zita belonged here far more than she ever would; and Kat was surprised at the sense of insecurity the thought brought with it.

The bar got busier. Ruth appeared for her espresso martini and sat on a stool sipping it slowly. More guests arrived and eventually left again, Ruth among them with plans for an early night before she started painting in the morning.

It was more than an hour later that Massimo made his return. He looked more exhausted than Kat had ever seen him and there was barely a flicker of surprise on his face when he saw Zita standing beside her, still clutching an order book.

'What happened?' Kat asked, as he sank down on one of the barstools. 'Where have you been all this time?'

'It's a disaster,' he replied.

'What?' Kat demanded, impatient for a proper answer.

Zita ducked behind the bar, poured a large brandy and handed it to Massimo. It wasn't something Kat had seen him drink before, but he slugged down most of it.

'Is Nico OK?' Zita asked.

'Not really,' said Massimo. 'He has been arrested.'

'And Adriana?'

'We managed to convince them to let her go. Nico, though, he is in trouble. It's a complete disaster.' Massimo splashed more brandy into his glass and gave Kat an anxious look. 'This isn't for the pages of your book, though. You must promise not to write about any of it.'

A Year at Hotel Gondola by Kat Black

CHAPTER 7

I've made the way it all began with Massimo and me sound so simple. But I had doubts, of course I did. There were sleepless nights when I tossed and turned alone in my bed and questioned everything. Then he would visit London for a couple of days and we would barely leave my apartment. That passion between us would flare again and it would all make sense.

My friends laughed when I said our relationship was going to be my new adventure. They talked darkly of the downsides of sharing a life, but it all seemed to be so trivial, dropped socks and fights about stuff that didn't really matter. Some had been married for twenty years or more and I had to concede they were the experts, and yet still I felt sure Massimo and I would be different.

Besides, this was the perfect time in my career to take a break. After so many years of long-haul flights and impossible deadlines, I was ready for a new challenge. I liked the idea of a slower pace, and of getting to know Massimo and his city deep down instead of hurrying off to new places and people like I'd always had to when I was filming my TV show *Black of Beyond*.

A year at Hotel Gondola, beginning in early spring, experiencing the seasons unfolding and our relationship growing and changing, that was my plan and Massimo liked it. Both of us agreed it was the length of time we would need to know if things were going to work in the longer term. There were other rules set. I would help out in the hotel since it was a family business and couldn't afford to carry me. Massimo would hold back from introducing me to his parents and his two adult daughters because he felt it wouldn't be fair until we were certain of each other. And the final rule, the most important one: however the year ended, we weren't going to regret a moment of it.

There were practicalities, although thankfully not too many. I had to find a tenant for my apartment since I didn't want to have it as a safety net. That meant things had to be packed away and put in storage or squashed into the single suitcase I was allowing myself. There were good friends I wanted to see before I left because I wasn't planning to return until the year was over. And then some old workmates threw a farewell party for me and I had a little wobble when I saw them all gathered together with drinks in their hands. Why did I have to leave? Why couldn't I be content to make a life here surrounded by all these people that I knew and liked?

It's just not in my nature, I suppose; never has been.

Venice greeted me with gloomy skies. The *passerelle* were laid out in Piazza San Marco – they're the platforms for people to walk on when the *acqua alta* floods in – and the tourists were all wearing plastic ponchos and disposable overshoes. I decided the first thing I was going to invest in was a stout pair of rubber boots for wading through the high tides. Because I was no longer one of the visitors, I was actually living here.

I gave myself a couple of weeks to calibrate myself to Venice. In those new rubber boots I did a lot of walking, splashing through the flooded lower parts of the city, braving rainstorms and chilled, misty mornings. Most days I found a reason to pass by Coco's little shop. She wasn't always there, of course, because she has a capricious attitude to opening hours. There is no point arriving before ten a.m. as she likes a gentle start, with time for lingering over what she is going to wear, for stringing on necklaces and stacking bangles. From mid-morning until lunchtime the shop is usually open, although you can't entirely rely on her not to have slipped out for a coffee. As for afternoons they generally depend on how lively Coco is feeling. She does enjoy a nap, particularly if she has plans to go out dancing that evening.

To begin with I pretended I was there to shop and bought things I didn't need – a scarf, a beaded evening bag, several more frocks, a hat. Coco took to removing items from my hands and returning them to the shelves or telling me outfits didn't suit me. She always seems pleased to see me, though, despite no longer wanting my custom, and likes to tell people how she helped me find the right man, so surely can be trusted to match them up with the perfect outfit. Whenever the shop is empty she suggests we go and drink a coffee, often served with her favourite *bussolà* biscuits, shaped like an S and flavoured with lemon zest and vanilla.

At this point Coco is my only Venetian friend but I'm finding that exciting rather than daunting. My life has so much empty space in it right now to be filled with all the new people and interests this city can offer.

Unfortunately there isn't quite so much free space at Hotel Gondola. On my visits to Venice over winter the place was never fully booked so we were able to use a guest suite. Now I'm officially living here which means I'm in the staff quarters: a small room on the top floor that I share with Massimo. As I was unpacking my suitcase into the half a wardrobe he had cleared for me, I realised for the first time in my life I didn't have a room of my own. In no particular order these are just some of the reasons that sharing can be challenging: I'm messy and Massimo is tidy; I lie in bed reading until late and he always falls straight asleep; I like a window open and he prefers the air conditioner; I always have music playing but he is a fan of silence.

There are bound to be other differences between us. We are operating a policy of dealing with each new thing as it comes along. I'm trying not to be such a slob; he's learning to enjoy listening to Adele, Lorde and Amy Winehouse. It all seems to be working out so far.

The advantage of being in cramped quarters is that it forces you out into the world. Venice is my living room, its wide *campi* and network of canals. I inhabit the *bacari* and the cafés. I call the green spaces my garden.

The days at Hotel Gondola have a regular rhythm to them. Everyone who works here is a part of the Morosini family, from the maid who tends your room to the waiter who serves your morning coffee. It's a very traditional place, a taste of the old Venice.

My time may be anchored by my regular evening shifts mixing cocktails in the bar but I have my days free and there is so much I want to fit into them. I hope to explore the lagoon, to row down the Grand Canal with one of the dragon boat crews. I haven't even been in a gondola yet! There are a lot of first-times ahead.

Let me tell you about shopping at the Rialto market. Coco insisted she should take me there, claiming that otherwise I'd be charged double or palmed off with inferior produce. She got up especially early to meet me. It wasn't difficult to spot her since she was the only one wearing a hot-pink woollen cape and an orange Hermès scarf.

On the edge of the Grand Canal, the Rialto market is a lively place to shop for food. The stalls are piled high with the freshest produce; some of it grown in the sandy, salty soil of the lagoon islands, which Venetians claim results in a more intense flavour.

That morning Coco led me excitedly from stall to stall, introducing me to all the most important people. 'This is Giancarlo, he always has the best radicchio in winter. And this is Michele, you must come to him for tomatoes over summer.'

Beneath the colonnades of the fish market Coco was especially beady-eyed. 'Only buy crab that smells sweet and fish that has bright eyes,' she instructed. 'Squid should have translucent flesh, prawns ought to look moist and the shells must never be cracked, scallops absolutely have to be pearly white.'

She made me get out my notebook and write down her words, repeating them to be certain I got it all right.

I bought too much of everything; I always do. Coco scolded me but I kept filling up my basket. The dish I wanted to make for our lunch was inspired by the classic *sarde en saor*. You will find this everywhere in Venice, from the humblest *bacaro* to the swankiest restaurant. It's really very simple, white onions slow-cooked in olive oil and good wine vinegar and flavoured with bay leaf. You can add raisins that have been soaked in white wine, and also pine nuts but you don't have to. The Venetian way is to steep sardines in the sweet/sour mix of onions and let them marinate at room temperature for at least a couple of hours.

I don't know about you but I'm hopeless at waiting for flavours to slowly infuse. I'm also not a great one for sticking to recipes – where is the fun in doing something the way it's always been done? I prefer to bring fresh ideas to each dish I cook. So I made several versions of *saor* for Coco's lunch and this is the one she preferred.

Yes, it's a recipe, but it's also only a suggestion. These onions would be just as good as a topping for grilled chicken or roasted eggplant; or stirred through a warm salad of white beans or waxy new potatoes. You could leave out the spices or add more, use red onions instead of white, include the raisins I've left out, whatever you like – your way of doing it may be better than mine and I won't be offended if you think so.

Coco says the main thing is to make sure the fish is fresh and your onions firm. She also wants me to add that this dish is very like life – you need to find the perfect balance of sweet and sour, too much of either is no good at all.

FISH SAOR

3 white onions
125 ml olive oil
125 ml white wine vinegar
a generous handful of pine
   nuts
2 bay leaves
5 whole peppercorns
1 tsp coriander seeds,
   ground

1 clove, ground
1 cm quill cinnamon, ground
pinch of salt
pinch of sugar
4 pieces of fish – white
   fillets, tuna steaks, even
   salmon

The important thing is to cook the onions so slowly that they
never brown. First halve them and slice thinly. Gently heat
olive oil in a heavy-bottomed pan. Add onions and fry for a
few minutes, then add peppercorns, salt and bay leaves, lower
the heat, put on a lid and let the onions sizzle slowly. Stir
regularly and add a little water if they seem to be drying out
or starting to brown. After 25 minutes add spices and fry for a
minute before pouring in the vinegar and throwing in a pinch
of sugar. Continue cooking, with the lid off, until the onions
are soft and a little gluey (at this point I like to inhale the
steam coming from the pan which smells divine!). Then take
off the heat, stir in the pine nuts and put aside to cool slightly
while you pan-fry your fish.

Plate up by topping each piece of cooked fish with a pile
of the onions and serve with steamed asparagus or French
beans, and buttery potatoes.

Serves 4.

So now I've caught you up on everything that has happened.
From this point on I'll be living this book as I'm writing it. I'll
be taking you with me wherever I go in Venice, you'll meet
all the people I do, taste the same food, hang out with me

and Massimo, share the ups and downs of my time at Hotel Gondola.

Often I think about that line of my mother's that so devastated me. 'Twenty good years' was what she claimed were left once I turned fifty. I'm devoting twelve months of that time to Venice. As beautiful as it is, I still have some doubts about settling for so long in one city when my habit of a lifetime has been to keep moving on to new places and people. And I don't know how things are going to turn out here, any more than you do.

7

Finding time to write as well as live was proving tricky for Kat. She kept sitting down at her laptop then being distracted by other things. Spring was starting to surrender to summer and the brighter days beckoned her outside. She could lose hours wandering through sunlit Venice or jumping on a *vaporetto* and going wherever it took her. Exploring was a part of her research; even so, it gave her an unfamiliar panicky feeling to arrive at the end of a week with so few new words written down.

Back in the days of her TV show, Kat had been part of a crew and problems were thrashed out together. As for her previous books, they had always involved working with a co-author, a photographer or food stylist. Now Kat was on her own, and this writer's block or lack of motivation ... whatever the problem was, she didn't know how to get past it.

Massimo kept telling her not to worry. 'You've got the whole year ahead. Just relax, enjoy *la dolce vita* and it will start to flow,' he would say and then inevitably the subject of their conversation would find its way back to whatever was bothering him.

His problems were always linked to the Hotel Gondola. Things had started going wrong after the street protest when Nico had been arrested for destroying the tourist menus outside several restaurants, knocking over stands and smashing glass. It might not have been too serious except Nico had struggled and become abusive when the police descended and they seemed to want to make an example of him.

Massimo did everything possible – helped the family pay

for legal advice, organised character witnesses, and wrote a letter portraying him as a prized employee. Even after his release, Nico wasn't especially grateful. Almost immediately he was caught up in two more protests, one in Piazza San Marco, the other involving a flotilla of boats that blocked the Grand Canal. And he was sullen with the guests and Kat, mixing up orders and spilling drinks so often it had to be on purpose.

'Perhaps you ought to let him go,' Kat suggested to Massimo. 'He's causing you so much stress.'

'But he's family.'

'I know, but even so, I'm worried he's becoming a liability. Who knows what he'll do next.'

Although he was reluctant, Massimo eventually agreed with her. However, letting Nico go only led to more problems. Almost immediately the Morosini family began fighting, with resignations among the younger members of staff who supported Nico's cause. Massimo had to hire a night manager from outside the family and Kat found herself temporarily working the breakfast shift as well as evenings. But the worst thing of all was Zita. She offered to help out in the bar until they found the right person to replace Nico.

'Kat and I make a great team,' Zita said cheerfully. 'We're having fun together.'

And although he must have suspected how Kat felt, Massimo hadn't argued. Nor was he showing signs of hiring anyone permanent. It was obvious why. He wanted things back the way they were, for the rift with Nico to be mended and the other staff he had lost to return. There were pressures from the family, with long phone calls that kept him distracted, and Kat noticed how often his brow was furrowed these days. She wished she could help fix things, turn back the clock, but couldn't see how.

'I was the one who talked him into firing Nico,' she told Ruth one morning. 'So I feel responsible in a way.'

Ruth was busy with her art now and producing canvases of smudged colour she only let Kat glimpse. Even so, most days they bumped into one another and went for an espresso, drunk swiftly standing up at the bar of the closest *pasticceria*.

Strictly speaking Kat shouldn't have confided the problems of Hotel Gondola to one of the guests but she wasn't sure where else to turn. And she trusted Ruth who, despite her woo-woo ideas, seemed both kind and wise.

'I need a plan,' Kat told her. 'But I'm at a loss right now.'

Ruth was convinced that Adriana was the key – she was Nico's sister, his companion on the protest march and remained a frosty presence on Hotel Gondola's reception desk.

'That puts her in the perfect position to act as a go-between, to smooth things over for everyone,' Ruth pointed out. 'If you need this situation sorted, she is the one to do it.'

'But Adriana hates me,' groaned Kat.

'That seems unlikely.'

'Really she does, she's never shown the slightest hint of friendliness.'

'Maybe that's because you've never shown any to her,' suggested Ruth.

So Kat approached Adriana warily. She started passing through reception with a warm smile and a cheerful *buongiorno*. She commented on the weather or admired what Adriana had done with her hair. She even asked for her opinion on the cocktail recipes she was testing. And when it seemed as if she was thawing, Kat carefully timed a chat with her.

'How is your brother?' she asked, pausing in the reception foyer mid-morning when there were no guests in sight.

'Why do you ask?' Adriana sounded mistrustful.

'I miss working with him. It's not that I don't get on with Zita but she's Massimo's wife and well … it's a little awkward as I'm sure you can imagine.' Kat's tone was confiding.

Adriana looked down at her computer screen, tapped out

a few words on the keyboard then looked back at Kat. 'Yes, I can imagine.'

'The only way she'll leave is if Nico comes back to work.'

'Massimo fired him.'

'I could persuade him to reconsider.'

'There is no need to bother. Nico isn't interested in coming back here. He doesn't miss working with you.'

'Oh ...' Kat was taken aback.

'He doesn't respect you,' Adriana said coolly.

Kat forgot her bid for friendliness. 'I've never understood why the two of you have such a problem with me.'

'It is not just you; it's everyone your age. You have taken the best of everything and left nothing for us. And now you want to silence us.'

'Is that what you think? How ridiculous.'

'I'll tell you what is ridiculous. Nico and I will never be able to afford homes of our own in Venice, not even to rent. When we get married and have our families, we will have to move to the mainland. Almost all our friends are in the same position. And what will happen to Venice then? It won't be a real city any more.'

'That's what Massimo said to me,' remembered Kat. 'It's why you went on the protest march.'

'Exactly. We must fight for what we want. It won't be given to us on a plate the way it was for your generation.'

'I've worked hard for what I have,' argued Kat, infuriated with her now. 'And actually I still do. I'm up there in that bar every night making cocktails, aren't I?'

'For now, yes, you are playing at living our life but you can walk away whenever you choose to.'

'So that's why you and Nico don't like me?'

'I didn't say that.'

'Why you don't respect me then?'

'It is why we don't respect people like you – because you

don't want to hear what we have to say. We are supposed to stay quiet and ask for nothing.'

The conversation had veered way off course but Kat wasn't ready to admit defeat.

'OK, I get that you're angry,' she said. 'But will you a least pass on a message to Nico? Tell him I'd like us to sort things out and for him to come back to work and I'm sure Massimo would too. Ask him to consider it.'

Adriana gave her a withering look. 'Signora, have you not been listening to me?'

The appearance of a group of guests clutching tourist maps ended their discussion before it could heat up any further. Kat left Adriana to deal with them. She needed a break from Hotel Gondola.

The little apartment above Coco's place was her bolthole now, as much as a place to cook. Kat liked to spend time there alone, lying on the old velvet chaise or sitting on the balcony on warmer, sunny days. She rarely got any writing done, just enjoyed the peace and the chance to think.

Today she didn't even bother taking her laptop. She walked there slowly, mulling over the talk she'd had with Adriana, stopping to drink milky coffee beside a canal, her thoughts rippling like the water. Perhaps every generation was destined to resent the one before, to feel misunderstood. Hadn't she once been the same? The thought made Kat feel so old.

At the apartment the first thing she did was throw open the doors to let out the musty smell that hung about the place whenever it was closed up. It had been a couple of days since she had visited last and when she looked out, Kat noticed a small change. There were three pots of herbs lined up on the window ledge opposite, obscuring her view into the room beyond, but only slightly. Kat couldn't help spying on the man who lived there. He was often to be seen taking a mid-morning nap on his sofa, or moving about his kitchen. Now it seemed he was growing herbs – flat-leafed parsley, sage and purple basil. At some point he would have to lean out of his window to water them, which might create a chance for them to exchange a *'buongiorno'*.

There was no sign of him now, though; the windows were shut and the sofa empty. Still feeling churned up from her exchange with Adriana, Kat sat outside and did the one thing that always soothed her – planned a menu. There were several in her notebook already, written out neatly by hand. She liked to plot a proper feast, beginning with an antipasto course and ending with a tiny sweet treat for after the main dessert. She put a lot of thought into dishes that might complement each other, to ingredients that were seasonal.

This time her imaginary menu was Venetian. It began with a cocktail to sip, a blend of puréed wild strawberries and ice-cold Prosecco. Then a *cicchetti* plate with tiny baby octopus dressed with chilli and a scattering of anchovies fried in a golden crust of polenta. To follow, rice rather than pasta, a soupy *risi e bisi* with its nutty flavour of freshly shelled peas. The main course took some deciding, should it be meat or traditional seafood? In the end Kat opted for a simple fish dish, fillets of John Dory dolloped in a sauce of sweet tomatoes that was pleasantly soured with chopped capers. Finally, for dessert a *zabaione*, a sweet warm cream of egg yolks and Marsala with plenty of amaretti biscuits to continue to nibble on over coffee.

Satisfied, Kat put down her pen. It was a good menu, perfect for late spring, ideal to eat al fresco. But just like all the others she had dreamed up, she would never cook it. In her tiny London studio there wasn't room to prepare several courses, never mind gather the friends to enjoy them. And here in Venice, she didn't know enough people, only Coco and Ruth, and would they have the appetite for so much food?

She might simplify it, serve a version of the rice and peas

with a few sautéed prawns and a salad of peppery leaves, and forget about the rich *zabaione* to follow. She could hold a lunch for the three of them up here in the apartment, with some of that wine that tasted like strawberries, if she could find it. A ladies' lunch – the more Kat considered the plan, the keener she was.

She was still preoccupied when she left the apartment. By now her thinking had moved on to brightening the bare room with vases of flowers, and how best she might set the scarred wooden table to make it look special. And then, just after she had crossed the bridge, a little way down the *calle*, she walked straight into him, the mystery man that she had been watching through the window of the apartment opposite. If he hadn't caught her, she might have stumbled on the cobbles.

Flustered, she apologised. 'I'm so sorry, I wasn't looking where I was going.'

'Don't worry, no one in Venice ever does, signora.' He smiled briefly, a flash of white teeth, a crinkle of the eyes and, releasing her, headed off down the *calle*. As he reached his front door Kat wanted to call him back, to introduce herself and ask his name, but instead she stood in the street, watching, until he disappeared inside.

Massimo was behind the reception desk when Kat trailed back into the Hotel Gondola. He smiled, pleased to see her, folding her in a hurried hug.

'Have you had a good morning?' he asked. 'Get any writing done?'

'Not a word,' Kat admitted. 'I didn't even try.'

'What have you been up to then?'

'Just wandering, as usual.'

For some reason Kat hadn't told him about renting the apartment. She wasn't sure why, as there was no point in keeping it a secret. Perhaps she liked having one thing for herself. Or maybe she was quietly angry that Massimo had never followed up on his promise to help her look for a kitchen and, too wrapped up in his own problems, had apparently forgotten all about it.

'Where is Adriana?' she asked, half-relieved not to find her there.

'Out on some errand,' he told her. 'She mentioned Nico and I didn't want to know any more. I expect they're both still involved in planning these protests.'

'I expect so,' Kat agreed, wondering if their little talk that morning might have made some difference.

The rest of the afternoon was spent struggling to make progress on the book. Every time she managed a paragraph, rereading it made her wince and Kat's finger pressed the delete key. She was struggling to decide exactly what she could share with her readers right now. That she and Massimo spent less and less time together? That his wife was a part of their life now? That Venice remained a mystery?

Kat had to make something happen, create a story she could tell; find a way into the life she wanted and the book she was trying to write.

A Year at Hotel Gondola by Kat Black

CHAPTER 8

If you're not careful, spring vegetable season can pass you by, especially in Italy where the summers are hot and seem to arrive suddenly. So when my favourite stallholder at the Rialto market told me to enjoy the tiny sweet peas from the islands of the lagoon because he wouldn't have them for sale much longer, I knew I had to hurry to make a *risi e bisi*. This is a very old dish, once enjoyed by the Doges that ruled Venice who made a ceremony of eating it for the festival of San Marco and had very strong opinions on how it should be prepared. Not that I care for their rules, naturally. I have my own ideas about how to marry rice and fresh peas most happily.

To my mind the whole point of cooking is feeding people, so my *risi e bisi* was going to be served at a ladies' lunch. I invited Ruth, a very lovely artist who has been staying at Hotel Gondola, and of course my friend Coco.

'A ladies' lunch, how nice, we must hold it in my garden,' she suggested when I mentioned my plan.

Coco's ground-floor apartment lies beside a backwater of a canal in Santa Croce, and is ridiculously cluttered. But attached to it is a small walled garden, very private and charming if rather overgrown. I don't think Coco sees the weeds. It's the blossoms on the tangled wisteria vines she exclaims over and the lavender springing from mossy urns, and the oleander climbing into the palms, and the scarred old wooden table beneath the twisting branches of a large fig tree.

'This is the perfect place for our lunch,' she declared. 'I think I will invite my favourite lover.'

'It's a ladies' lunch,' I reminded her.

'We need a little male company,' she insisted. 'And you will like Vittorio; he is completely charming.'

So far I'd heard lots of talk from Coco about her lovers, but never actually met one. It was impossible to determine how many she had, but they all adored her, apparently. They took her out dancing, to concerts and suppers. I assumed these men were actually companions, and Coco used the word lover because she liked the sound of it.

'OK, invite him along and we'll have to hope it's not raining,' I said.

'It won't be.' Coco sounded certain.

Sure enough, on the day of my little party Venice was bathed in sunshine. I like lunch to be a long affair that stretches on till dinner time, or at least until everyone is craving an afternoon nap, so my plan was to tempt my guests slowly with flavours rather than fill them up all at once. I spent hours designing the perfect menu and then, of course, changed my mind about almost everything at the last moment.

I was up early to arrive at the Rialto fish market as soon as it opened. I wanted some of the *moeche*, the soft-shelled crabs only available for a few weeks in spring and autumn, as they are wonderful soaked in egg, dusted in flour and crisped in hot oil. Plenty more seafood found its way into my basket. Lots of *moscardini*, the tender brown octopus with their delicate taste of the sea, bags of clams and mussels that I would mince with garlic and parsley to spread onto crostini. And then there were the vegetables: the first tiny courgettes of the season to be grated and turned into bite-sized fritters, the last of the Treviso radicchio to be roasted and drizzled with vinegar, violet-coloured artichokes, and of course the fresh peas, which were to be the star of the meal.

Lunch always feels like such an indulgence, something you are doing in time stolen away from work or boring chores,

and I love to make it special. It seems that Coco is of the
same mind as she had decorated a beautiful table. It was
covered in a white cloth edged with old Burano lace, with
flower-sprigged napkins and jugs overflowing with herbs (and
possibly a few weeds) she had picked from her garden, along
with mismatched vases of blowsy pale pink peonies that were
already dropping their petals.

Coco herself was a vision in mint green with a cashmere
wrap resting round her shoulders.

'You will be dressing properly, won't you?' she said, casting
an anxious glance at my jeans and marl-grey T-shirt. 'I have
told Vittorio to wear a suit.'

'Don't worry, I won't let you down.'

'What colour are you wearing?'

'Bright pink, a dress I bought the other day, but not from
you, I'm sorry.'

'Pink,' she repeated approvingly. 'We should look good
together.'

Some people like to cook alone, others prefer to be
surrounded by helpers; I'm happy either way. So Coco podded
the peas and Ruth, arriving early and equipped with an apron,
pitched in by cleaning the mussels and toasting slices of
French bread for the crostini.

As we neared the time her lover had promised to arrive,
Coco started repowdering her nose and fussing over the shade
of her lipstick.

'Most men don't like a woman to wear too much make-up
but without it I look like I have no lips,' she despaired.

'You look lovely,' Ruth told her. 'I don't know what you're
worried about.'

Coco frowned. 'Vittorio is younger than me.'

'How much younger?' I asked, busy chopping shellfish flesh
into tiny pieces.

'It is hard to know. I have never told him my age and he has
never mentioned his.'

'Where did you meet him?' Ruth wondered.

'I can't remember any more. I have known him for a long, long time. For years we were friends and then his wife died, and afterwards he was lonely so ...'

'You got it together,' I finished for her.

'That sounds unromantic,' Coco complained.

'Oh really?' I teased her. 'How would you put it then?'

'Something more dignified ... more ... oh, I don't know, what is the English word?' She looked at Ruth, who laughed.

'Don't ask me. Since I lost my husband I haven't got it together with anyone, I haven't even been out on a date.'

'No?' Coco sounded shocked. 'But how long have you been alone?'

'Long enough to know I'm perfectly fine by myself,' Ruth said briskly.

'Life is about more than being perfectly fine. Where is the excitement, the spice, the mystery?' asked Coco. 'Where is the passion?'

'I don't need any of that,' Ruth told her. 'It's all safely in my past.'

Coco's eyes widened, but she said nothing. Instead she occupied herself dusting blusher on her cheeks and blotting her lipstick with a tissue. I wondered about this man Vittorio who she wanted to look her best for. In my head I pictured someone white-haired and stooped, dapper in an old-fashioned suit. Even though she had said he was younger, I imagined him as birdlike and walking with a stick.

It turned out Vittorio does carry a stick; it is highly lacquered and silver-tipped, and he mainly seems to use it to wave about and point at things. He arrived at Coco's place, right on time, wearing a Nehru jacket in a deep maroon, a pair of well-cut black trousers and a wide-brimmed panama hat.

First he produced gifts. A posy of spring flowers, a bottle of vintage champagne, a flask of fragrance for Coco, three boxes of chocolates; all of it presented with a beaming smile. As soon as his hands were empty, he clasped them round Coco's waist and pulled her towards him, delivering a kiss that went beyond companionable. Oh, and he isn't stooped or frail, Vittorio is a handsome man, with a good head of steely grey hair, lightly tanned skin and a generous set to his shoulders.

Once I had changed into my pink frock, we sat down together in the garden to graze on the first course – the seafood crostini – and allow Vittorio to charm us. He was especially attentive to Ruth, asking questions in his slow, careful English, and nodding interestedly at her replies. Coco seemed impatient at his attention being drawn away from her. She kept interrupting with comments that didn't entirely belong in the conversation and, when Ruth mentioned she was an artist, gave a long and rather stagey sigh.

'I suppose you want to paint me? Everyone always does,' she said.

Ruth looked a little startled. 'Oh, I hadn't—'

'I've been painted many, many times,' Coco interrupted. 'There were lots of nudes done of me when I was younger but I didn't like them much. You don't paint nudes, do you, Ruth?'

'No, I—'

'Because the body looks better clothed, and the way we dress says so much more about us than our skin does. The portraits I liked were the later ones but I always hated sitting for them. Hours and hours in some draughty studio and nothing to do but be still.'

'That does sound awful,' I agreed.

'It is why I decided: no more. No matter how much an artists begs me, I always refuse to sit for them.'

'Oh, what a shame,' Ruth said. 'Still, I do understand and I don't have people sit for me, not usually.'

'Do you paint from a photograph rather than life?' Vittorio asked.

'No, I form impressions and often paint from memory. It's a different process because my work is more about emotion.'

'What have you been focusing on in Venice?' he wondered.

'Mostly strangers that catch my eye but I've also done quite a few of Kat,' Ruth admitted.

That was a surprise as the only canvases I had seen so far were of groups of people sitting outside Venice's cafés or wandering beside the canals and they were blurs of colour rather than distinct forms.

'Were you planning to show me?' I asked.

Ruth laughed a little nervously but didn't reply.

'I too would love to see your work,' said Vittorio. 'We must arrange to meet again. How much longer are you here for?'

'Not long, I'm afraid. I'm booked into the Hotel Gondola for another week. I may return to Venice in the autumn, though. I've been thinking about renting an apartment.' Ruth gave me an apologetic glance. 'It's so much cheaper.'

'Autumn was always my favourite season.' Vittorio sounded wistful. 'It was when my wife Laura and I celebrated our wedding anniversary. She used to bake a cake of chestnuts, chocolate and rosemary. I haven't tasted anything like it since.'

Ruth nodded, sympathetically. 'My husband enjoyed a carrot cake with buttercream icing. I'm not much of a baker but I always made one for our celebrations. It's funny how food can end up reminding you of people, isn't it?'

Vittorio gazed at her. 'I'm not sure I could eat that cake now even if I found one. It would taste too sad and—'

Covering his hand with her own, Coco quickly said, 'My darling, this is not the time for melancholy. We are here, together on a beautiful day, and your Laura would want you to make the best of it.'

'My husband would want that too,' agreed Ruth. 'He'd be pleased I'm in Venice rather than at home, feeling lonely.'

'And I'm quite sure he'd want you to come back here in the autumn,' I put in. 'I could get Massimo to do you a deal if you'd prefer to stay at Hotel Gondola rather than be in an apartment on your own.'

'And I might agree to sit for you so long as it doesn't take for ever,' Coco added graciously. 'You could paint Vittorio too.'

At that point I had to leave the table to prepare the next course. The soft-shell crab, the octopus and the courgette fritters were quickly fried and arranged on a platter. I pulled a bottle of wine from the fridge, tucked it under one arm, and managed to make it back to the garden without mishap, although I did almost lose a couple of fritters off the edge of the crowded plate.

The conversation stopped the moment I appeared, in that awkward way it always does when people are talking about you, and I wondered what they'd been saying. Only Coco seemed unembarrassed. The others turned quickly to the food, exclaiming at how good it looked, piling their plates with crisp crab and golden fritters.

Twenty minutes later when I returned to the kitchen to make the *risi e bisi*, Ruth insisted on coming to help. I think she wanted to get me on my own for a chat. As I stirred saffron-spiked broth into the bubbling rice, she talked about her paintings, stressing they were her vision rather than reality, and I might not recognise myself.

'I've never had my portrait painted before,' I told her. 'I'm intrigued.'

'I hope you're not disappointed. I'm only an amateur artist.'

'Will you paint Coco?' I asked. 'It didn't seem to me as if you wanted to.'

'I suspect I may not have much choice.'

We both laughed then, because Coco really is an unstoppable force, and if she wanted a portrait of herself, then she was going to get one.

The *risi e bisi* was almost ready. I tipped the peas in with the soupy rice and gave them a few moments to bubble away so they were barely tender. It's not the way the Venetians do it but I wanted to retain all of that nutty, sweet flavour. Finally I stirred in scandalous amounts of freshly grated Parmesan cheese, and spooned the creamy, steaming rice into four bowls.

Ruth helped me carry it all into the garden, along with the roasted radicchio salad and the artichokes. Again silence fell the moment we appeared, but this time Coco seemed uncomfortable. She was quiet as we ate, not joining in when we discussed the fresh peas and the importance of choosing plump, unmarked pods. Although she pronounced the dish delicious, she didn't manage much of it.

Vittorio mirrored her distraction with anxiety, constantly stealing glances at her face.

I wondered if perhaps they had argued while we were in the kitchen. There was certainly something amiss. To soften the mood I topped up everyone's glasses with more wine and insisted on a series of toasts – to Venice, to Ruth, to Vittorio, to Coco, even to Hotel Gondola – and then I filled the glasses again. It's all a bit hazy after that but I remember Coco made coffee and brought out sablé biscuits we were all too full to eat. There were more toasts, and it was absolutely agreed that Ruth would return in the autumn and she would paint Coco and Vittorio, separately and together.

Then Coco got rid of Vittorio. She did it diplomatically, declaring that it had been a lovely party and she wished it could go on forever but he looked so very tired and she didn't want him to overdo things and perhaps he ought to take a water taxi straight home, right away.

She took his hand and encouraged him up from his seat, held onto it while he said his goodbyes, and led him from the garden. Ten minutes later she reappeared, sank into a chair, and said rather shakily, 'Is there any more of the wine?'

I poured what was left and Coco finished it in a few gulps. 'Oh dear,' she said.

'Do you want me to get another bottle?'

Coco shook her head. 'No, best not.'

'Are you OK?'

'I am not entirely sure.'

I went and fetched that other bottle anyway, and when I got back found Coco and Ruth in a huddle.

'What's going on?' I asked.

'Coco's had a bit of a surprise, that's all,' said Ruth.

'Quite a big shock, actually; it was the last thing I expected.' There was a quiver in Coco's voice. 'My darling Vittorio proposed. While you and Ruth were off cooking, he asked me to be his wife.'

'What did you tell him?'

'That his proposal was unexpected and I needed time to think; what else could I say?'

'You might have said yes,' I told her. 'You do seem very keen on him, after all.'

'I adore him, he's wonderful, but I don't want to be married,' declared Coco.

'Then you should tell Vittorio that.'

'But he made a long speech about how much he loves me. He had a ring in a velvet box, an emerald. He wants to cherish me ...'

'Oh dear,' said Ruth. 'Still, I suppose you're going to have to find a way to let him down gently.'

'He is lonely. He wants a wife to wake up with every morning, someone to make a fuss over what he eats, to help him choose which shirt to wear, all those little things. He thinks I am that person.' Leaning back in her chair, Coco closed her eyes.

'And you're definitely not?' I asked. 'You're sure about that?'

'I don't want to spend the rest of my life with him or any man. Hopefully there is another woman who might.' Coco opened her eyes and stared at Ruth.

'Not me,' she said. 'I've had the love of my life. I'm not interested in trying to replace him.'

'You are sure? Yes? Ah well.' Coco sighed and changed the subject. 'Kat, why was the *risi e bisi* so yellow?'

'I put saffron in it.'

'What else was different?'

'A tiny pinch of chilli, some sugar snap peas for crunch, smoky pancetta.'

'Interesting ... What a shame Vittorio had to choose right then to propose and I wasn't able to eat more of it.'

'It was pretty good,' I told her.

'Ah, my lovely Vittorio, I expect he thought it was the perfect moment. And now I will have to find the poor man a wife.' Coco sighed again. 'Perhaps I will have a little more wine after all.'

VENETIAN RICE & PEAS

¾ cup of Arborio rice	100 g sliced pancetta
500 ml chicken stock	1 tsp saffron threads
2 tbsp olive oil	tiny pinch of dried chilli
1 chopped onion	100 g freshly grated
2 chopped cloves garlic	Parmesan cheese
800 g peas in pod	salt
100 g sugar snap peas	black pepper

Put the chicken stock in a saucepan and bring to the boil, reduce to a simmer and add the saffron. Fry the onion, garlic and pancetta until the onion is soft, being careful not to brown. Add the rice and fry for a minute, stirring to coat it in oil. While stirring, slowly add the stock one ladle at a time, allowing it to absorb before adding more. You will most likely need more liquid so boil the kettle or make an extra stock by boiling the empty pea pods in water. Add a pinch of chilli, black pepper and then taste and add salt if needed (pancetta and bought chicken stock are both salty so more may not be required). Once the rice is very nearly soft, add the podded peas and the diced sugar snap peas and allow them to cook until they are barely tender. The finished dish should have a slightly soupy consistency so don't worry if the liquid hasn't all been absorbed. Remove from the heat, stir in the grated Parmesan and serve. If you're feeling especially indulgent you could also stir in a chunk of butter.

Serves 2–3.

8

Kat was pleased with the chapter she had just written. The descriptions of the blowsy, overgrown garden gave it colour; Vittorio's unexpected proposal added drama and, most importantly, the readers would assume the lunch had been prepared in Coco's kitchen. She wasn't going to reveal she had rented an apartment; it would spoil the whole concept of her book. Much better not to mention that Coco's oven was filled with shoeboxes, her cooktop piled with silk scarves and beaded bags, and who knew how long it had been since food was prepared there. Or to let her readers know that the three of them had kept on drinking wine all afternoon, until the sun moved on from Coco's garden and the sudden chill reminded Kat she had a job to go to.

Leaving Ruth to clear up the dirty dishes, she had half-run back to Hotel Gondola and even so was late. That had given Zita the perfect opportunity to make it clear she had everything under control. The bar was tidy, the guests had a drink in front of them and she was busy chatting to Massimo about the changes they might make in time for summer: planters filled with scented flowers, lots more fairy lights, replacing the cocktail glasses with vintage Murano.

Zita was running through her ideas when she paused and gave Kat a careful look. 'Are you OK? Do you feel well enough to work?'

'I'm absolutely fine,' insisted Kat, who had developed a piercing headache. 'Won't those cocktail glasses be a fiddle, though? We'll have to wash them by hand.'

'People come to Hotel Gondola to experience a little

Venetian glamour so we must give them a taste of it,' Zita had replied. 'I'm sure we'll find time to wash a few glasses, Kat. It's not so difficult, after all.'

There was a dismissive tone to her voice and she shot Massimo an exasperated glance as if they were dealing with yet another idle staff member. Kat seethed quietly for her entire shift. As soon as it was over she went to bed, without saying goodnight.

In the morning she pretended to be asleep until Massimo left for work, then dressed quickly and escaped Hotel Gondola. The apartment was a nicer place to write, she told herself. Sitting on the chaise beside the open doors, her laptop on her knee, listening to the soft chug of motorboats and smelling the briny canal water they stirred up, the words had come easily for once.

Constructing the recipe left her feeling irritated – so many grams of this or that, taste it before adding salt, don't let the onions brown ... It was as if people were idiots and Kat preferred not to think that of her readers. Still, the lunch had provided plenty of material, which was the whole idea really.

Closing her laptop, Kat wandered out onto the balcony to stretch and yawn, taking a moment to glance through the windows opposite and see if there was any sign of her neighbour. The place looked deserted and the potted herbs on the window ledge were parched and wilting.

She leant on the balustrade, looking down over the canal with its rows of motorboats moored along one side, some sleek, others shabby. Perhaps she should see about buying one. Kat wasn't convinced she would ever have the confidence to manoeuvre a boat alone through the busy canals, but it might be something else to write about. It was all very well promising her readers they could live the adventure alongside her, but there had to actually be some adventures.

Kat felt a pang of hunger. She had skipped breakfast and it

was nearly lunchtime now. On her way out to find food she knocked on Coco's door. She hadn't been expecting to find her at home, but a voice called out something in Italian, then the door opened a crack and a wan-looking Coco peered through it.

'Ah, *buongiorno*.' As she opened the door wider, Kat saw she was wearing a faded blue kimono and an orange turban that she must have thrust on hastily because it was lopsided.

'Are you OK?' asked Kat.

'I may have been a little delicate earlier but now I feel fine.'

'Why not get dressed and come out to lunch with me?'

'At my age a woman doesn't simply get dressed. It is a process and it takes some time.'

'I assume that's a no to lunch then?'

'Would you bring me something back?' asked Coco. 'No hurry at all, though, I might lie down again for a little while.'

Instead of taking her usual route back towards the Rialto market, Kat turned into a tangle of canals and back streets she hadn't yet explored. There were fewer tourists here and more bars with old Venetian men passing time at their tables.

Kat was looking for an interesting place to eat, not the usual *bacaro* with endless plates of meatballs and things skewered onto crusty bread with a toothpick. She was beginning to think this part of Venice had nothing else to offer when she came across an *osteria* that looked intriguing. It was only a small room with a banquette running along one white-painted wall, and oversized bunches of dried flowers hanging from the ceiling. The place was empty, even though it was nearly midday, but Kat could smell something good cooking.

She wandered in and, since there was no sign of a waiter, sat herself down. After five minutes of being tormented by the scent of things being caramelised and braised, turned in butter and soused in wine, she went and found a menu. Her impatience ratcheted up another notch when she saw the whole thing was written in Italian, with no English translation, and filled with words so unfamiliar she couldn't guess at their meaning.

'Hello,' she called out, then again. 'Hello, is anyone here?'

No one appeared and Kat was really exasperated now. Leaving her table, she marched over to the swing doors that led through to the kitchen and pushed her way in. The chef was standing with his back to her, hovering over a stove covered with steaming stockpots and pans full of simmering sauces.

'Are you open?' she asked crossly.

It was only as he turned that Kat recognised him. Dark blond hair, fair skin, fine features – it was the man from the apartment opposite, dressed in chef's whites, holding a sauce-glazed spoon that he was about to take a taste from.

'Oh.' She stepped back in surprise. 'You're my neighbour.'

'Am I?' He sounded confused but then a moment later added, 'Ah yes, you are the one who is always tap-tapping on your laptop. Why are you here?'

'I came to eat lunch. But perhaps you're closed? If so you probably shouldn't have left the door ajar.'

'No, signora, we are open, most certainly open.' He put down his spoon and quickly wiping his hand on his apron, took her elbow and steered her back through the swing doors. 'Please sit down, anywhere you choose, and in a moment I will return to take you through the menu.'

'Is there no waiter?'

'There has been a small issue. But today is not busy so it will not matter.'

His eyes were green, she realised. No, they were hazel. Or maybe like Venice's canals they changed colour depending on the light that fell on them.

'Don't worry about the menu. Why don't you just feed me?' Kat suggested. 'Bring whatever is most delicious.'

He treated her to a smile. 'Do you have an appetite?'

'Always.'

'Then I would be delighted to feed you.'

What he produced was Kat's kind of food, hearty and imaginative. Plump pasta parcels stuffed with roasted cauliflower and lemon cream, resting on a bed of butter-poached leeks. Fish for the main course, sea bass crusted with shrimp and chorizo. And finally a deconstructed tiramisu dressed with tart wild strawberries, dusted with smashed pistachios and teased with a thin drizzle of *zabaione*.

He brought out every course himself, topped up her water and took away the dirty plates.

'Why don't you sit down?' Kat suggested when he appeared with her dessert. 'You can help me eat this. I know I said I had an appetite but you've more than satisfied it.'

He glanced around at his empty dining room and shrugged. 'Why not?' he said, taking the chair opposite.

'I'm Kat Black, by the way.'

Often her name was familiar but clearly not to him. 'I'm Dante Berardi,' he replied. 'Tell me, how was your meal?'

'Amazing. I can't understand why you don't have queues out the door.'

'I opened only this week.'

'What you are doing here is exciting, you need to tell people ... and get some wait-staff obviously ... and maybe translate the menu so tourists can read it. Everything else is great: the simplicity of the décor, the complexity of the food. I love how you've taken traditional ingredients and mixed in other influences but not overdone the whole fusion thing. You've made each dish entirely your own.' Kat was enthusiastic and Dante's green-then-hazel eyes lit in response. 'I've eaten some good meals in Venice but it's all been same-same. This is the first that has surprised me.'

'That is what I wanted, to modernise Venetian food but still respect our traditions.' He leaned across the table towards her, his look intense. 'My food has a story to tell and every single ingredient has a message and a meaning, a purpose for being on the plate. Each dish should surprise people a little, but not too much.'

'What people?' Kat asked, gesturing at the empty tables. 'There is no one here.'

'They will come,' Dante said, sounding certain. 'They will find me.'

'Well I'll certainly be back soon,' she told him. 'I want to taste more of your food, lots more.'

He smiled at her. 'There will always be a table for you.'

This man was definitely going to feature in her book, decided Kat. His ideas, his passion, his sheer Venetian-ness would all leap from the page. He might even let her include a couple of his simpler recipes. Once she knew him better, she would ask but for now she had another favour.

'I promised to take lunch over to a friend,' she told him. 'Would you make me some more of the ravioli perhaps?'

Dante agreed, even letting her back into the kitchen to watch him work. He was one of those chefs who cooked in a quiet, considered way and neither of them spoke until the ravioli was packaged up and ready to go.

Kat paid the bill, which was fairly steep but worth it. 'Please tell me you're going to get some help around here. Kitchen hands, wait-staff, that kind of thing.'

'It's a matter of finding exactly the right people and I haven't had much luck so far,' admitted Dante.

Kat had a good idea. 'I might know a waiter who could start pretty much straight away. He's local and experienced.'

'I'd want him to tend the bar as well as wait on tables, at least until business picks up. Is he any good?'

'His name is Nico and I think he'd be perfect,' she promised.

*

Eating well always made Kat feel the world was a nicer place and wandering back to Coco's apartment, clutching her takeaway package of ravioli, she was infused with a sense of well-being. Venice was brash in its beauty, all blues and pinks in the bright afternoon. Summer felt only a few breaths away. She was enjoying the pleasant buzz of chancing on a cool, new restaurant no one else had found. And she was hopeful of finding Massimo's nephew a decent job.

Kat delivered the pasta to a sleepy Coco, packed up her laptop, and turned towards home. As she reached the Hotel Gondola it seemed clear what she needed to do.

Adriana was behind the reception desk. She looked up with the same dutiful smile that she offered all the guests, dropping it when she saw it was only Kat.

'Where's Massimo?'

'Office.' Adriana gestured with a flick of her head.

'I need Nico's number from you.' Kat held up a hand to stop her arguing. 'I may have found him a great job. I'm assuming he does actually need one?'

'A job in another hotel?' Adriana asked.

'A restaurant, a really brilliant new one.'

'OK then.' Adriana's expression didn't change as she scribbled the number on one of the hotel's cards and passed it over.

'You could say thank you. I'm trying to do a nice thing here,' Kat told her.

'I'm sure you have your reasons.'

Kat was too exasperated to reply. Ducking beneath the reception desk, she knocked on the door of Massimo's claustrophobic little office. 'Got a minute?'

'Of course.' He seemed happy to see her. 'I need a break from staring at this computer and I'd far rather look at you instead. Come and sit down.'

'No, let's get out of here, I need to talk to you properly.'

'You want to go upstairs?'

'Out of here altogether,' said Kat. 'We should head down to that little *bacaro* on the corner for ten minutes. I know you probably have accounts to do but we really need to talk.'

'Not accounts, just the list of guests to register with the police and give to the statistics office and that job can wait.'

By the time they reached the *bacaro*, Kat had worked out exactly what she needed to say to him.

'Nico won't be coming back,' she declared, as she sipped on a sparkling water. 'You know that, don't you?'

Massimo sighed then nodded. 'I guess you're right.'

'We need to find a replacement for him and then Zita can go back to doing whatever it is she normally does, which I'm sure will be a relief to everyone.'

'But she hasn't mentioned being in a hurry to leave.' Massimo sounded surprised. 'And the two of you are getting along so well. She is always telling me how much you love running the bar together.'

'Seriously?' Kat was so astonished she forgot the rest of her speech. 'Do you think she actually believes that?'

'Why would she lie?'

'I don't know, but, Massimo, I'm hating it.'

He looked shocked. 'Has she done something to upset you?'

'Yes.' Kat searched her mind but couldn't come up with anything specific. 'No, not really, but it's awkward and I think it would be so much better to bring in someone who isn't still married to you.'

'Zita told me it wasn't awkward at all. I asked her about that specifically.'

'You didn't ask me, though,' Kat pointed out. 'I don't want her here every evening. I can't get away from her. She makes me feel ... I don't know ... like she's the one that really belongs here – which is true in a way, isn't it?'

'Not even slightly true,' he promised her. 'But I didn't realise that's how you've been feeling. I feel very bad, Kat. I'm sorry.'

'Now that you do realise, please will you find a way to get rid of her?'

Massimo was white-faced. 'This is going to be tricky. You will have to be a little patient.'

Kat gave him a look that was intended to convey just how short on patience she was.

'I can't risk upsetting her,' Massimo argued. 'I have the girls to consider and our good relationship is important to them. If they think I have fired their mother ...'

'I understand that but you also have me to consider now,' argued Kat.

'Are things so bad?'

'They might be pretty soon if we don't do something. Remember how you didn't even want to introduce Zita to me at first?'

'True, and I wish this situation hadn't arisen but it did and now I am asking for your patience while I try to find an elegant solution.'

'An elegant solution?' Kat softened a little. 'This is awkward for you too, I know. OK then, I'll do my best to be patient.'

'Thank you. And if there is something else bothering you, if ever you are unhappy, then please, Kat, tell me straight away. I can't promise life here will be perfect for you, but I will try to make it as good as I can.'

He hugged her and as she leant in, breathing the clean, cut-grass smell of him, feeling the strength of his arms, Kat reminded herself how lucky she was to have him.

She kept reminding herself later in the evening, while working the bar with Zita who seemed to be doing everything possible to test her patience. Issuing instructions for the sake of it, disappearing in the middle of a busy spate without giving a reason, criticising the amount of peach nectar poured in the Bellinis, complaining the orders were mounting up and Kat needed to work faster. Nothing awful, not worth complaining about, just that same low-level sense of being played that Kat always seemed to have with Zita around.

When Ruth popped in, only for a glass of lemonade because she wouldn't be drinking alcohol again for a while, Kat asked a question that had been on her mind for a while.

'Take a look at Massimo's wife, over there on the terrace. I was wondering, what colour is she?'

Ruth didn't bother turning round. 'That one is interesting. Usually colour swirls round people like an aura. But Zita has a solid column of red running right through her centre. I've never seen anyone else like her.'

'What does it mean?'

'You always ask me that and I never have a straight-forward answer for you. There isn't one this time either, I'm sorry. But she is an impressive woman, I think.'

Kat watched Zita clearing away the empty glasses from a table. The way she walked and held herself, her careful smile, her air of coolness and confidence ... There was no need for psychic powers to see Zita was impressive.

For once Kat felt like writing. It seemed like an escape to be working on her book, to be thinking about food and her new discovery, to forget about Zita for a while and focus on the beginnings of a new friendship she had great hopes for.

A Year at Hotel Gondola by Kat Black

CHAPTER 9

I always say food is a bit like fashion; it's not necessarily about whether it's any good, but if it's the right moment. How else do you explain the extraordinary emptiness of Locanda Dante?

I suspect I may have been the first person in Venice to discover this amazing new *osteria*. I ate a lunch there so delicious that I woke up still thinking about it the next morning. The chef is modern and exciting, the food is an experience, and it ought to be a fight to get a table. But I was the only customer in there and I don't entirely understand why. Possibly because the place is much too new to be in any of the guidebooks, or not a well-known name like Harry's Bar; at least not yet. Or maybe this is not the right time for Dante Berardi's kind of food, although I'm hoping that's not the case.

He is so good he could be cooking in any restaurant you care to mention; at least in my opinion. He is not one of those chefs who hovers at the pass and tweaks the odd micro-green as the plates are presented. He likes to feel the heat of the gas jets, to get his hands into the food, to know his ingredients. Every morning he is at the Rialto market choosing the freshest produce. He serves what is harvested from the lagoon and its islands season by season, and creates dishes that remind him of his childhood, growing up in the back streets of San Polo, which is where I found his unassuming little *osteria*.

'It takes a certain person to want this life,' he told me when I returned to eat there again, this time with Coco in tow, and eager to see what she made of the place.

I led her into the modest room and refused to let her see a

menu. Then Dante came out of the kitchen and made a fuss
of us. Coco loved that, of course. There were none of her usual
demands to check the freshness of the seafood, no haughty
reminders that we wouldn't be paying the tourist price.
Instead she agreed that Dante should choose what we ate.

The first course appeared, a bite-sized tart filled with
creamed cod and subtly flavoured with ginger. Next we were
served a small plate with three fat scallops nestling in a small
tangle of anchovy-spiked spaghetti and drizzled with a salsa
verde. And then the sea bass with a light sauce of gently
poached strawberries, mint and basil. I closed my eyes and
savoured each new mouthful.

When she had finished eating, Coco put down her fork with
a sigh. 'I am a little sad.'

'Sad? But why?'

'This food won't work, not here. What tourists want from a
simple *osteria* in San Polo is a menu with all the usual things:
sarde in saor, cuttlefish cooked in its own black ink, artichokes
in garlic and lemon. And if they are honest, this is what the
locals want too; food that tastes as if their *nonna* might have
made it in her kitchen, flavours that haven't changed in a
century or more. Perhaps if the place was grander, close to
Piazza San Marco or somewhere more exclusive, but hidden
away here it will be a challenge.'

'You are right, signora.' Dante had overheard her. 'These
are the problems I must fight, but I have to believe I can. It is
why I wake early every morning to go to the fish market, why
I am here all day and into the night, why I am putting my love
into Locanda Dante.'

'But what if it doesn't work?' I asked, wondering if Coco
might be right.

Dante looked serious. 'It cannot fail.'

That's when he said all that stuff about only a certain sort
of person wanting a chef's life. He brought out a Murano glass
platter covered in petits fours and talked of the long hours of

work, his drive for perfection and how he could never cook food he didn't believe in. He has the curious mix of arrogance and vulnerability I've seen in other chefs I've met and I'm always fascinated by it.

Later, as Coco and I strolled across a wide *campo* and beside the shadowed waterways, I wanted to talk about Dante, his food and his chances of success, but she cut me off.

'It is only cooking and every woman in Italy does it without any fuss. Then a man comes along, puts on a white jacket, serves strawberries with the fish and we are supposed to admire him.'

'But you liked the food.'

'I did,' she agreed. 'Still it was only food that I ate and then forgot about.'

'It was incredible,' I objected. 'Beautifully thought out and executed, perfectly presented, food with—'

'I am not so impressed with this man Dante either,' she interrupted. 'I think he would be a very selfish lover.'

I spluttered a bit. 'Who exactly is going to be making love to him?'

Coco was dressed in white, with a wide-brimmed hat, oversize sunglasses and a scarf tied at her neck. It was a stylish outfit that took at least a decade off her, but still it was a jolt to hear a woman her age talking like that.

'I was only thinking,' she said mildly. 'Doesn't it cross every woman's mind when she meets an attractive man?'

'Are you saying these things to shock me?' I asked, laughing now.

'Of course not.' Coco didn't seem amused. 'I may be old but I have the same thoughts I had when I was a girl. And the same feelings.'

'That's good to know ... I suppose.'

I may have sounded flippant because Coco peered at me disapprovingly over the dark lenses of her sunglasses. 'You think this chef Dante is so courageous?'

I nodded. 'Yes, actually, I do.'

'What you don't realise is that at my stage in life, everything is courage.'

I didn't understand what Coco meant, not right at that moment. None of us wants to spend too much time imagining being old, do we? We ignore those alarming clicking sounds our knees begin to make. We steer clear of mirrors unless the light is kind, and are sucked into buying almost anything if it's labelled anti-ageing. We look at those other people, the ones who are stooped and thickening round the middle, the colour leaching from their wrinkled skin and thinning hair, as if they're another species rather than what we'll become some day.

Thankfully, I can mix a negroni in my sleep by now because I must have been distracted during my shift behind the bar. I kept thinking about Coco and how it must be for her to have that old, frail body. Was it depressing? Did she feel as if she had left her real self behind somewhere? Could she even look at a younger woman without being slightly envious?

When my friend Ruth came by she asked me twice if anything was wrong, but I wasn't ready to share the thoughts that were running through my head. As I sent out tray after tray of cocktails, I had that sense of life rushing by. Very soon I'd have burnt through those twenty good years my mother had promised, and there would be fewer remaining. Then I'd be old like Coco and with so little of life left ahead of me.

As soon as my shift was over I went back to see Dante. I wanted to tell him that he was doing the right thing, taking risks, chasing the life he wanted. There was so little time, why spend it doing a single thing you didn't believe in?

A couple of Americans were leaving his *osteria* when I arrived. They were discussing the size of the bill and how they could have eaten at Harry's Bar for not much more.

I found Dante alone in the kitchen, loading the dishwasher. To help, I began scraping the plates clean. Far too much of the sea bass remained on one and there was an almost untouched tart of creamed cod on another.

'Just one table in tonight?' I asked him.

He nodded.

If my TV show had been running I'd have featured Dante for sure. *Black of Beyond* made stars out of many of the people who appeared on it: a chef in an obscure ramen bar in Tokyo, a creator of incredible dumplings at a shabby joint in some Chinese town, a barbecue pit master in Tennessee. Their places were packed after the episode had screened. If only I could do the same for Dante.

Hoping to help in some smaller way, I had recommended a waiter.

'Did you call him?' I asked now.

'Yes, but he isn't right,' said Dante.

'Why not?'

'There isn't enough passion there.'

'Is anyone ever particularly passionate about being a waiter?'

'If they work here, they need to care as much as I do.'

His refusal to compromise dazzled me but even I could see he was being unrealistic.

'If that's your criteria you may not find any staff,' I pointed out.

'Then they will find me, just as the customers will.' He sounded so certain about it.

He cooked me a late supper, a simple plate of *bigoli in salsa* that we ate from a pan in the kitchen, leaning where we stood. It wasn't the kind of food Dante wants to be famous for, no subtle twists, no ingredients to surprise the palate, just thick strands of chewy wholewheat spaghetti in a rustic sauce of anchovies and onions.

After we'd finished I had him write down the recipe because it deserves to be shared. It's a meal you can cook when there is barely anything left in the cupboards. It's an honest dish, with robust flavours, to stave off your hunger and make you feel warmed inside. It's the sort of food you can taste the love in.

BIGOLI IN SALSA

If you're not a fan of oily, salty food then move on quickly; this pasta dish is not for you. Also, a word about *bigoli*. You're unlikely to be able to find this thick, wholewheat Venetian-style spaghetti in your local store. You could substitute with a regular wholewheat spaghetti but I think that tastes like cardboard so I prefer a thickish white spaghetti, or even tagliatelle at a push. Some people go with *bucatini* but in my opinion that's the most annoying pasta shape ever invented.

60 g jar anchovies in oil
1 large onion, finely chopped
1 clove of garlic, finely
  chopped
olive oil
250 g spaghetti

white wine
black pepper
salt
bunch flat-leaf parsley
  (optional)

Put a big pan of salted water on to boil for the pasta. Heat a little olive oil in a skillet (I always use the anchovy oil too) and slowly fry the onion and garlic over a low heat until very soft. Add the anchovies and break up with your wooden spoon. Then add two to three tablespoons of white wine and simmer. Season with black pepper. You shouldn't need to add more salt.

Cook the pasta until al dente, drain, return to the pan and stir in the anchovy sauce. You can add some chopped parsley for extra flavour but it's fine without. How easy is that?

Serves 2, unless you have the appetite of a small bird.

9

Summer brought to Venice all the things everyone complains of. Muggy days, stinky canals, street hawkers, slow-moving crowds and an unbearable crush on the *vaporetto*.

Kat managed to ignore most of it. For her, summer in Venice meant bright skies and heat-soaked days. As she wandered through the city's back streets she collected snippets of other people's lives from the sounds that drifted through their open windows. Here they were listening to opera, there clinking plates as they cleared up from lunch, somewhere a baby was crying, the TV was turned up too loud, a couple were laughing together. Venice in summer seemed less mysterious, more prepared to include her.

At the Hotel Gondola they were fully booked and in the evenings the bar was jammed. Kat had learned to tell from the way a person was dressed which places she ought to suggest they visit. If they were wearing the things that made Coco wince – baggy shorts, trainers and money belts – then she offered the basic combination of the Basilica and the Doge's Palace plus a little local knowledge about the best shops for carnival masks. The women in stylish dresses and interesting pieces of jewellery Kat always directed to Coco's store. Others she pointed towards the areas that were still very Venetian – to the far canals of Cannaregio, to the hidden gardens, hard-to-find *bacari*, to the fruit and vegetable barge in Dorsoduro that would look so picturesque in their Instagram posts.

Many asked for restaurant recommendations – where do the locals eat? they always wondered. Kat was careful which guests she sent to Locanda Dante, although the food there was better than ever, riskier and more brilliant. Other people had found it now and there was a steady stream of customers, with even lunchtime busier. Kat still wandered over most days. It had become part of the rhythm of her new life, like a visit to Coco or a quick coffee with Ruth.

Sadly, Ruth had left just as summer arrived. It had been such a wrench helping her pack up her canvases and saying goodbye. Kat extracted a promise she would return once the hottest weather was over.

'You have to come back to paint Coco,' she had reminded her.

Ruth had frowned. 'I'm very much hoping she'll forget about that. I don't know how I'd paint someone who has no colour. A grey canvas wouldn't be very exciting.'

Kat was missing all her talk of colours. Sometimes she squinted at Zita, trying to find that column of red running right through her, or she imagined the angry shades swirling around a hard-to-please guest.

There was a portrait Ruth had painted of her hanging above Kat's bed now. At first she wasn't sure how much she liked it. None of her features were recognisable; it might have been anyone really. But Massimo thought the bright canvas captured a movement that was completely like her. And it was nice having the painting there, a reminder of an unexpected friendship.

Kat couldn't imagine growing so close to any of the other guests. Most only stayed for a couple of days and then they were off to Florence, Pisa or Siena, to tick more must-sees off their lists. What would they remember of Venice? A jumble of canals? That afternoon they got lost? A tour they had taken? Kat felt sad for them not having the time to soak the place in through their pores like she could.

Life here ought to have been perfect. Every morning she woke to the sound of gently lapping water and the murmur of a breeze through her open window. She felt Massimo beside her, his hand resting on her hip or his ankle criss-crossing hers. There was a whole day ahead to do anything she pleased: take a boat out to the islands, eat lunch at some new place, visit friends or write her book. If it hadn't been for the evenings and that heart-sinking moment when she arrived in the bar to find Zita there, efficiently filling dishes with olives or making sugar syrup, then she would have nothing to complain about.

Massimo hadn't found the promised elegant solution and his ex-wife seemed more entrenched than ever at Hotel Gondola. On the face of it she was charming but still Kat was collecting small reasons not to like her. Her bossiness, her habit of acting as though she was the one in charge and deciding on things without checking first, and increasingly how so many of her comments seemed loaded in some way when Kat analysed them later.

Often Zita managed to find her most sensitive spots then appeared to delight in needling them. There was her tendency to go on and on about being a mother, for instance. Not that Kat was sensitive about being childless. After all, it would have been irresponsible for a woman who travelled as much as she did to have babies. Some of the *Black of Beyond* crew used to say their kids thought Dad lived at the airport because they dropped him off there so often. Kat never wanted that for a child of her own and reminded herself of it whenever she did feel a pang.

So she wasn't sensitive, exactly, but certain things did rile her, in particular anyone who acted as though you didn't quite count as a woman unless you had experienced motherhood. Zita, it seemed, specialised in that.

'Family is everything, isn't it?' she would comment, smiling fondly at a group of parents and teenagers sitting together out on the terrace. 'My girls are my life. It's such an extraordinary bond that Massimo and I have with them.'

She was always cooing over babies or pinching the chubby cheeks of toddlers. 'Such a blessing; the love of a child is like nothing else in the world,' she would say to the proud mother before giving Kat a look that clearly said, 'You're a career woman and you missed this.'

Then there was her easy camaraderie with Massimo. Perhaps she was doing it on purpose, maybe not, but Kat had noticed how she touched him more than necessary – her hand on his chest as she greeted him with a kiss on both cheeks, a casual lean against his shoulder, a fond rumple of his hair. Massimo insisted it meant nothing; Zita was Neapolitan and they were all like that. But Kat wasn't entirely convinced. At times it felt as if Zita was competing with her for Massimo's attention.

'What does she want? Why won't she just go away?' she asked Coco one morning when they were at the shop together.

Her friend shrugged. 'Perhaps she is bored. Or she wants her husband back. Or she is jealous. Maybe it is even because she likes you. Anything is possible. But why question me? It is her you should be asking.'

'I can't do that.'

'Why not? She is the only one who knows the answer.'

'If she is trying to get Massimo back she's hardly going to admit to it, is she?'

'Who knows?' said Coco. She was sorting through evening bags, searching each fold and pocket carefully for anything that had been left behind. There was a small pile on the counter: a few old coins, a miniature gilt-edged mirror, a key and some beads from a broken necklace. 'Why do you dislike this woman so much? Is it only because she is Massimo's ex-wife?'

'It's a feeling she gives me,' Kat tried to explain. 'Like she's in control and I'm being manipulated, or she knows something I don't. Maybe I'm being oversensitive but still I'd prefer her not to be such a part of our lives.'

'It is a difficult situation,' Coco conceded. 'She has children with him. She was his family long before you met him and having her there must be a constant reminder of that. But why assume the worst of her? Why worry so much?'

'I'm not worried.'

'Yes, you are, and it is pointless. Either you talk to her and ask your questions, or you accept that she is a part of life at Hotel Gondola and there is nothing you can do.'

'Massimo would hate it if I talked to her,' said Kat. 'I don't see how I can.'

Coco was about to respond when a customer appeared. She was young and barefoot, and came in hesitantly, as if unsure she was in the right place.

'*Salve*,' called out Coco.

The girl seemed startled. 'Is everything in here old?'

'Vintage,' Coco corrected.

'Oh, right.'

'There will be a dress here that is perfect for you,' Coco promised. 'But, signorina, first you need to put on some shoes. You cannot walk around Venice like that. It is not clean and more importantly it is not respectful.'

The barefoot girl backed out of the shop without another word and Coco gave a long sigh. 'This is why it is better not to try to give advice ... because you can't make people take it.'

Kat felt restless. She didn't want to go to the apartment to write, or pause for coffee in any of the usual places; she couldn't be bothered sitting on a bench and people-watching. For a while she wandered aimlessly and then, nearing a *vaporetto* stop and seeing one of the ferryboats idling, she ran to jump aboard without any idea of where she was going.

At the Arsenale stop she disembarked. This was a Venice she didn't know so well. She had walked past the high brick walls of the old shipyard and through some of the quieter *campi* but hadn't spent too much time exploring because it was where Zita lived and she didn't want to risk bumping into her.

Now she wondered if Coco was right, if all the holding back her words and damping down her feelings was a bad idea. Kat hadn't come to this part of the city on purpose but, as she walked through the unfamiliar back streets, it occurred to her that she ought to have. Why was she waiting for Massimo to sort things out? She had never expected a man to fix her problems before.

Kat didn't know how to find Zita's place, only that she owned a ground-floor apartment with a small courtyard garden. One time she had mentioned being close to the walls of the Arsenale, but so were lots of people. Kat spent an hour wandering about, vaguely hoping to glimpse her, but there were no sightings so she didn't have to test her courage. What would she have said anyway? That she wanted her to leave the Hotel Gondola and not come back? That she would rather tend the bar alone than have her there? That she put her on edge? That she didn't want to be her friend after all? These things were true and yet Kat couldn't possibly say them. She was beginning to see why Massimo might be struggling.

Kat walked slowly, letting herself get lost. In the middle of this sun-baked day the *campi* were deserted and the neighbourhood seemed slower and sleepier. Only as she skirted Piazza San Marco did she strike the other Venice, with its streets clogged with tourists, brash waiters calling out for customers and shop doorways strung with the same cheap leather handbags that were sold all over the city.

She spotted the teenage girl who had been in Coco's shop earlier that morning. She was sitting on the edge of a canal, her bare feet dangling down towards the water. 'You can give advice but you can't make people take it,' her friend had said. And it was true but the trouble was even the best advice wasn't always so easy to follow.

Kat didn't see Zita until half an hour before their shift in the bar was due to start. She had arrived early and was busy restocking bottles, a list in her hand and a frown on her face.

'We need to get more Prosecco delivered,' she said. 'And some of the peach nectar.'

'I'll sort it out,' offered Kat.

'No, no let me,' countered Zita. 'There will be less chance of a mix-up. They don't speak such good English at the suppliers we use.'

Kat sat on a barstool, the one that had always been Ruth's favourite. 'Fine,' she said. 'But I'm perfectly capable of putting in an order.'

'Of course you are. I'm trying to help.' Zita stopped arranging bottles of wine and gave her a long, steady look. 'I'm only ever trying to help. You know that, don't you?'

'The thing is—' began Kat.

'I know,' interrupted Zita. 'I've been thinking exactly the same thing.'

'You have?' Kat was surprised.

'I thought working together would be a chance to get to know one another but it hasn't really worked out, has it?'

'Not at all,' agreed Kat, suddenly hopeful that Zita was about to offer the elegant solution everyone was looking for.

'We need to spend some time together away from Hotel Gondola to really become friends,' she announced instead.

Kat had no words. She stared at Zita with her too-sleek hair and her too-smooth skin, and the clothes that clung more than they should have, and wondered what she was playing at.

'I'd like you to come over to my place for lunch. I'll cook Neapolitan food for you. What about tomorrow?'

'I was in your neighbourhood this afternoon actually,' was all Kat managed to say.

'Really? I was at home for most of the day. What a shame you didn't come by to say hello.'

'I didn't know your address.'

'I'll write it down for you, with some directions too, of course, although it's not so hard to find. And then you can return to my neighbourhood for lunch tomorrow.' Zita smiled. 'And we can sit in my little courtyard and talk all afternoon until it's time to come to work. It's so peaceful and private there.'

'Oh … OK.' Kat couldn't find a way to refuse.

Zita smiled again. 'I'll look forward to it.'

The bar was slammed that evening so there was no chance to pull Massimo aside and talk to him until her shift was over. Tiredly, she suggested they went to a small *bacaro* that stayed open later than most. It was the sort of place Kat had longed to be taken to when she first arrived, small and un-remarkable, filled with old men and women who still spoke the Venetian dialect. As well as the usual crostini they served zucchini flowers, stuffed with ricotta, laced with nutmeg and deep-fried in the lightest of batters.

Kat always ate them greedily. She had finished one plate and ordered another before she got round to raising the sub-ject of Zita. When he heard about the invitation to lunch, Massimo looked uncomfortable.

'That might be my fault,' he admitted. 'I tried to talk to her and must have done a terrible job because she seemed to think she needed to make more of an effort with you. I'm sorry, Kat.'

'It's OK, I can see that it's difficult. I'll just have to go along and find a way to explain to her that we need some space, you and I. That having her here is awkward and while I'm happy to be friends eventually, I'm not ready yet. That's how I'll put it.'

Massimo seemed anxious. 'Do you think so?'

'I won't upset her,' Kat promised.

He rubbed his eyes tiredly. 'The unfortunate thing is I think she really does enjoy working with you. This is the happiest I've known her in a long time. Zita needs a purpose in life.'

'Oh well.' Kat wasn't going to feel guilty. 'I expect she'd enjoy working somewhere else with another person.'

It wasn't often that Kat found herself dreading a lunch. Usually, thoughts of what might be on her plate filled her mind and there was scant concern about the conversation. But this meal was about everything but the food. She dressed carefully for it in a floaty frock she had bought from Coco. And she took a water taxi to the address she had been given, rather than walk or ride the *vaporetto* and end up crushed or sweaty.

Zita had made an effort too. She had tonged her hair into loose curls and was wearing a dress that revealed her tanned shoulders and cleavage. She kissed Kat on both cheeks as she welcomed her inside her small apartment with its low, wood-beamed ceilings and uneven floors.

'Go through to the courtyard.' She pointed towards some French doors. 'It is the only place to be when the weather is this hot.'

Kat sat in the shade of a sun umbrella and sipped a chilled Pinot Grigio as Zita brought out the meal she had already prepared.

'I have kept this lunch very simple so there is more time for us to talk but I have shopped carefully for it. There is fresh buffalo mozzarella from Campania, tomatoes and basil grown on Sant'Erasmo, some bread I bought still warm from my favourite *panificio*. I know how important food is to you and I wanted you to have the best. So eat, please.'

The mozzarella was amazing, so soft it almost melted to cream when it met the warmth of Kat's mouth. The cherry tomatoes were jewels of sweetness, the basil's flavour sang. Despite herself, she closed her eyes as she tasted it all.

'Good, yes?' Zita sounded pleased. 'I buy the mozzarella

from the Casa del Parmigiano beside the Rialto market. You know it?'

'Yes, I often go there for cheese,' Kat told her. 'Their pecorino is amazing.'

'Everything is the very best quality. You should try their olives,' said Zita. 'But, Kat, I didn't ask you here today to talk about food. I have something important I want to say.'

Kat froze, a forkful of mozzarella halfway to her mouth.

'When you arrived in Venice no one knew what to make of you, this famous person from the television who had crashed into Massimo's life and decided to stay. We were shocked. I am talking about his family now – me, his parents and sister. The conversations we had! Everyone reacted differently. His mamma and papà are very Venetian. It took them a while to accept me so you can imagine how they feel about you. His sister cares about money more than anything and she worries that you might too.'

'And what about you?' asked Kat.

'I have been waiting for someone like you to appear. Massimo is a good man, attractive, kind. There was always going to be another woman after me and I am realistic enough to accept it. So when you arrived I was curious to meet you. I decided straight away that, whatever you were like, we should be friends; it seemed the best thing for everyone. So I made a very big effort. But you, Kat, you made no effort at all, did you?'

Everything seemed very still. No breeze ran through the garden, no leaf on the lemon tree trembled, no curl of Zita's hair moved even a fraction. She held Kat's gaze and the only sound was a cicada singing.

'Maybe I didn't,' Kat admitted.

'That was stupid. Don't you remember how the first time we met I said you ought to be my friend because I can help you? And you do need my help, *cara*, because you are struggling and it is only going to get worse.'

Kat wasn't going to let this woman think she needed anything from her. 'You're wrong. I'm not struggling. Massimo and I are happy, I love Venice and my book is going really well. It's all fine.'

Zita speared a tomato and a tiny piece of mozzarella with one swoop of her fork. 'As fine as it can be when he works all the time and you hardly see each other and you feel as if all he cares about is the Hotel Gondola.'

'Why do you say that?' asked Kat.

'I struggled with all the same things. It wasn't so bad when the girls lived at home. Then they grew up and left and no one needed me any more. Just like you, I worked at the hotel because it was a way to be a part of his life. And we kept going for a little while, Massimo and I, but it had to end eventually.'

'And you've never found anyone else?'

'No.' Zita's gaze shifted from Kat's face. 'No one else, not yet.'

'So now you want Massimo back?' asked Kat, since it appeared this was the time for brutal honesty.

Zita threw her hands in the air. '*Mamma mia*, do you ever listen? I am trying to tell you to spend some time with this man and you think I want him?'

'I do spend time with him,' said Kat defensively.

'Does he take a weekend off work for you – even a day a week? Have you been together out on his family's boat to picnic on one of the islands, or to fish or search for clams? Have you been to the beach at Alberoni for a swim?' Zita shook her head. 'I don't think so. You must make Massimo do these things with you. They are important. The hotel will keep running. Everyone will cope. And you will be happier.'

Kat felt as if something was caught in her throat. She choked a little then found herself crying and for some reason couldn't stop.

'Is it so bad? You should have talked to me before now,' said Zita softly.

'I don't know why I'm crying,' said Kat, because honestly she didn't.

Zita ignored her. 'We can sort it out. I will help you.'

She sounded so determined, and Kat remembered the column of red that Ruth had seen running straight through her.

'Why would you do that?'

'Why wouldn't I?'

Zita fetched more food. Tender slices of veal rolled tightly round a mix of pine nuts, salty cheese and prosciutto then braised until tender in a rich, highly seasoned sauce of tomatoes and wine. She spooned some on a plate, along with fried courgettes and a few peppery leaves. Kat felt so churned up she didn't think she could manage anything but she tested a mouthful, then another until somehow she had finished a meal.

'I need to know something,' Zita said, when her plate was empty. 'Are you planning to stay in Venice?'

'I made a commitment to be here for a year,' Kat told her.

'And after that?'

'I don't know. I expect we will talk about it closer to the time.'

'So Massimo has no idea where he stands with you.'

'It's what we agreed at the very beginning,' said Kat defensively. 'Both of us.'

'Ah, now I understand,' said Zita.

'You understand what?'

'Some things.' She spooned a little more of the veal onto Kat's plate. 'But perhaps not all of them yet.'

A Year at Hotel Gondola by Kat Black

CHAPTER 10

On a warm summer evening the terrace bar of the Hotel
Gondola is a lovely place to be. You can watch the sky turn
pink and gold then sit beneath the stars. Soft music plays,
fairy lights twinkle and people are relaxed and happy.
Nevertheless, you won't find any Venetians drinking here. It's
not a haunt for locals. So when Coco and Vittorio turned up at
cocktail time I was surprised to see them.

They came and sat beside the bar, since every outside table
was taken, and both ordered a negroni.

Coco looked around despondently as I was busy preparing
the drinks. 'There isn't a soul here,' she declared.

'What do you mean? The place is packed,' I pointed out.

'And yet nobody at all is here,' she insisted.

She started asking questions about various people at the
tables. Who were they? Where had they come from? Were
they married or single? Since guests come and go quickly at
the Hotel Gondola I couldn't provide very much information.

'Is there no one here like Ruth?' she hissed at me, and
finally I understood what was going on. Coco was hoping Hotel
Gondola would supply Vittorio with a potential wife, a single
woman in her sixties ready to be charmed by a suave Venetian
man. She had assumed there were lots of Ruths staying with
us but of course that isn't the case.

'We don't get many long-stay guests like her,' I explained.
'And hardly anyone seems to come to Venice on their own.'

I don't think Coco believed me because she ordered a
second negroni, and remained at the bar, watching people

come and go. Vittorio seemed oblivious to what was going on and was enjoying himself hugely.

'I am so often alone these days I relish these evenings being out in the world,' he told me. 'Coco always takes me somewhere interesting but we've never come here before. It is very nice, your hotel. I should like to stay here if I were a visitor.'

'Were you born in Venice?' I asked, as I loaded more drinks onto a tray.

'My family comes from Chioggia, one of the villages of the lagoon.'

'You must have seen many changes since you were a boy,' I said, topping up flutes of peach nectar with Prosecco.

'Venice never changes really. People wash through her like the tides, but the city stays the same.'

Coco said something in Italian that made Vittorio smile. 'She is telling me I should have been a poet instead of a lawyer.'

'It's probably not too late,' I told him.

He glanced at Coco. 'I am hoping it is not too late for many things.'

They left shortly afterwards but early the next morning Coco returned to Hotel Gondola to find me. The situation was desperate, she claimed. Vittorio was pressing her for a response to his marriage proposal and she was certain it would break his heart completely if she turned him down.

Over coffee and brioche at the nearest *pasticceria*, she outlined her plan.

'I have to find someone he can fall in love with; a woman like your friend Ruth. Pretty, kind, not moody, ideally a better cook than me, oh, and nicely groomed; that is what would be perfect for Vittorio.'

'Where are you going to find this paragon?' I wondered.

'This is my big problem. I have played the matchmaker before but it was easier when we were young and there were so many parties and outings. Now everyone stays at home.

And Vittorio doesn't need some person who wants to sit and watch television all day long. He loves me because I am always interesting.'

'That's your problem,' I told her. 'It's you he wants, not some other woman you throw in his path. You're just going to have to explain that you don't want to be married.'

She dismissed my words with a flutter of her hands. 'Not until there is a distraction for him. Surely your hotel, all those guests coming and going, that has to be a good place.'

I was dubious. 'We do get small groups of older women coming through but they're looking for history, architecture and Tintoretto paintings rather than love.'

'They are looking for love, even if they don't know it,' she said stubbornly.

'I'll keep an eye out for you,' I told her. 'But if I do happen to find this kind, attractive creature you're seeking, how are you going to bring them together?'

'Leave that part to me. I will find a way.'

So we have been looking, Coco and I. She has been back to the Hotel Gondola several more times and has taken to wandering the tourist trails – the Piazza San Marco, the Peggy Guggenheim Collection, the route past the Bridge of Sighs – always with her little dogs at her feet. And, of course, you can't browse through a rail of dresses in her shop any more without being peppered with questions. Where are you from? How long are you here for? Where is your husband today?

I suppose most people think she is eccentric – after all, that is what I assumed at first – when in fact she is scarily shrewd. She is weighing you up and if there is a flaw she will find it. Ragged fingernails, chunky ankles, an unwise choice of lipstick shade, a laugh that is too high-pitched, or if you're too pushy or too timid, she notices it all.

'You're very fussy,' I told her.

'This is for Vittorio; he deserves someone who is right for him. It is a shame about your friend Ruth. I am convinced she is the perfect type. And he was so interested in her art, remember? That is a good start.'

'Ruth will be back in the autumn. But she did seem very adamant that she wasn't keen.'

'She doesn't know him yet.'

'You know him, and you don't want to marry him,' I pointed out.

'That is entirely different.'

'I don't see why.'

'I am much older than Vittorio and Ruth. It is too late in my life for more new beginnings.'

And that's when Coco told me the story behind her shop. She described it as her final new beginning and as she spoke it was like seeing a curtain lift and glimpsing some of the sadness behind it.

'I kept walking past that shop and noticing it lying empty,' she began. 'Eventually I had the idea of renting it for a week or two to sell some of my own belongings that I didn't need any more. Then people started bringing me their treasures. Evening bags they would never carry again and gowns they couldn't wear, things that still had so much life in them while those that owned them didn't.'

'So that's why you have so much stuff cluttering up your shop and your apartment?'

'No, the deaths are the reason for that – so many deaths. When you are my age there is always some old friend passing on. They leave behind the hats they wore to parties, the shoes that took them to weddings, christenings and funerals, all the clothes they lived in. And so I continue to have my shop and give these things another life ... at least until it is my turn to die.'

'Don't say that,' I said, because I hated to think of it.

'But it is true. Some day I will be gone and then perhaps another person will sell this blouse.' She fingered the vibrant peacock print. 'I hope so.'

'Is that why you won't marry Vittorio, because you worry you might die and he's already lost one wife?'

'It is not the whole reason.'

'What then?'

'I want to be free to be myself. To choose how I spend my days and nights.' Coco shot me an impish look. 'And more importantly, I don't want to give up my other lovers.'

Summer evenings in the bar at Hotel Gondola are busy. There often isn't time for me to pause and talk. But when Coco comes in I always steal a few moments. She brings her little dogs, and sits on one of the high stools. I make her a negroni and she keeps a careful eye on me to be sure it's exactly how she likes it.

Then she takes her drink and wanders from table to table chatting to people. Massimo thinks she's fabulous. He says the guests love it and we ought to put her on the payroll. He has no idea what Coco is doing – no one does but me.

I wonder if she will ever find a match to make. Tonight was an unsuccessful mission. She made a circuit of the terrace then came back for a second negroni. I placed it on the bar in front of her and she frowned as she told me, 'There isn't a soul here.'

THE HOTEL GONDOLA NEGRONI

This is the classic Italian cocktail with my own small touch – a dash of Prosecco to give it a flavour of the Veneto. Coco prefers me to have a heavier hand with the gin than the Campari and the sweet vermouth. Also, she demands a slice of orange rather than the traditional twist of peel (yes, she is demanding).

1 part gin	*1 part sweet vermouth*
1 part Campari	*a splash of Prosecco*

Put the first three ingredients into a cocktail shaker with some cracked ice. Shake well. Pour into a chilled glass, top up with a little Prosecco and garnish with a twist of orange peel.

It was the tears that had confused Kat; the way they coursed down her face as Zita talked in that soft and reasonable voice. She remembered tasting their saltiness then eating the over-seasoned food, and confiding in Massimo's wife things she was only just beginning to realise she had been thinking. That she wanted more of him, that she was lonely, that falling in love wasn't quite how she had expected it to be.

Zita had promised to help. And in the warmth of the afternoon, when Kat was filled with wine and food, it had seemed as if she meant it. Now, though, she wasn't so sure. The more she thought about that day, the more it felt as if Zita had managed yet again to find a tender spot and taken pleasure in probing it.

Had Kat even meant all the things she said? Loneliness had never been her problem. She had travelled the world, relying on herself in all sorts of situations, rarely feeling she needed anyone. Why would that have changed? And those tears that had come so easily, flowing over her cheeks – that wasn't like her either.

Kat woke early the next morning, rolled away from Massimo's side, and was dressed before he had stirred. Grabbing her laptop she went straight to the apartment because it seemed the safest place. She didn't even stop for coffee but rushed to be there, with the door closed against the world. She kicked off her shoes and moved quietly, hoping if Coco were below she wouldn't hear her footsteps.

Out on the small balcony she began to write. It was a chapter she knew would be deleted as soon as it was finished because it was too raw, too honest, and not how Kat wanted the world to see her.

More tears came, blurring her eyes so she couldn't see the screen. Kat wiped them away impatiently with the edge of her T-shirt, mystified by their arrival. There was no reason to feel so low. Things weren't perfect, but when had they ever been? She had been stranded by erupting volcanoes, had her luggage stolen or lost, been let down, cheated and mugged, and one time even abandoned. She had never cried about any of it. Furious at herself, Kat stabbed at her keyboard.

'*Cara*, what is wrong?'

Dante was leaning out of his window, staring at her, concerned.

'Nothing,' Kat said hurriedly. She had forgotten it was a Monday, which meant the Rialto market was closed, and so was his *osteria*.

'But you are crying.'

'It's an allergy,' Kat lied.

Dante shook his head, disbelieving. 'If you say so. But no one is allergic to Venice.'

Kat put her finger on the delete key and the words she had written began disappearing one by one. 'I'm just feeling a bit blah today for some reason.'

'Blah?' he asked, evidently not understanding.

'Yes, you know. Flat.'

'Flat?' He seemed even more confused.

'Low, blue, down.' Kat tried to come up with a word he recognised.

'Ah, depressed,' Dante said cheerfully, clearly pleased to have got it at last.

'Not as serious as depressed ... Just a bit blah.'

'That is not good.' Dante cocked his head to one side, as if trying to see her from another angle. 'I am making coffee. Why don't you come over?'

'To your place?' Kat had never been inside his apartment and was curious.

'Yes, come now. I will run downstairs and open the door for you. Maybe I will even slice up some fruit for our breakfast.'

'OK then. Thanks.'

Dante's apartment was surprisingly untidy and filled with little piles of things Kat hadn't noticed when she was trying to peer in through his windows: coins and keys, newspapers, biros and cookbooks. He cleared a space on his dining table for the coffee cups and a plate of sliced melon.

'What are you going to do with your day off?' she asked him.

Dante yawned in reply.

'More sleeping?' Kat guessed.

'Usually, yes, I would take a morning nap on my sofa, and maybe another in the afternoon. But today I have promised to go and see my family. So I must stay awake.'

'Where do they live?'

'In San Polo, not far away, my father and brothers have a *squero* … a boatyard. They are gondola makers.'

'Really? How interesting.'

With a casual shrug, Dante poured coffee and passed her the melon.

'I've never been in a gondola,' Kat admitted. 'It seems like such a touristy thing to do.'

'That's because it is the best way to experience Venice.'

'I suppose I'll give it a try eventually.'

'I could take you out,' Dante offered.

'Do you know how?'

'Of course! I am the son of a boat maker. I learned how to row them as well as build them.'

'And your family has one you could use.'

'Of course,' Dante said again.

'Then I'd love to come with you some time, thanks.'

'What about today? I have to visit the *squero* because I've hardly seen my family since I opened Locanda Dante. And it would be fun, yes? We will have a nice time.'

'It would be great,' she told him, brightening at the prospect of an adventure.

Kat realised she had walked past the Berardi family's boatyard many times. She must have seen the stacks of timber left outside to season, the gondolas lying on their sides and the way the mossy ground sloped down into the canal, but still hadn't registered this was a place where boats were built and repaired.

Dante took her inside the workshop and introduced her to his father Enrico and his two brothers. These men were plainer versions of him with work-roughened hands and they spoke in a staccato of Venetian dialect Kat couldn't hope to catch a word of.

'What are they saying?' she asked Dante.

'They are asking if I am ready to stop playing in my kitchen and do some real work here. It is what they always say.'

Kat cast a sympathetic glance his way. 'Do they not think being a chef is a proper job?'

'They think I am wasting my talent.'

For a while they watched the men work. Kat was surprised to see Dante's brothers were setting fire to old-fashioned torches, just bundles of sticks really. Once they were blazing, they passed the flaming ends over the wooden sides of the half-built gondola, their brows furrowed in concentration.

'Are they scorching the wood?' she asked Dante, confused.

'No, they are curving the oak planks. First one side is soaked in water and then the other heated by fire. It is the traditional way and if you can get it right then the wood is perfectly curved without any of its fibres being damaged.'

Kat watched, fascinated. 'And you learned how to do this?'

'When I was an apprentice I was taught it all – how to choose wood without any knots or white edges, how to prepare the frames and curve the sides, and add layer after layer of black varnish. But my real skill was the carving.'

Enrico had been watching his sons but now he looked up and muttered something to Dante.

'He wants you to know that it takes two months to build a boat like this and there are eight types of wood to be used. That he works in the old style and does everything by hand.'

'Tell him I think it's amazing,' said Kat.

'Papa understands English he just refuses to speak it. And what he isn't telling you is that they rarely build a new gondola here these days. Now it is mostly maintenance and repairs – not so amazing.'

Kat stole another glance at him. 'And not the life you chose for yourself?'

Dante shook his head. 'You have to love it, and I didn't.'

His brothers had sweat dripping from their faces now. When the firing was finished and the torches plunged into a trough of water, Enrico inspected their work. Finally he nodded, his expression not changing, and that seemed praise enough for Dante's brothers who grinned and punched each other's shoulders in congratulation.

'Good, now we eat,' said Dante.

While they had been watching, his mother had slipped in quietly with a basket full of *tramezzini* – triangular sand-wiches of soft crustless white bread generously filled with creamy mayonnaise, smoky ham and preserved artichoke hearts. Kat hung back, assuming there wouldn't be enough for her since she hadn't been expected, but Dante's mother beckoned her over and insisted she took one.

Clearly this was who he took after, this pale-skinned woman with her angular cheekbones and full lips. As she ate, Kat watched the two of them sitting side by side. They had so much to say to one another, in contrast to the other men of the family who were entirely focused on their chew-ing and swallowing.

Only once he had finished eating did Enrico speak, directing a long and rapid spate of Italian at Kat, apparently assuming she understood every word. She turned to Dante to translate.

'He is telling you that each boat is unique,' said Dante. 'It is customised to the gondolier's height and weight, and crafting one is an art. He is saying this *squero* has been in our family for over a hundred and fifty years and the skills have been passed down through the generations. Two of his sons will continue the legacy. Of this he is proud.'

Kat realised how difficult it must have been for Dante to go his own way and become a chef. She liked him all the more for having had to struggle.

'Surely he is proud of you as well?' she said.

'He is the reason I cannot fail,' responded Dante in a low voice, as his father moved away.

The gondola they took out was old but still entirely seaworthy. Dante rowed Kat through the quieter back canals and every now and then she turned in her seat to watch him, perfectly balanced on the stern, arms muscular as though they always wielded an oar. It was a peaceful way to see Venice. Passing slowly beneath bridges, gliding through still water past the scarred walls of houses and grand *palazzi*, and then out into the Grand Canal, choppier and busy with other craft. Dante steered carefully around a delivery barge stacked with casks of wine, a speeding police boat, ferries and other gondolas manned by men in straw boaters and striped tops.

'I love to be on the water,' he told her. 'We Venetians need it. When I was away from here I physically missed it.'

'Were you gone for a long time?' asked Kat.

'For several years, while I was learning about food. I travelled to Paris, London, Madrid, and spent some time in Asia and Australia. Cooking was a passport for me to see the world.'

'And you loved it,' assumed Kat.

'This job is hard,' said Dante, shifting his body and working the long oar as he manoeuvred the gondola into a quieter canal. 'You cut yourself, burn yourself and work crazy hours. The longer I cooked, the more I hated it and the more I realised I could never do anything else.'

Kat laughed. 'That sounds crazy.'

'I know,' agreed Dante. 'It is like an addiction. What I dreamed of was coming back to Venice and having my own place where I could cook the food I believed in. That dream never changed.'

'And now you've managed it.'

'Yes, thanks to my father. It is his money backing Locanda Dante and he has an opinion on everything. Just like your friend Coco he believes I should serve the old favourites because they are what people want. Papa would prefer to see pork loin simmered in milk and *fritto misto* on the menu. He doesn't understand that my food is me; you can feel my heart in every single dish.'

To be sculling through the almost silent canals listening to Dante talk about food was the ultimate Venice moment, thought Kat. She had never felt happier to be here.

'You have to follow your passion, even when it's a struggle,' she told him.

'But if I fail then I will be back working in the *squero* until I've paid my father back. That was my promise to him. So I can't fail.'

Dante tethered the gondola to a mooring beside a small *bacaro*. He came and sat beside Kat on the battered red leather seats and called out to a waiter to bring cold beers and a plate of crostini.

'I haven't rowed for a while and I am out of practice,' he admitted. 'Let's rest here for a while before we head back.'

Dante laid his arm behind her and they drank their beers as the boat gently rocked on the lapping water. 'We should come out late at night some time,' he said. 'That is when it is really beautiful to be in a gondola.'

'It's pretty good right now,' Kat told him.

'No more feeling … what was the word?'

'Blah? No, you've cured me completely.'

'Of course,' said Dante, with his usual certainty.

He fed her crostini covered in fried sardines, creamy salt cod and smoked trout with its roe.

'They use the very best ingredients here,' he told her. 'Even when a place offers the most simple food it is an opportunity to be excellent.'

Listening to him talking so softly and seriously, Kat thought about all the brilliant chefs she had met over the years, so many of them, all around the world, some quietly intense, others stormy and impatient, but always highly creative, driven and exacting. As he took up his oar again and prepared to row her back, Kat decided that none of them had ever been quite like this man Dante.

Later, walking back through the doors of Hotel Gondola felt a bit like re-entering an old life. Everything was the same as always. Adriana on reception staring at the computer, guests checking in, a loaded luggage trolley waiting to go into the lift, a hum of conversation in another language.

Adriana glanced up. 'Massimo is looking for you. He's been trying to call you.'

Kat's phone had been on silent while she was with Dante and she hadn't noticed the missed calls. 'Where is he now?' she asked.

'In the bar, I think. Zita hasn't arrived yet.' Adriana gave her a look that was almost complicit.

She found Massimo unpacking the new delivery of Prosecco. He stopped when Kat appeared. 'I've been trying to get hold of you.'

'I know, sorry, I've been busy doing some research for

my book.' It wasn't a lie, but still Kat felt guilty. 'What's wrong?'

'Nothing.' He gave her an odd look. 'But I can't imagine what you said to Zita when you had lunch at her place yesterday.'

'Oh no, what has she done now?'

'She has been very busy organising our lives,' Massimo told her. 'Apparently, tomorrow will be a holiday for us. Adriana will manage perfectly well alone on reception and Nico has been persuaded to help Zita in the bar. Meanwhile, you and I will be taking the boat out into the lagoon to visit some of the islands. Apparently this is what you have asked for?'

'I might have mentioned that it would be nice ...' Kat said weakly, trailing off.

'You mentioned it to Zita but not to me?' Massimo sounded hurt.

'I didn't mean to, it just came out.'

'But, Kat, if I'd known this was what you wanted I would have made it happen. Why didn't you tell me?'

'You're always so busy, caught up in the hotel,' said Kat defensively. 'And whenever I ask you for anything it doesn't happen.'

'What hasn't happened?'

'It doesn't matter now,' said Kat.

'If you don't tell me things how can I—'

'I assumed if you wanted to spend time with me then you would. I didn't think I had to make a special request.' Kat knew she sounded defensive.

Massimo stared at her and she couldn't tell if he was angry or upset. 'So you asked Zita instead.'

'We were talking ... things came up. I didn't intend for her to interfere like this, though.'

'I see.' Massimo's brow furrowed. 'But now that she has, and it seems everything is planned, do you actually want to come out in the boat and spend some time together?'

'Yes,' said Kat, trying not to think of the afternoon she had just spent on the water with Dante. 'Yes, of course I do. I'd love it.'

A Year at Hotel Gondola by Kat Black

CHAPTER 11

Venice is a city of boats. It's not until you are out on the water that you realise how many different types there are. Yesterday I had my first gondola ride – one that lasted for most of the afternoon – but even then I don't think I fully understood how important the relationship is between Venetians and the boats they own.

Today Massimo took me out in his motorboat. It is sleekly beautiful with polished wood and soft leather seats and he introduced me to it like it was a member of the family. As we slowly chugged through the canals he pointed out some of the other boats. The *sandalo*, flat-bottomed like a gondola but better for fishing, the slim and elegant *pupparin* that's often used for racing, and the larger but still handsome *caorlina*. He spoke of them affectionately, describing the regattas and races of his youth. It seems he once had quite a talent for what the Venetians call *voga*, their traditional style of rowing, standing up and facing forward.

This was the beginning of a day when I saw a different side to both Massimo and Venice. He took me across the shallow waters of the northern lagoon out to Mazzorbo, a small island where many of the vegetables I've been eating are grown. We strolled along a pathway past walled vineyards and market gardens and then across a long bridge to Burano, famous for its lace-making and brightly coloured houses.

Next he took me to the island of San Francesco del Deserto where we headed up a cobblestone road to a monastery shielded by an army of tall cypress trees. He rang a bell and a monk appeared to show us around the cloisters and gardens. It felt like walking through history.

Afterwards he navigated the channels through the marshes and mudflats, past wading herons and screeching seabirds, until we moored beside an island that seemed wild and overgrown, which was where Massimo unpacked the picnic he'd brought.

He chose a spot with far-reaching views across to the spires of Venice and laid a rug in the shade of an old fig tree.

'Remember how once you asked which was my favourite view?' he said. 'Well this is it. I've been coming here at least once a summer since I was a boy.'

'It's so peaceful,' I told him, gazing back at the blue of the lagoon and Venice shimmering in the distance.

'There are never many people because you can only reach it by private boat,' he explained. 'It's not really a secret place, but it feels that way.'

Massimo unpacked the picnic from a cooler bag. He had been to my favourite *bacaro* and had them package up so many treats. Marinated anchovies, grilled squid, sardines fried in a coating of polenta, tender meatballs. There was a crusty loaf of bread, creamy stracchino cheese and parcels of waxy paper filled with cured meats. We ate slowly and lazily, picking at little bits of this and that, twining our bodies between mouthfuls. Yes, it was ridiculously romantic.

Massimo talked about his youth, rowing out to the islands with friends for picnics, going clamming in the shallows, finding any excuse he could to escape for a day.

'I need to make the effort to do this kind of thing more often,' he admitted.

When he's not caught up with the day-to-day demands of Hotel Gondola, Massimo seems younger. So much of his life is about processing reservations, paying bills and managing staff, answering questions and solving problems, so much of it seems to be the one thing I've spent my own life trying to avoid – routine.

'It's nice to have a day where there is nothing for me to do but talk to you,' he said.

Our lives haven't had much in common so far, but stretched out on a picnic rug, in the dappled sunshine of his secret island, it didn't seem to matter.

'Do you love running the hotel?' I asked him.

He shrugged. 'It is a job, there are good days and bad.'

'But was it what you truly wanted when you were younger, to go into the family business? Didn't you have other dreams at any stage?'

'That is all so long ago I can barely remember. I expect I thought I was lucky that my father owned a hotel and there was a good, reliable job waiting for me. What about you? Did you always want to be a writer and work in television?'

'I think it might have been my way of avoiding having a good, reliable job,' I admitted.

Massimo smiled. 'I don't suppose you ever planned to be a bartender in a small hotel.'

'Not at all, but it was an opportunity that came along and I took it. That's how I've always lived.'

'And what about the future?' Massimo wondered.

'I could ask you the same thing. How much longer will you run the Hotel Gondola? Right up until you retire?'

Frowning, Massimo propped himself up on his elbow. 'Actually, my sister would like to see it sold once my parents are gone so she can have her share of the money. But how could we sell a place like that? Once we lost it we would never find anything like it again.'

'You do love your hotel then?'

'I can't imagine life without it.' He sighed then reached down, tangling a hand in my hair. 'I'm beginning to not be able to imagine my life without you either, Kat.'

Massimo promised me passion and he is a man of his word.

There on the island, at risk of being spotted by a passing fisherman, listening to birdsong and the shallow waves of the lagoon meeting the shoreline, smelling sun-warmed grass, my eyes closed and my other senses worked overtime.

'We'll come back here soon,' Massimo promised later, as we were packing up the picnic things. 'There are other islands too, places I haven't visited in years, I'll take you to all of them.'

We travelled the long way home, across the lagoon and into the quiet backwater canals, exploring Venice until Massimo suggested mooring beside a small *bacaro* that I've only been to once before.

'The *cicchetti* are famously good here. They use only the very best ingredients,' he told me.

The waiter brought our drinks to the boat and we ended the day with glasses of Prosecco and a plate of crostini while listening to music from a jazz band playing outside a neighbouring café.

My skin felt salty after so much time on the water. I was peaceful, relaxed. As the evening light turned golden, Venice took on a dreamlike quality. Leaning my head on Massimo's shoulder, it seemed like this was exactly where I was meant to be.

By the time we moored outside Hotel Gondola, it was dark. While Massimo fussed with the boat, stowing gear and covering the seats in case it rained, I headed into the hotel. There was a woman standing at the reception desk. Neatly cropped hair, smartly dressed, luggage that matched. She turned and smiled at me a little hesitantly.

'Excuse me, but are you staying here?' she asked, her accent plummy English.

'Actually no, I'm on the staff,' I told her. 'Is everything OK?'

She looked anxious. 'I'd like to check in but there's no one around. I've been waiting at least fifteen minutes. I did email to say I'd be arriving quite late.'

'There ought to be a night clerk.' I ducked beneath the reception desk. 'I've no idea where he's got to but I can check you in now. I'm so sorry you've had to wait.'

Since I've helped out on reception a few times, I know how the system works. Logging on to the computer, I found the correct form to be filled in and checked her passport – Rosetta Rees, aged 65, and looking pretty good for it, I decided, glancing up at her face.

'Are you in Venice alone?' I asked.

'Yes, I'm here for two weeks. It's my first visit.'

'That's a good amount of time. You'll be able to see so much. And you'll be here for the Festa del Redentore, Venice's big celebration. Everyone tells me the firework display is amazing.'

'I'd like to experience some of the real Venice, the parts tourists don't always find,' she said.

I took another look at her. Her clothes were understated but stylish, her figure trim, her hair a carefully maintained light blonde and her wedding finger bare. She seemed exactly the type of woman Coco wanted for Vittorio.

'Why don't you come and find me in the bar tomorrow evening?' I suggested. 'I'll make you a welcome drink and share some local knowledge.'

'That would be wonderful,' she said warmly. 'I'll be sure to do that.'

Massimo appeared, his arms full of things I had left behind on the boat. He raised his eyebrows enquiringly when he saw me standing behind the reception desk.

'This is Massimo Morosini, the hotel's owner, who will take your luggage and show you to your room,' I told Rosetta. 'I'll see you tomorrow. Sleep well.'

Passing me the chiller bag, a tube of sunscreen and my cashmere sweater, Massimo bent to pick up her bags.

'Signora, welcome to the Hotel Gondola. This is a family-run hotel so you must make yourself completely at home. Coffee and pastries are served from seven a.m. to ten a.m. and there is also a cocktail bar that is open every evening from five thirty …'

It was his usual patter delivered with the charm Massimo offers to every guest. Rosetta Rees seemed completely entranced. She dimpled a smile then followed him to the lift.

'The reception desk should be staffed twenty-four hours and if you need help or advice our team are always happy to provide it,' continued Massimo, turning to me with a nod of thanks.

It felt good for us to be working together like that, to make sure this woman's holiday got off to a good start, to help her have the best time in Venice and take home beautiful memories. I think I'm starting to see why Hotel Gondola matters to Massimo so much.

CROSTINI

Cut a baguette or ciabatta-style loaf into slices about 1 cm thick and lightly toast. Top with any combination of cheeses, cured meats, grilled vegetables, pesto, etc. You can go fancy with blue cheese and thinly sliced figs. Or mash up some tinned cannellini beans with lots of garlic and a dash of red wine vinegar and top with diced parsley.

Seafood also works. One of my favourites is really good-quality sardines that have been packed in olive oil, drizzled with a piquant salsa verde. I also love tuna and creamed horseradish. Everyone tells me the important thing is to choose the very best ingredients.

Only when she had finished writing the chapter did it occur to Kat what a risk she had been taking. This was Venice, a city where people's lives criss-crossed all the time. It was one thing to visit the same *bacaro* with two different men on separate nights, but what if those two men were to meet some day? And what if Dante should mention to Massimo the things he didn't know? The apartment she had been renting for months now, the time she had spent at his *osteria*; all the parts of her life she had stayed quiet about and kept separate. It was the kind of thing that might easily happen.

'You are playing a dangerous game,' Coco agreed, over coffee. 'I always make it very clear to my lovers that I am not exclusive.'

'But I am exclusive,' Kat pointed out. 'It's not as though Dante's my lover.'

'You want him to be.'

'No I don't, not at all.'

Coco gave her a disbelieving look.

'He's much too young for me. Anyway, I'm perfectly happy with Massimo.'

'Really? Then why did you ask me not to mention the apartment? Why spend so much of your time there without telling him? You are lying to him, Kat.'

'Not really lying,' she protested. 'Aren't I allowed a part of my life that's private?'

'It is not how relationships work,' Coco told her. 'There is meant to be sharing ... honesty. But, Kat, I think you are not even being honest with yourself.'

Kat felt tears pricking at her eyes again. She wiped them away roughly with the back of her hand. 'Oh, for goodness' sake. I need more coffee, and cake ... very sweet, gooey cake, preferably with some chocolate involved.'

She went up to the counter to choose from the laden cabinets. There were pastries swollen with cream, plump doughnuts dotted with sweet custard, dainty tarts, biscuits crusted with nuts, slabs of tiramisu and *torrone*. Normally Kat wouldn't have been too tempted since sugar wasn't her usual addiction. But today was different; she didn't feel like herself. She picked a large confection of choux pastry, *zabaione* and chocolate.

'I absolutely don't want to sleep with Dante,' she repeated, when her cake arrived, on its gilt-edged plate, with a special fork, and a dusting of icing sugar and one of those paper doilies, because no food in Venice was ever served without ceremony. Kat dug into it and took her first rich mouthful. 'But I do admire him and I think he's intriguing.'

'And attractive?' Coco prompted.

'Well obviously he is but that's not what I'm interested in.'

'Men like that ...' Coco made a tutting sound. 'By your age I had learned to avoid them. Selfish, arrogant, the type that break women's hearts without noticing.'

'What about men like Massimo?' Kat asked. 'How would you sum him up?'

'Intense, sensitive, the type whose heart it is all too easy to break. I would probably avoid them too.'

'He's a really great guy,' Kat said, and she meant it. 'He's kind, he's thoughtful, he's funny and when I do get him away from that hotel we enjoy each other. I don't want to hurt him.'

Coco didn't respond, just watched her devouring the cake and dabbing at her lips with a paper napkin.

'So I guess you're right about the apartment,' admitted

Kat, between mouthfuls. 'I should have told him about it at the beginning but I didn't. I'll have to find a way.'

'What is so difficult? Just say you have only just rented it this week.'

'That would be another lie.'

Coco shrugged. 'Sometimes they are necessary.'

'Maybe it's what I'll do then.' Finishing her cake, Kat ran her finger over the plate and licked it clean.

'You enjoyed that,' Coco observed.

'I seem to be craving sugar at the moment. Also, I've cried three times in the last few days. I don't know what's wrong with me.'

'These things happen,' Coco murmured disinterestedly.

'Oh, and I meant to tell you. A woman checked into the hotel last night – mid-sixties, staying in Venice for longer than five minutes, would love to meet some locals.'

'Really?' Coco perked up. 'Is she pretty? Cultured? Did she seem kind?'

'I was only with her for a few moments. I told her to come to the bar this evening so I'll find out more then hopefully.'

'In that case I think Vittorio and I need to drink cocktails together tonight. What time should we be there?'

'Aren't you rushing things?'

Coco treated Kat to one of her looks. 'Yes, of course I am.'

Walking off all that rich cake seemed a good idea so Kat said goodbye to Coco and struck off with no destination in mind. She kept up a brisk pace, darting round clusters of slowly ambling tourists, and ended up on the Zattere, one of the neat edges of Venice where it meets the deep Giudecca Canal.

There was a cruise ship passing through, a monstrous thing that dwarfed the graceful spires of the surrounding buildings. Watching it, Kat began to worry that Venice was

176

being crushed beneath the weight of all the people who wanted to see it.

Reaching the Punta della Dogana, Kat saw another sight, this time one that made her smile. A group of women, all dressed in pink, wielding their oars in a dragon boat. She had heard about this rowing squad, all survivors of breast cancer who dubbed themselves the Pink Lionesses and competed in the regattas. Kat waved as they passed and several of the women smiled in return. Venice's heart was still beating, she decided. Its spirit had survived so far.

Kat walked past the church of Santa Maria Della Salute and turned back into a network of quieter canals. At first she didn't recognise Nico. He was sitting with two other men outside a *tabacchi*, a small local shop selling cigarettes, phone cards and lottery tickets. His hair was longer than before, he looked thinner and was wearing ripped jeans and a slouchy T-shirt. She might not have noticed him if he hadn't muttered something that made his companions laugh as she walked by.

'Nico,' said Kat, pausing in surprise.

He gave her a nod and then turned away.

'Hey, thanks for working my shift for me last night.'

'I did it for Zita,' he replied, his tone sullen.

'Might you consider doing it again some time?'

Ignoring her, Nico pulled out a packet of cigarettes. He offered them round his friends then lit one himself.

'Do you have a job yet?' she asked.

'Why do you care?'

'We still need a bartender at the Hotel Gondola. Zita was only ever a temporary replacement.'

'This is not what she told me. But in answer to your question I will come back to cover a shift if she asks me to ... not for you.'

Kat noticed that Nico's hair needed washing and his jeans were torn. He lit a second cigarette as soon as the first was finished, then shook the empty packet, before slipping it back in his pocket.

'Are you OK for money?' she asked, certain Massimo would want her to help if she could.

Nico stared and didn't reply.

Kat dug into her bag for her purse. Pulling out all the cash she had, she offered it to him. Nico didn't move so she put it in his lap.

'Take it. Buy yourself some food, get cleaned up and come and see Massimo. He misses you,' she said.

As she walked away, Kat heard the men laughing again. She hoped it wasn't at her this time.

It had needled Kat being accused of lying by Coco because she considered herself an honest person. Neglecting to mention one or two things to Massimo hardly seemed the greatest sin but it was a risk, and he would be hurt if he found out, so she decided not to waste any more time.

She found him in his office as usual, staring at a spreadsheet filled with figures that would have made Kat's eyes glaze over in a minute.

'Hey, baby,' he said, as she rested a hand on his shoulder. 'Yesterday was great, wasn't it?'

'Really great,' she told him.

'It wouldn't have happened without Zita. I guess we should thank her.'

She may have been helpful but Kat still wasn't sure how she felt about his ex-wife. She couldn't bring herself to trust Zita a hundred per cent.

'I'll thank her, of course,' she said quickly to Massimo, 'but I wanted to talk to you about something else. I rented an apartment this morning. A place with a decent kitchen where I can test recipes and make a mess without anyone minding.'

Massimo screwed up his face. 'Oh no, I promised to help

you with that and it slipped my mind completely. I'm so sorry, Kat.'

'That's OK. Coco put me onto this place. It's right above her own apartment so perfect really.'

'I expect you'll be spending lots of time there?' There was a hint of concern in his voice.

'I shouldn't think I'll be away any more than usual,' said Kat, battling a wave of guilt at how easily the lie had been told. 'I'll hang out there during the day, writing and cooking. You can come over and I'll make you lunch. I'm going to need someone to test my recipes on.'

'I'll be happy to help with that.' Massimo gave her a quick hug. 'Oh, and thanks for looking after that guest last night. Guido had a bad stomach upset. Apparently he had been stuck in the bathroom for some time.'

Guido was the night manager, and usually reliable. 'Will he be OK to work tonight?' wondered Kat.

'I hope so, otherwise it will be down to me. I'm planning to take a nap this afternoon just in case.'

'I could come and take a nap with you,' Kat offered.

'I do actually need to get some sleep,' said Massimo, then he gave her a slow, smile. 'OK, maybe I don't need quite so much.'

What was worrying Kat was the state Nico had been in and whether he had been quite so shabby the night before while he worked her shift behind the bar. The thought nagged at her as she lay in bed with Massimo that afternoon, listening to his soft snores, and the sounds of Venice drifting in through the open windows. Massimo liked his staff to look immaculate. He wouldn't be happy to think standards had slipped.

She talked to Zita about it when she saw her that evening in the bar.

'Nico seemed unsavoury. We can't have him working here like that.'

'I smartened him up,' Zita promised. 'He wasn't too bad once he was in clean clothes. But I am worried about him. Ever since he was arrested he's been different.'

'He's made it pretty plain that he hates me,' said Kat.

'He is full of hate for everything, it seems. I have known him since he was a little boy and it is sad to see him like this.'

'Perhaps if he came back to work here it would help,' Kat suggested. 'Could you talk to him?'

'I could try but he only helped last night as a special favour since I am his favourite aunt.'

'What about talking to his mother? Do you have much to do with Massimo's sister?'

'I talk to Anna all the time. She is concerned but he is a grown man so what can she do?'

Kat felt responsible. If she hadn't pushed for Nico to be fired in the first place then most likely he wouldn't be at such a low ebb.

'Never mind all that for now.' Zita interrupted her thoughts. 'Tell me about your day out with Massimo. Did you have a good time? Was it perfect?'

Kat was saved from responding by last night's new guest, Rosetta Rees, appearing in the bar on the dot of opening time, notebook in hand, ready to jot down some local wisdom. Dressed in silk, she looked elegant. Kat found herself hoping Coco and Vittorio weren't planning on making too late an entrance.

A Year at Hotel Gondola by Kat Black

CHAPTER 12

The arrival of Rosetta Rees has created more of a stir than is usual when a new guest checks into the Hotel Gondola. While she may be thinking she is here to visit the churches and galleries, Coco has other plans for her.

The matchmaking efforts began in earnest this evening. Rosetta appeared in the bar keen for me to share some of my Venice must-dos as promised. I gave her the cocktail of the week – the Hugo, a delicious blend of Prosecco, elderflower and mint – and managed to keep her in conversation while juggling other orders until Coco arrived with Vittorio; unaware he was to be the night's romantic interest.

I acted surprised to see them, just as instructed, and then casually made an introduction.

'Rosetta, these are some good friends of mine. They're Venetians born and bred so know the city's best secrets. You should talk to them.'

'I understand very little Italian,' said Rosetta, apologetically. 'Do you speak English?'

Vittorio, ever the gentleman, reassured her that both he and Coco were fluent and would be delighted to chat to her about their beautiful city.

'But first tell us something about yourself,' Coco interrupted. 'Where are you from? What are you interested in?'

I eavesdropped when I could, dipping in and out of their conversation as I mixed drinks. At one point I heard Rosetta telling them she was a yoga teacher.

'I mostly take classes for seniors now. It's so good for the balance and posture.'

A little later I picked up that she lived in north London, had always dreamed of visiting Venice and had decided to brave a trip alone.

'So you are unmarried, signora? Or divorced?' asked Coco. 'There is no man anywhere?'

Rosetta seemed not to mind such devastating directness. 'I'm single and very much hoping Venice is safe for a woman alone.'

Vittorio was all charm. 'Yes, yes, but you are not a woman alone in Venice now, signora, because you know us.'

'Exactly,' agreed Coco. 'And if you have no plans for the rest of the evening then you must join us for dinner. Don't you think so, Vittorio, *caro*?'

'A wonderful idea.'

'Thank you so much, I'd be delighted.' Rosetta sounded thrilled. 'Dining out on your own in the evenings is always so tricky, isn't it?'

'Vittorio and I will take you to a lovely little local place where the gondoliers like to eat,' Coco promised.

At that point I had to suppress a laugh and move away. I couldn't believe how easily Coco had manipulated the situation. As for that nonsense about the gondoliers, she herself has told me there are hundreds of them and they eat pretty much everywhere. The woman is shameless.

The bar got super-busy after that and I missed the rest of what was said but, glancing over from time to time, it seemed the three of them were getting on well. Coco was at her most vivacious and Vittorio looked delighted to be escorting two women for the evening.

At one point I went over and topped up their water glasses so I could check in on them properly.

Coco gave me a rather smug look, clearly thinking her plan was working.

'Have you ever done any yoga?' she asked me. 'Rosetta is going to teach us some. She says it is never too late.'

'I've never tried it.'

'Then you must join us,' Coco said. 'We are going to have an al fresco class in my garden early one morning and then while I am busy working in my shop Vittorio will show Rosetta some of the sights.'

I glanced at Rosetta, hoping she wasn't feeling too steamrollered, but she was smiling and appeared happy enough.

They left for dinner after their second cocktail. Massimo was on the front desk by then and called them a water taxi. When I caught up with him later and explained what was going on he was hugely amused.

'So let me get this straight,' he said. 'Your friend Coco doesn't want to marry this man so she is finding someone else to be his wife? *Madonna mia*, I love how women's minds work.'

'My mind doesn't work that way.'

'You don't plot and scheme to get what you want? I'm not sure I believe you.'

'I'm most definitely not like Coco,' I insisted.

'I wonder if her plan will work.'

'I suspect the only thing we need to wonder is what we'll wear to the wedding.'

That made Massimo laugh. I lingered in reception and spent more time chatting with him. Guests came in and out. They stopped and asked for new maps because their old ones had disintegrated, they thanked him for a restaurant recommendation or made some sort of complaint, usually the noisy plumbing or problems getting on to the Internet.

Massimo dealt with them all so smoothly. He apologised about the plumbing but explained it was an inevitable part of life in an old Venetian building, he handed out maps and cards printed with the hotel's name, and he offered to help people access the WiFi or made a suggestion for a wonderful place to eat tomorrow night. He is a man who seems to have endless reserves of patience, which I suppose he needs in a job like his.

Now he is still working, pulling a night shift, and I'm up in our room putting the finishing touches to this chapter. In a few moments I'll climb into bed. It will feel strange to sleep alone. I've grown used to having him beside me, to hearing the sounds he makes while he sleeps, to knowing I can roll into his arms at any stage and he'll wrap them around me.

I wonder if Rosetta will be lying in Vittorio's arms tonight. Not so soon, surely, as she seems fairly proper. But if anyone can make it happen it has to be Coco. Massimo agrees with me. He is all for them holding their wedding on the terrace of the Hotel Gondola.

COCKTAIL OF THE WEEK – THE HUGO

If you're looking for a refreshing summer cocktail it's hard to go past this. Elderflower syrups/cordials vary in potency so you may find you want to use more or less. What you're aiming for is a fresh burst of elderflower, not an overload of sugar. Since I don't tend to drink when I'm working behind the bar I often make a non-alcoholic version with soda water and lots of mint.

7 parts Prosecco   *lots of ice*
3 parts elderflower syrup   *bruised mint*
2 parts soda

Put ice and bruised mint in glasses. Mix Prosecco with elderflower syrup and soda. Balance to your own tastes and add a squeeze of lime if you prefer your drinks on the sour side.

Kat woke in the grip of another bout of apathy. She propped herself up on the pillows, sipped the coffee Massimo had brought, and wished she could spend the day lying there, reading and dozing. Everything else seemed much too hard.

She remembered the old Kat. The one with the boundless energy, who loved to plunge into each new day and see what it might bring. Had Venice altered her so much? Was writing a book and mixing cocktails day in day out crushing her? Kat wasn't certain; all she knew was that often she didn't feel at all like herself.

This morning Massimo seemed perkier than her, despite having had no sleep. He showered and dressed, chatting away as he put on his neatly pressed shirt and trousers.

'It is good to do a night shift every now and then,' he said. 'The hotel feels different when all the guests are in bed.'

'It must be deathly quiet,' said Kat, with a yawn.

'Not really,' Massimo told her. 'The building creaks and the plumbing clanks and that old clock on the wall seems to tick so loudly. I never hear those sounds during the day.'

'Weren't you bored?'

'No, I enjoyed my night. It felt as though it was just me and the ghosts.'

'Ghosts?' Kat sat up and showed some interest. 'Is the building really haunted?'

Massimo laughed. 'This is Venice. I'm sure everywhere is.'

A ghost would be a great addition to her book; perhaps she should invent one. Lately she'd had doubts about what she was writing. It seemed more Coco's story than her own and Kat worried about finding enough to interest her readers. People loved spookiness, didn't they? She considered introducing a haunted room, some unexplained bumps in the night or even reports of a sighting.

Eventually she managed to roll out of bed. As her feet touched the ground her spirits lifted a little. She decided to approach the day like Coco might, taking time to choose the clothes to face it in, bothering to tame her hair and put on make-up, trying to think of something she might enjoy doing. This apathy had to be smothered. She hated it.

It was mid-morning by the time she emerged from her room and the Hotel Gondola was bustling. Kat exchanged a nod and a *buongiorno* with several guests on the stairs, and found the foyer filled with a noisy tour group checking in.

Rosetta Rees was standing off to one side, beside a curtain-swagged window, flicking back and forth through the pages of her Fodor's guide.

'Good morning,' Kat called to her.

Rosetta looked up, her expression distracted, and then smiled. 'Oh, hello, I'm so glad I've bumped into you. Thank you for introducing me to your friends.'

'Did you have a nice dinner with them?'

'A lovely dinner in a place I could never find again if you paid me a million pounds. Afterwards we had a *digestivo* at a bar where they all seemed to know Coco and Vittorio, then I came back in a water taxi rather late which is why I'm not making an early start.'

'Where are you planning to go?' Kat asked her.

'That's what I can't decide. I had intended to visit the Accademia Gallery but I think it deserves an entire day so I'm wondering if I should check out the Peggy Guggenheim Museum instead.' Rosetta looked at Kat, as if hoping she might have the answer.

'Actually, I've never been to either place.'

'Truly?' Rosetta seemed astonished.

'I've heard the Peggy Guggenheim has a nice café,' Kat offered weakly. 'One of the guests told me it's pricey but they do a decent cup of tea.'

'Tea is always welcome after a viewing of twentieth-century paintings. Perhaps I'll go there. I don't suppose you'd care to join me? If you've never been and would like to ... But I expect you're terribly busy. Actually, last night I realised where I recognise you from. Are you here working on another TV show?'

'A book, actually.'

'How exciting.'

'Not really,' said Kat. 'It's mostly involves me sitting alone in a room with a laptop; so it's the opposite of exciting. Perhaps I should come to the Guggenheim, just for an hour or so. It might be something to write about.'

They took the no.1 *vaporetto* that zigzagged down the Grand Canal, pressed uncomfortably close together as more tourists piled onboard. Rosetta seemed not to mind the crush.

'I'm used to it,' she explained to Kat when they disembarked. 'For years I commuted to work by Tube at rush hour every day. At least on a boat there is a view to look at.'

'Didn't you say last night that you're a yoga teacher?'

'Yes, but back then I taught history in a secondary school. Yoga was just a hobby until I decided to retire early and retrain so I could teach it. Best thing I ever did.'

'It must be why you have such great posture.'

'It's good for the body and the mind,' Rosetta told her. 'Are you going to come along and try it? We've arranged to have a class in Coco's garden tomorrow morning. She was certain you wouldn't want to miss out.'

'I'm sure she was,' Kat said wryly.

Seeming to pick up on her tone, Rosetta smiled. 'She's a real character, that's for sure.'

*

Kat found, to her surprise, that she loved everything about the Peggy Guggenheim Collection. Many of the paintings reminded her of the art Ruth had made, abstract shapes, blazes of colour and filled with energy and movement. Kat especially liked how the palazzo was furnished, so it felt like looking at art in someone's home rather than a vast, soulless gallery. And the sculpture garden, while packed with visitors, was curiously peaceful. Once she'd had her fill of paintings, she sat for ages in an old stone pergola beneath the trees, thinking about her book mostly, but not in the half-panicked way she usually did.

Rosetta's voice startled her. 'You look deep in thought.'

'Oh, hi. Yes, I was actually.'

'Do you want to get that cup of tea now? I could do with a break before I start on the futurists.'

'Sure,' Kat agreed.

The café was starkly white and modern, with framed prints of the rich art collector Peggy Guggenheim hanging on the walls, and a glassed-in terrace overlooking the leafy courtyard. They ordered tea, along with some sweet treats at Kat's insistence.

'I'm really glad you asked me along,' she told Rosetta.

'It's rather special, isn't it?'

'Yes, and it was what I needed. I don't seem to be able to settle and write first thing any more. This morning I woke up in a particularly odd mood, everything seemed much too hard.'

'I know those moods.'

'Do you? It's not like me to be like that at all. But lately I've been all over the place: up, down, tearful, these crazy mood swings that come for no reason and without any warning,' Kat confided.

'I was exactly the same at about your age. The menopause is no fun.'

'The menopause?' Kat's head jerked back. 'I don't think so.'

'How old are you?'

'I'm fifty and everything else is still normal so that can't be it.'

'Yoga can really help,' Rosetta continued. 'Some of the restorative and supported poses are—'

'I'm not having the menopause. Not yet.'

'Perhaps just the beginning of it, the very early stages,' Rosetta said gently. 'I think they call it perimenopause.'

'No!' Kat put her hands over her ears. 'I'm not listening.'

'OK, but it's completely normal.'

She dropped her hands and looked at Rosetta in genuine horror. 'I don't want to be normal.'

Kat returned to the hotel on foot in a bid to clear her mind. She went for her usual Venice walk, darting through shadowed passageways and round corners that looked interesting even if they didn't lead in the right direction. Rosetta's words were on her mind. How could she be going through the menopause? There hadn't been a single hot flush or any of the other symptoms women talked about, the dry skin and sleeplessness, the lost interest in sex. No, this had to be something else surely.

Heading across a spacious *campo*, Kat realised she had walked this way several times before. She was beginning to recognise all the corners of this city. Getting lost in Venice had become more difficult and Kat missed it; she liked not knowing exactly where she was.

She was so deep in thought she didn't notice the sky darkening. She heard the rumble of thunder, though, low and long, and felt the wind pick up before the rain came storming down. People on the street around her were struggling with umbrellas or trying to shrug on plastic ponchos. Kat ran to a shop doorway for shelter and huddled beside an old

Venetian woman and her shopping trolley. These summer storms seemed to come from nowhere, she remarked to Kat in Italian, mistaking her for another local. And Kat, who could understand a little Italian now but still struggled to speak a word, nodded and smiled.

The rain eased but showed no signs of stopping. Realising she was close to Locanda Dante, Kat decided to make a run for it. A glass of wine and something good to eat would make up for getting wet.

By now she was a familiar visitor at the *osteria* and in the habit of waving at the wait-staff that had been hired at last, and then heading straight through the double doors into the kitchen. Dante always seemed pleased to see her. If the place was busy then Kat might put on an apron and help him by chopping onions. When it was quieter he often tested out new dishes on her, knowing he would get an honest opinion.

Today Kat arrived in a lull. Dante was drinking coffee and talking to the kitchen hand about cuts of pork, and how best to use them.

'Ah, this terrible weather today,' he said as she appeared, her hair all damp ringlets. 'I hope it is not going to be this way for the Festa del Redentore.'

Lately, people had been discussing their plans for Venice's big festival, how they were going to celebrate and their preferred viewing position for the Saturday night fireworks.

'Will you open the *osteria* that evening?' wondered Kat.

'Yes, but we will close early because no one will want to miss the display, me included. It is magical to see the spires and domes of the city lit up.'

'It will be my first *festa*,' Kat told him.

'Then you should also watch the regattas and walk across the pontoon bridge to the Giudecca to buy bags of sugared nuts from the stalls there. We loved all those traditions as children. But for me it has always been about the fireworks most of all. They are spectacular.'

'Where will you go to watch them?'

'The best view is from a boat. Maybe this year I will take out the gondola. You should come too.'

'I'd love to,' said Kat, then a beat later realised she shouldn't have accepted the invitation because surely Massimo would be expecting them to spend that evening together.

'Great, we'll have a good time I'm sure.' Dante smiled at her. 'Now, have you eaten? No? There is a dish I have been playing with that I want you to try.'

He fed her roasted summer vegetables freshened with a light sorbet of oregano and enriched with a dense cream of almonds and she ate the entire plateful standing beside an open window, the breeze hot and damp on her face, her hair drying into a frizz while Dante continued to talk about the festival.

'When we were younger my brothers and I used to go to the Lido to swim once the fireworks were over and we'd stay up all night on the beach. Now I prefer to take a picnic out in the boat and eat it beneath the stars.'

'That sounds amazing,' said Kat, wondering if there was any way she could manage to go along.

'It will be, I promise.'

A Year at Hotel Gondola by Kat Black

CHAPTER 13

Have you ever tried yoga? It's harder than it looks. Even lying on the mat with my arms at my sides, I could feel my left hip hurting and my back creaking. And as for bending forward with our fingertips touching the ground ... I stole a glance at Coco and was mortified to see she seemed more flexible than me.

The morning hadn't started so well. Rosetta and I arrived at Coco's place to find her with a face like thunder. It turned out that Vittorio had just phoned, complaining of a summer cold, and he wasn't coming.

'And after me going to the trouble of borrowing special mats, and buying these stretchy clothes,' complained Coco, who was dressed in Lycra.

It wasn't the real reason for her crossness, of course, but Rosetta still had no clue about the matchmaking scheme. She thought we had gathered purely to do yoga.

'Perhaps he'll be better in a day or so and we could have another class,' she said soothingly. 'Just the three of us today will be lovely, actually, very peaceful.'

And it was particularly peaceful in Coco's garden, with the birdsong and a slight breeze tousling the leaves of the trees. After a while my body started to stretch into the positions a little more easily and there was a calming quality to Rosetta's voice as she described how we should be breathing and moving.

At the end she asked us to lie quietly on the mats and let our minds empty. My mind is always buzzing with a hundred thoughts and I can't slow it down, never mind quieten it completely. Lying there, I was aware of every ache and knotty muscle in my body. Wriggling uncomfortably, I glanced at Coco and was irritated to see her stretched on her mat serenely, eyes closed, belly rising and falling with each breath.

We finished the session sitting with our hands pressed palm to palm.

'*Namaste*,' said Rosetta, and we echoed the word back at her.

I couldn't wait to get up off that mat, but Coco held her position for a few moments longer. 'A wonderful way to begin the day,' she said.

'You move very well,' Rosetta told her admiringly. 'It's hard to believe you've never done any yoga.'

'I have always been a dancer,' said Coco. 'Always loved to use my body for all the things it's meant for.'

'Are you not sore at all?' I asked, somewhat bitterly.

'If any part of me hurts then I ignore it,' Coco declared. 'I don't want to be that person who groans whenever she stands up from her chair.'

'You're so inspiring. How old are you?' asked Rosetta, much to my joy because I've been dying to know but haven't dared to pose the question.

Coco refused to give her a straight answer. Instead, with a laugh she said, 'There is no point in making such an effort to stay young if I am going to give away my age.'

While Coco went about her getting-ready rituals I made us a healthy post-yoga breakfast, Rosetta chatting to me as I chopped fruit. She was interested in how I had ended up in Venice so I gave her the edited highlights.

'It seems such a bold move,' she said, when I'd finished. 'I admire your courage but I'd never do it myself.'

'Really? You wouldn't move to Venice for a passionate love affair?'

'God no, absolutely not, I'm far too cautious.'

'But you chucked in your job to teach yoga,' I pointed out.

'That's different; it was my reward for all those years of hard work and it involved a lot of planning.'

'What if you happened to meet a really great guy while you were here?'

'I'd never take apart the life I've worked so hard to create since I got divorced, and risk all my happiness,' Rosetta said, with certainty. 'No matter how great he was.'

I was very glad that Coco was locked away in her bathroom, smearing on creams or plucking stray hairs, or whatever it is she spends all that time doing. She wouldn't be pleased to know how bad a candidate Rosetta seemed for her matchmaking plans.

We ate breakfast in the garden. The day was shaping up to be a scorcher and Rosetta had plans to seek the air-conditioned cool of some museum or gallery.

'First you must visit my shop,' Coco instructed. 'It is full of beautiful things and I want to give you something special as a thank you for this morning.'

'Oh, you don't have to, I was happy to do it. I never expected anything in return.'

'I know that. But there is a dress in there that is only for you. I am sure of it.'

As usual my friend was right. Rosetta looked stunning in the Moroccan-style dress, with billowing sleeves and intricate embroidery. Coco strung some of her own beads around her neck to complete the look.

'More necklaces?' Coco wondered, standing back. 'Maybe not.'

Rosetta stared at her reflection in the mirror. 'I look—'

'Beautiful,' I put in.

'I was going to say, not like myself at all. My daughter would love it, though. Would you mind taking a picture with my phone so I can send it to her?'

'I didn't realise you had a daughter,' I said.

'Yes, and a son too,' said Coco. 'But they are grown up now and have their own lives. Isn't that right, Rosetta?'

'It is. I'm hoping for grandchildren some day but neither of them seems keen to supply me with one right now.'

'Do they both live in London?' I asked.

Rosetta nodded. 'I'm very lucky that neither of them has strayed too far from home and I get to see them all the time.'

I'm not sure if Coco is starting to realise her plan is in ruins. I suspect she still thinks she can push them together, her lonely lover and this very elegant, sorted woman. But you can't force things that are meant to happen naturally, at least in my opinion. Not even if you're Coco.

'You should wear that new dress on a romantic night out,' she was saying to Rosetta as I left the shop. 'It is exactly what it was made for.'

Kat was longing for a change of scene and realised she'd have to travel further afield to find it. She asked Massimo to suggest a place not too far away that didn't feel so much like Venice.

'You want to get away from the crowds?' he guessed. 'I always feel the same this time of year when the city seems to be bursting at the seams. There is a place that is beautiful and still quite local. It's called Serra dei Giardini and is hidden away near the Biennale gardens. They have a café and a flower shop, and often there are exhibitions. I think you'd like it there.'

'Will you come with me?' asked Kat.

'I would love to but I can't take the day off.'

'Not the whole day, just a few hours?' she asked hopefully.

'The hotel is full and we've had staff calling in sick. I'm sorry, Kat. Once summer is over we'll have more time together, maybe even take a holiday.'

Kat shrugged off her disappointment. 'You know me. I'm always fine on my own.'

'You are the most independent woman in the world,' he said, smiling his thanks before kissing her goodbye. 'Come and tell me what you think of it when you get back.'

Serra dei Giardini turned out to be a greenhouse, an art nouveau building of glass filled with light and plants. Inside this oasis Kat found the café and ordered a herbal tea then sat for a while on a wrought-iron chair, her laptop open on the table in front of her. She people-watched more than she worked. There were children charging round the play-ground outside, customers buying flowers and potted plants, a couple at one table, a group of young mothers at another. No one else was here alone, noticed Kat.

It didn't feel like Venice, Massimo was right. If it hadn't been for the Italian voices echoing around her she could have been in almost any European city. Kat was beginning to miss the world and all its variety. How good would it be to stand on a street in some noisy Asian city eating slippery fried noodles? To be surrounded by skyscrapers rather than crumbling *palazzi*, to hear cars roaring down the streets rather than the rumbling of suitcases? Venice was magical, but it was also stifling, a city that barely changed.

Kat had committed to spending a year here and she was determined to manage that. She had arrived in early spring and now it was high summer – a fair stretch of time to spend in one place for someone who had spent years on the move. Lately she'd had the sense that her life was on train tracks, always heading to the same places, always doing the same things. As much as she loved Venice, there were times she felt trapped by it.

Often Kat found herself dreaming about going travelling again. She had been making a list of destinations she had never visited and planned to get to all of them some day. She would find a way to make it work. Maybe she could shoot a web-based show? Or host intrepid travel tours? Or hop around the world working in hotel cocktail bars; anything that involved different sights and new people, uncertainty and excitement.

She thought about Massimo and how much they would miss each other. For two people who shared such a small space, they managed to live quite separate lives much of the time. And yet when they were together, that day of the boat-trip, for instance, or at night in bed, they fitted like a jigsaw. There was something about him that calmed her; that slowed Kat down. She liked watching him as he slept beside her, liked the way he looked at her when they hadn't seen each other for a few hours, liked sitting with him outside a *bacaro* and watching people go by. He made her feel happy and peaceful.

And then there was a more unfamiliar feeling that rushed her at unexpected moments; an almost physical sensation, a needing and wanting that spooked her. Was that how love felt? Kat still wasn't certain. Neither was she sure what would happen when they reached the end of their year together. She had always imagined that by then it would all seem so much clearer. She continued to hope so.

Sighing, she closed her laptop. Then she heard a voice calling her name.

'Kat? Kat Black? Ah, it is you.'

He was tall, in a chequered shirt and dark-framed glasses, head shaved, face smooth. Definitely a television executive but she couldn't place him.

'Garry Clarke,' he reminded her, holding out his hand.

'Of course,' she said warmly. 'What are you doing in Venice?'

'Here with the family.' He nodded towards the playground where presumably some of the high-energy children were his. 'Just for a mini-break. And you?'

'Working on a book and spending a whole year immersing myself in the place.'

'God, that sounds great.'

'Yeah, it is. I was just thinking about putting together a web series actually. Something really nimble, without a proper film crew involved, secret Venice, the places only the locals know about, that kind of thing,' she improvised wildly.

'What and just put it up on YouTube?'

'Yeah, why not? The book is the real reason I'm here but this could be a really cool passion project.'

'And would you be the presenter?'

Kat sensed she had caught his interest. 'No, I'm thinking just a voiceover, Venice would be the star.'

Dipping into his pocket, he pulled out a small silver case. 'Let me give you my card. I'm always looking for fresh content. And your old show is finished now, isn't it? So you're free to move on to something new?'

'Absolutely, I am.' Kat glanced down at the words embossed on the square of heavyweight paper: Garry Clark, senior commissioner, factual programmes. At some point she must have sat across a boardroom table from this guy or beside him on a brightly coloured beanbag in his office's creative zone.

'Flick me an email and outline a few of your ideas,' Garry suggested. 'This may have potential to be more than a web series. Obviously we've got our official pitching process but let's keep things informal for now.'

'Thanks,' she said casually. 'I'll do that.'

'You could always shoot a few sample scenes, put a short clip together and give me an impression of the look and feel you'd be going for. I can't guarantee anything but Kat Black in Venice definitely has potential.'

'It has loads of potential,' agreed Kat. 'And I've got some great ideas that I know you're going to love. I'll put some of them together for you in the next few weeks.'

They chatted for a little while longer – Kat recommending a few places to eat and a tour she'd heard was fun with kids. 'Have a really great holiday,' she finished, as Garry turned to find his family.

'And you have a great year. I'm envious.'

It almost killed Kat keeping her expression neutral. She was fizzing with excitement, and the moment he had disappeared, she grabbed her phone and texted her agent.

Call me! I just accidentally pitched a series to a commissioning editor called Garry Clark and he seems interested.

She signed off with a thumbs up, a smiley face and a gondola. Hopefully her agent would take the bait.

Kat had never stopped hoping she might find a way back into her old life. When *Black of Beyond* had been canned the year before it hadn't come as the biggest surprise. Ratings were falling, the show was expensive to make and Kat was an old face when there were plenty of fresher, younger ones coming through. She had seen other people's careers stutter to a halt but that didn't make it any less devastating when her turn came along.

Her agent had been bullish at first but soon stopped returning emails quite so quickly. Kat wasn't one of her big stars any more and the knowledge had hurt. So she seized on this chance meeting as the start of things turning round. All she needed was a great pitch that grabbed Garry Clark's attention and Kat would be heading back where she belonged at last.

On her way home to the hotel she sifted through ideas. Should she shoot some initial footage on her phone or source some camera gear? And where would she start? By filming Coco in her shop, perhaps, or Dante in the kitchen of his *osteria*. No, the obvious beginning was the Festa del Redentore. It had history, colour and excitement, and if she took up Dante's invitation to go out on his family's gondola she would be right in the middle of it all.

Back at Hotel Gondola she hurried straight to Massimo's office. He was there, as expected, mesmerised by the columns of figures he had up on his computer screen.

'How was Serra dei Giardini?' he asked, without looking up.

'Great, really great and I had this amazing idea while I was there. Could we go for a glass of wine and I'll tell you about it?'

'Kat, I really need to—'

'Please?'

'OK,' he agreed, 'a quick *ombra*.'

They went to their usual *bacaro* and Kat insisted on ordering paper cones full of fried squid and stuffed piquillo peppers. As they ate and sipped glasses of yeasty, dry white wine she described her plan.

Massimo seemed bemused. 'How will you make a TV show all by yourself? For your old series didn't you have a crew to travel with you?'

'Yes, but *Black in Venice* will be different, raw and immediate, with shorter episodes. And at this stage I'm just putting together a pilot, remember?'

'Have you ever done any shooting or editing?' Massimo still sounded dubious.

'No, but I've watched enough other people. And these days there's a YouTube tutorial to show you how to do just about anything so I'll pick up skills as I go along. I'm sure I can make it work. I'll do a few trials in the next few days then start shooting properly at the Festa del Redentore. A neighbour of Coco's has got a gondola he can take me out in.'

'Why not film it from my boat? I could help you.'

Kat felt torn, but the work took precedence. 'Thanks, but a gondola would be better, no noisy motor. Plus it's more Venetian.'

'That's true.' He sounded disappointed.

'I'd definitely love to go out in your boat and shoot some of the islands, though. And don't worry, if we film any of your special places I won't give away their exact locations.'

He smiled at her. 'Secret Venice again?'

'I'm afraid so. But also the hotel – I could shoot it at night when only the ghosts are around. Or very early in the morning out on the terrace when the light is so soft and pink.'

Massimo grasped onto that idea, just as Kat had known he would.

'Not the guests, though,' she added, 'or at least not

without their permission, but all of the staff would be fine. Maybe even do a day in the life of the Hotel Gondola, with time-lapse photography.'

'This filming, it won't distract you from your book too much?'

'No, I can do both,' Kat said, with certainty. 'It might even help with the book, who knows.'

The truth was that the book, with its recipes that needed testing and the concentration required for writing, was nowhere near as interesting as filming. Kat was happy to be distracted. She bought a tripod for her phone and then discovered her camera shot decent video too.

Dante was enthusiastic about helping her film the Festa and Kat was determined to capture plenty of footage of him helming the gondola. With his even features and that flash of green in his eyes he was bound to look amazing on film.

She had bumped into him at the Rialto market very early in the morning as she was filming practice shots of the vendors setting up for the day. When she explained her plan, he had been full of ideas.

'You will want to get footage in the *squero*, of course,' he said.

'Yes, what a shame I missed the opportunity to film them firing the new gondola.'

'They won't be building another one for some time but maybe we can arrange something. Let me talk to my father. And Locanda Dante? Were you thinking of doing something there?'

'Shots of you buying seafood then preparing it back at the *osteria*, plates going out full and coming back empty, lots of movement.'

'Maybe there is a way to incorporate a recipe in with that,' Dante suggested.

'That's a good plan.' Kat had missed brainstorming like this.

'Is food very tricky to shoot?'

Kat nodded. 'It's hard to do it well. Ideally we'd have a decent cameraman. If I can get my TV executive onboard then I'll have the budget but for now I'm assuming it's just me.'

Even Kat's agent had been encouraging. She was replying to messages more speedily now, like she had in the old days, and was keen on the idea of a short pilot to whet Garry Clark's interest.

Everything was starting to come together really nicely and Kat felt as if Venice might be exactly where she needed to be after all. The city was working its magic for her, throwing her in the path of a TV executive just when she needed a new project to energise her.

She felt exactly like she had in the early days of *Black of Beyond* – the same sense of doing something new, of risk and adventure. That night, working behind the bar of Hotel Gondola, nothing ruffled her. Guests with obscure cocktail demands, a sudden rush of orders, Zita fussing over stuff that really didn't matter, running out of elderflower syrup and having to change the cocktail of the week mid-evening, none of it seemed as much hassle as it normally would.

Kat felt properly alive again and it was such a relief.

A Year at Hotel Gondola by Kat Black

CHAPTER 14

The Festa del Redentore is the way Venetians have celebrated the end of a terrible outbreak of plague in their city ever since the sixteenth century. Each year in July, a pontoon bridge is built from the Zattere to the church of the Redentore and a day is devoted to religious festivities. The Saturday is party time, with boat races and a spectacular firework display that everyone gathers to see.

If you're a local and own a boat then the water is the place to be. Luckily I know someone who has access to a gondola. A little while ago I visited a *squero*, one of the few remaining boatyards where these uniquely Venetian craft are still made in the traditional way. I arrived in time to see the master craftsmen bend the wood using the heat from flaming torches.

A gondola ride has always seemed far too touristy a thing, but when the chef Dante Berardi, who happens to be the son of the gondola maker, offered to take me out, I jumped at the chance. And I certainly wasn't going to turn down an invitation to go with him a second time and watch the Redentore fireworks.

We packed a delicious picnic. I brought a focaccia covered in onions that I had caramelised in balsamic vinegar and thyme along with a bottle of very good Prosecco. Dante outdid me with a salad of luscious summer tomatoes and chargrilled squid as well as a pasta al forno stringy with melted cheese and dotted with balls of fennel-spiked meat.

As we set off from the *squero* the back canals seemed quiet. There can't be a more peaceful way to travel than gondola.

With no chugging motor you can listen to the sounds around you, the echoes beneath the bridges, the buzz of conversation and music from the bars you pass.

Reaching the San Marco basin, we saw the crowds lined up along the banks and a flotilla of moored boats decorated with lights and streamers, noisy with music and people.

Everyone was waiting for eleven thirty when the fireworks would begin. Right on the dot the ancient spires and domes were illuminated with showers of bright colour and shining white. There was so much beauty everywhere it was difficult to know where to look. I felt lucky to be here, living this quintessentially Venetian moment, with my very own gondolier to guide me.

Of course, Dante sees a display like this every year. He's been coming to the Festa since he was a little boy and can't remember missing one in the years he has lived in the city. But I don't recall seeing anything quite like it. To me it felt as if Venice was exploding with joy.

Afterwards the parties started up again; we could hear them echoing across the basin. So we moved further on, until the music was a murmur. Dante found a place to moor and we ate our midnight picnic – although it well past midnight by then. Flavours always seem more intense when I'm on the water and I ate while staring up at the sky, all inky blackness and bright diamonds. The night air was cool and Venice shone.

For our dessert Dante produced some crumbly almond biscuits he called *fregolotta* as well as raisins soaked in grappa. We ate a little more, talked about this and that, and let time get away on us. Daylight was brightening the sky by the time we made our slow return to the city. We had stayed out far later than intended, and the day ahead was undoubtedly set to be a quiet one.

Venice showed her approval by giving us a glorious morning. It was very still and in the dawn light the palaces that line the Grand Canal glowed with soft pinks and old gold, and the water reflected them like glass.

It had been such a memorable night and I'll always be grateful for it.

FREGOLOTTA RECIPE TO COME
(*maybe see if Dante will share his?*)

14

There were too many gaps, far too many details she couldn't share with her readers, and Kat could see she was going to be glad of the recipes now for at least they stretched the chapters out a little longer.

Even writing about the Festa had been tricky. It seemed better not to mention filming it because there was every chance her TV series wouldn't happen. Besides, when Kat downloaded the footage, most of it was disappointing. What she saw on the screen didn't match the images in her mind.

And there was something else she was reluctant to touch on. Out there in the almost dark, the waves gently rocking their gondola, Kat had felt freer. As they grazed on the food they had brought, she and Dante talked and talked, greedy for conversation, eager to share their thoughts, their stories and opinions. Kat couldn't recall ever having that much to say to a man in a single night. For a while she had let herself forget the gap of years between them. How old was Dante anyway? Perhaps in his early thirties, a generation apart.

Nothing had happened that Kat needed to feel guilty about, and yet still she did. When Dante dropped her off at the small landing outside Hotel Gondola she hurried inside like a wayward teenager, trying not to meet the night clerk's eyes as she passed through reception.

She had managed to slip between the sheets without waking Massimo. Sleep didn't come, although she closed her eyes and pressed her face into the pillow. Before long the alarm clock was ringing and Massimo was swinging his legs out of bed.

'Good morning,' Kat said softly.

'Ah, you're awake. How was last night? Did you get back late?'

'It was pretty fantastic. Did you see any of it?'

'No, but all of the guests went. Zita came up with the idea of offering them hot chocolate when they got back so I stayed here and helped her.'

Kat felt even guiltier. 'She didn't mention that to me. I should have helped too.'

'And miss your first Festa? It was only a few cups of hot chocolate. We managed fine without you.'

In the days that followed, Kat kept filming. She recorded endless scenes of gondoliers in their striped tops and straw boaters, spent a morning following one of the rowing clubs practising for a regatta, stalked Coco in her shop, shot sunsets and sunrises. She was getting better at it but still not good enough.

If there was one thing she had plenty of, it was contacts. She sent emails to the cameramen she had worked with over the years, asking for advice. Several came back saying she would never manage to achieve what she wanted, that she needed a professional, then quoted their rates and gave the dates they were available. That only made Kat more determined.

Late one afternoon Zita found her in the bar, with her camera on a tripod, filming close-ups of herself making a cocktail.

'What are you up to?' she asked.

'Did Massimo not tell you? I'm working on shooting a TV pilot.'

'About cocktails?'

'No, about Venice, sort of a video blog of my time here.'

'Why?' asked Zita, sounding surprised.

'It's what I do – film-making.'

'But I thought you'd given up on that now?'

'I'm trying a different approach. It's all still in the experimental stages at the moment.'

'Can I help you at all?'

Kat wasn't keen on the idea. 'Well, I—'

'Probably I'd be no use,' Zita added quickly. 'I haven't had any experience at all with filming. But I'd love it if there was something I could do.'

She sounded so desperately keen and Kat remembered that day boating round the lagoon with Massimo that had only happened thanks to Zita. She found herself relenting. Surely it wouldn't do any harm?

'Actually, you could help me right now. I'm trying to shoot some close-ups of my hands mixing cocktails but they're not my best feature.' She held up her bitten fingernails for inspection. 'Yours are more elegant, so would you be my hand model?'

'Absolutely. Just tell me what to do.'

Zita's fingernails were lacquered and her hands smoothed from years of being lavished with rich creams. Instantly the shots looked much better. And Kat found that standing behind the camera made it easier to see how best to compose the scene. Simply moving a cocktail glass or a bottle by a few millimetres seemed to make a difference.

'This is such a learning curve,' she told Zita when they finished. 'Thanks for helping me; you were great.'

'Really?'

'Yes, I'd have been messing around for ages by myself and the results wouldn't have been half as good.'

'Is there anything else I can help with?'

'I'll think about it,' Kat said, although she wasn't keen. 'At the moment everything is a bit trial and error and I'm not sure whether I'll be able to use a lot of what I've shot. Also, I need to teach myself to edit. I haven't even started on that yet.'

'Is it difficult?'

'I expect so but I'm confident I can learn.'

There was still some time before they needed to set up for the evening so Kat took a few shots of Zita out on the terrace, sipping one of the cocktails she had mixed. Then she put herself into the scene, sitting side-on to the camera, so she was a part of things but not the main focus. She had a feeling that was what Garry Clark would prefer.

'What else have you been filming?' Zita wanted to know.

Kat listed a few of the places she had been. 'Once I'm a bit more proficient I want Massimo to take me out in the boat to film on the lagoon islands. Do you think Nico might cover my shift again?'

Zita frowned. 'Maybe. He does have a job now; although I'd be surprised if he is being paid for it.'

'What kind of job?'

'It is with the group he is involved with, the one that stages the protests. They have set up a website called Respect Venice that's full of advice to visitors on how they can experience the city without harming it. Nico is helping with that and doing other things for them; Facebook and so on.'

'Sounds better than shouting on the streets and getting arrested,' said Kat. 'Have they stopped all that?'

'I doubt it. They are determined to be heard one way or another.'

'And what if he gets arrested again?'

'It's a risk he's prepared to take,' Zita told her. 'Nico believes this is what he is meant to be doing. It is his real passion. In fact, in some ways I think he is very like you – committed, driven, not prepared to let anything stand in his way.'

'Is that how you see me?' Kat was surprised. She thought of herself more as the spontaneous, creative type, a person who took opportunities as they chanced along.

'I think it's how we all see you, *cara*.'

*

Kat was reluctant to involve Zita in any more of her filming. She didn't want to spend more time than necessary with her. But when it became obvious exactly how much she could help, it seemed worth overcoming her misgivings. Zita was Italian, after all, and while Kat didn't need a translator exactly, there was no doubt having one smoothed the way immensely. With Zita at her side Kat got a warmer welcome from those vendors at the Rialto market who still treated her like an outsider, the men who farmed the vegetable gardens of Sant'Erasmo, the father and son who ran a tiny locals-only *bacaro* on the edges of Cannaregio.

Best of all, no situation fazed her. She was willing to approach newly-weds posing for photographs in Piazza San Marco. She charmed a snooty waiter at Caffè Florian and even talked some gondoliers into giving them a lively rendition of 'O Sole Mio'. At times it was actually quite good fun being with her on the streets of Venice. Kat loved never quite knowing how a day was going to pan out.

There was a downside, though; Kat was collecting far too much footage. She tried not to think about the moment she would have to sit down and plough through it all.

'I'll help you with that too if you like,' Zita offered.

She was smart and enthusiastic, and Kat, who had been missing working with other people, found there were moments when she almost stopped thinking of her as Massimo's wife. They were becoming a crew now, albeit a very small one, and Kat always formed a fast, firm bond with the people she went out filming with, even if they had nothing much in common in their real lives and she never saw them again after the shoot had wrapped.

As for Massimo, he seemed bemused but didn't complain. Each morning he asked where they were planning to head that day and often made suggestions, sending her to the best *gelato* shop in town, an amazing glass artist in Dorsoduro and to the cemetery on San Michele at dawn when the mist was rolling off the lagoon and over the graves. Late every night Kat and Massimo sat in bed together, her laptop on his knee, and looked through what she had shot.

Those days were among her happiest so far in Venice. Kat was full of purpose, with no time to waste mooching around Coco's shop or distracting Dante from his work. She couldn't believe she hadn't hit on doing something like this much sooner. Life seemed altogether shinier.

The part she had been dreading most was sitting down and writing a script for the pilot episode Garry Clark was waiting to see. Aware it was time to stop procrastinating, Kat took her laptop to a quiet *pasticceria* and fuelled up on coffee and cake. The trick was going to be identifying the best scenes and finding a way to link them together. Her head hurt just thinking about it.

She had been sitting, staring of out the window rather than at her screen, for quite some time when she saw them. Massimo and Zita walking together down the *calle*, talking and smiling. Kat wondered where were they going. No one had mentioned any joint appointment and it wasn't like Massimo to abandon the hotel in the middle of the day for anyone. A sense of unease needled her. Impulsively she snapped her laptop shut and set off to follow them.

It helped that Massimo was tall, so even hanging back and hidden amidst a crowd, Kat could see him head and shoulders above almost everyone. She kept pace with them, crossing a bridge and walking beside a canal, then down a quieter *calle* where she stayed in the shadows close to the buildings and hoped neither would turn and spot her. They were walking faster now, side by side, not quite touching.

Kat asked herself what on earth she thought she was doing and then she heard the sound of Zita's laughter echoing back at her. She kept following and, a short time later, watched the two of them duck through a doorway and disappear. Hugging her laptop to her chest, Kat halted, unsure what to do next, then decided she had come this far so might as well go on.

It was a restaurant, she realised, as she neared the doorway. She walked slowly now and, as she passed the window, glanced inside hoping to get a glimpse of them. Sure enough they were sitting together, Massimo with his back to her, Zita beside him, their attention focused on two much younger women also at the table.

Kat's feet slowed then stopped. She took in everything she could of the scene in a few short moments. These pretty girls must be their daughters, she guessed. Both were very like Zita, with slender figures, olive skin and long, sleek hair. Together they looked a happy family, a middle-aged couple out for lunch with their grown-up children.

One of the girls glanced up and stared blankly towards her then looked back at the menu. To her Kat was just another tourist, not anyone significant.

She felt a fool for spying on them. Forcing herself to move on, Kat wondered why Massimo hadn't told her that his daughters were in Venice. Had he been worried she would ask to meet them and it might be awkward? At the very beginning of all this they had agreed Kat wouldn't get involved with his family until they were surer of their future. It had seemed so sensible back then but now, walking slowly away from the restaurant, the image of them gathered round the table seared in her mind, Kat felt left out.

University holidays must have begun and they would stretch on at least until September. As she walked, Kat imagined more lunches and parties she wouldn't be invited to even though the girls surely must know about her by now. The family might even go to the beach together for a short holiday – didn't Zita have a place in Calabria? And Massimo, always too busy to leave his hotel, would find enough time for his daughters. Of course he would and it was ridiculous for Kat to be jealous; she had no right at all to this hollowed-out feeling.

Locanda Dante hadn't been the destination she had in mind, she wasn't heading anywhere in particular, but her feet took her to the little *osteria* and once inside the familiar pale-walled room, she felt less unsettled.

A few of the tables were occupied and automatically Kat checked the food on everyone's plates, noticing the octopus dish Dante had been trialling on her last visit seemed to be popular. Flash fried and served on a purée of salty, citrusy *bottarga*, she had tasted only a forkful and been left wanting more.

'I'm here for lunch,' she told the waiter, who was hovering nearby. 'Tell Dante I'll have the octopus, a green salad, a glass of a really nice white wine and anything else he thinks I should try.'

'Only you today, signora?'

'Yes, I'm alone.'

She took a table, pulled out her laptop in an attempt to look busy and tried not to think about Massimo and his family lunching together. Before too long, her food arrived. The octopus was perfectly tender, the wine just chilled enough and the simple salad of crisp peppery leaves dressed with a grassy olive oil. Whatever those others were eating at their furtive lunch, this was bound to be better.

By then the people around her had been served dessert. Dante brought out a new dish for Kat to taste – a lake of puréed potato swimming with lobster, clams, mussels and cuttlefish. He grabbed a spare fork from an empty table and, still wearing his chef's whites, sat down beside her. Kat was aware of a few curious glances but he seemed not to notice.

'Eat,' he said, digging his fork into the food. 'Taste it and tell me what you think.'

The purée was silky and smooth, rich with butter and

smoky with beef broth. The mussel flesh was sweet, the clams tender and the lobster tail juicy.

'Things are pretty quiet here today,' Kat remarked.

Dante gave an unconcerned shrug. 'August will be worse. That's when everyone who lives here disappears to the beach and surrenders Venice to the cruise ships and the day-trippers. I'm thinking of closing, at least for a couple of weeks.'

'Will you go away?'

'I haven't decided. Maybe I'll stay here, sleep a lot and cook what I want when I feel like it. I have plenty of friends with boats I can take out if I need to escape the city.'

'A holiday at home then.'

'Exactly.' Dante smiled and his eyes found hers. 'Are you staying in Venice too?'

'I'll be here,' said Kat. 'I may be available for some hanging out if I've managed to edit my film by then.'

'Ah, your new project. You've been working hard. It's why you've been such a stranger lately, yes? I've missed you.'

Dante dipped his fork into the dish and speared a bite of sweet-fleshed scampi, then offered it to her. Opening her mouth, she accepted the food and closed her eyes as she chewed, to make the most of every flavour. When she opened them again, Dante was staring at her.

'I like seeing you eat,' he said. 'I like the way you focus on the flavours I've created. I can tell how delicious you are finding the food just by watching your face. It's very sexy, actually.'

Kat felt herself flush. 'No one has ever said that to me before,' she murmured, patting her mouth with a napkin.

Dante offered her another morsel of the scampi and this time Kat chewed with her eyes open, and he held her gaze.

Flustered by the attention, she dabbed at her lips again. 'I've never thought of eating as being particularly sexy.'

'Neither had I, not till now.'

Kat knew it didn't mean anything – Dante's obsession

was with food, not with her. Still, she couldn't help feeling flattered.

'It's your great cooking,' she told him. 'The texture, the taste, everything ... You just keep getting better.'

His lips curved into a smile. 'I hope so. That's what it's about, after all. Bringing people pleasure; helping them to feel good.'

'You've definitely made me feel better.'

Dante stayed with her while she finished eating then took the empty plate away and had the waiter bring her coffee and a dish filled with salty, nutty chocolates that she kept coming back to until she'd devoured every one and there were no more reasons to linger.

She paid her bill and kissed Dante goodbye, pressing her cheek to his and feeling the warmth of his breath as their faces crossed to touch on the other side. As they parted there was a brief instant when she found herself wondering what sort of lover he might be? A selfish one, as Coco had imagined? For some reason she didn't think so.

And then Kat checked herself because she recognised this moment. As a traveller there were often forks in the road and so much about your journey depended on the one you chose. Walking away from the little *osteria*, her appetite sated by Dante's cooking, Kat reminded herself why she had come to Venice in the first place. This adventure wasn't about experiencing yet another casual fling, she was here for a love affair, real passion – and wasn't that supposed to mean Massimo?

Even so, as she walked back towards Hotel Gondola, it wasn't only him that occupied her thoughts.

A Year at Hotel Gondola by Kat Black

CHAPTER 15

Sometimes summer seems too bright for Venice. It lights up corners that might be better softly shadowed and steals away some of its mystery. I think I preferred spring with its high tides and low mists. And I'm looking forward to the golden days of autumn. But for now life in Venice is bright and it's very busy.

Every time I've seen Coco lately all the talk has been of sun salutations and warrior poses so clearly there have been more morning yoga sessions in her garden. But I fear time is running out for her. Rosetta Rees must be due to check out of Hotel Gondola any day now and there has been no hint of success with the matchmaking plan.

Rosetta is one of those conscientious tourists; you notice them in every city. She has a list of things she is determined to see and is efficiently ticking them off: the Accademia Galleries, the Tiepolos at Ca' Rezzonico, the Titians at the Frari. Her Venice is stitched together with frescoes and canvases, imposing Gothic churches and hushed museums; it's very different to mine.

I did manage to make it to her final yoga class but chose to watch instead of taking part. Recovered from his summer cold, Vittorio was tackling the poses with great gusto. Now and then Rosetta intervened, correcting his position with gentle, guiding hands and then Coco would catch my eye, in the hope this was a good sign.

Apparently there have been more evening cocktails, more dinners together and a night out dancing. Vittorio has even accompanied Rosetta on a sightseeing tour. But there seems no chemistry at all between them, and Coco must have noticed that.

'There will be someone else if this doesn't work,' she told me later. We were drinking coffee together before she opened up her shop. Meanwhile, Vittorio and Rosetta had headed off on a walking tour of Venice's religious art (surely the ultimate passion killer).

'So you're back to square one,' I said.

'No, no, I see this as progress. Vittorio has enjoyed having her company. He is more open to meeting the right woman now.'

'But you have the same problem as before: where will you find this woman?'

Coco's eyes narrowed. 'Your friend Ruth, she is the one, I am sure of it. When will she return to Venice?'

'I have no idea; all she said was some time in the autumn. I haven't heard from her but I can check to see if she's made a reservation yet.'

'If she hasn't then you ought to get in touch, offer her that good rate you promised.'

'I will, but I think you're wrong about Ruth. She said she wasn't interested in men, remember.'

'She may change her mind,' said Coco, and I didn't bother trying to argue.

I'm more concerned with my own relationship at the moment. When Massimo and I embarked on this year together I knew there might be times when it wouldn't be easy. And right now, peak tourist season with the Hotel Gondola bursting at the seams and Venice exhaustingly hot, this is looking like one of them.

Summer is when most residents escape the city and head to the beach. The few shops still serving the locals close up their shutters, and all that remain are the souvenir stores. You see fewer familiar faces on the streets and more strangers posing for selfies. That almost secret greeting, the discreet nod Venetians give each other amidst a crowd of visitors, rarely ever happens.

For those left behind, like Massimo, there are no lazy, blue-sky days. It's all work, work, work for him from now until the holiday period ends and inevitably this means we're not seeing enough of each other.

Even he has to eat at regular intervals and so I began to plan a lunch to tempt him away from his busyness for an hour or so. I wanted to prepare dishes he couldn't resist, his favourite foods, but realised I didn't know exactly what they were. Was he a pasta lover or a fan of risotto, more passionate about seafood, crazy about meat? When we've dined out together I've never noticed a pattern to his ordering or heard him express a particular preference. Massimo eats just about anything with an equal amount of enjoyment and I don't know what he prefers.

To me this seems a sign we haven't got to know one another in the almost five months we've been together, not properly anyway. So I asked a few searching questions: what would he choose for his last supper, what was the meal he remembered best from his childhood, that sort of thing. And then I checked with Coco that I could borrow her garden for an afternoon.

I wanted to this to be a proper occasion, one to remember. So I sent Massimo a written invitation. *Please join me for the best meal of your life* ... it began and attached was a copy of the menu I had planned as well as the dress code – very smart.

'What is all this about?' he asked, waving it at me. 'It's not my birthday. Or are you celebrating something?'

'Do we need a reason to have a special lunch together?' I asked.

'No, I guess we don't.'

'Well then, are you going to rsvp?'

'In writing?'

'Yes, of course.'

The next day I received a letter. *My darling Kat, I would be delighted to accept your invitation ...*

The day of the lunch dawned hot and cloudy. I woke early to get to the market and was dismayed to find some of the best vendors were missing. It took me longer to shop than usual but at last I had my ingredients.

Next I decorated Coco's garden, hanging colourful bunting from the leafy fig tree, putting a vase overflowing with rosemary on the table, and laying out freshly pressed linen. Then I took my time to prepare the food, finding a sort of calm in all the frenzy of chopping and stirring.

Massimo arrived looking handsome in an ivory-coloured linen suit and a pale blue tie. I laid out all the dishes I had cooked and settled down to enjoy his company. There was just enough of a breeze, the cicadas were playing their creaky music and the air was scented with food. A lasagne made with thin crêpes and wild mushrooms, a stew of seafood with plump tomatoes and sweet spices, a salad of ripe peaches, shavings of fennel and shredded red basil leaves.

'These are some of my favourite flavours,' Massimo said, amazed.

It was good to be away from Hotel Gondola for a while. As much as I do love the place, it's hard to see how it consumes Massimo. While it's easy for me to finish a shift behind the bar and not give it another thought until the next evening, his job is more difficult to escape. Even relaxing over a meal in Coco's garden he seemed distracted now and then by his phone or some thread of thought running through the back of his mind.

There was no dessert as it turns out that Massimo doesn't have an especially sweet tooth. Instead I brought out a creamy mountain cheese and some seedy crackers I had baked myself.

'I can't imagine a better meal,' Massimo declared.

Coco had promised us privacy and said we should treat

her garden as our own and so after lunch that's exactly what we did. We took the cloth from the table and laid it on the ground, stripped off some of our very smart clothes, dozed in the heat of the afternoon and then when we woke … Well, I think it's fair to say Massimo managed to forget about work for a while.

SEAFOOD WITH VENETIAN SPICES

Venice was built on the spice trade and near the Rialto market I chanced on a shop that sells mounds of every sweetly scented spice you could ask for. But I've actually made different versions of this dish all over the world. You can leave out the spice mix altogether and instead use a spicy chorizo sausage boosted with a teaspoon of smoky paprika. And it goes without saying that you can chuck any fresh seafood you fancy into the delicious broth. Adding that hint of acidity at the very end lifts the dish, but don't overdo it.

8 big juicy prawns
400 g white fish fillets, cut into bite-sized pieces
2 medium leeks, finely chopped
2 small carrots, finely chopped
2 ribs celery plus leaves, finely chopped

500 ml chicken stock
700 g cherry tomatoes
butter
olive oil
salt & pepper
white vinegar or fresh lime
fresh herbs – basil or parsley – chopped

Spice mix

1 tsp coriander seeds
1 tsp cumin seeds
4 cloves
small pinch ground ginger

big pinch crushed chilli
1 tsp nutmeg
seeds of 1 green cardamom pod

Grind up spices roughly in a pestle and mortar. Fry leek, carrot and celery over a medium heat in a big knob of butter and plenty of olive oil, for about 10 minutes until soft. Add spices and cherry tomatoes and fry for another minute. Add chicken stock and simmer, squishing tomatoes as they cook. Add salt and black pepper to taste. Simmer for 15 minutes. Add prawns and, when they are just cooked, add fish pieces and give them a moment to cook through. Remove from heat and add a dash of white wine vinegar or lime and some fresh herbs. Serve with lots of crusty bread or with rice if you want to stretch to feed more people.

Serves 2 fairly greedy adults.

Alone in the garden together, with nothing to do but eat and talk, Kat had thought Massimo might drop into the conversation that his daughters were in Venice. She gave him plenty of chances, even asking after them at one point, but he didn't take the bait.

'They're fine, studying hard as usual,' was all he said, before changing the subject.

She wondered what else he was keeping from her. After he had left and she was in the kitchen clearing up the mess she'd made, it occurred to Kat that he was doing exactly as she had – holding things back, fencing off a part of himself and keeping it hidden. This seemed a bad sign. Hadn't Coco told her it wasn't at all how relationships were meant to work? Kat's good mood was unsettled by a sudden sense of unease.

She finished stacking the clean plates, hung the saucepans on the rack then tried to lose herself in writing. After half an hour of tussling with words she gave up and fetched the leftovers from the fridge to take downstairs to Coco. A good chat with her was what she needed.

Kat knocked on her door twice without getting a response and was about to walk away when she heard a voice calling faintly, 'It's open, *cara*, come in.'

She found Coco stretched out with her dogs on the small sofa that was jammed in between the overloaded racks of clothes. Her face was pale, her ankles swollen; she looked older and more tired.

'Are you OK?' asked Kat, concerned.

'It is much too hot,' Coco complained. 'These summers sap all my energy.'

'It is rather stuffy in here,' Kat agreed. 'The garden is cooler. Why don't you come down and sit in the shade with me for a while before I head into work?'

'I can't bear to move.'

'Yes, you can. I'll get you a drink. And have you eaten anything – no? A little food then as well.'

Taking a deep breath, Coco sat up. 'You are right. I will feel better if I move, I always do.'

Even so, she didn't object when Kat offered her a steadying hand on the short flight of steps down to the garden then fussed about with cushions as she settled into a chair.

Was she thinner? Did her hand tremble a little as she accepted a glass of iced water?

'It is only the heat,' Coco insisted. 'At night it is difficult to sleep and then I feel exhausted during the day. I am going to close the shop for the rest of the summer.'

'That's a good idea, take it easy.'

Coco sighed. 'It is boring taking it easy, such a waste of time. But yes, I will have to, at least for a while. Once it is cooler then I will feel better, I always do.'

Kat brought out some salad and a slice of the crêpe lasagne then sat with her while she grazed on it.

'You gave Massimo a good lunch,' Coco remarked, putting down her fork. 'Did he appreciate it?'

'I think so.'

'And the other one, what of him?'

'You mean Dante?'

Coco leaned back in her chair, closed her eyes and nodded. 'You are seeing him as well, I suppose?'

'I've seen a bit of him,' Kat said defensively. 'I know what you think but it isn't like that.'

'No?'

'Dante and I, we have a different sort of connection. He's a friend. We talk a lot. It feels as though we can say absolutely anything to one another.'

'And with Massimo it's not like that?'

Kat thought about it. 'Not always,' she admitted.

'Oh dear.'

'Even today at lunch we had a good time together but ...' Kat wondered whether to tell Coco about his daughters, then thought better of it. 'There are things we don't say. Both of us are holding things back.'

'So there is one man you make love to, and one you talk to. I suppose it might work, at least for a while,' said Coco.

'It's not ideal, though, is it?' Sitting on the ground, Kat hugged her knees to her chest.

'Are you going to do something about it?' Coco asked.

'Such as?'

Kat hoped her friend might have some advice to share. But Coco yawned and with her eyes still closed, let her hand drift down to rest on the head of the dog beside her chair. 'I don't know, really I don't.'

At the Hotel Gondola the ceiling fans were whirring and the air conditioner working at full blast so walking into the foyer was like hitting a wall of frigid air.

Kat paused beside the reception desk to enjoy the cool and Adriana glanced up at her.

'I thought Massimo was with you. I wanted to talk to him about something,' she said, with a frown.

'Isn't he here?' Kat was confused. 'He left me a couple of hours ago.'

'I haven't seen him all afternoon.'

A familiar hollowed-out feeling started in Kat's stomach. 'Have you checked with Zita? Or is there no sign of her either?' she asked.

Adriana gave a slight shake of her head and said nothing.

'Maybe they've gone somewhere together. Why don't you text or call him?'

'It's not urgent,' muttered Adriana. 'I just wanted to ask if it was OK for me to put out some leaflets for the guests.'

'What leaflets?' asked Kat.

'Nico dropped them off earlier. He's handing them out everywhere, I think.' Adriana pushed a blue card over the counter towards her. It was emblazoned with a silhouette of a gondola and the words 'Respect Venice!' Kat read through a bullet-pointed list of instructions for visitors.

'That all seems pretty fair,' she remarked.

'So you think I'm OK to put some out? Also there's a problem with the bathroom sink in Room 6, it blocked up for the third time this week and I want to know whether to call a plumber. And we have several guests requesting a late check-out and usually Massimo works out how best to manage that.'

'Well he's not here,' Kat said, irritated that it was always left to him to sort things. 'I guess you'll just have to decide for yourself.'

There was still an hour or so before she needed to start work so Kat went up to her room and fiddled round with her book for a while, deleting words then changing her mind and typing them back in. If she was trying to distract herself from thinking about Massimo's mysterious disappearance, it wasn't working. Kat wondered where he had gone to when he'd left her after lunch claiming he needed to hurry. Was he with his daughters again?

Glancing at the clock, she decided to take a quick shower before the evening of work ahead. As she soaped her body she remembered the heat of the afternoon, lying half-dressed on a tablecloth beneath a tree with Massimo. For a short while everything had felt so good between them. He always knew exactly how to touch her, when to hold back, when to give a little more. Once things began they didn't need to talk. Slow moments, rougher ones, skin to skin, mouth to mouth – that was how it went until the last few seconds when neither of them could help crying out. Afterwards they lay in a dazed silence, until Massimo had been the first to move. 'I have to go, I'm late,' he had told her.

He hadn't actually said he was going back to work, although he must have realised it was what she would assume.

Kat was running late now. She put on a mint-green frock that Coco swore looked good on her. While the colour was pretty, she was less convinced the shape was flattering but there was no time to run an iron over anything else. Piling her hair on her head and dabbing on some lip gloss, she raced to the bar.

There were already people waiting to order drinks. The faces of most guests were blurs to her now and Kat hardly recognised anyone from day to day. Since Rosetta had left, with effusive thanks and small gifts for them all, there hadn't been anyone who had stayed more than a couple of nights as far as she could tell. Nico had a point, she conceded. How were these visitors going to experience Venice if it was just another quick stop on a frantic itinerary? Surely the city deserved more than that.

Zita arrived late too, flustered and apologising. 'I completely lost track of the time,' she claimed.

'That's not like you,' Kat said pointedly.

'I know. But you've managed OK?'

With a brisk nod, Kat turned back to her work. The bar was full so it was easy to avoid saying much to Zita.

When Massimo came by to make his rounds of the tables, Kat kept her head down and managed not to meet his eye. She wiped the bar, polished glasses, replenished the ice, sliced more oranges – anything to be as busy as she could.

'What's wrong?' Zita finally asked.

'Nothing,' said Kat.

'Are you annoyed with me for being so late?'

'Of course not.'

'Then why are you sulking?'

'I'm not ... I never sulk. I'm busy, that's all.'

'Fine,' Zita said coolly. 'I'll talk to you later then.'

Kat threw her an exasperated look, but didn't bother replying.

When the last guest had left, Zita came and sat at the bar. 'I'll have a negroni,' she told Kat, 'and some honesty too, please. What has been the matter with you this evening?'

'Honesty?' Kat gave a dry laugh. 'Perhaps you should try some of that yourself.'

'What are you talking about?'

'I saw you having lunch with Massimo the other day. And this evening the reason you were late was because you were out together, isn't that right?'

'We were with our daughters who are home from university. I thought that Massimo had told you.'

'No.'

'Ah, I see. And you are upset because you think he is keeping secrets from you?' Zita guessed.

'I'm not upset,' Kat insisted. 'He has every right to see his daughters.'

'But you feel left out?'

Kat set the negroni down a little too heavily and some of it spilt. 'Sorry,' she said, automatically.

'No, I am sorry,' replied Zita steadily. 'It is a shame you are feeling hurt. But you created this situation, Kat. You can't blame me for that.'

'I'm not blaming anyone.'

'Good, because if Massimo isn't telling you things then you need to ask yourself why. Maybe this arrangement is hard on him, this waiting until the end of a year and seeing how things turn out. I think he would feel better knowing how he stands with you.'

'Has he said that?'

'Not to me,' Zita said. 'But I know this man well and it is obvious he is crazy about you. What I can't tell is how you feel. Do you care for him or are you only here for the sake of your career?'

Kat mopped up the spilt negroni, unwelcome tears pricking at her eyes. She dabbed at them quickly with a clean cocktail napkin.

Zita sighed. 'I have upset you again. But really, Kat, you have to commit one way or another. You can't expect any more of Massimo if you don't.'

'We made an agreement,' Kat said stubbornly. 'He seemed happy with it at the time.'

'But now he isn't happy and neither I think are you.' Zita took a long sip of her drink. 'So what are you going to do?'

Kat wondered what game Zita was playing as she sat there, her face smooth and untroubled, waiting for an answer to the question she had posed. Was she trying to come between Kat and Massimo, or help them? It was impossible to know.

'It's not as simple as it might seem.'

'It shouldn't be as complicated as you're making it.' Zita's tone was infuriatingly reasonable. 'Either you're planning a future with Massimo or you're not.'

'I don't see what this has to do with you.' Kat was angry now, speaking without thinking.

'You don't? Truly?' Zita sounded disbelieving.

'Can't you stop interfering with his life and find one of your own?' Kat had wanted to say it for ages and it was almost a relief now the words were out.

Zita's expression hardened. 'But I am a part of Massimo's life. There is no doubt about that. What I still don't understand is if you intend to be?'

Kat stared at her but didn't dare reply.

'Or are you planning to walk away from him once this year together is over?'

'Neither of us knows yet how things are going to turn out.' Kat was struggling to keep her cool. 'If my TV project goes ahead—'

Zita interrupted her. ' Can't you see how selfish you are being?'

'Selfish?' Kat was indignant.

'Yes! It's always all about your career – your book, your film. Nothing else matters as much, does it?'

'That's not true.'

'I think it is.'

'You don't know me at all,' Kat bit back. 'You don't know anything about me.'

'But like I said, I do know Massimo. I was hoping he'd found someone to make him happy but I was wrong.' Pushing aside her drink, Zita stood up. 'While you're busy making up your mind about my ex-husband, please stay away from the rest of my family. Leave my girls alone while they're in Venice, OK? I don't want them upset by this.'

Kat watched her turn on her high heels and storm away. For a while she felt shell-shocked and then, replaying the exchange in her head, grew angry again and began to wonder how far this woman's interference stretched. What had she been saying to Massimo? To their daughters and the rest of them? Had Zita been working against her from the very start?

She poured herself a glass of Pinot Grigio and drank it far too quickly. Massimo was always saying she shouldn't let his ex-wife get to her. But Kat's moods swung around untethered these days; it was unsettling and confusing. And she couldn't shake the feeling that Zita had been trying to cause trouble all along. She found herself regretting all the time they'd spent together out filming. It had been a mistake to trust her, to let her get so close.

Sitting out on the terrace in the warmth of the night as the fairy lights flickered, Kat kept sipping until she had finished the whole bottle. By the time she went up to bed the wine had dulled her worries a little.

Massimo was sleeping deeply. Easing into bed beside him Kat listened to the rhythm of his breathing. Surely when summer was over they would have more time together. Then they'd escape the Hotel Gondola and Zita too, have a chance to talk properly and everything would sort itself out. Until then she would try to focus on the things that were important – her film and her writing. She fell asleep thinking about them.

A Year At Hotel Gondola by Kat Black

CHAPTER 16

August in Venice is even slower and stickier. It feels as if a storm should blow through to clear the air but it never seems to happen. I feel sorry for the crowds out in the heat of the day on their walking tours and souvenir hunts. August is a time to find some shade and lie down in it.

That is what Coco is doing. Her shop is closed and she seems to have decided to sleep through the rest of summer. I can't even tempt her out to drink a coffee or eat a light lunch. Some days she has visitors. I've seen Vittorio once or twice, a few other old friends and a younger man she says is her nephew, but they never stay for very long. Whenever I check on her she tells me not to worry, but it's hard to see her so lacking in her usual vitality.

'Go to the Lido,' Coco keeps saying. 'The air is fresher there. That's where all the young people will be.'

The trouble is I have a very low tolerance for lounging about in the sunshine – a day at a beach, smearing on creams and rinsing off gritty sand, lying on a lounger lined up with hundreds of others like a regiment of soldiers? No thanks. Far nicer, I think, to take a boat out to some quiet part of the lagoon and search for a breeze. So that's what I've been doing, whenever I can find someone who will take me.

Not all Venetians bother owning boats these days, according to my friend Dante Berardi. Many find their way about the city on foot and use a *vaporetto* for longer trips. He is the son of a gondola maker so of course he loves to be on the water and can turn his hand to piloting almost any small craft.

The other night I took time off work and went out on the lagoon with him. We sat beneath a lavender sky and he talked about the sea creatures that live in its shallow, brackish waters and how he likes to prepare them. The brown-skinned goby fish from its muddy depths that are so good for making a delicate broth for risotto, the big juicy *mazzancolle* prawns, the red mullet fished from the rocky waters, the spider crabs and baby cuttlefish.

There is this thing that happens when you meet someone else who loves food. You kind of accept that everything is seen through a lens of how it can be cooked and eaten. Dante loves to catch his own fish, to forage for edible weeds on the islands, to create new flavour combinations. It's his driving force in life. And out there on the water chatting with him, I realised how much I need that same passion and excitement.

Up till now I've been so uninspired with my cocktails. No wonder I'm getting a little bored behind the bar, all I do is mix pre-prepared peach juice with Prosecco because that's the way it's always been done at the Hotel Gondola. There has been so much opportunity to shake things up, to be creative, pair interesting flavours and make the most of the ingredients I come across as I wander through Venice, and I've been letting it pass me by.

So that's what else I've been doing with my August. I picked some lavender flowers from Coco's garden and infused a bottle of gin with their old-fashioned fragrant flavour. I bought a crate of over-ripe sweet plums from one of the vendors at the Rialto market and cooked them into a syrup. Then I experimented with shrubs – mixtures of cherries, sugar and balsamic vinegar. I puréed summer fruits for daiquiris, adding a tiny pinch of salt to add a crispness that left people wanting more. I infused vodka with rosemary I foraged on one of my walks and toasted sesame seeds to marry with a shot of bourbon.

Every day I've been trying some new combination and

Massimo has become my chief tester. Occasionally he frowns at his first sip of whatever I have concocted, and suggests I add less of this or more of that. Some of my more successful inventions have made it to the menu and while most visitors still prefer the classics (I'm sure there would be a riot if we took the Bellini off the menu), the people who do order something different always seem to enjoy it.

The Hotel Gondola is still fully booked and the bar is humming every night. This is the time of year that fills the coffers and makes up for those quieter winter months and no one seems to mind working longer and harder. But I think we're all longing for autumn, looking forward to the cooler temperatures, but also to Venice belonging to us again, rather than mostly to the tourists.

It's not that Venetians hate having visitors but at this point of the year the place does feel overwhelmed by them. Lots of the locals are worried about it. Dante says his father believes the solution is to charge an entrance fee to the city, but the younger people are wary of turning their home into a sort of Disneyland. They want to keep it as a living city where there are still people going about life, and shops selling everyday items, not only souvenirs. They fear losing their identity as Venetians.

Everyone you speak to here has some opinion on the situation. It's what those two old Italian men at the bar beside you at the *bacaro* are probably talking about; and the groups of young Venetians standing about on corners smoking; and the shop assistants gossiping together in between serving customers. We need these tourists, but how are we going to survive them?

Some of the younger ones are taking action. Massimo's nephew Nico is involved with a group called Respect Venice, who have put out this list of instructions on how best to enjoy and support this city and I thought I'd share it with you.

RECIPE FOR VISITING VENICE

*Spend time in Venice and have a meaningful experience, don't come and go in a day.
*Book into a hotel rather than renting an apartment that a Venetian could be living in.
*Shop mindfully for products that have been crafted in Venice, not cheap, imported souvenirs.
*Fill your water bottle from the fountains rather than buying more plastic.
*Keep to the right on our narrow streets and don't stop on the bridges.
*Find a bench to sit on if you want to eat a picnic.
*Don't walk around shirtless, barefoot or in a bathing costume unless you're at the Lido.
*Take off your backpack when you're on the vaporetto. And please don't block our way with your luggage.
*Remember that it is forbidden to swim in the canals.
*Help us by signing our petition to ban cruise ships from Venice.

And don't come in August, that's my own piece of advice. This is a month for beaches or shady forests, not a city that's been built on a network of swampy islands. If there is any time that the streets will smell of sewage and the still water of the canals turn fetid, this is it. Tempers shorten and visitors get crankier about the high prices and the long queues, or the way a waiter treated them in some overpriced *trattoria*, or the crush on the *vaporetto*. So I'm with Coco, actually. August is a time to stay at home and sleep away the heat.

Venetians start to reclaim their city on the first Sunday in September. That is when they hold the Regata Storica, a pageant on the water, with costumed gondoliers and ornate boats in the style of the sixteenth century. Flags fly, the Grand Canal is filled with colourful craft and people cram onto bridges, balconies and in windows wherever they can to watch the races.

Massimo and I had a prime vantage point from aboard his motorboat, which he had moored the night before not far from the gondola stop of San Tomà. We stole a few hours from work and joined the party. I think Massimo misses his rowing days. He says some day he'd like to join a crew again because being out on the water is something every Venetian needs to be truly happy. I can't imagine when he'd find the time. The Hotel Gondola is always demanding his attention. It eats up his life and I don't see how it could ever be less hungry. He loves it, though, just as he cares fiercely for every corner of this city from the pink marble façade of the Doge's Palace to the narrowest stone-flagged passageway.

I think if you asked Massimo what he loves most in the world, he would say Venice.

Kat was trying to be more reasonable. She wasn't finding it easy. The smallest things might pull her mood down and her energy levels had plummeted; everything seemed more difficult. Like Coco, she blamed the heat. But there was no time for her to lounge about beneath the shade of a tree all day, however much she might like to. She had a book to write and a pilot TV episode to edit.

Every day she woke early, and escaped the Hotel Gondola as quickly as she could. After a breakfast of coffee and brioche, dispatched quickly while standing at the counter of her favourite *pasticceria*, she took her usual route through the twisting *calli* towards the narrower back canals.

For most of the day she holed up in the apartment with all the doors and windows open to catch any hint of a breeze, and forced herself to work, reviewing footage and making notes. It felt as if Venice was outside, quietly going on without her. From time to time she would hear the dull thud of an oar as a gondolier passed along the canal below, or foreign voices raised in overloud conversation as they crossed the nearby bridge, but mostly this part of the city was inhabited by locals and for now it was closed up and hushed.

To begin with Kat went far too slowly for her liking. Editing wasn't her skill and she was impatient to learn and be good enough. But after hours and hours of watching dreary how-to clips on YouTube, the film took shape and she began to get excited. The raw quality of the sound and images seemed to work. It felt more intimate than *Black of*

Beyond ever had, and her hope was that it lent some immediacy to what the viewers would be seeing.

Kat lost herself in the work. She liked being busy and besides it provided the perfect excuse to avoid the rest of her life. Massimo, Zita … She would deal with them later. The one person she had time for was Coco, and only since she seemed to need her so much right now.

'I am perfectly fine,' her old friend kept insisting but Kat wasn't convinced.

'Are you sure you don't want to see your doctor?'

'My doctor would tell me to rest which is exactly what I am doing. It is very dull, though, Kat. I miss my life.'

Coco had given up making an effort to face the day. Often Kat found her dressed in the same things – a loose kimono and turban – her face bare of make-up and arms free of bangles. Her appetite had waned; while always appreciative of the small meals Kat brought, she rarely cleaned a plate. As for her matchmaking scheme, Coco seemed bruised by her failure with Rosetta Rees and refused even to think about it.

'Vittorio will have to look after himself until the autumn when your friend Ruth returns,' she said.

'I'm not sure that's going to happen,' Kat admitted. 'Massimo offered her a really great room rate but she hasn't committed herself to a booking yet.'

'Ah well.' Coco gave a resigned sigh.

'Did you break the news yet to Vittorio that you won't marry him?' wondered Kat.

'Not exactly. All I have told the poor man is this is a bad time. That I can't think about anything important right now, not while I am feeling so very unlike myself.'

That worried Kat, who made sure to check on her often, popping in several times a day, taking snacks, topping up her water jug, even cleaning her bathroom a couple of times. She did her best to cheer her up, and when the TV pilot was near to being finished, Coco was the first to see it.

Clad in a loose cotton smock dress, she sat expectantly in front of the laptop. 'How exciting.'

'The music isn't necessarily my final choice,' Kat warned her. 'And it's very rough in places. Also there are still a couple of scenes I'm not sure should be included.'

'Stop talking, *cara*. Press a button and make it play.'

Coco gave a small squeak every time she recognised a place or person. And when she saw herself, she put her hand over her mouth. 'How do I look? Do you think that dress is good on me? Oh and see, there is my shop, how lovely. What is it I am doing now?'

She watched it four more times before sinking back down on the sofa. 'So much fun,' she sighed. 'When will this film be shown on the television?'

'That's out of my hands,' Kat told her. 'It might not ever be. But I can always put it on YouTube or something.'

Coco gazed at her blankly.

'On the Internet,' Kat explained.

'And does that mean everyone will be able to watch it?'

'Yes, whenever they want to.'

'Do you think I will be recognised?' Coco sounded thrilled.

'I suppose you might, if enough people see it.'

'How exciting. I must be back on my feet by then.'

Massimo was the next to get a viewing. Kat showed the film to him just before rushing off for her shift in the bar and it was even more nerve-wracking than it had been with Coco.

'Don't expect too much. It's just a rough cut,' she stressed.

He watched it with great focus and when it was finished, to her relief, he was smiling. 'This is great. I love it. You're very clever.'

'Really? Oh thank God. I showed it to Coco but she was so overexcited about seeing herself on film it was hard to get any sense out of her.'

Massimo wanted to watch it again so Kat left the laptop

with him and headed off to work. The cocktail of the week involved some fuss to make but that was fine by her. She was happier working than caught up in conversation. Mixing drinks was one thing; dealing with so many people night after night was quite another. Kat had a new respect for anyone who managed a lifelong career in hospitality.

A few of the guests still recognised her, but often were confused about exactly where they knew her from.

'What's your real job?' they asked sometimes. 'What do you really do?'

The customers she actively disliked were the ones who clicked their fingers or whistled and waved money in the air to attract her attention. Or those who wanted her to run through the details of every cocktail on the menu before they ordered the Bellini they were planning to have right from the start. Some were visibly impatient if their drink wasn't in front of them within seconds of ordering. And then there were the bores, drinking too much and too fast, cornering her and endlessly talking nonsense.

But the person she was keenest to avoid engaging with was Zita. Massimo's ex-wife had apologised for calling her selfish, but hadn't seemed contrite for long. In fact, she had tried several more times to discuss Kat's relationship with him – where was it going, what was she planning.

Kat refused to be drawn because she didn't see how it was anyone else's business, but particularly not Zita's. And the truth was, everything seemed to change from day to day. Sometimes the sun shone on her moods, but more often her brain clouded and then all she could be certain of was that Massimo deserved what they had promised each other right at the very beginning, a year before they made up their minds. She couldn't think beyond that.

So if the cocktail of the week was a little too complicated and left no time to stand about talking, Kat didn't mind at all. Besides, what she had written in that last chapter of her book was true. Being creative made bartending much more bearable. Some of her concoctions turned out pretty much undrinkable, but others worked and, with Massimo's help, she enjoyed coming up with Venetian names for them – the Doge's Secret, the Gondolier's Ruin, the Guggenheim's Fling.

By the end of an evening's work, Kat was tired but there was a sense of satisfaction that had been missing before. And sometimes guests – often Americans – asked for the recipes and it amused Kat to think of one of her cocktails being mixed up on the other side of the world.

She never lingered in the bar once a shift was over. Tonight, she paused only to grab a couple of bottles of Peroni from the fridge, before heading up to her room. Kat really wanted to talk to Massimo about her film. Had she tried to include too much? Was the pace of it OK? Had she picked the right sort of music? His were fresh eyes and she valued his opinion.

She found him sitting in an armchair beside the window, her laptop still in front of him. He looked up and raised his eyebrows as Kat walked in. There seemed something out of kilter, but she wasn't sure what.

'You're not still watching the clip?' she asked.

'No,' he said shortly.

Suddenly Kat had a very bad feeling. 'What then?'

'I've been reading your memoir – *A Year at Hotel Gondola*. It's all very interesting.'

'I didn't say you could do that. It's still a very rough draft, it isn't ready to be seen yet.'

His mouth a thin line, he tossed her laptop on the bed.

'So you hate it,' she said.

'I come across as a dull workaholic.'

'No you don't,' Kat countered uncertainly.

'And I'm not sure I know this woman who is telling the story or the life she describes. She seems like a stranger to me. Is it really you?'

'It's a version of me.' Kat jumped to her own defence. 'I'm curating my life; it's what everyone does these days. Don't you ever look at Instagram?'

'So you are proposing to publish this?'

'Of course, once it's finished.' Kat was at a loss. 'My readers want a story and I'm giving them one.'

Massimo stood up. 'It's your book so I guess you can write whatever you want.'

'It hasn't been easy, you know—' she began.

He cut her off. 'I'm going out for a while. My head is aching and I need some fresh air.'

'Please wait,' she called after him, but the door closed and he was gone.

Sitting down heavily on the bed, Kat picked up her laptop. She hadn't read back through the chapters for a while, and now she began to, trying to view them through Massimo's eyes. It didn't seem enough to provoke such a strong reaction. Yes, she had played down some things, steered clear of mentioning any tensions between them, skipped over Zita's interference, but she had assumed Massimo would prefer that. And he had warned her not to write about Nico's problems, after all. So what was so wrong, she wondered as she continued reading, why was he being so unreasonable?

Kat experienced an uncharacteristic urge to call her mother. Generally the last thing she sought was her advice – there had been far too much of that growing up as the only child of an anxious solo parent. But now she needed someone to talk to.

Her mother was the wrong person, of course. Relationships were hardly her area of expertise. After leaving Kat's father she'd had nothing to do with men at all. In fact, she made a point of saying a woman didn't need one. She and Kat had moved to the far end of the country so she could guard the independence she was so proud of, and Kat could imagine exactly what she'd say now. I told you so, didn't I? Men are all the same. You're strong and self-reliant; you're better off without one.

Perhaps there was a friend she could reach out to, instead. Lying on the bed alone, Kat ran through the options in her head. It was a fairly long list; she had plenty of friends. But all those years of travelling hadn't encouraged much closeness. There was a neighbour she went walking with, friends that were always good for a couple of wines, there were several who loved to lunch, a few that invited her for weekends at their houses in the country. But was there a single one who was especially close? Who wouldn't tell her she was living the dream and she should try on their life for size? Kat didn't think so. What she needed was a proper best friend, a confidante, and, to her surprise, no one back in London seemed to fit the bill.

Kat dozed for a while and woke a couple of hours later to find the bed beside her still smooth and empty. She hoped Massimo was OK. Fumbling for her phone she tried calling him, but he didn't answer.

Rolling off the bed, she opened the window and stood staring out into the night. Salty, humid air rushed into the air-conditioned room. She leaned out a little and looked down at glints of rippling water and the dark shape of a barge passing. She had been in Venice for almost six months now. In March she had arrived, so sure she was ready for whatever lay ahead. Now she wondered if it had all been a mistake, particularly for Massimo. He had given her all he'd promised and what had she offered in return? A few cocktail recipes, a book it seemed he hated.

For the first time Kat thought properly about what she had done, leaping into this year at Hotel Gondola as if it was just another adventure – a new city; a new experience; inspiration for her work. She had been so eager for the opportunity. Had she recognised that this time it was different because it involved someone else's feelings? Had she been concerned about hurting Massimo? No, she didn't think so; not enough, anyway. Instead, she had assumed his thinking was the same as hers.

Now Kat stared through the open window and wondered, What if it wasn't? What if it had never been?

She remembered Zita calling her selfish and how shocking that had been. Kat had never seen herself that way before and the idea was unsettling. Now, as she began to find the truth in it, she felt awful, hollow and empty.

Alone in the small room at the top of the silent hotel, gazing into the dark, Kat felt the sadness creep over her. She was sorry for herself and for Massimo. Tears pushed at her eyes yet again and, resting her weight against the window sill, she didn't bother trying to wipe them away.

A Year at Hotel Gondola by Kat Black

CHAPTER 17

Autumn is whispering to Venice. The locals have already
changed their clothes for the season; jackets are being worn
now, longer trousers rather than short, proper shoes not
sandals, even though the days are still warm.

This morning I went for a walk and tried to lose myself but
it was impossible. I know Venice now; not so well as someone
who has always lived here, but I can find the quickest route
from place to place; the hidden passageways for short cuts;
the quiet back alleys that bypass the main thoroughfares. I
still love to walk this city but after six months of exploring it
on foot, Venice is not a mystery any more. Often it feels more
like home than any other place I've lived.

Today, turning back towards Hotel Gondola, my walk took
me past Coco's shop. I was concerned to see the door ajar
although the closed sign was still hanging and the lights
switched off.

The shop seems an unlikely place to get burgled (what thief
wants to ransack someone else's faded grandeur?) but still I
was cautious as I pushed open the door a little further, calling
out, 'Hello ... is there anyone there?'

'Kat, cara, is that you?' It was Coco's voice. A minute later
she pushed her way through the racks of dresses. She was
wearing a smart suit, dusky pink and in the finest wool, with a
hint of Chanel about it.

'You're very smart,' I told her. 'But aren't you meant to be
at home resting?'

'I cannot rest any longer; the boredom will kill me. And it is a little cooler, no? I wanted to come and make sure my shop was all in order.'

'Are you sure you're OK?' I asked, because Coco has seemed so much frailer lately.

'I am upright and it is a good day,' she said firmly. 'What I would like right now is to go somewhere lovely then I can rest again this afternoon if necessary.'

I took her to a favourite café where they have tables alongside the canal with fluttering red-striped sun umbrellas and an especially handsome waiter. He must be at least forty years younger than her but Coco flirts with him and he seems to love it, always making a fuss and bringing out a small vase with a single flower on the tray with our coffee and biscuits.

'It is such a relief to be in the world again,' Coco said, when he'd ushered us to a table.

'I've missed our coffees and lunches,' I told her.

'I have missed everything – the streets, the people, life all around me. I have missed going out dancing and gazing in shop windows and looking at art and all this beauty. Most of all I am longing to see my darling Vittorio and Roberto, and Silvio, too, of course. All my lovers.'

'You might have asked them to come over and visit you.'

Coco pursed her lips and shook her head. 'They are my lovers, Kat. I would never let them see me that way.'

'Surely they wouldn't care?'

'Perhaps not, but I would care because I want them to desire me. We are still passionate people even if we don't have young bodies any more.' Coco's voice was easily loud enough for the couple at the neighbouring table to hear. 'You may struggle with that now, my dear, but when you are old hopefully you will feel the same.'

'I'm hardly young now.'

'You are in your prime,' Coco insisted.

'No, I'll be fifty-one very soon and things seem to be

changing, things I have no control over. I'm getting older and not liking it much,' I admitted.

Coco balanced her coffee cup on the saucer carefully, and it struck me that her hands might have been trembling slightly. 'So you have a birthday coming up. How lovely, we should have a party.'

'I don't feel like celebrating.'

'In that case you need to change your attitude,' she said crisply. 'How could you deprive your friends of a party?'

'I don't actually have very many friends in Venice,' I pointed out.

Coco seemed entirely untroubled. 'You have me, that is enough, surely.'

I laughed and agreed not to let my birthday slip by without some sort of celebration. The truth is, I've been dreading fifty-one; it seems just another stride towards the finish line, and the thought of running out of time is what panics me. There's so much more to do, places to visit, experiences I want to have, and the years seem to be concertinaing up on one another, with no space to cram enough in.

'It's completely weird getting older, isn't it?' I said to Coco. 'Something is happening to the skin on my arms and I'm convinced one of my eyes is becoming bigger than the other. Is that actually a thing? I keep plucking these long hairs from my face. And I can't decide whether I should keep dyeing my hair or go grey gracefully?'

Coco glanced at me. 'Never mind all those things. Your biggest problem right at this very moment is the dress you are wearing.'

I was in a mint-green frock that is gathered round the front, creating a slightly puffed-out effect I had been concerned was rather unflattering.

'It looks terrible,' said Coco, confirming my suspicions. 'What on earth made you think it was a good idea?'

'You did. You said the colour was lovely on me and I seemed fresh and cool?'

'I don't think so.'

'You did,' I insisted.

'Did I have my eyes open?'

'Absolutely.'

Coco gave her head a small shake, as if trying to clear her mind. 'I am so sorry, I can't have been feeling at all well that day,' she apologised. 'We must go back to the shop and swap it for something better. And we need to make plans. A treat for your birthday, a cocktail somewhere glamorous before then.'

It was so good to see Coco more like her usual self. Her higher spirits were infectious. Later, walking back to Hotel Gondola in a different frock – one that Coco assured me was a vast improvement – I started to think that autumn in Venice feels more like a beginning than an ending.

The crowds have ebbed, the little local shops have reopened, my favourite stalls at the Rialto market are piled high with produce that I can't wait to take into my kitchen. Plump pomegranates and persimmons, colourful pumpkins and squashes, pears with their stems dipped in red wax to keep them fresh.

Coco has got me excited about all the possibilities of the shift in seasons. She talks about the sugar-crusted paste I can make from the quinces that grow on the lagoon islands. She says when winter comes there is a chance of seeing snow falling on Piazza San Marco. She is making me think the darker, shadowy days might bring some of the mystery back to Venice.

This city may seem frozen in time but it does change if you watch it properly. As the weather chills and the sky clouds over I can see the blue of the lagoon turning steely grey. The daylight seems more silver now, the sunsets deeper and pinker and, in the parks, the trees are beginning to weep their leaves.

My year at Hotel Gondola is half over. I'm hoping the best is still to come.

Kat finished writing the chapter and wondered how much longer she could go on like this; giving her readers this idyllic view of a life filled with food, fashion and matchmaking, creating a fantasy of Venice as she thought they'd want it, when there was so much tension at Hotel Gondola.

Each evening in the bar felt more strained than the last. The autumn chill in the air had made it obvious Zita was avoiding her. Even though there were heaters on the terrace, most guests preferred to occupy the indoor tables once the sun had gone down, and in that smaller space it became clear she was keeping her distance. Beyond a few sidelong looks, and the bare minimum of talk needed to keep the bar running, not much passed between them.

Things were still off balance with Massimo too. He hadn't mentioned her book again, and was acting almost as normal, but some of his warmth seemed to have seeped away. This showed itself in small ways. There was no cup of strong black coffee put into her hands before he went to work in the morning, no stolen hour in bed together up in their room in the afternoons, no more talk of where they might take a holiday once winter set in. At times he seemed so withdrawn she struggled to get him to say much at all.

Sick of trying to work through all of this alone, Kat called a couple of her more sensible London friends. Neither seemed surprised to hear she had run into difficulties.

'You've done really well to make it this long. I had money on you only managing a couple of months,' said one.

The other was more sympathetic, but still unhelpful. 'The

thing you need to understand about men, Kat, is that you're not meant to understand them.'

There was no advice to be had from Coco either; she wasn't interested in hearing about troubles, only talk of parties, outings and shopping. She had bought an expensive Marni jacket and insisted on taking Kat out to lunch at Harry's Bar so she could wear it. 'Don't worry so much,' she kept saying. 'You don't have any problems, not really. Relax and enjoy life.'

Kat was trying to but the problem was she felt on edge the whole time, and her moods still soared up and down unpredictably.

When she heard Ruth had booked a room at Hotel Gondola, it was as if Kat had been tossed a life jacket. She might have her quirks but she knew how to listen; and surely if anyone had some useful advice it would be her.

So Kat was already feeling more upbeat and then Massimo boosted her mood by suggesting they take a night off and go out for dinner.

'I'll organise Nico to cover for you and book a table somewhere interesting.'

'What about Quadri?' she said eagerly. 'I love it there.'

'I'm not sure,' he said vaguely. 'Leave it to me. I'll surprise you.'

'That would be nice.' She smiled at him. 'I love surprises.'

That night they made love and it felt as good as ever. Kat lay awake afterwards, hoping she had overreacted. There were all sorts of reasons why Massimo might have seemed chillier – a work worry he was grappling with, fatigue after the busy summer, family pressures he hadn't mentioned. Tomorrow night they could go out for dinner, have a really good talk and sort things out. Maybe she'd have to rewrite bits of her book to keep him happy but that wouldn't be the worst thing ever. And they'd speak about the future and the way the rest of their year together was going to play out; it was time for that now. They shouldn't put it off any longer.

It started like a repeat of their first date. At six p.m. they met in reception; Kat dressed in tight capri pants and an off-the-shoulder top that Coco had promised didn't look too young on her. She had left her hair loose and dusted bronzer on her cheeks to make up for her summer tan fading.

Massimo put his arm around her shoulders as they walked together, and she leaned into him, breathing the fresh scent rising from his warm skin, feeling the firmness of his body. He asked what was happening with her film and she became absorbed in discussing it with him.

'My agent loves it, but she's not the important one. It's the programme commissioner I have to get interested. It's with him at the moment and even if he does give it a thumbs up there is a whole process we need to go through, so it could take ages.'

'There is nothing you can do in the meantime?'

'Just try not to think about it and get on with writing the book.' Kat gave him an anxious glance. 'There's still lots of work to do, recipes to develop as well, so it will keep me busy.'

Massimo nodded, but didn't speak.

'I suppose things should quieten down soon at Hotel Gondola,' she said.

'We will be full for a little while longer, hopefully,' he told her. 'But yes, in a month or two there will be time to breathe.'

They turned a corner into a narrow *calle* and Kat realised their route was a very familiar one. 'Where are you taking me?' she wondered.

'I thought we'd go to your friend's place?' he told her. 'The one you've written about so much in your book.'

Kat felt her stomach give a lurch. 'Locanda Dante?'

'That's right.'

'What about Quadri instead?' she suggested quickly.

'It will be busy; we'd have to queue for a table. And you gave Locanda Dante such a rave review, I can't believe I haven't been there yet.'

'You don't want to swing by Quadri first just to see if there's space?' Kat pressed him hopefully.

Massimo was insistent. Quadri would be packed with tourists and besides, he wanted to eat somewhere different. Locanda Dante it had to be. The way Kat had written about the food was so tempting. It was almost like he could taste the flavours.

To Kat this seemed like an olive branch. If Massimo was making an effort to be positive about her writing then she couldn't find a way to argue.

But as they drew nearer, Kat began to panic. This was what she had so wanted to avoid, for the two men to meet – the dark one she lived with and the fair one she spent so much time with. She had been careful to keep them apart. Now Kat considered feigning a headache or sore stomach but it seemed too late for that. Maybe it would be OK, she reassured herself. She would introduce Massimo to Dante, they would eat a good meal and then they'd leave. Why did it have to be such a problem?

They walked into the familiar room with its long banquette and swathes of dried flowers and Kat saw that almost every table was occupied. The *osteria* was so full Dante might be too busy to come out of the kitchen to greet her.

As they studied their menus, Kat tried to focus, to see if new dishes had been added, or any of her old favourites removed. But her thoughts were too scattered. She kept watching the doors that led to the kitchen and very much hoping Dante wasn't about to sail through them.

'You order for both of us,' she told Massimo.

'Are you sure don't want to choose since you know what's good?'

'No, surprise me.'

While Massimo looked over the menu carefully, Kat stared about the dining room and tried to settle her thoughts. The buzz of conversation was loud and there was a convivial atmosphere. She saw the waiter ferrying full plates from the kitchen and imagined Dante must be working hard.

Massimo ordered, speaking in rapid Italian, so Kat wasn't certain exactly what he had chosen.

'It all seems very seasonal so hopefully there will be some new dishes for you to try,' he said, as the waiter filled their wine glasses with a fresh, young Soave classico.

Kat had felt hungry earlier but now her appetite was gone. Thankfully, the first course, a platter of autumn vegetables and smoky cured meats, was easy to graze on. The second was heavier, fat pillows of handmade ravioli stuffed with herbs and ricotta and garnished with clams swimming in a buttery sauce.

'You're not enjoying it?' Massimo asked as she picked around the edges of her plate.

'It's delicious,' she reassured him. 'The wine is lovely too. Everything is perfect.'

'Perfect? Are you sure about that?' he asked.

'I'm sorry?' Kat was almost certain he wasn't only talking about the food.

'Because lately I've been worrying that everything is far from perfect. It's why I wanted to eat dinner together this evening. We need to talk.'

'My book?' she supposed. 'You completely hate it.'

'I am confused by it,' Massimo admitted. 'It took me by surprise.'

'It's a first draft. Nothing is set in stone yet. I can change it.'

'Can you make me less dull?'

Kat laughed. 'You're not dull, I promise.'

'What concerned me most is there's so much in there I didn't know about.' He shook his head ruefully. 'It's like

I'm not completely a part of your life or your book. I hadn't realised how I've let work take over lately. But there is a reason for it, Kat. Some day, when my parents are gone, I will have to buy my sister's share of the Hotel Gondola. And the price she will want and what is fair are two different things. So I work long hours, keep costs down, save as much as I can.'

'You can't imagine your life without that hotel, can you?'

'I don't want to imagine it.'

'So you'll grow old there?'

'Yes, I hope so.'

Kat could almost see him, his still-dark hair gone grey, his wide shoulders a little stooped, taking a turn round the terrace on summer evenings, charming the guests as he always had. Somehow she couldn't quite put herself anywhere in that picture.

'For both of us work is what comes first,' she said. 'Perhaps it's inevitable if you get together when you're older.'

Massimo stretched a hand across the table and his fingertips touched hers. 'For once let's not talk about work. There's something more important to discuss.'

Kat braced herself, wondering what was coming.

'My daughters were in Venice for a short while during their summer holidays. Zita says you saw us together and were upset I hadn't told you.'

'She shouldn't have mentioned it. I was just having an oversensitive moment … It's not important.'

'But I think it is important. I'd love to introduce you to my daughters. It's proving much too difficult for me to keep you apart. I've been avoiding things – celebrations, gatherings – and it can't go on. I'm starting to think about Christmas – do I leave you alone and spend the day with my family? My parents keep asking to meet you, my sister.'

Kat wasn't sure what he was trying to say. 'So you mean you want us to meet?'

'Yes, of course I do, but first I need to know exactly what is in your mind.'

She stared at him blankly.

'I want us to be a real part of each other's lives now. Not just a year together, but a future. What I'm trying to ask is if you want that same thing too. To make a life with me.'

Kat took a deep breath. 'Massimo, I'm crazy about you, I really am but ...'

She hesitated and he prompted her. 'But?'

It was better to be honest. 'I don't think I could ever love your life. Running a hotel, every day the same routine, trapped by it.' Kat saw the hurt in his eyes and almost faltered. 'It's not your fault. I understand this is what you love. It's just that I'm different.'

'Perhaps you are not as different as you think,' he said evenly. 'Maybe you want the same things most of us do.'

'I want to travel, to see new places and have new experiences.'

'And do you imagine I would ever stop you doing that?'

'Well I—'

'Even you need a home to come back to, Kat.' His voice almost seemed to break on the words. 'Don't you?'

Dante chose that moment to sweep through the kitchen doors, overjoyed to see her, carrying a new dish he had been longing for her to try because didn't Kat know her opinion was essential to him now and why had she stayed away so long?

'Working.' She was curt, hoping he would take the hint and go away.

But now he was introducing himself to Massimo, shaking his hand and being pleased to meet him. Helplessly, Kat watched as the two separate parts of her Venice life merged.

Massimo recovered himself and began chatting to Dante, complimenting the food, asking him questions.

'Yes, my little *osteria* is doing really well,' Dante was

saying. 'Kat was so great in the early days; her enthusiasm helped keep me going when it seemed the customers were never going to come. She has an excellent palate and is not afraid to say exactly what she thinks. She is one of the few people I know who is as passionate about food as I am.'

'So you two are good friends?' Massimo asked, glancing at Kat, who shifted in her seat nervously. She wondered how far into her manuscript he had read before she'd interrupted him. Had he come across her description of the night she'd spent in Dante's gondola watching the Redentore fireworks, or that evening out on the lagoon in his boat talking about food? Kat had thought she'd been discreet, avoiding any hint of a flirtation, but now wasn't so sure.

'Yes, we're very good friends.' Dante seemed oblivious to her discomfort. 'We've had lots of great times together over the past few months. Actually, Kat, I was wondering if you wanted to come out fishing one morning. I thought we could take a boat out to my usual spot on the lagoon, bring a picnic, of course, and see if we can catch some red mullet.'

Kat fiddled with her napkin and gazed down at the dish Dante had brought out that was fast cooling on the table. 'Tell me what this is?' she asked, hoping to change the subject.

'Roasted pigeon, a raviolo stuffed with its offal, on a bed of foie gras with just the tiniest hint of truffle. Eat, eat,' Dante urged. 'Tell me what you think. Is it too rich? I thought so at first but then I changed my mind because this is for my winter menu and it is the season we long for these sorts of deeper, more robust flavours.'

Kat forked up a small amount and put it in her mouth. Chewing the lump of food, she found it fatty and unpleasant. 'Yes, much too rich,' she said, feeling her throat constrict as she tried to swallow.

'OK, OK.' Frowning, Dante turned back towards the kitchen. 'Don't forget about the fishing. We'll leave early so let me know what morning suits you.'

After he had gone there was silence. She and Massimo sat with plates of barely touched food between them, a hum of conversation all around, and nothing to say to each other.

At last Massimo spoke. 'It's been six months and I still don't know you, do I?'

'Of course you do.'

He shook his head. 'All this time I have been boring you with my dull job and my routine and my hotel that you have felt so trapped in and I haven't realised it.'

'No,' she began, 'it's not like that at all.'

'You've been busy with your life, your friends, your world – you've made it very clear it's so much more exciting than mine. I understand. I don't blame you.'

Desperately Kat searched her mind for the right thing to say.

'But this Dante – chef, gondolier, whatever he is – surely there is only one reason why you haven't introduced me to a man you've spent so many great times with.'

'We're friends, that's all,' Kat insisted. 'Nothing has happened between us.'

'When I read your book, that's what I hoped.' His tone was disbelieving. 'But now ...'

'Is that why you suggested coming here? You suspected something?' Kat couldn't believe he'd be so devious, then understood what must have happened. 'You've been speaking to Zita. This was her idea.'

'She thought you and I needed to talk properly and she was right,' said Massimo defensively.

'You told her about reading my manuscript?'

'I had to discuss it with someone. I didn't know who else to turn to.' His voice was low and Kat thought he sounded enormously sad. 'No one should blame Zita for this.'

'But she interfered?' Kat was incensed. 'What did she say to you?'

Massimo sighed heavily. 'Mainly that it was my fault.

That if I've been left out of the life you've been leading here then it must be because I haven't made enough time for our relationship. She gave me quite a lecture.'

'And then suggested coming to Locanda Dante for dinner tonight?'

'I described what you'd written about this place and him.' He nodded towards the kitchen. 'I told her I couldn't stop thinking about it, wondering what you might be leaving out, not telling me or your readers. Zita said I should come and see for myself, that it might put my mind at rest. Only it hasn't. Not at all.'

Kat felt shattered. All these things had been in his head and he'd told his ex-wife rather than her.

'Nothing happened,' she repeated. 'Dante and I went out on his boat a few times, that's all.'

'Maybe that's the truth but I'm not sure how much it matters now.' Massimo stood and tossed some cash on the table. His eyes were hooded and his voice was growing hoarse. 'I thought it was possible to make things work, but I was wrong. You don't want to be with me, do you, Kat? That's the real problem. It's time we ended it, don't you think? Why struggle on for a whole year together just because it's what we agreed at the start, if neither of us is happy? The worst thing would be to end up hating each other. So let's stop this before that happens.'

'Is that really what you want?' Kat asked numbly.

'It's what makes sense.' Massimo exhaled a ragged breath and seemed as if he was about to say something else then stopped himself and with an implacable shake of his head strode out of Locanda Dante without another word. Kat didn't try to stop him. For a few moments she sat very still before filling her wine glass almost to the brim and drinking it down with quiet determination.

The maître d' was staring over at her, so were the couple

at the neighbouring table. Probably they had overheard everything but Kat didn't especially care.

'Excuse me,' the woman said, her accent English. 'I recognise you from somewhere. Have you been on television? Oh yes, I know. It's Kat Black, isn't it? I used to watch your show every week. Is it coming back on soon? I miss it.'

By now Kat was practised at deflecting strangers who recognised her, but her presence of mind had deserted her. Dully, she nodded at the woman, signed an autograph on her tourist map of Venice and even managed a few moments of forced, polite chat.

'How great to meet you,' the woman said, as Kat stood to go. 'I had no idea you lived in Venice. This has completely made our evening.'

With a weak smile, Kat backed away. She hurried out of Locanda Dante, half running down the *calle* and away from the place, only stopping when she reached a wide *campo* dominated by a Gothic basilica. A canal curved through one corner, wide steps leading down to it, and Kat sank down on one, her head falling into her hands.

She stayed there for a long while. People passed by – couples going to and from dinner, noisy groups who'd had too much to drink, tourists wearing gaudy front packs. As it grew late and darkness fell there were fewer of them, until Kat was completely alone.

Every morning Kat woke up feeling disoriented. Her first thought was that she was alone in bed and then she remembered she was in the apartment. There was no hotel beneath her; no hive of visitors poring over maps and planning their day, there was no Massimo.

She had come straight here after that disastrous dinner at Locanda Dante and slept on a bare mattress. Now there were sheets and pillows on the bed, and her clothes were hanging in the wardrobe. The portrait that Ruth had painted of her was on the wall and Coco had lent her a vase to put flowers in.

Aside from a volley of texts she had barely been in touch with Massimo. He had sent over her belongings and settled up for her final week of bar shifts. His final message had read, *It may not have worked but I'm glad we gave it a try. Take care of yourself wherever you adventure to. Goodbye and good luck.*

Kat reread it at least once every day and each time her heart felt just a little heavier.

Coco kept telling her that Italian men were proud and Venetians most of all. She put herself in charge of cheering Kat up. Every chance for gaiety was taken. There were cocktails at the Gritti Palace and concerts at La Fenice; there were art exhibition openings; even an outing with Vittorio to listen to the Gregorian chant at the monastery of San Giorgio Maggiore. Kat went along with whatever was suggested.

Today it was raining and the clouds hanging low were as

dark as her mood. Kat lay in bed trying to resist the urge to check her email and see if her agent had been in touch. It had all gone ominously quiet. Nor was she making progress with her writing. She couldn't bring herself to pretend any more. The year at Hotel Gondola was over, it had come to a premature end and so had her book about it. Idly she wondered if her publishers would expect her to pay back the advance she had received.

Money was shaping up to be a problem. She had some savings left, and once they were spent, she would have to find a Plan B. Kat had no idea what that might be but she had always been good at thinking only as far ahead as the next problem, so put it out of her mind. For now what concerned her most was the frayed edge of her life in Venice. This wasn't how she wanted to leave things.

As grey as the morning had turned out, there was some light ahead. Ruth was in Venice. She had checked in to Hotel Gondola the evening before and, learning Kat had left, texted to ask what had happened.

Come to the apartment for lunch tomorrow and I'll explain everything, Kat had messaged back.

Having a meal to prepare gave her some purpose. It forced Kat to get up and dressed, to walk the rain-slicked streets to the Rialto market, haggle with the vendors there for bitter radicchio and sweet autumn squash and buy a lump of cheese she couldn't really afford from the Casa del Parmigiano. Back in the apartment, while the rhythm of chopping and stirring might not have shifted her sadness entirely, it did help lift it a little.

By the time the door buzzer sounded everything was ready. Kat waited impatiently, listening to Ruth's footfalls as she climbed the steep stairway with care.

'Oh!' said Ruth, setting eyes on her. 'Oh dear.'

'Don't tell me what colour I am, because I don't want to know.'

Ruth leaned in for a brisk hug and then Kat stood back so she could pass through the doorway. 'Come in. You'll see the place is looking a bit different.'

Ruth stared at the bright canvas on the walls and the clutter of Kat's belongings that she hadn't bothered tidying.

'You're living here now. What happened? What went wrong?'

'Let's eat then I'll explain. Tell me about your life first. How was your summer? What's been happening?'

'My life is the same as always,' said Ruth, settling at the table and accepting a glass of Prosecco. 'I've been longing to get back here and looking forward to seeing you. When they told me you'd gone, at first I assumed they meant you had left Venice altogether.'

'I've thought about it,' admitted Kat. 'But my flat in London is rented out and besides, I don't feel ready to go yet.'

'Coco must be pleased to have your company. How is she?'

'Better but still not fully recovered from whatever was wrong over summer. Her hands tremble at times; I'm sure they didn't used to.'

'Her age is catching up with her.' Ruth didn't sound surprised.

'I think I'm in denial about that,' Kat admitted. 'It turns out I've been in denial about rather a lot.'

Once they finished eating Kat poured out her story while Ruth leaned forward and listened with her usual intensity. As she spoke, Kat began to see herself through her friend's eyes. She was a woman who had turned fifty, panicked, and plunged into the first relationship that came along; it had been a mistake, but she hadn't listened to anyone who tried to tell her. Navigating that relationship had proved harder than finding her way through any maze of Venetian back alleys. She hadn't handled it well.

'I've hurt Massimo so badly, that's the worst thing,' she said. 'I keep thinking about the last time I saw him. I feel so sorry and sad.'

Ruth sat back in her chair. 'I suppose that explains it then.'

'Explains what?'

'Your colour – it's a thick band of dirty yellow and it hasn't moved since I came in.'

For once Kat didn't dismiss her talk as woo-woo. She felt as if she could almost sense the colour pressing in and smothering her.

'How strange but I think you're right,' she admitted. 'What the hell am I going to do?'

'I guess that depends on what you want,' said Ruth thoughtfully. 'First you need to remember that all relationships go through difficult patches, even the happiest ones. You can stay together or you can walk away. Neither is an easy choice.'

'Did you and your husband ever have problems?' Kat wondered and then immediately apologised. 'Sorry, that is such a nosy question.'

'It's OK, and of course we did. We fought, we hurt each other's feelings, we misunderstood each other all the time. Often we argued about trivial stuff and didn't say the things that were important.'

'Like Massimo and me,' Kat realised. 'I keep wondering what I should have done differently. If I'd let him read the book at the beginning, if I hadn't kept my friendship with Dante a secret, if I hadn't made him feel as if the life he's chosen is dull and pointless ... But maybe it would have all gone wrong at some stage anyway. I mean the whole idea, a year together, without giving any thought to what would happen when it ended. It was crazy, wasn't it? Looking back, lots of people did try to tell me but I wasn't interested in listening.'

Ruth gave a faint smile. 'Yes, I remember.'

'I thought love would be this thing that would either happen or it wouldn't, and then it would be obvious where we should go from there.'

'And did it happen? Do you love him?'

'I think I do but ...'

'Go on,' Ruth encouraged her.

'If I loved him enough wouldn't I be prepared to give up everything else – my independent life, my career, being able to pack up at a moment's notice and head off into the world? I'd want Massimo more than any of those things.'

'But you can still feel the pull of them?'

'All the time,' admitted Kat. 'As much as I care for Massimo I don't know if I could ever be the person he needs. Maybe he was right, it was time to end things. There was never any future for us. I just wish we'd been able to do it in a better way instead of it all being so messy and painful.'

They chatted for the rest of the afternoon over pots of camomile tea. Ruth didn't have any answers but the talking seemed to help Kat thread together some of the strands of thoughts unravelling in her mind. As the evening closed in she felt better than she had in a while.

'I've taken up too much of your time when you could have been painting,' she said to Ruth guiltily.

'Don't worry about that, I'm not in any rush to start. This summer I've barely pulled out my paints and the longer I leave it the harder it gets. I seem to have lost all the creativity that flowed so easily when I was last here. I'm hoping being back in Venice will change things.'

'Coco is determined you are going to paint portraits of her and Vittorio.'

'Ah yes.' Ruth sighed. 'I had conveniently forgotten about that. Did they want me to do them together?'

'No, she has decided it will be separately and beginning with Vittorio. Coco has it all planned. You are going to paint him in his apartment, which is rather grand, apparently. She has even picked out what he'll wear. I can't see how you'll get out of it.'

'Painting Vittorio might be rather nice,' Ruth admitted. 'He is the most beautiful russet colour. It is Coco I will struggle with – all that grey, I'm not sure how I'll manage it.'

'Then you had better take a really long time over Vittorio,' Kat advised, laughing.

By the time Ruth left the rain was easing off and the clouds had lifted enough for pinpricks of stars to be shining. Kat walked with her most of the way back to Hotel Gondola, nodding as she passed an old Venetian woman who often frequented the same stalls at the market, a butcher she bought meat from, and the man who sold tickets for the *traghetto* boat she often took across the Grand Canal.

'This was what I wanted when we first met,' she told Ruth. 'To be a part of Venice, to get to know the people who lived here, and it's happening now when it's all too late.'

'So you have made up your mind then. You're going back home?'

Kat gave a sad shake of her head. 'I think it's going to feel more like leaving home than returning.'

She stopped short of walking all the way to the Hotel Gondola because she didn't want to see its familiar front-age: the arched windows lit up from within, the Murano glass chandeliers dazzling in the foyer and the tangle of fairy lights gleaming up on the terrace. Zita would be behind the bar by now, Massimo either still in his office or with her greeting the guests that were filtering in. It was an unsettling feeling, knowing she wasn't a part of it all any more.

Once she had said goodbye to Ruth, she began to retrace her steps. There was a street vendor selling hot roasted chestnuts on a corner and she stopped to buy a bag. Hugging the warm package to her chest she hurried on, eager to be indoors, to curl up on the old chaise and think some more about what Ruth had said about relationships, the difficult patches they went through and how best to decide what was worth fighting for.

Kat didn't realise she was being followed until she turned back towards a shop window display that had caught her eye, bumping into a black-clad figure behind her as she did so.

'Sorry,' she apologised automatically then, recognising the face shadowed by the brim of a black woollen cap, 'Adriana, is that you?'

'Yes,' said a familiar husky voice.

'Are you on your way home from work? I didn't know you lived over this way.'

'I don't,' Adriana admitted. 'I was coming after you. I need to talk.'

'About Massimo?' It was Kat's first assumption.

'No, I have something important to ask. Can you spare a few moments?'

'I suppose so.'

'This way then.' Adriana pointed towards a tiny *bacaro* that Kat didn't usually bother with because there were only ever a few tired crostini on its scuffed wooden counter. 'I will buy you an *ombra*.'

She ordered two glasses of red wine, chatting to the proprietor in Venetian dialect as she unbuttoned her coat and took off her cap. He seemed vehement about whatever he was saying; putting down the bottle at one point so his hands were free to gesture.

'He doesn't seem happy,' remarked Kat, when finally he finished pouring the wine.

'He says he's had a bad season. The passengers from the cruise ships don't spend the money. They stand here making one *ombra* last as long as they can, taking selfies and posting them on Instagram. They never buy anything to eat.'

'Perhaps he needs to offer better food,' suggested Kat.

Adriana frowned. 'You have no sympathy?'

'The good *bacari* are always busy,' Kat pointed out. 'This isn't one of them.'

'Perhaps that is true,' Adriana conceded, 'but the point is these people from the cruise ships are choking the life out of Venice. In a way that is what I wanted to talk to you about. I need your help.'

'You do?' Kat was surprised.

'Not me, personally,' Adriana added hurriedly. 'The organisation that Nico and I are working for, Respect Venice. We produced the leaflets I showed you a little while ago. You remember?'

'Yes, but I didn't realise you were still involved with them.'

'I work behind the scenes. Massimo knows. He is OK with it.'

'How is Massimo?' wondered Kat.

Adriana shrugged. 'Fine ... working hard as always.'

'I'm not being missed then?' said Kat, with an awkward laugh.

'Massimo talks about you. That is how I heard about your TV series. He said you have already shot a pilot episode and it's really great.'

'He did?' Kat couldn't help feeling pleased.

'Yes, and then we thought wouldn't it be good if you made one of your programmes about Respect Venice. Our aims, our protests, all the reasons we must fight for our beautiful city so that we never have to leave it.'

'Massimo suggested that?'

'It was Nico's idea. He says we have to make a noise that is loud enough for the world to hear us.' Adriana was more animated than Kat had ever seen her. 'And you can help us.'

'I'm sorry but I can't,' said Kat.

The sulky look dropped back onto the younger woman's face. 'I told my brother you would say that.'

'It's not that I'm not interested, but I don't have a TV show yet and it's probably not going to happen.'

'Massimo is telling everyone it is why you left the hotel. Because you need to go back to your career.'

'That's not exactly how it is,' Kat said carefully. 'It's more complicated.'

Adriana gave her a shrewd look. 'I see.'

'For what it's worth I agree with you. Venice might be ruined if something isn't done. I will help if I can. But right now nothing is settled ...'

'Things are difficult, I understand,' Adriana said. 'If that changes you know where to find me. I would be happy to hear from you any time.'

'In the unlikely event my show gets the go-ahead, I'll be in touch,' Kat promised.

Adriana treated her to a smile. 'Thank you.'

'Say hi to everyone at the hotel for me,' Kat said, and then added, 'Is Zita still there?'

'No, she left not long after you did. Nico is back now. I thought you knew that.'

'You mean she's not working in the bar at all?'

'Things are quiet over winter,' Adriana told her. 'Nico will easily manage until business picks up again in spring.'

Kat felt a surge of anger. 'She was only ever there because of me, wasn't she?'

'Zita? Yes, of course.'

'And now Massimo and I have broken up, I suppose she has achieved what she set out to with all her interference.'

'No, you are drawing the wrong conclusions as you always do.'

'Zita wants Massimo back. Isn't that obvious?' Kat was entirely furious now.

Adriana shook her head. 'You don't know her. If she wanted Massimo then she would have him. She is a strong woman, determined; she almost always gets her own way.'

'What was she doing then?' Kat demanded. 'Watching me? Claiming she wanted to be my friend. Why?'

'You are misunderstanding the whole situation,' Adriana insisted.

'So explain to me what was going on.'

'It seems obvious enough.' Adriana was as blisteringly condescending as ever. 'Her daughters are everything to Zita. She is protective. When it seemed you might become a part of the family she wanted to get close, to know everything important about you. Now that you're not, you no longer matter to her. And so she vanishes from your life ... *pouf*.'

'Seriously?' Kat was incredulous. 'She is that manipulative?'

'She will be the same with the next woman that appears in Massimo's life ... if there is another.'

Adriana buttoned up her coat, put her hat back on and took a scarf from her bag to wind round her throat. Nodding at Kat's flimsy clothing she said, 'It is getting cold out there. You will need to find some warmer things if you are going to stay in Venice all winter.'

'Maybe.' Kat fingered the light chambray of her shirt. 'I'm not sure whether I'll be here for much longer.'

Finishing the last of her wine, Adriana stood up. 'He misses you,' she said quickly. 'He may not ever say so but it's obvious.'

19

Coco was in a good mood; some days she was so insistently upbeat that Kat could only cope with her in small doses. Once again most of her attention was focused on her match-making scheme. Having finally refused Vittorio's proposal of marriage as tenderly as possible she was more determined than ever to see him happily settled with someone else.

'I'm not making the same mistake I did with that yoga woman,' she said, on hearing that Ruth was back in Venice. 'So much effort and no result at all. This time I intend to move fast and you will help me.'

'Isn't it risky meddling in people's relationships?' asked Kat, who had a fresh appreciation of how complex they could be. 'Shouldn't we let things happen naturally?'

'Happen naturally?' Coco sounded perplexed. 'Don't be ridiculous.'

There was quite some effort involved in preparing Vittorio for his portrait to be painted. Coco sent him to have his hair trimmed, his skin exfoliated and his nails buffed. She changed her mind several times about the outfit he should wear and the ideal background to set him against.

'It won't matter,' Kat kept telling her. 'Ruth focuses on the colour she sees in a person. Vittorio is russet, apparently. She says it's a beautiful shade.'

'A little grooming won't hurt,' Coco argued. 'Ruth will spend a lot of time staring at him while she is making this portrait. Trust me, I have experience of artists. If there is a flaw their eyes will find it.'

'I don't think Ruth is like that,' Kat argued, but Coco wasn't interested.

'My Vittorio will look his best. As she paints him they will talk. An attraction will form … naturally. Just as you said it should.'

'It all sounds very straightforward.'

'Why shouldn't it be?' asked Coco airily. 'These two people are meant to be together. All we are doing is helping them.'

The day of the first sitting happened to be Kat's birthday. She was turning fifty-one – already eroding the slab of twenty good years her mother had said were all she could hope for. Despite having promised Coco a party, Kat decided to let the day pass like any other. No cards, no cake, no champagne.

She woke early and had her usual breakfast of milky coffee and a plain brioche, standing beside the counter of the nearest *pasticceria*. Coco appeared, dressed in cream wool and multiple long strands of iridescent pearls.

'Hurry,' she urged Kat. 'I want to make sure we get there before Ruth arrives. Everything must be perfect.'

Despite her demand for haste, the walk with Coco was slow going. Her little dogs strained on their leashes, pulling her forward, and several times while climbing the steps of a bridge she needed to pause to take a breath.

'Are you OK?' Kat asked. 'Should we get a water taxi?'

Leaning on the balustrade, Coco shook her head. 'I am fine. It is not much further.'

Vittorio's apartment was on the ground floor of a palazzo in Dorsoduro. It was large but most of the rooms had the cool, damp feel of spaces that were rarely used. There was a layer of dust over the shelves of glassware and ornaments. Only a few of the photo frames had been polished to a high shine, the ones containing shots of the wife that had died and the grown-up son who had moved away to Rome.

'Come through, come through.' Vittorio seemed delighted to see them. 'I have set up the room just as you told me to. How am I? Smart enough?'

He was dressed in a bone-coloured suit, a gold cravat at his throat, a matching handkerchief peeping from his top pocket, and carrying a polished wooden cane with a decorative golden handle.

'You look like you've made a big effort,' Kat said tactfully.

'Of course!' He beamed at her.

The background that had been carefully prepared was just as formal. There was a family crest hung on the wall behind where he was intending to pose. A large potted fern on a high stand had been placed on one side of the chosen spot, a marble sculpture of a lion on the other.

Ruth had arrived a little earlier and was looking flustered. She hadn't set up an easel yet or unpacked her paints and brushes.

'This isn't how I usually work,' she muttered to Kat, while Coco was busy fussing with the fern, spraying its leaves with a mist of water.

'What do you want me to do?'

'Creativity creeps up on me when I'm not trying too hard to find it,' Ruth told her. 'I need to feel relaxed and for Vittorio to be too.'

'I'll get rid of Coco, then, shall I?'

'Yes please. That would definitely help.'

Coco refused to take any of Kat's hints to leave. She was convinced things wouldn't go smoothly without her interference and clearly planned to stay for the duration.

Finally Kat hissed at her, 'Nothing is likely to happen between them with us here. We need to go and leave them alone.'

Reluctantly, Coco collected her handbag and clipped her

dogs onto their leads. After issuing some last instructions –
Vittorio should be sure to stand up straight, and Ruth must
make him look handsome – she let herself be led out of the
apartment.

Kat found a water taxi to take them back and Coco
seemed relieved to be helped onboard. The day was misty
and moody and, as the boat skimmed slowly down the still
canals, she sat quietly, gazing off to one side, her dogs en-
circled in her arms.

For once Kat was the chattier one. 'Wouldn't it be great if
your plan actually works?' she remarked. 'Ruth and Vittorio
do really seem to like one another.'

'Of course they do,' said Coco, and there was a shakiness
in her voice that prompted Kat to look more closely. She
saw her friend's eyes looked watery and her cheeks a little
moist.

'Are you crying?'

'No, it is the mist stinging my eyes.'

'What's wrong?' Kat touched her shoulder gently. 'I
thought you would be happy to see they are getting on well.'

Coco gave a small sigh and turned her head away.

'Isn't it what you wanted?'

'This may be a new beginning for Ruth but for me it is
an ending. I will miss my Vittorio. I am allowed a moment's
sadness.'

'Whatever happens between them, you can still see him,'
Kat pointed out.

'Yes, but it won't be the same. My time is over.'

'You have your other lovers, don't you?'

She nodded. 'For now.'

Coco asked the driver to drop them beside her shop. These
days it was rare for the *Closed* sign to be taken from the
door but she tried to get there every day and sometimes, if
a certain kind of woman stopped to gaze in at the window,
she might find herself being beckoned inside. 'I have an

outfit that is perfect for you. I couldn't let you go by without trying it,' Coco would say.

Today she seemed restless, pacing the cluttered space, rearranging garments on the rails and changing the frock on the mannequin that was now positioned inside, half blocking the door.

'It's so stuffy in here,' said Kat, fanning herself with her hand. 'Did you leave the heating on overnight?'

'There isn't any heating.'

'There must be; I'm sweating.' She wiped her hand across her suddenly damp forehead.

'I am not at all warm, *cara*, only you.' Coco tilted her head. 'But I think this is not the first time you have felt very hot for no good reason?'

'What do you mean?' asked Kat, although she suspected what was coming.

'I had assumed it is why you insist on wearing the wrong clothes for the season?' Coco told her.

'I am English,' Kat said testily. 'We don't all change into wool the moment the calendar tells us summer is over. We wait for it to actually get cold.'

Coco's laugh tinkled. 'For you, that might not happen so much this winter. You will need to invest in layers, *cara* – little cashmere cardigans, wide scarves and shawls you can easily take off. Don't worry, it can look very stylish.'

Kat sank back against the counter and fanned at her flushed face. 'Oh God, the terrible mood swings and now this.'

'It happens to all of us.'

'This is a hot flush.'

'Yes, yes, but there is no need to make such a fuss.'

'I can have a moment of sadness, can't I?'

A moment, yes,' Coco agreed. 'We are all allowed that.'

The heat seemed to rush through Kat's body and set her heart hammering. She had to escape the shop. Out on the street the cool air may have chilled the moisture on her skin but it couldn't settle her. One word loomed in her mind: menopause. Walking back to the apartment, she tried not to look at the women she passed; the younger ones she was envious of and the elderly reminding her of what was coming.

At home she stripped off her clothes and took a shower, catching sight of her reflection in the speckled bathroom mirror as she wrapped a towel around her wet body. Nothing had changed. Her waist seemed no thicker, her shoulders weren't stooped, her 51-year-old body still looked strong and healthy. Viewed from the right angle the softening of her jaw wasn't as noticeable and in a good light the lines around her eyes didn't appear etched so deeply. Kat wasn't old yet; she refused to be.

Dressed in a slip and her bathrobe, she opened the French doors to the balcony and sat with her laptop on her knee, looking with a sinking heart at websites about menopause symptoms and hormone therapy.

'Hey,' came a male voice and Kat glanced up to see Dante leaning out of his window, staring across at her.

'Hey,' she replied.

'Aren't you cold sitting out there like that?'

'Perhaps a little but it feels refreshing.'

'You English people ... very strange.'

'Why aren't you at work?' she asked.

'It is Monday, my day off,' he reminded her. 'I was planning to get up early and go out fishing but then my alarm went off and I couldn't seem to open my eyes. So I've had a lazy few hours and now I want food. Are you hungry?'

Kat hadn't eaten anything since her morning brioche. 'Yes, I think I am.'

'My fridge is almost empty. What do you have over at your place?'

'Not much ... some of the new season radicchio di Treviso,

a wedge of cheese, fresh walnuts and porcini mushrooms, olive oil, of course.'

'That is plenty. Stay right there, I'm coming over.'

Dante arrived with a tub of frozen chicken stock and a packet of *carnaroli* rice and, while Kat stretched out on the chaise, he took over the kitchen, chatting as he cooked.

'How is your friend?' he asked, splashing the radicchio with olive oil and putting it in the oven to bake. 'Massimo, isn't it?'

'Not my friend any more,' she said, lightly enough. 'We fought.'

'Ah, I see.' He poured more of the oil into a pan, lit the gas and began chopping an onion. 'You are sad?'

'Yes, but a part of me thinks it may be better this way. I'm not going to stay in Venice much longer.'

'You don't want to get too serious with anyone then.' Dante tossed the onions into the hot oil, and Kat smelt them begin to sizzle. 'Not if you'll be moving on soon.'

'Exactly.' She got up to give the onions a stir, while Dante began cracking walnuts.

'It is exactly the same for me,' he told her. 'I can't expect any woman to wait while I work these crazy hours. Better not to get serious right now.'

He made a risotto with the porcini and walnuts, tossing in the last of Kat's expensive cheese so it was richly creamy. The roasted radicchio he dressed with a little balsamic. They ate hungrily, sitting side by side on the chaise, Kat closing her eyes to experience every layer of flavour.

When they had finished their food they put the empty bowls on the floor, too comfortably full to move. Kat's phone beeped with texts several times but she didn't bother to get up and check them.

'It's my birthday,' she confessed to Dante. 'I'm trying to ignore it but my friends keep sending messages and reminding me.'

'Happy birthday.' He leaned over and his lips touched her cheek. 'You should have told me. I feel bad that I don't have anything for you; not even a bottle of Prosecco.'

'There's no need.'

'Maybe not, but we ought to make the day special.' He gave her a slow, lazy smile. 'Don't you think?'

'What did you have in mind?'

He reached over and brushed her neck with his fingers and she felt a tingling down her spine.

'Dante ...' she began.

'You know how sexy you are when you eat.' His fingertips slipped beneath her bathrobe.

She was flattered enough to be tempted for a moment and that was all it took for Dante's lips to fall on hers. He kissed her hard then pushed her back onto the chaise and tugged the bathrobe free of her body. In one fluid movement he was on top of her and she heard a tearing sound as the delicate silk of her slip gave way to him.

'Dante,' she said again, half-helplessly.

Kat felt the urgent pressure of his fingers and breathed his muskiness, her torn slip round her waist, the rough bristles of his skin chafing her face. His touch was quick and impatient. Now he was unbuckling his belt and trying to shrug free of his jeans.

'Dante, stop.' She wriggled out from under him, smashing one of the dirty plates as she landed on it.

His face was flushed. 'I thought you wanted this.'

'I may have thought so too for a few moments. But I don't, I'm sorry.'

Dante pulled his jeans back over his hips. 'Why not?' he asked.

'It doesn't ... feel right.'

'But it's your birthday and we were having a good time, nothing serious.'

'I'm sorry,' she repeated.

'If you don't want it, fine. It's up to you.' His voice was tight, his expression sulky.

Kat pulled the bathrobe round her body. 'We're still friends, right?' she said awkwardly.

'Sure.' Dante stood up and straightened his clothes.

'I'm sorry,' she said again.

'Hey, stop apologising, it's no big deal.' He gave a careless shrug of his shoulders. 'I'll see you at the *osteria* some time, OK? Enjoy the rest of your birthday.'

After he had gone Kat cleared up the broken plate and washed the rest of the dirty dishes. Then she went and looked at her reflection in the bathroom mirror again; really examined it this time. She saw how the skin above her upper lip was puckering. That there were brown blotches of sun damage on her cheeks and her forehead looked sort of corrugated when she frowned. Her jawline was softening no matter how she angled her face and the lines scored beneath her eyes had deepened. She was starting to show her age.

Most likely Kat wouldn't be attracting younger men like Dante for very much longer. Still, she wasn't sorry to have stopped him.

20

There was at least one moment in every day when Kat thought about contacting Massimo. Often she picked up her phone to send a text or dreamed up scenarios where she went to the hotel and surprised him. She wasn't sure what stopped her from actually doing it, but each day that went by the harder it became to imagine being face to face, talking in a way that wasn't loaded with resentment, making things better rather than worse.

Venice was wintry now; its few trees were stripped of their leaves and the sun low in the sky, casting long, dramatic shadows. Kat knew she ought to be leaving. There was nothing to keep her here.

Her days were short and aimless. She slept a lot and punctuated the hours she was awake with mealtimes. A late breakfast with Coco at the usual *pasticceria* before walking together to her shop, then a lunch assembled from what was to be found at the market on the way home. As twilight closed in Kat would head to whichever *bacaro* she and Ruth had chosen, her footfalls echoing in the quiet streets, to make an early dinner out of an *ombra* or two and a plate of *cicchetti* while they talked.

Ruth had extended her stay in Venice. She had been here for over a month now and her portrait of Vittorio had turned into a series. Each day the pair of them wandered somewhere new, and every evening she told Kat all about it. She had painted him set against the glittering interior of Caffè Florian, flocked by pigeons in a misty early-morning Piazza San Marco, standing on a bridge beneath a yellow umbrella, sitting beside a canal reading his newspaper. She painted him on fine days and wet ones, as a brisk wind whipped in from the Dolomites and a cold afternoon faded to grey.

'I've never focused so much on any one person before,' she admitted. 'It's intense and also fascinating.'

No one had seen the work yet but Coco had begun talking excitedly about friends who had galleries and the chances of an exhibition. Ruth was more cautious. 'It may be the best thing I've done or it might be the worst. I can't tell yet,' she said.

Kat was envious as she missed having a project to be absorbed in. She was still practising her film editing skills but there seemed no point in shooting anything new until she heard back from her agent. As for her book project, it had foundered completely; she couldn't stand to think about it.

'I'll be moving on soon,' she kept telling Ruth over crostini loaded with creamed salt cod and endless plates of meatballs. 'On to my next adventure.'

The truth was, Kat felt stuck. If only she could buy a backpack and a plane ticket then disappear, as if she was nineteen again and dropping out of college. There were times she panicked about the way one day seemed to blend so easily into the next. But mostly Venice was an easy place to do nothing. The city seemed to be slowing down with her. The people on the streets warmly wrapped in puffa jackets were more likely to be locals, the *bacari* were half empty and their proprietors ready to stop and chat. There was time to linger over a cup of richly dense hot chocolate, to enjoy the company of a friend or gossip with a neighbour.

Apart from Coco, the only neighbour Kat knew well enough to talk to was Dante. She had seen him on a couple of occasions since that awkward fumble in her apartment and both of them found it easier to pretend nothing had happened. He still spoke about going out fishing on the lagoon and waved whenever he glimpsed her from his window.

'What you need is a lover,' Coco told her, one afternoon when they were bundled up in old eiderdowns, sitting in a shivery patch of sunlight out on her balcony. 'It may as well be him.'

'I thought you didn't like Dante?'

'He is vain, arrogant, self-obsessed, humourless.' Coco ticked off his worst qualities on her fingers. 'But he is also convenient. And you need to do something, *cara*. Moping like this doesn't suit you.'

'I know it doesn't,' Kat admitted. 'But Dante isn't the answer.'

'Who then? Massimo?'

'That won't work. And anyway, it's too late; he's not speaking to me. I should have gone to him straight after that stupid fight. If I'd sorted things out then ... if I'd made him understand, then maybe it would have been OK.'

'But you didn't,' Coco said mildly, 'which must mean you didn't want to.'

'It's not that simple.'

'Yes it is.'

'Massimo asked me a question that final night over dinner,' Kat explained. 'He wanted me to be a part of his life for ever, not just a year. He asked me to make a commitment but it seemed like I had so much to lose if I did. I said all the wrong things and then there was so much hurt and I didn't know how to fix it. So I stayed away.'

'You hoped he would come to you?'

'Maybe,' Kat admitted.

'And now you miss him?'

Kat missed the smell of him, sharp and clean. She missed kissing the top of his head as he frowned over his work, the trace of a smile on his face as he teased her, the sound of his voice. She missed drifting off to sleep with him each night and waking every morning, his body tangled with hers. Most of all she missed his goodness.

'Yes, I miss him,' was all she said to Coco.

'I miss Vittorio too. But these things run their course and there is always someone new – that is what makes life exciting.'

Kat didn't want anyone new. She had realised that during the messy tussle with Dante. Afterwards, the more she thought about Massimo the more she understood what she had lost. What was it he had said? Even she needed a home to come back to. Perhaps that was true but there seemed no way to salvage anything now.

What Kat had to do was to shake herself out of this torpor and find a way back to the person she used to be – independent and fearless, a woman who didn't need a man to be happy. That was how she remembered herself.

'I must be terrible company. I'm even boring myself.'

'Then cheer up,' Coco suggested. 'Get a haircut. Buy a new lipstick.'

'I think it's going to take more than that.'

'Go and see Massimo if that's what you want. You know where to find him. He'll be at that hotel of his like always.'

Kat wrapped herself more tightly in her eiderdown and sank into her chair. 'No, I don't think so. I can't.'

'In that case come out dancing,' said Coco, undeterred. 'It always lifts my spirits no matter how bad I feel.'

Throwing off her covers, the old woman got to her feet and danced a few tottery steps across the balcony, humming tunelessly.

'I can't dance,' Kat told her.

Coco stopped mid-step and frowned. 'I am a little tired of hearing what you can't do, *cara*.'

Coco really was going dancing. Her excitement grew over the course of the afternoon as she described the outing that one of her lovers had planned. There would be a glass of Prosecco, a light supper, a few good friends, wonderful music, and an hour or so of being whisked around the floor in his arms.

'So much fun.' She smiled. 'I can't think of anything nicer.'

She was vibrating with happiness as she headed downstairs to choose what she would wear. There was talk of skirts that flared and swirled as she moved, of silk stockings, strappy shoes and feathers in her hair.

'I intend to look marvellous,' Coco declared. 'I will see you in the morning and tell you all about it.'

Kat's plan was to meet Ruth as usual. By now they had a few favourite *bacari* and would text each other at some point in the day to agree on which one to head to. Kat checked her phone to see if Ruth had been in touch yet but there were no messages.

Where tonight? Do you fancy All'Arco? she tapped out.

The reply came five minutes later. *Vittorio invited me out to dinner. He wants to take me to Harry's Bar. Sorry! Tomorrow evening?*

Sure, no problem, Kat sent back. *Have fun!*

At a loss, and sick of being cooped up in the apartment, she headed out alone. She walked through the empty square where the market had been packed up for the day, and over the Rialto Bridge. It was a cool, clear night and Kat kept walking, through narrow streets of smart boutiques, across Piazza San Marco where a café orchestra was playing to a scattering of onlookers, and further into a quieter, more local part of Castello.

She chose a *bacaro* at random, an overheated place lined with wine barrels. Standing beside the counter, she downed a glass of red wine and grazed on some unimaginative *cicchetti* – sour onions and sardines on a slab of chewy bread, a meatball that had been fried some time ago, roasted vegetables sopped with oil.

'Another *ombra*?' the proprietor asked, refilling her glass without waiting for a reply.

Kat drank quickly, barely tasting the wine but enjoying the effect it was having, the loosening of muscles and the easing of her mood.

'Did you hear the latest news?' the proprietor asked, his elbows on the counter and keen for conversation.

'No, what's happened?' asked Kat.

'They want to ban you tourists from wheeling your suitcases through the streets of Venice. Noise pollution, they are calling it.'

'I'm not a tourist, I live here,' Kat told him.

'Oh yes?' He sounded unconvinced.

'Those suitcases do make a terrible sound when people trundle them along. I'm not sure how else they're meant to move them though.'

'Well you can blame that group ... what do they call themselves ... Love Venice.'

'Respect Venice?'

'That's right. They are campaigning for this.'

'Do you think it will happen?'

He tipped more wine into her glass and shrugged. 'Who knows? These young people want Venice how it used to be. But you can't turn back the clock so there's no use in trying. That's what my wife always says.'

His words may have been a cliché but they stayed in Kat's mind as she bundled herself into her jacket and headed back out into the night. Shivering a little she walked briskly, sticking to the better-lit *calli*. Was that what she was trying to do, turn back the clock? Is that why she couldn't bring herself to leave Venice?

Ahead of her, a brightly lit *bacaro* spilt out a crowd: women warmly wrapped in quilted coats, men with their chins lowered into woollen scarves. People were calling goodnight to each other, kissing cheeks and embracing. A man was laughing.

Her eyes followed the sound and she found a face she

recognised – Massimo. He was with a younger man and they were moving away from the group and still laughing together about something. Kat's footsteps faltered. She had forgotten how handsome he looked, the reassuring breadth of his shoulders, the way he wore his clothes, neatly pressed and tailored to fit.

She realised the younger man was Nico. He must have seen her because he touched Massimo's elbow and said something that made him look over. Kat's feet took her forward.

'Hi,' she said, almost shyly.

'You're still here,' Massimo replied. 'I thought you must have gone back to London.'

'I couldn't go without saying goodbye.'

An odd expression flickered across his face. 'You look cold,' he said. 'Where is your coat?'

She tugged at the thin wool collar of her jacket. 'I'm OK,' she lied.

'Here.' He unwound the scarf from his neck and offered it to her. 'Don't worry about giving it back; I have another.'

She must have looked doubtful because he pushed it into her hands and stood watching as she wrapped herself in the soft wool still warm from his body.

'It suits you.'

'Thanks.'

'It's good to see you, Kat, take care.' His hand on Nico's shoulder, he turned and began to walk away.

'Massimo,' she called after him.

He looked back. 'Yes?'

'Thanks,' she said again, 'for everything.'

Walking home, sinking her face into the scarf and breathing his familiar scent, Kat wished she hadn't repeated herself, sounding like an idiot. Thanks, thanks – as if there weren't so many hundreds of better things to say.

She knocked on Coco's door when she got back but there was no response so she assumed her friend was still out partying. Climbing the stairs to her own apartment, she made a few promises to herself. In the morning she would email her agent and say if she didn't hear something then she was going to post the footage she had shot onto YouTube and forget about it. She would read through the chapters of her book and find a way to finish the thing because the advance had been spent and she couldn't afford to repay it. She would make a plan for her next step; there were places to go and friends to visit. And then Venice could just be a memory.

She slept still wrapped in Massimo's scarf, a deep and dreamless sleep, and when she woke to the smell of him, opened her eyes in confusion, thinking for a moment or two that she was back at the Hotel Gondola.

A dull light creeping in through the shutters meant another grey winter's day was waiting. Kat closed her eyes for a few more moments, tempted to stay in bed, cosy and warm, safe from life. Remembering last night's resolutions, and her plan to meet Coco for breakfast, she eased out from under the covers, wincing as her bare feet met the chill of the parquet floor. The scarf stayed draped over her shoulders as she brushed her teeth and splashed water on her face. And when she dressed she chose clothes to match the burnt orange shade of its deeply piled wool.

Kat waited at the usual *pasticceria*, nibbling on a brioche and drinking several cups of coffee, but Coco didn't appear. Perhaps it had been a late night and she was tired; or more likely her friend couldn't brace herself for the damp wind whipping up from the canals. Kat decided to take breakfast to her and bought a couple of pastries and a few sugar-crusted biscuits, the waiter laying the sweet treats in a box and tying it with gold ribbon.

'These are for the signora, yes? She likes things to look glamorous.'

Outside it seemed even frostier and Kat was glad of the

scarf. She hurried through the almost empty streets, clutching the box, the whitened tips of her fingers tingling. Detouring past the shop she checked for signs of Coco but the door was locked and the windows dark. There was still no answer when she knocked at her apartment, although she heard the yipping of her dogs inside.

Kat went up to her own place, emailed her agent then forced herself to open her laptop and click on the file for her book. Reading through its first few chapters took her back to those first weeks of falling in love with Massimo and Venice. How naïve she had been, how puffed up with herself. Surely without Coco she would have floundered so much earlier.

For lunch she snacked on a couple of biscuits then took the rest back down to her friend. The dogs were whimpering behind the closed door now. Kat hammered on it harder than she had before, calling out, 'Coco, are you in there? Hello?'

Unsure what to do, she stood listening to the plaintive howls for a few minutes. Then she made up her mind and, running back upstairs to her apartment, grabbed her phone and called Ruth's number.

'Hi, I was going to text you,' Ruth said, when she answered. 'I'm definitely on for tonight. Let's go to All'Arco like you suggested yesterday.'

'Actually that's not why I called. I'm a bit concerned about Coco. There's been no sign of her all day. I've checked several times.'

'Perhaps she's gone out.'

'The dogs are there; she almost never leaves them, and they don't sound happy. I don't know ... probably I'm over-reacting but I've got a bad feeling. What should I do? I don't have a key to her place and I can hardly kick the door down.'

'Hold on a moment, let me check with Vittorio.'

Kat heard a short, muffled conversation and then Ruth

said to her, 'OK, we're coming right over. Vittorio has a key. We'll be no more than twenty minutes.'

'Thanks.' She was relieved. 'I'll listen out for you.'

Kat tried knocking several more times then sat on the steps to wait, her anxiety mounting. Coco had definitely said she wanted to meet for breakfast. There was no mention of any other plans for the day. This wasn't like her.

Ruth and Vittorio arrived as quickly as promised, both swathed in warm layers and carrying painting gear.

'I'm so sorry to have interrupted you,' said Kat.

'We weren't too far away,' Ruth reassured her. 'And we're sure everything is fine but there's no harm in checking, is there?'

Even so, Vittorio seemed sombre as he told them to wait. He unlocked the door and, as he went in, Kat heard him muttering to the dogs. '*Va bene, va bene.*'

There was the noise of a door opening and closing, then silence. No sound at all for a long time.

'Do you think we should go in?' Kat asked.

Ruth shook her head. 'Not yet, let's wait like Vittorio said.'

'But where is he, what's he doing?' she asked impatiently.

Ruth laid a restraining hand on her arm. 'Just wait.'

'Either Coco is there or she isn't.' Kat searched Ruth's face and didn't like the expression she found. 'Oh God, you don't think …?'

When Vittorio reappeared, he was pale and his eyes reddened. Kat tried to push past him and into the apartment, but he blocked her, saying hoarsely, 'She wouldn't want you to see her like this.'

'Like what … what's happened?'

'She has gone, Kat, my dear. Coco has gone. She is at peace now.'

'No!' Kat tried again to get past him and this time Ruth held onto her. Turning, she pressed her face into the other woman's shoulder and said, more weakly, 'No.'

'I'm so sorry, my dear, I'm so, so sorry.' Ruth's arms pulled her away and guided her towards the stairs. 'Come with me and leave Vittorio to deal with things here. He will know what to do and who to call.'

'I want to go to her.'

'I know, I know.' Ruth steered her upwards until somehow Kat was in her apartment and sitting at the table while the kettle boiled for tea.

'She can't be gone. Yesterday she was happy and going out dancing.'

'Vittorio thinks she has been sick for some time. Coco was old, her body was failing.'

Kat had a recollection that seemed important. 'Her colour was grey. You told me that.'

'She made herself colourful, she put on a brave face, that's how she would want us to remember her, don't you think?'

'But when did it happen? How long do you think she has been lying there all alone?' Kat's voice broke and she pushed her face into the wool of the scarf that was still resting round her shoulders.

Ruth made cups of tea that neither of them drank and they sat together at the table waiting for Vittorio because it seemed the only thing to do.

'I can't bear to think I'll never see her again or hear her voice,' said Kat.

'I know, believe me I know,' Ruth replied, her voice gentle. 'This is what it's like when you lose someone you love.'

Finally Vittorio appeared, exhausted and tear-stained, the dogs at his feet. He was holding a large stack of envelopes that looked like invitations.

Ruth gave him a quizzical look.

'Letters,' he said, placing the pile on the table.

'From Coco?'

'That's right. She has been busy writing. There is one for everyone she considered important.'

'However did you find them amidst all that clutter?' wondered Ruth.

'She told me where to look for them if something ever happened. She knew this day was coming for her sooner or later.'

Kat stared at the cream envelopes and the names printed on each one in purple ink. 'You've opened one.'

'It was for me and it says almost exactly what I thought it would. There is a letter for Ruth and I can imagine some of what is written in that. But I don't know what she might have wanted to tell you, Kat.' He rifled through the pile, pulled out an envelope and pushed it over to her.

She held it to her nose as if there might be some trace of Coco's powdery fragrance there but all she smelt was paper. 'Who else has she written to?'

'Family, friends, lovers; my task is to deliver each letter and make sure everyone finds out what Coco wanted them to know.'

'I can't believe she's gone,' said Kat numbly.

'Neither could I at first,' Vittorio told her. 'She was in bed, in her nightgown, I thought she was asleep but ... then I saw the life had gone. Her face was different; not her any more, not really.'

'What happens now?' asked Kat.

'I have called the undertakers and they will come soon to take her. She has left us plenty of details about what she wants.'

'For the funeral?' Kat felt chilled.

'Not exactly.' There was the trace of a smile on Vittorio's lips. 'This is my darling Coco so of course what she expects is a party.'

There were two things for Kat to open now: Coco's letter and the email that had come from her agent earlier that afternoon. Sitting in front of her laptop, the envelope on the kitchen table beside it, she braced herself for the final words from her old friend and the message that might hold a clue to her future.

It was the envelope she picked up first. Ripping into it, she found a sheet of notepaper covered in Coco's semi-legible script. She had to strain to decipher it.

My friend Kat

This life of mine has been filled with interesting people – thank you for being one of them. Grazie mille for all those little things you have done that have added up to so much. The day you came into my shop to try on a dress – the one that was so wrong for you, remember – I was sure we would be friends. I never guessed how much you would mean to me.

I wanted to take this chance to tell you one last thing. I have tried not to give you too much advice unless it is about fashion. But it is more important to find a life that suits you than it is a frock, and for both it is necessary to look at yourself with your eyes wide open.

You, Kat, tend to see the person you long to be rather than the one you are. I understand why; I have done the same. But before you give up on Venice I hope you will begin to recognise yourself a little better.

Stay here for a while longer ... for as long as you like. Don't worry about the apartment. The place belongs to me and I have arranged things so you can continue renting it.

It has all been such fun, hasn't it? How sad that it must come to an end. Still, mine has been a good life mostly and I don't regret any of it. I hope you will be able to say the same one day. I very much hope so.

Goodbye, my dear. With much love, Coco.

She read the letter several times, frowning over it, unsure what Coco was trying to say. Her advice might have been well meant but it didn't resonate at all. Of course Kat knew the person she was, of course she recognised herself. She had been hoping for something more from her friend and with a sense of disappointment set the note to one side.

It was time now to find out about her career. Putting Coco's letter out of her mind for a moment, she turned her attention to her laptop, double clicking on her agent's reply to her email.

Dear Kat,

My apologies for taking so long. It is such a busy time of year. I have encouraging news for you, however. There is interest at the network about your idea. They see it as having potential. My understanding is they think you could apply the same approach to other cities – Black in Paris, Barcelona, Rome and so on – giving an intimate and alternative view of places we might think we already know.

The first step is to set up a meeting. When are you in London next? Try to give me a few weeks' notice so I can make sure everyone is available.

Hope you are well and having fun in Italy. Talk soon – Penny.

It was what she had been desperate to hear but Kat was less buoyed than she had expected. She went back to Coco's letter and read it for a fourth time. Then she lay on the chaise, curled up beneath Massimo's scarf, and tried to make sense of it all.

Kat drifted off to sleep and woke in the dark. Feeling for her phone she saw it was only just evening. After holding the scarf against her face for a few moments, she made up her mind about one thing at least; she wanted Massimo right now, no one else. She needed to see his face and hear his voice, to tell him everything.

21

Outside, a sleety rain was falling. Kat half-ran the familiar route back to Hotel Gondola. She was flushed and breathless as she burst into the foyer, standing for a moment, dazzled by the brightness of the chandeliers and unnerved to be back there again.

She didn't recognise the man behind reception who greeted her with a perfunctory, '*Buona sera.*'

'Is Massimo around?' she asked.

'I will have to check if Signore Morosini is available,' he said, his tone starchy.

'Is he in his office?'

'I am not sure, signora.'

'I'm a friend, I really need to talk to him.'

'Is he expecting you?'

'No, but it's important.' Kat realised she was sounding desperate but still couldn't stop herself leaning onto the counter and calling, 'Massimo, are you back there?'

She must have raised her voice loudly enough because a moment later Massimo appeared, looking tired and un-characteristically rumpled.

'Kat? What are you doing here? There was no need to bring back the scarf.'

'I know but I had to see you.'

'OK,' he said evenly. 'Here I am.'

'I wanted ... the thing is ... my friend Coco died,' Kat managed to say before the tears she had been struggling to hold back escaped her.

Massimo's arms were around her before she knew it. 'Oh, Kat, I'm sorry.'

'No, it is me that's sorry,' she told him, her cheek pressed to his chest. 'I should have come ages ago. I was too proud or stupid or ... I don't know. But I'm sorry.'

'We need to talk,' Massimo said. 'Not here though.'

'If this isn't a good time,' began Kat, 'if you're busy ...'

He wiped a tear from her face gently with his thumb. 'Busy?' he said, as if he hated the sound of the word. 'Yes, I'm always busy. That is another thing to be sorry for.'

Sheltered by one of the hotel's umbrellas, they walked to the *bacaro* they had always preferred and sat in a quiet booth in the furthest corner. For a long time Kat talked about Coco, her shock at losing her, her sadness, her regrets.

'There were things I should have said to her. I never thanked her properly; told her how much her friendship meant and how grateful I was. I thought I had more time.'

'She knew those things without you telling her,' said Massimo.

'I can't be sure. That's why I'm here. There are things I should have said to you too and I need to make sure you know them.'

'Kat, you don't have to—'

'Yes, I do,' she insisted. 'I hurt you. It was all my fault.'

'No it wasn't.'

'I was selfish.'

'And so was I. There has been plenty of time for me to think about what I ought to have done differently. If I had found us an apartment instead of expecting you to live at the hotel, if I had made more time to be with you, worked fewer hours, listened to what you wanted. But no, I expected you to fit neatly into my life without disrupting it at all. We never gave ourselves a chance, Kat, I realise that now.'

Kat stared at him. It was so good to see his face, to listen to his voice, to be close enough that they could reach out to each other.

'All that is in the past and what I care about is the future,' Massimo told her, and then more softly, 'I've missed you … I love you.'

'I love you too.' The words rushed from her and only as she heard herself say them did Kat realise how much.

'In that case let's not give up so easily. Can't we find a way to make this work?' Massimo wondered.

'I'm still not sure.'

'But we don't need to be sure, Kat. We only have to try.'

Kat felt a spark of hope light inside her. What if it wasn't necessary to let go of all the other things that made her happy to be with this man she loved? What if she could have it all?

There were so many flowers. They covered the coffin on the funeral gondola and every boat in the slow procession following it. Only white flowers – lilies, roses and orchids – for this was to be a stylish occasion, as Coco had decreed.

Kat was glad her friend wasn't alone on her final journey to the cemetery of San Michele. Four gondoliers were manning the boat that carried her and there was a whole flotilla accompanying it: sleek motorboats, shabby old barges, traditional rowing craft, even a dragon boat. The traffic on the Grand Canal moved out of their way as a sign of respect, even the waterbuses stilling and their passengers forced to wait until the convoy had passed.

Church bells tolled as they neared the brick archway of San Michele and it began to snow. Kat waited beside Massimo in his boat, with Nico at the wheel, while those ahead disembarked: aged women in plush furs, men in dark capes, sombre-looking families, boat after boat filled with people and flowers.

'Coco knew all these people,' Kat marvelled. 'And I thought of her as being just my friend.'

'She was a part of the old Venice,' said Massimo. 'She lived in this city all her life. Almost every family was connected to her in some way.'

Snow was settling on the white marble headstones as they walked along pathways lined with tall cypress trees. Flowers had been left on many of the graves, their colours bright against the frosted grass. To Kat the cemetery felt almost like a garden and the thought made it easier to bear the idea of Coco inside a wooden box being lowered into the cold, hard ground.

Leaning into Massimo for comfort and warmth, she looked for faces she recognised. Ahead she saw Dante and his family. Beyond them were Vittorio and Ruth holding two small dogs clad in dark plaid coats. She saw people who had been visitors to Coco's apartment and men who might have been her lovers.

At the gravesite Kat hung back while others tossed white blossoms and handfuls of earth onto the casket. Then she heard a voice start to sing 'Ave Maria' sweetly and strongly and, stepping further forward, she saw a woman with long dark hair standing between two children, holding tightly to their hands, eyes closed as she delivered her lament.

Handkerchiefs were held to faces and couples moved closer to each other for solace. Glancing at Massimo, Kat saw that he too was crying. The singer held the final note then took a single dark red rose from her son's hand and tossed it into the grave.

'There is champagne waiting for us,' she announced. 'But first I will give Coco one last song, "Porgi Amor" by Mozart, because it was one of her favourites as well as mine.'

The woman was still singing her aria as she turned from the grave and slowly began to move away. The crowd followed the sound of her voice along the pathways, as the snow fell on their black umbrellas and dusted the cedar trees.

'That was so beautiful. Who is she?' Kat asked Massimo.

'Valentina di Malapiero. I'm not sure how she is related to Coco but she is from one of Venice's old noble families. The party later is being held at their palazzo.'

'Vittorio says it's going to be a huge celebration.'

Massimo lowered his voice. 'And people are scandalised,' he whispered. 'I've been eavesdropping on their conversations. Champagne and dancing? It is not traditional, not how things are done here.'

Kat found herself amused at the thought of Coco planning a funeral that was bound to shock people. 'She never did like to do what everyone expected of her.'

Despite their disapproval it seemed almost every true-born Venetian had flocked to the imposing palazzo on the Strada Nuova. Its rooms were large and high-ceilinged, lit by candles and dusty chandeliers and decorated with faded frescoes. White-jacketed waiters were serving champagne and tango music could be heard above the roar of conversation.

Kat pushed her way through the hordes, trying to find Ruth. At last she came across her standing in a corner of the ballroom watching the dancing.

'This is extraordinary,' Ruth said. 'All these people dressed in black and yet shimmering with colour. I'm trying to take it all in so I can paint it later.'

'I keep expecting to see Coco,' Kat told her. 'She should be out there on the dance floor, looking impossibly glamorous.'

Ruth nodded. 'Or upstairs in the salon surrounded by adoring men.'

'All her many lovers.'

'Yes, poor Vittorio, I think he hated having to share her.'

'How is he doing?'

'Very sad to lose another woman he loved. But Coco's letter said he mustn't waste time mourning her so he is trying to show a brave face.'

'What did she write in her letter to you?' Kat wondered. 'I'm sorry, maybe you'd rather not tell me?'

'That's OK, I'm sure you can guess at least a part of it. Coco wanted two things. One was for me to deal with all those clothes in her shop and the apartment.'

Kat groaned, sympathetically. 'On no, that will be a huge job. How did she expect you to get rid of them all?'

'She decided I should take over the work of finding them new homes.'

'Coco wanted you to run her shop?' Kat was surprised.

'Apparently,' Ruth said drily. 'And it's not such a big problem that I have no flair for fashion since I can use my natural eye for colour.'

Kat smiled; she could almost hear Coco saying the words.

'The second thing she asked was for me to look after Vittorio. She has even arranged for me to rent her apartment ridiculously cheaply to make it all possible.'

'What about her dogs?' Kat had forgotten they would need a new home.

'I will take care of Vittorio and he will look after them. Coco thought of everything.'

'She was matchmaking all along but you must have known that?' said Kat. 'She was determined you and Vittorio would be together even though you'd made it clear you didn't want another man.'

Ruth smiled. 'Ah, but Vittorio isn't just another man, as I have discovered.'

'So she was right, the pair of you are—'

'We are taking it slowly,' Ruth interrupted. 'But yes, I think Coco might have been right.'

'Oh my God I *so* wish she was here. I can't believe she is missing this; any of it.'

'Actually, I feel as if she is here,' Ruth said. 'Not grey any more but shining silver. I can very nearly see her.'

'So can I,' Kat replied. 'Right over there, at the very centre of things.'

Leaving Ruth to watch the dancing, Kat went down to the kitchen in search of food. She found Dante and another chef duelling over the stove, turning out platters of *cicchetti*.

He seemed pleased to see her. 'Taste my *sarde en saor* and compare it with this one. Tell us which is the best.'

Kat took a bite of each. In one the flavour balance tipped a little too far to sweet. 'Both are good,' she said tactfully.

'Is mine better?'

'Not necessarily.'

'Are you sure?' Dante frowned.

'They're both completely delicious,' Kat reassured him. 'But I didn't expect to see you here. You weren't especially close to Coco, were you?'

'She was my neighbour and my family knew her – my parents and grandparents. She was a part of the old Venice and so we are all come to say goodbye and honour her memory ... Which is lucky because there are many hungry people and my good friend Carlo here needed my help.'

The other chef looked up from his work and shrugged. 'I am letting him help me,' he told Kat. 'The man insisted.'

Kat smiled. 'I can imagine. It looks like a feast, though. Coco would have approved.'

'You have lost your friend. You are feeling blue?' asked Dante.

'Yes, I am.'

'Then you must come by the *osteria* very soon. I will make you feel happier with my food. I am changing everything, you know. No more heavy meats, only foods from the islands and the lagoon, local vegetables and seafood. Come and taste the dishes I am creating. This is my best work ever.'

Kat murmured her agreement, took a large plate of the crostini and moved on. He might be arrogant as Coco had always said, but Dante was charming and he could cook, she conceded, as she munched on the crostini.

'Oh thank God, some food,' said a woman with a London accent, reaching over and scooping up a large handful of the crostini. 'I'm completely starving. Hey, aren't you Kat Black? Coco told me about you. She said you're going to put her in a book and make her famous on the television.'

'Possibly,' Kat said awkwardly. 'I'm working on it anyway. I didn't realise she'd been telling people about it.'

'She's spoken about almost nothing else lately, hasn't she, Valentina?' The women turned to the dark-haired singer from the cemetery who was standing beside her.

'She has been very excited,' the singer agreed. 'My aunt Coco always did think she was born to be famous.'

'I guess I had better finish my book then?'

Valentina nodded. 'Don't let her down. Or Coco will almost certainly come back and haunt you.'

They tilted their champagne glasses at her, and moved on as partygoers do, looking for the next interesting person. To Kat, with every passing moment this was less a wake and more a celebration. It seemed as if Coco was still there but she was moving to the edges now, leaving her friends to carry on, all of them laughing and dancing, shouting to be heard above the music, filling their glasses.

In the middle of the crowd a wave of sadness passed over Kat. She felt a sudden need for Massimo. She looked but for a long while couldn't find him, walking through rooms filled by women glinting with diamonds, through clouds of fragrance and tobacco smoke, up and down the stairs then back through the same rooms again.

At last there he was, framed by an arched window looking out on the snow-blanketed branches of a tree. Already the light was dying and lanterns had been lit. Massimo was talking to an older couple, a woman in fur, the man an older version of himself. These must be his parents, she realised.

Noticing her, Massimo held up a hand, spoke a few last words to the couple and then came over.

'Are you ready to meet my family?' he asked.

'Do you really want me to?'

'Yes of course, my parents, my daughters, my sister – they are the other important people in my life beside you. I was stupid ever to imagine it was a good idea keeping you all apart.' He took her arm.

'Wait, there's something I need to tell you first.' Kat felt panicked. 'I heard from my agent and there's a chance this TV show might happen. If it did then there would be lots of travel involved. I'd have to leave you … leave Venice.'

'Why is it you think you must choose between your adventures and me? Didn't I say you could have both? So long as you always come home, I'll be happy. Go anywhere you want to, Kat, but promise that you'll always come home.'

'I promise,' she told him. 'I absolutely promise.'

Massimo pulled her closer. 'Then come with me. I don't want to wait any longer.'

CHAPTER 18

There are all sorts of meals to be cooked in a lifetime; meals
to celebrate or comfort; to reunite people, to show them love,
appreciation and kindness; meals to nourish, to laze over and
delight.

The meal I am cooking this evening needs to be all those
things and more.

For the truth is, neither this book nor my life has turned
out as I planned. Lately, things haven't been good at all.
Now, though, I'm in my tiny apartment, cluttered with
sauce-spattered pots and pans, messy with bags spilling over
with far too much food, with yellow squash, purple fronds of
radicchio, tentacles of seafood, meat to braise slowly, fruit to
bake in red wine and sugar.

Outside, Venice is icy, but these rooms are softly lit,
warmed by the heat of the stove and scented by all that is
bubbling away on it.

Massimo is here with me, stretched out on the velvet
chaise, eyes closed, a rug half falling from his body. In a
moment I will start to feed him, slowly, course by course. We
will eat together for half the evening, we will celebrate and
commiserate, show our appreciation, and most of all we will
love each other.

Remember how I used to think there was no sadder feeling
than being jealous of your own life? I wrote that at the very
beginning of this book. Since then I've known a lot of sadness
and things have changed; I've changed too.

Have you ever looked back at the woman you once were,

so sure of herself, so fixed in how she saw everything, so absolutely wrong much of the time? Have you ever been that way?

Because I know I have … and right now I'm doing my best to make sure I won't be any longer.

Thank you ...

I'd like to thank everyone who has helped me get to this point in my writing career. That's a lot of people – publishers, booksellers and readers – and I wish I could name you all.

For this book specifically a big thank you to my friend and fellow Auckland author Stacy Gregg for keeping me company *and* keeping me sane (mostly) and to Brodie McDonald from Sea Breeze café in Westmere for allowing us to be his unofficial writers in residence and supplying excellent coffee and emergency carrot cake.

Thanks to Lucio Zanella for talking to me about life as a Venetian hotelier, to Jeremy Nivern of Mea Culpa bar in Ponsonby for sharing his passion for cocktails and to Jenni Abdelnoor for telling me about the way she sees the world.

Thanks as always to my agent Caroline Sheldon. To my editors Laura Gerrard and Rebecca Saunders – and my previous ones Genevieve Pegg and Yvette Goulden who taught me so much. To everyone at Orion, Hachette Australia and Hachette New Zealand for your support and kindness – Louise Sherwin-Stark, Mel Winder, Gemma Finlay, Alison Shucksmith, Suzy Maddox-Kane, Jennifer Breslin, Elaine Egan, Tania Mackenzie-Cooke and many more. And to Kevin Chapman for Chardonnay and wise words.

Most of all to my husband Carne Bidwill who has stuck with me through thick, thin and ten novels and whenever he hears me complaining that, 'I just can't do this' always says, 'Well don't then' which is a lot more helpful than it sounds.

ALSO BY NICKY PELLEGRINO

*Two feuding families, two love stories
and a lot of delicious Italian food . . .*

Although settled in London, the Martinellis are a typical Italian family: fighting, eating and loving in equal measure. Now Pieta's sister is getting married and she will make the wedding gown. But she is distracted by a series of mysteries. Why is her father feuding with another Italian family? Why is her mother so troubled? And could the man she's always secretly cared for really be getting married to someone else?

As the wedding draws nearer, Pieta uncovers the secrets that have made her family what it is – and may stand between her and happiness . . .

'*The Italian Wedding*, a feast of food and love, a terrific read.'
Beattiesbookblog

'If your soul needs some nourishing, *The Italian Wedding* is a great pick.'
MiNDFOOD Magazine

'Nicky Pellegrino has crafted a feast not just for the mind but the mouth.'
boomerangbooks.com

'The elements of drama, history, romance and passion are layered, flavoured, tasted and left to simmer, not unlike the Italian recipes which are scattered throughout the book . . . I absolutely loved it!'
Stephanie Zajkowski, tvnz.co.nz

Luca Amore runs a cooking school in the Sicilian mountain town of Favio. He's taught many people how to cook the dishes passed down to him by generations of Amore women. As he readies himself for yet another course he expects it to be much like all the others. He will cook, he will take his clients to visit vineyards and olive groves, they will eat together, become friends, and then, after a fortnight, they will pack up and head home to whatever corner of the globe they came from.

But there is a surprise in store for Luca.

This time there are four women booked in to The Food of Love Cookery School. Each one is at a turning point in her life. Each one is looking for something more than new cooking skills from her time in Sicily. Luca doesn't realise it yet but this group of women is going to change his life. And for Moll, Tricia, Valerie and Poppy, after this journey, nothing will ever be the same.

'Nicky Pellegrino not only knows her Sicilian recipes and cooking traditions, she also keeps an immaculate beat throughout her tale.'
Sainsbury's Magazine

Two women, one house – one at the beginning of her life, one nearing the end. Alice is in London, working in the kitchen of a top restaurant and determined to live life fast and to the full. Babetta is living in a lonely house in southern Italy and trying to hang on to the quiet life she has made for herself.

When the two women meet one summer life changes for both of them. This is a novel about what we run from, and the places that make us stop and consider. Drenched in sunshine, it's about friendship and growing up, food and love.

Can a city
hold the key
to happiness?

One Summer in Venice

Nicky Pellegrino

*In the maze of Venice's canals, one woman sets
herself a goal to find the ten things that could be
the key to her happiness*

*'This isn't a mid-life crisis OK? For a start I'm not old enough yet to have
one of those. I'm calling it a happiness project. I've stolen an entire summer from my life and by the time it's over I plan to leave this place with
a list in my hand. The ten things that make me happy, that's all I want to
know.'*

Addolorata Martinelli knows she should be happy. She has everything
she thought she wanted – her own business, a husband, a child. So why
does she feel as if something is missing? Then when her restaurant, Little
Italy, is slated by a reviewer, she realises that she's lost the one thing she
thought she could always count on – her love of food.

So Addolorata heads to Venice for a summer alone, aiming to find the
ten things that make her happy. Once she's found them, she'll construct
a new life around her ten things, but will they include her life in London?

'Genuine heart and true observation.'
Elizabeth Buchan

Imagine swapping your
house for a stay in an Italian villa …

Nicky
Pellegrino

Under Italian
Skies

"The food, scenery
and language leap from
the page" YOURS

Stella has life under control and that's the way she likes it. When her boss dies suddenly, Stella starts to question her life choices and finds that she has little to show for herself other than her poky London flat.

In order to build the life she has always dreamed of, Stella impulsively joins a house-swap website. When she stumbles across a beautiful villa in southern Italy, she packs up and moves before she can talk herself out of it.

Here she tries on a stranger's life and begins to imagine the man who lives there. As she feels herself falling for someone she has never met before, she has to wonder, can an idea of someone ever be matched in reality?

'This book will make you want to chuck it all in and run
away to Europe for a house swap of your own'
Weekend Herald